Done is Done

A Year and a Day: Part Three

Lisa Courtney

Cover design by Sally A. Sloley of daisyprincess.com
(Guitar photo: Sally A. Sloley; Bokeh background image:
Matt Higby: https://www.facebook.com/matthigbyphotos);
Illuminated "O" by LeAnne Constantine:
https://www.facebook.com/leanne.constantine.16

First published in 2015
ISBN 978-0-9971968-3-2

Table of Contents

one

CALLIE HAD INCREASED her running speed, turned her head forward, and crashed headlong into the High King.

Had the King not seen her racing blindly toward him, the collision might have knocked them both down.

He braced himself, moved with the impact, and caught her safely in his arms.

"Hello," he said, all courtesy as he looked down at her.

Dazed and disoriented, she looked up at him. A slow smile grew across her face as she caught her breath.

In the silence, he stared at her with such intensity that she squirmed, suddenly uncomfortable in the once-familiar strength of his arms. He released her and took a step back.

"You're staring," she pointed out, rubbing her bruised forehead. "I must look like last week's fright."

The King smiled, but looked over her head, surveying the forest for any sign of trouble. "Where is Mazzin now?"

"About a mile and a half northeast of here. He's got about two hundred shadow soldiers, badly made, obeying him."

The King considered this. "You were running. Was someone chasing you?"

Callie shook her head and almost laughed. "No. No one will come after me. They're otherwise occupied. And since I am not there to give Mazzin reasons to use the Green-crystal against me, we have a little time to talk. He knows you are coming; he is waiting for his encounter with the High King of Faerie," she added, her eyes resting reassuringly on the royal oak leaf circlet in the King's hair.

Satisfied that there was no immediate danger, his gray eyes studied her.

She spoke lightly, despite her serious and truthful admission: "I was beginning to fear that you were not coming."

It was not delivered as a criticism, and he did not react as though it had been. "I know," he said. "Every place I stopped on the way here, the Folk needed my reassurance that the Mischief is not going to do further harm to them, or to the mortals or to the land itself. The Folk needed care and comfort; it is my duty to provide it. I swear to you that I came as quickly as I could.

"By the way, your chin is bleeding."

She nodded, rubbing the blood off onto her sleeve. "I flew into the top of a tree. I'll tell you later." She started to turn around to find a place to sit, but swung back to face him, her dark eyes bright with relief. "Oh, Garrhyn, I am so very glad to see you!"

"And I you, Your Grace. I am grateful that you are, more or less, unharmed."

They moved toward a felled tree. He slipped out of his brown leather jacket and placed it on the tree bark for her to sit on, then he sat beside her.

Something occurred to Callie. "How did you find me? I didn't even know I was coming this way until I did, and you were already here..."

The King reached into the pocket of his black jeans, and pulled out what Callie recognized at once as one of her favorite embroidered handkerchiefs. He opened the handkerchief to reveal the presence of a Dunnor's Bell. He slid a finger across it and spoke to it as though it were a petulant child. "Go ahead and sing to her. You no longer need to be silent." He handed the handkerchief and the singing Bell to Callie; it was, after all, the very one he had given her, once upon a time, to celebrate their love.

The Bell was made of silver, and was approximately the size of Callie's thumb. Occupying the Bell's front was a delicately carved harp, the filigree so fine that it appeared that the harp's strings could make their own sweet music. The back side held the entwined initials of the King and Queen, surrounded by two crowns and a subtle line etching of the Elvenhome crest in the background.

The Bell, in the presence of the people whose love it heralded, rang in giddy delight as it sat on Callie's open palm. The Queen's brown eyes were fixed solidly on the Bell. And if her lip quivered, or if her eyes threatened to fill with the longings of lost memories or the sadness of choices made, neither she nor the King acknowledged it.

He gave her a moment to watch and warm to the Bell she'd loved and worn for so many years. Then he spoke. "I asked your Ladies to get it from your Tower Room, so that I could locate you." He did not meet her eyes. "I needed the cloth to remind the Bell of your scent. Do not be angry with Your Ladies for my intrusion; I was somewhat insistent."

The Bell sang a little louder. "Hush now," Callie told it. "Thank you for helping him to find me." She closed her hand, gave her husband a soft smile, and pocketed her Bell and the handkerchief. "It was a good idea. In fact, that was how I found Arrendel, using the Bell he had made for Maggie."

The King nodded his approval, but Callie sensed that he was studying her face. "What is it? Is my chin more damaged than I thought?"

"No. At least I don't think so." He lifted her chin with his hand, and examined the wound. It was deep, and a bruise was forming, but the bleeding had slowed down. He touched the wound with his thumb, and she winced. She saw that he was fascinated with her face, and then realized what he was, or was not, looking at.

"Oh. My skin, my markings. That's what you're looking for."

He nodded. There was a deep, unspoken sadness in his eyes that tugged at some vague and unused space in her heart. "It is strange to me," he murmured, "discovering you this way. Do you know, I have never seen your face without the sacred images."

"I had not thought of that," she said, kindness filling her voice as she acknowledged his private distress. "When I travel Upworld, I hide the markings so that I will not be noticed overmuch. I have always done so."

"They are not gone, then, only hidden?"

"Only hidden, Your Grace."

"I thought for a moment that perhaps Mazzin had..." The King shook his head, as if to clear it of a horrific thought. "I must admit, it is somewhat disconcerting, Madam. I barely recognize you." A smile twitched at the corners of his mouth, and his eyes sparkled as he set his uneasiness aside. "You know, if you had not thrown yourself at me just now, I might not have recognized you at all."

They laughed companionably, then moved into the serious matters at hand.

"Where is Arrendel now?" he asked.

"I expect that he has arrived at Maggie's cottage by now."

The King listened as Callie explained how she, Thomas, and Cassane had come looking for Arrendel, and how Callie had found him. The King's eyes narrowed as she described the physical damage that Mazzin had either directly or indirectly caused her cousin. He remained patient and silent as she recounted her instructions to Thomas and Cassane about tending to Arrendel's wounds and getting Arrendel home to Swiftaine's and Maggie's care.

Callie added that she had instructed the Wood Elves to watch for Cassane as he raced through the greenwood, to insure that no Mischief attempted to prevent Thomas

4

from protecting Arrendel. "It took us several hours to move through the woodland to find Arrendel. Cassane will only have needed three-quarters of an hour to fly them to safety. I have no reason to believe they are not already there."

She couldn't help it; her eyes filled with tears, and they spilled down her face. "Garrhyn, the violence and harm Mazzin's servants did to Arrendel...it was horrible. I have to believe that he will live, and he will be well. If he were to die..." Callie's voice broke; she looked away, and continued. "In any case, if Mazzin did not hold the Greencrystal, I would have ended him. And it worries me that I would have enjoyed it."

She looked back at the King, her eyes filled with misery. He reached over and took her hand. His voice was both gentle and strong. "You would have enjoyed punishing him, but only for a moment. Your compassion always overrules your rage, so do not torture yourself with wondering if you, too, are a monster. We know that you are not.

"We must have courage, and remember that Arrendel is surrounded by Folk who have great love for him. That love will sustain him as he heals and grows stronger. I have not yet met his Maggie, but from what I have heard from him of her, I daresay she will not let him go without a fight. And as for Swiftaine..."

The King knew his Queen; she smiled in spite of her tears. The King gave her hand a tiny squeeze, and released it. As she brushed the wetness from her cheeks, the King asked Callie to tell him everything she'd seen Mazzin do with the Greencrystal.

As is generally the way, the telling of the thing took far less time than it had taken for it to actually transpire in the first place. Callie informed the King not only of what had happened, but also why she had chosen the diversions she had: first, the creation of the huge avian to deflect attention from Thomas' rescue of Arrendel, and then the smaller distractions of her shape-shifting to fly out of reach (here she explained how she'd banged her head and

5

cut her chin), the calling of the butterflies, the insects, the rearranging of the soldiers' feet.

"I toyed with him," she concluded, "and his response to my actions was swift. He successfully quieted all of the root magic he could recognize, though."

"You played children's games with Mazzin to assess his ability to use the Greencrystal. That was wise. You protected your light, too?"

"Yes. I knew I might have to save that for a final gambit, which I ran into these woods to plan, since I didn't know when you might arrive. But you're here."

The King nodded, his expression grave. "Is there any remaining light, or has Mazzin silenced all of it?"

"Other than yours and mine, it has all been quieted. He has a strong bond with the Greencrystal. I have not had a chance to consider why that is."

"The Greencrystal loves the Word, and had not heard it spoken in a long time, Your Grace," said the King with forced neutrality. "There was, at the time of the Greencrystal's making, joy in the Word, for obvious reasons. So it follows that the Stone would respond favorably to the one who reunited it with the Word it loves. We never intended for anyone, let alone a creature like Mazzin, to encounter the Stone in the first place, so I did not consider very much in the way of protection at the time."

Callie nodded, understanding. "I said the Word, to get the Stone's attention, and to complicate the process for Mazzin." She searched his gray eyes for acknowledgment of what the effort had cost her.

"Does it hurt?" he whispered.

"Yes," she whispered back. "But it is the price we must pay. I have not had time to think about it, but I shall, later."

"So shall I."

She moved them away from the dangerous precipice of their emotional past, and back toward dealing with Mazzin. "The Greencrystal responds to that damned

Goblin, and he has managed to learn *making* fairly well. Given time, he could master it. I don't want to give him that time."

"How does he fare with *unmaking*?"

Callie frowned. "I don't know. And that has me nervous."

"Still, the Stone heard you, and played along with your games." The King was thinking aloud. "Did the Stone refuse to do anything Mazzin commanded?"

Callie shook her head.

"Did Mazzin call on the Stone to do something it would not choose to do?"

"Not that I know of." She stood up, and handed the King's jacket to him. Rising from his seat on the tree, he slipped it back on. "Do you think there is a chance he might, and it might not?"

"We won't know until it happens," the King replied.

"How worried are you?"

"'Worried' may be too strong a word. 'Cautious' might be better. Anyone who has the Word can learn to use the Greencrystal quickly. Mazzin is clever, he is strong and has ambitions; he wants to rule a kingdom, and will do crazy and evil things to make it happen. But he knows what he's about, since he is demanding this." The King touched the oak leaf circlet in his hair. "Mazzin is also weak, for he is hungry for power, focused only on his own goals, and it would not surprise me to learn that he is maddened from the continuous scrying. He comes by the gift honestly enough, but he is incautious about his use of it. He is also vulnerable to drunkenness because of his overindulgence of the Northern Wine he uses to aid him in his divination. Horshog told me these things when he wished me good fortune in destroying the villain."

Callie's mind raced to the arena of kingly politics. "Horshog is going to step aside and have you deal with Mazzin without him? Isn't he obligated to participate in some way that is useful? He is your vassal, a lesser king of the Realm. He needs to obey you, not barter with you to deal with his own domestic problems."

The King shrugged. "Horshog's participation will only involve not challenging me when I have ended his only remaining heir."

Callie's eyes widened as she considered the additional political repercussions. "Oh..."

A late-afternoon sunbeam streamed through the trees and shone across the King, making the golden circlet in his long, dark hair sparkle.

The Queen looked at the King, her question as direct as her gaze. "What are we going to do now?"

"*We* are not going to do anything. This work falls fully into the province of the High King, Madam," he told her with a wry smile. "I have perhaps been somewhat lax in my responsibilities of late. Pray allow me to set a few things to rights."

He punctuated this with a nod of his head as she lifted her chin, about to object. "But—"

He cut her off with a shrug and a smile. "If anything happened to you, the Lord High Chamberlain would lose his mind and might very well thrash me within an inch of my life. Then your Ladies would gather together to destroy what was left of me. How you have managed to surround yourself with such temperamental Folk has mystified me for some time."

Callie couldn't help it; she giggled.

"Truly, Your Grace," he said, "This work is mine. Let us say I have responsibilities to catch up on, for the Folk." A thought occurred to him, and he seemed to smile to himself as he added with another shrug "...and perhaps even to myself.

"You should join the others at Maggie's cottage, and see to Arrendel. Go, off with you now...if it please Your Grace."

The day was considering diffusing into a misty twilight; in its wake, darkness would descend quickly. In silence, they walked a few more steps together.

8

She turned to face him. "Do you know what you're going to do?"

"Not yet. I imagine it will occur to me in due course."

"You are impossible," she groaned.

"So you have pointed out on occasion."

Callie put her hands on his arms, locked her eyes on his and commanded fiercely, "Don't lose."

"I won't."

"End him."

"Without question, Your Grace."

"And try not to get hurt in the process."

"I will."

"Do you need me to—"

The King gave his wife an endearing, very private smile she hadn't seen on his face for more than six hundred years. "Your Royal Majesty, it is time for you to depart. I will join you all presently. Go now."

To her complete surprise, Callie had nothing to say: no gentle taunting, no regal commanding, no friendly advice. Not for the first time lately, she wondered who her husband truly was now. He had changed in subtle ways that made him seem far more like the man and the King he had been before the loss of their son. That he would be here, prepared to protect the Folk and the land, facing more than just the uncertain outcome of a mad Goblin wielding the Greencrystal, all of this made her proud. She was aware, too, that the King was facing private demons from his past and his present; she could tell by the set of his chin, and the conviction that burned in his determined gray eyes.

Yes, she was proud of him in this moment. She was also sad, somehow, weighted down by an unbidden, uncomfortable feeling that all that had been lost long ago was trying valiantly to awaken and return to its place in her heart.

She had nothing left to say to him and, looking up into his eyes, she realized that he did not expect her to speak, nor did he need her to.

Biting her lip, Callie reached for the King's hand, and squeezed it hard. She had no doubt that he understood her.

In response, the King traced her face with the index finger of his free hand. "Without your markings, you look so very pale," he told her. "Still and ever a warm and beautiful Midsummer Night, My Lady, but without the stars..."

She smiled and let go of his hand.

"Go now," he repeated, his voice softer, nodding his head.

With a last look, Callie nodded back, and vanished in a flash of shimmering green light.

THE HIGH KING of Faerie, Garrhyn son of Garrick, noiselessly appeared behind a wide-trunked oak tree that stood less than ten feet from where Mazzin was seated on the ground. From this vantage point, Garrhyn could see the Goblin scrying in the slowly fading light with a wide wooden bowl that held what appeared to be the last bit of Northern Wine he used for this purpose. Two empty bottles lay dry in the dirt near where Mazzin sat gazing deeply into the bowl.

Garrhyn looked around for evidence of the strange army Mazzin had created; there wasn't any. Surprised by this, the King checked for the presence of anyone else nearby. He sensed no one, not even the Wood Sprites who lived in the trees. If the Sprites and their trees were awake at all, they were silent.

Mazzin began to laugh at what he saw in the bowl. "Hmmmm...excellent. The King approaches!"

Amused in spite of himself, Garrhyn stepped unheralded from behind the tree. "Not bad. See? I approach. On the other hand, I had already arrived."

With deliberate calm, Mazzin turned to face the High King of Faerie, his head automatically nodding in vague respect.

Garrhyn offered the Goblin a smile and a light toss of his head. "It's all in the semantics."

Mazzin's eyes moved from the King's face to the regal circlet in the King's hair. "I see you have brought the ransom, Your Majesty. That is well. I did not wish to cause the damage that not proffering it would require."

If Garrhyn had not believed that Mazzin was irreparably insane before, the casual look in the Goblin's black eyes and the quiet, self-assured tone of his voice as he delivered these words fully clarified the fact of it.

If Garrhyn had had a specific plan in mind for retrieving the Greencrystal and dealing appropriately with Mazzin a moment before this, it was gone now. The King was a natural diplomat, and was as effective in discussion as he was in wielding his personal power. He knew he would have to end Mazzin. He also knew that he would have to do it in a way that was consistent with the laws and sensibilities of Faerie. More than that, he knew he had to do it in a way that he could live with. This unexpected realization jolted itself, uninvited, into his awareness; he tucked it away for later, and focused on the calm, patient, insane Goblin who now stood before him.

"You do not truly believe that you will hold both the Greencrystal and the circlet, do you, Mazzin?" Garrhyn asked, his tone deceptively light. "I cannot allow you to hold the one, or keep the other. Surely you must understand that. And you must also understand that the theft of the Greencrystal, and the Mischief you created, and the mortal and the Fair blood on your hands, to say nothing of the damage done to Lord Arrendel and his Lady, are high crimes. They come with the penalty of death, whether you return the Greencrystal to me or force me to take it from you."

Mazzin smiled. "Your Majesty, I have no intention of giving you the Stone. And before this day is done, I will have your circlet, and your title as well." He paused, patting the Greencrystal, which hung around his neck and rested under his vest. "I would have you know, before you die, that I bear no ill will toward you, or toward Lord Arrendel, for that matter. Slole and Treln did, though, for Rierg's execution. They were quite fond of the princeling, and hoped to improve their circumstances when he ascended to Horshog's throne."

Garrhyn looked around. "Where are they now? Slole and Treln?"

"Slole seems to have disappeared. He is brutal when empowered and somewhat craven when bested, so he may have run away to temporary safety. If he crosses my path, I may kill him for desertion. As for Treln, he has ended, but I do not know the details."

"I understand it was "death by Spriggan'," said Garrhyn. He did not attempt to hide a broad smile.

"Ah," Mazzin shrugged.

The King took a step back, and surreptitiously checked the surrounding trees to see if any of them were paying attention to the conversation. Everyone seemed to be asleep, trees and their Sprites, even the woodland's animal residents.

Mazzin noticed the King's subtle movements. "Your Majesty should know that I have quieted all the life around us, so that we can deal with each other without unwelcome interruption."

Garrhyn nodded acknowledgement. "So we will fight, rather than resolve our 'differences'?"

Nodding, Mazzin grinned. "A pity, perhaps, that we will be unseen and unheard. The tale of my victory should be a most worthy one."

The High King was thinking, but he covered that with a stray question: "I have been curious, Mazzin. Was Horshog party to your plan to take the Greencrystal?"

"No. I do not believe he had the wit to be of use. I confess I considered making a gift of the High King's circlet to my dear uncle to atone for my part in his son's end, so that I might return to his good graces. It seemed a wise idea. But as I am now Horshog's sole heir, and the circlet would have come to me in time anyway, I may as well keep it."

"I see," Garrhyn murmured, as he considered then tossed away ideas about how to handle the coming fight. "Did you and your scrying bowl look into the future to see if you will indeed hold the Greencrystal and the crown? Will you rule the Northern Kingdom, or all of Faerie?"

Mazzin had moved back against a sleeping tree, to rest. "While there are many ways to scry, of course, my preferred method is to attend to events that are close at hand. Especially when the distant outcome is already clear to me, as this one is. I confess that I was about to divine my full future, just before you arrived, but I ran out of wine for the bowl." He laughed, with genuine amusement. "I have not seen my future as High King, yet it will come to pass. I have the Stone, as you see."

With that, Mazzin pulled the Greencrystal out from under his vest, and raised it to show Garrhyn. "Your Majesty: hand me the oak leaf crown, and prepare to die."

THE HIGH QUEEN of Faerie, still dressed in jeans, boots and a black leather jacket and, overall, only a little worse for the wear, materialized without a sound just inside the door of Maggie's cottage. She was exhausted.

The flurry of activity around her moved in sharp contrast to the stillness with which she observed it.

Two Water Sprites—wise, ancient Naiad healers—walking fast, were speaking in hushed wisps of their native tongue, their conversation intense. They each carried two large plastic buckets of loch water up the stairs toward the bathroom, which they entered together, and then closed the door behind them.

A Spriggan's shout from outside the large living room window pulled Callie's focus. As she turned and looked, she saw Swiftaine jumping up onto one of Maggie's kitchen chairs, giving orders and supervising the work that was going on around him. He called to a small group of approaching Dryads, who were carrying armloads of fallen bark, and pointed them to two other Dryads filling in the broken spaces in the outside wall of the cottage. The Sprites sang a Carrying song, and the air was filled with the sounds of Fey music blended with the noise of construction.

Moving toward the window, Callie saw yet another group of Dryads putting the finishing touches on a makeshift shelter for Cassane. The stallion had obviously been brushed and cared for. At the moment, he was eating apples proffered by an aged Tree Sprite and watching the proceedings with whickers of approval.

At the sound of dishes clattering, Callie moved toward the kitchen.

Maggie was at the sink, her back to Callie, washing dishes with manic, desperate urgency. As Callie entered, she looked around. The kitchen was literally spotless. Her eyes flew to the white cabinets where Arrendel's blood had remained splattered yesterday. It was gone. The cabinets all but sparkled with crisp cleanliness.

The High Queen was not alarmed by the absence of the blood marking Arrendel's live presence. There was no question that the blood had been purposefully washed away. Callie knew for a certainty that if Arrendel had died, she would have felt it. The presence of the healer crones in the house only confirmed what she already knew. Still, Callie breathed a sigh of relief as she watched Maggie reach into a cupboard for another stack of dishes and put them in the soapy water.

As Maggie extended her arms, Callie caught the flash of a silver necklace around Maggie's neck, and heard a faint, slow, but comforting chiming. Maggie had her Bell back, and she she had Arrendel, too.

Callie cleared her throat loudly, gave Maggie a second to register the sound. Then she walked across to greet her new friend, who dropped the sponge into the dish water and turned off the faucet.

Maggie turned and gave Callie a tired but hopeful smile.

Callie smiled back and asked, "What does a Queen have to do to get a cup of tea around here?"

THERE WOULD BE a duel to the death.

The High King of Faerie and the maddened Goblin did not need to agree on terms or rules. There were none.

As he walked to the far end of the clearing, almost one hundred feet from where Mazzin was still settled against the tree, Garrhyn wondered what he was going to do. He was Fey enough to lean toward the playing of the game he found himself in, but there was no true merriment in it; the Mischief had been serious, and its resolution would carry equal gravity. He had a clear image of how he expected this encounter with Mazzin to end, but he did not know yet how he was going to get there, which posed a philosophical problem or two that he didn't have time for. He smiled to himself as he cast the thought aside, and turned to face the Goblin across the long thicket.

A heartbeat later, the duel began.

Mazzin was ready, and he grinned as he commanded the Greencrystal. "Stone, quiet the King's golden light!"

The Goblin looked expectantly at Garrhyn.

After a pause, the King flicked a little golden light from his right hand, sprinkling it on the ground. A dozen daisies sprang up by his feet.

Mazzin frowned.

Garrhyn smiled, the soul of patience. "Sorry, Mazzin. The Greencrystal cannot quell the energy that originally created it. You're going to have to work a little harder than that if you are going to play this game."

Frustrated but not dissuaded, Mazzin raised the Greencrystal high above his head. He whispered to the Stone, and suddenly the shadows of fifty archers with loaded longbows shot very real arrows through the air, each aimed at Garrhyn.

In the instant before the first rain of arrows reached him, Garrhyn raised his hand, and gold flame shot from his palm, setting fire to the arrows and frying them to dust before they touched him.

Since there were no rules, Garrhyn felt no need to retaliate, at least not yet. He would play for time, perhaps push Mazzin to burn himself out on his own. He did not want to give the Greencrystal's energy and his own golden light too much room to spill into the forest. Better to hold himself in check, and keep the overall rush of power under control.

He hoped he could do that. He remembered what kind of magic had gone into the creation of the Greencrystal, forever ago, and he knew how strong it was. And, he thought with a sigh, he was about to find out what kind of damage it could do in the wrong hands.

MAGGIE AND CALLIE filled each other in as they prepared the tea together. Afterward, Callie went into the downstairs bathroom and washed the dried blood off of her chin, examining the slice. It hurt, but it wasn't serious, and would heal quickly. The bruise on her forehead ached, and she had a bump. She ignored it, and returned to the kitchen just as Maggie was putting the tea pot and some toast and marmalade on the table. They sat down and talked some more.

Cassane had brought Arrendel and Thomas home nearly two hours before Callie's arrival. A very worried Swiftaine had gone to the loch earlier in the day, and pleaded for help from the resident Sprites. The Naiad healers had shown up to aid Elvenhome's Heir Apparent forty minutes before Callie's arrival. Thomas had carried Arrendel upstairs and helped Maggie put him in their bed. But at the command of the Old Ones, Thomas carefully moved Arrendel from the bedroom and into the bathtub, where the Old Ones were now caring for him. They had suggested somewhat tersely that Maggie let them do their work with Arrendel in private.

Maggie had volunteered to fetch the loch water for them. They declined her offer, explaining that they needed to choose the water themselves, which they did. They had been back and forth from the loch no less than five times.

In an attempt to stay busy from the moment Callie and Thomas had left to find Arrendel that morning, Maggie had cleaned most of the house from top to bottom, even clearing out drawers and dusting the books in her extensive library. When the Naiads closed Maggie out of the bathroom, she had fled to the kitchen. Finding nothing new to scrub, she had pulled all of the clean dishes out of the cupboards and washed them, dried them, put them away, and then started over again.

"I am insane," Maggie told Callie with a tired grin.

"Perhaps. But you have a very clean home."

Maggie nodded and chuckled, but this did not mask her sarcasm or her anxiety. "Yeah. That will help." She poured more tea, and looked at Callie, unable to hide her fear and sadness. "Arrendel hasn't been conscious, at least not that I know of. Thomas said they talked a little on the ride home, but not much. He's worried, too—Thomas, I mean. After he moved Arrendel to the tub, we came downstairs, and I made Thomas some coffee. He was pretty shaken up, Callie. He told me that Arrendel didn't weigh much, that he'd weighed more when Thomas first got him onto Cassane's back. Something's wrong...I mean, so many things are wrong, and..." Maggie's voice trailed away.

Callie put her hand on Maggie's arm, and met her eyes. "Water Faeries 'dry out' when they are injured or ill. That's why we took loch water with us when we went to find him. As he dries out, he's going to weigh less."

Maggie forced herself to ask. "I know he's badly hurt. I saw a lot of what they did to him. Is he going to die, Callie? The Naiads didn't say, and I couldn't make myself ask them."

Callie shook her head and answered honestly. "I don't know. All we can know is that he's alive in this moment. And that counts."

"Does it?"

"It does."

They were silent for the space of a full minute.

Finally Callie asked, "Where is Thomas?"

"Asleep, in the guest room. He tried to hang out with me as long as he could, but he was really tired, and edgy, so I let him go. That's when I started washing my clean dishes."

Hesitating only a little, Maggie told Callie that Thomas had admitted to her that he'd been upset about leaving Callie alone to deal with Mazzin. Then Maggie asked about the King.

Fair Folk do not lie. They do, however, tend to gloss over things that mortals do not really need to know. Callie told Maggie about finding Arrendel and instructing Thomas about how to help him. She also told Maggie about much of her encounter with Mazzin. She even told her about running into the King, and shared a portion of their conversation.

It was fully dark when Swiftaine came in through the front door, just as Callie was telling Maggie that the King had requested that his Queen return to the cottage.

"I did not know you were here, Your Grace," the Spriggan said with quiet respect, glancing up the stairs to see if there was any movement.

"Yet here I am, Swiftaine," Callie declared with a raised eyebrow.

Swiftaine bowed, and looked up the stairs again, his unease evident in his black eyes and twitchy, darting fingers. "Most of the Dryads have gone back to the forest. They completed the enclosure for Cassane, and have seen to the damage to the outside of the house. The holes have been filled until the walls can be fully repaired."

"Well done, worthy Spriggan," Callie commended.

"Thank you," Maggie added.

Then the emotional dam broke as Swiftaine and Maggie spoke at the same time, each looking at Callie with anxious and unhappy desperation:

"Your Grace, can you not command the healers to tell us of his condition?"

"Callie, aren't you going to pull rank and get those Naiads to tell you what's going on up there...with him?"

The Queen looked at the weary woman sitting beside her, and then over at the worried Spriggan standing before her, and with determination in her eyes, rose from her chair. "Yes."

two

IN THE FOREST, uneasy thunder crackled ominously overhead. Invisible but agitated energy swirled around them, stirring up the elements.

Mazzin, sweating profusely, kicked his scrying bowl out of his way. It had rolled toward him, dizzy and directionless, when he had called for the ground to roll like wrath-filled waves. More ocean than earthquake, he had not succeeded in smashing Garrhyn against the trees, and this enraged him.

The High King had merely elevated himself a yard or so off the ground, standing on air, watching Mazzin's growing frustration with unfeigned interest.

Once the forest floor ceased rolling and churning, Garrhyn lowered himself back down, and waited while the exasperated Goblin threw his next punch.

It was an effective one, and it caught Garrhyn off-guard.

At a word from Mazzin, a huge brindle wolfhound ran at full speed toward Garrhyn.

Garrhyn's heart skipped a beat as the huge dog came toward him. "Cav...?"

Of all the dozens of dogs Garrhyn had ever owned and loved, Cav was his treasured favorite. He'd come to Garrhyn as a puppy, a gift from Terena, the first year they had lived together as lovers in his castle at Elvenmere. The

King and the huge wolfhound had often been inseparable, and Garrhyn's memories of Cav blended with his happiest memories of his time with Terena. The dog had lived to the ripe age of twenty-four, quite old for even a Fey-born wolfhound. Garrhyn and Terena had both grieved terribly when they lost him.

And here he was, in his prime, beautiful and strong, and racing at Garrhyn with a look of love and excitement in his bright eyes.

Time and place froze as Garrhyn was emotionally transported to one of the most contented and carefree periods of his long life.

Cav bounded at his beloved master, and Garrhyn opened his arms, watching for the dog to slow down before greeting him.

But the wolfhound didn't slow. Instead, he slammed hard against Garrhyn, knocking him to the ground. Winded, Garrhyn was shocked and confused as pain roared through his body. The dog was biting him, tearing at the flesh of his neck and hands with teeth somehow larger and more deadly than Garrhyn could remember.

He pushed the dog away with all of his strength, slamming the canine head hard with a bleeding fist, then rolled out of the way and staggered to his feet as Cav positioned himself for a lunge.

Eyes wild now, Cav trembled with resolve as he crouched to spring. Beloved dog and cherished master made firm eye contact. As the wolfhound plowed toward Garrhyn to attack again, Garrhyn made a fast, squeezing gesture with his hand. Gold light sprayed between his fingers as he crushed the dog's heart.

Dead instantly, Cav fell heavily to the ground, inches from where Garrhyn stood trembling in renewed grief and deep, desperate loss. He took a couple of breaths, stifled a sob, and ignored the tears that sat on his eyelashes. He chose not to pay attention to either the physical or the emotional pain that threatened to smother him.

The High King of Faerie was angry now. Very angry.

Thunder roared through the sky, and an irritable wind had begun to blow and intensify as the seconds grew into long minutes.

Garrhyn wiped his bleeding neck on his bleeding hands, and wiped his hands on his jeans. And then he began to walk across the clearing toward an extremely nervous Goblin.

CALLIE STOOD IN the doorway of Maggie's bedroom as two strong male Dryads positioned an unconscious Arrendel on the bed, bowed to Callie, and left. The Naiad Healers fussed a bit, getting Arrendel settled, and then pulled the sheet and blanket up to cover him. From the corner closest to the bed, Maggie stood silent, fingering her quieted Bell as she waited.

"Water, every hour," the elder of the ancient Water Faeries commanded, nodding at Callie.

"Do not tell *me*, Mother Healer," Callie returned with a raised eyebrow. "Tell Maggie."

The Crone turned to look at Maggie and repeated herself, ignoring the High Queen's subtle rebuke. Arrendel was to drink a full glass of fresh loch water every hour until he could walk easily on his own. Otherwise, he was to sleep undisturbed until he woke on his own. He was to rest and remain untroubled by others for a week. Under no circumstances was he to be put in a situation where he would perspire, either from heat, or from *any* physical activity. The younger of the Ancient Ones waggled a finger at Maggie, who immediately assumed a facial expression of unqualified innocence. The Naiads' surprise at Maggie's wide-eyed ignorance of their intended meaning left them speechless. Callie was hard pressed to stifle a snort and a giggle.

As they left the room, Callie touched each of the Naiads on their stooped shoulders. "We thank you for your aid, and for coming so swiftly when you were needed. Will he mend, truly?"

The Naiads nodded. The elder spoke to the Queen. "With the right care, he will mend. It will be slow at first, but he is strong and will recover all that he has lost."

The younger of the crones added, "If he has need of us, ask for us at the loch, and as soon as we have word, it will be our honor to return and help."

Callie bowed and spoke the ritual words with sincerity and pride: "You and your kind, Mothers, are the strong magic in the water; water is sacred, and water is life." She smiled warmly. "I thank you."

"It is our honor to serve." They bowed, and left.

"Maggie...?" Callie asked the frazzled woman still standing in the corner by the bed, staring at the sleeping Arrendel.

Maggie forced her gaze from him and looked over at Callie.

Callie smiled, affection beaming in her eyes. "Why don't I shut the door, and check on you both later?" She turned and left the room, pulling the door shut behind her.

As the door closed, Maggie carefully got onto the bed, slid under the covers, put her arms around the man she loved, and held him while he slept.

MAZZIN WATCHED AS the King approached. The Goblin cupped his hands around the Greencrystal, and muttered to himself as he tried to decide what to do next to keep the King from getting too close, but the thoughts didn't come. The fire in the King's eyes was as intense as the twitching of the long scar on his face. The closer the King got to him, the more visible the royal rage was, and Mazzin began, for the first time, to falter in his firm conviction that he would easily win the day.

Worried now, Mazzin whispered to the Greencrystal. "Give me wings, Stone, and I will fly from here!"

In less than a heartbeat, Mazzin had wings. It is not so sad a thing that Goblins are not natural shape-shifters. Since he had not been specific with either his words or the image of himself with wings, he was shocked by the strange reality he had created: two small, black wings that might have proudly adorned the body of a large crow protruded from Mazzin's chest, flapping wildly but taking him nowhere.

Garrhyn was less than thirty feet from Mazzin when the Goblin countermanded his useless wings, but was unable to *unmake* them. After several seconds of confusion, he gave up, and instead, in desperation, commanded the Greencrystal to make his final play: "Stone, destroy him utterly! Kill him! End him now, in pain, and forever!"

The Greencrystal pulsed in Mazzin's hand, summoning energy at such an intense rate that the earth shook again, violently, and several very old, tall trees toppled helplessly to the ground. One nearly hit the King as he strode closer to Mazzin.

The air was thick with energy, making it seem almost too heavy to breathe.

"Take his life!" Mazzin screamed at the Stone, shaking it in the direction of the approaching King. Lightning crackled from the Stone, dancing dangerously out of control as it shot out in every direction.

Garrhyn was still so angry that it took him a moment to register the crushing pain in his head, and the sharp slices of agony suddenly alive in his chest.

IN MAGGIE'S DOWNSTAIRS guest room, Thomas was asleep. Callie watched him for a few minutes, then left him and closed the door. She didn't know whether she was disappointed or grateful that she couldn't talk with him at the moment. She had much on her mind, and was too tired to sort it out on her own. Yet, the idea of actually putting energy into a discussion made her groan with exhaustion.

To clear her head, she decided to walk outside in the cool night air and revel in the silence.

The living room was mercifully peaceful as Callie walked through it. All of the Folk who had helped today were gone, back to their homes in water or tree. A glance out the front window revealed a gray and white Fiat parked under the enclosure the Dryads had built. Swiftaine was curled up under one of the couches with Maggie's cats, and she almost laughed aloud at the comic sweetness of it. All in all, he chose his friends well.

Once outside, Callie found her way to the side of the house, and sat on the oak swing that beckoned from the overhang. She tucked her legs under her, and let the swing rock her in the darkness as she took a few deep breaths and forced herself to relax and empty her mind.

After a few quiet minutes, Callie pulled her Bell out of the pocket of her jeans, and admired it as it sat in the palm of her hand, twinkling in the dark. Once upon a time, in the part of her history when the Bell had been always with her, her life had seemed merry and uncomplicated, filled with love and laughter. She had not been naïve, but perhaps she had been blinded by her tendency to see the world the way she had wanted to see it, the way she sometimes commanded it to be, rather than the way it was, both in Faerie and Upworld.

She had been happy, entirely happy, once upon a time.

She'd been happy enough since, certainly. And she was happy now, with Thomas.

She wondered, though, if she would ever be as happy and as completely in love with anyone else as much as she had been with the King.

Callie closed her eyes, and bright memories danced, reminding her of small, private, wonderful moments she had not thought about for centuries. He had loved her then, and she had loved him, and together, they were joined by the strength of their commitment to the Fair Folk.

Or, they *had* been.

Once upon a time...

It was at that moment that her eyes flew open. She alone had felt it. There was a heavy, soundless crash of malevolent thunder that would have frightened anyone who had heard it or perhaps only sensed it.

25

Clasping her Bell in her hand, she got up from the swing, and listened.

There was nothing to hear, which made Callie listen that much harder.

She couldn't hear him, but she instinctively recognized the source of the energy that she felt: Garrhyn. She sensed a strained, agitated flicker just beyond the edge of her awareness. She was sure that he wasn't calling out to her—or to anyone—for assistance, but she knew that he was doing battle with the damned Goblin, and that the work was strenuous, taking a great deal of energy.

He was strong, capable, powerful, and clever. There was no question that the High King of Faerie would deal with Mazzin appropriately.

Mazzin had the Greencrystal. What if the King had not yet taken it from him? What if Mazzin was able to use it against the King, and harm him? Was this unlikely situation the cause of her sudden apprehension?

Callie felt another ripple of energy slip across her consciousness.

If he needed help, and he did not call to her, how would she know?

He is proud, she thought, *and would not ask. He would presume that he could master the situation, as would anyone else who knew him.*

He had made it clear to her that he would fight this battle alone. For a fraction of a second, she considered going to the forest anyway, and seeing for herself that he did not require her aid.

She realized vaguely that she was pacing as she decided what to do. As usual, it did not take very long for her act.

"All right, Garrhyn," she whispered into the night air, her dark eyes shining as she raised her hands over her head, pointing her fingers in the general direction of the forest where she knew the King fought with Mazzin. "This is your battle; you have so claimed it. But I send you a bit of a cheat, if you find you have need of it. If you will have it, accept this gift...in memory of our wee Garrhydan."

Dazzling and almost blinding green light shot through her fingertips and sped through the night toward its destination.

Callie watched it go, and then sat back down on the swing, where she let herself have a much-deserved little cry.

GARRHYN COULD NOT breathe, and part of his mind found a small interest in the reality of this. He was only a little surprised to discover that he was on his knees in the darkness of the forest clearing. He was vaguely aware that Mazzin, some distance away, was screaming in maddened rage at the Greencrystal, demanding the King's death. Garrhyn could not quite understand why he was still conscious, and still alive.

His head hurt. It felt like it might simply burst. His heart was constricted in his chest, and he did not mind overmuch that it had been perhaps too long a time since he had taken a breath.

The oak leaf circlet in his hair pulsed, and he could feel a small tug as it seemed to try to move from its place on the royal head. This struck Garrhyn as strange, since the crown could only belong to him.

And then he remembered that Mazzin wanted it, the supposed ransom for Arrendel, the symbol of the High Kingship of all the Fair Folk.

He could not breathe. He thought he should want to or need to, but the pain told him not to bother.

In a haze, Garrhyn gave up on bothering, so the pain would go away. He was tired, and sad, too. Perhaps it was time for him to finally end, and sleep.

Then, from the corner of his closing eyes, he saw it: a wild rush of bright green light hurling across the night sky, headed straight for him. If he could have taken a breath, he'd have laughed. He knew exactly what it was, and who had sent it.

The green light threw itself around him, wrapping him in a protective verdant flame as it helped resuscitate his own flickering internal golden light. Unexpectedly, he found his breath again. The pain in his head and chest evaporated as energy both gold and green joined and revitalized him. Power surged through his body, his mind, and his soul.

Garrhyn shook his head to clear it, took another long, delicious and most welcome breath. A steady heartbeat later, he discovered that he was doing something close to unbelievable: he was smiling. The smile was small, to be sure, but it was a smile, and it began to light up his face. Without sadness, rage or regret, he whispered a once nearly-unspeakable name: "Garrhydan, my beautiful wee boy..."

Glowing in a majestic fusion of shimmering green and golden light, the High King of Faerie rose to his feet.

And then he looked directly at Mazzin, and began to walk toward him again.

Frightened now, the Goblin tore his eyes away from Garrhyn's, and gaped at the Greencrystal in his hand. He shook the Stone, and cried "Stone! Rip the earth to protect me from the King! Make a gulf he cannot cross, for he means me harm!"

The ground between Garrhyn and Mazzin seemed to clench itself before it began to shake. The earth groaned, then called out in an angry, thunderous roar as the Greencrystal obeyed the master who held it. The quake was shallow, but it did the trick. In moments there was a gaping crevice between the King and the Goblin.

Undaunted, Garrhyn kept walking toward his enemy.

Relieved that the Greencrystal had responded to his will, Mazzin gave a convulsive laugh. "Stone!" he commanded, shrieking on the edge of hysteria. "End the King! And end the Queen! Destroy all who love them, and then destroy Elvenhome! And give me the circlet of the High King, at once!"

Garrhyn reached the crevice in the ground that separated him from Mazzin. It was too wide to step over.

The oak circlet struggled to leave him, pulling at Garrhyn's long hair as it tried to obey Mazzin's command.

Satisfied that he was in control, Mazzin danced in a delighted frenzy, urging the Stone to instantly obey him in all things. As he skipped around, he waved the Greencrystal high in the air above his head, glancing only fractionally at Garrhyn.

Bathed in gold-green light, the King stood still, and lifted his voice above the din as he said a single word: "Enough."

Nothing much happened. Mazzin continued to dance and issue raving commands. The forest floor quivered beneath their feet, unsure of what to do next.

Garrhyn sighed, then smiled as he shouted. "Greencrystal, hear me. I too speak the Word, and also the *rest* of the Words: *for Garrhydan, son of Garrhyn, King of the Faeries.*"

The gold-green light around Garrhyn burst into brilliant splendor, brightly illuminating the entire clearing as if were actually closer to noon than after nine in the evening.

"Come home," Garrhyn said to the Greencrystal, and held up his hand.

The Greencrystal ripped itself from Mazzin's manic grip and flew straight across the clearing so quickly that the Goblin did not understand at first what was happening. He watched in growing horror as the Stone slammed itself into Garrhyn's open hand and he closed his fingers around it.

Mazzin's scream was frantic. "I am the Stone's master! I have the Word!"

Garrhyn shook his head.

The Goblin roared in disbelief. "I have studied and planned this for a hundred years! It is not possible...you cannot win! I have the Word!"

"Long ago, when I confessed to my men that there was a Word to awaken the power of the Greencrystal, perhaps I failed to mention that the Stone's full might was actually tied to a phrase that *included* that Word. But then, I never intended that anyone else would attempt to use the Greencrystal's power. I was wrong about that. Your greed and theft and Mischief have taught me much, Mazzin. I already knew that the Stone could harm me if commanded to, but it could never obey a command to destroy me, since my energy was part of the making of it. So it may be fair to say," Garrhyn shrugged, and barely covered a rueful smile, "I cheated. You lose. I have grown weary of this game, and even more weary of you."

Mazzin gasped, and turned to run.

"Hold," Garrhyn suggested, and Mazzin froze, unable to move.

The King took a moment to address the Greencrystal he held in his hand. "All is well," he murmured.

Looking around, Garrhyn inspected the clearing, the sky filled with uneasy clouds, the forest around them, the chasm in front of him, and finally at Mazzin. "I shall not *unmake*, for *unmaking* has the potential to cause additional harm. Instead, I shall renew, for that is my birthright, my duty and my honor."

Holding the Greencrystal in front of him, Garrhyn spoke to the forest floor. "Mend the tear with fresh earth and clean, healing water." The forest floor hesitated. Garrhyn smiled. "Go on, then."

Gold-green light flooded the wide crevice, and in a moment, the ground exhaled its tension and filled its own raw wound.

He could not restore the five elderly trees that had fallen. But he encouraged the other trees to welcome the renewed earth by stretching their roots comfortably into it, and thus become more strongly anchored.

Garrhyn moved to where Mazzin stood, eyes wide with terror, furry hands grabbing helplessly for the Stone that was no longer within his reach.

The oak leaf circlet in the King's hair glistened. "I am the High King, the protector of the Fair Folk, the land, and all who inhabit it. I must also protect this world, when the Fey do harm. You have given me much to do, and have

30

caused broken faith, fear, the shedding of innocent blood, and death.

"For your greed, your Mischief, and the crimes you caused, I must act as your King, your judge, and your executioner. Do you understand?"

Garrhyn gestured, and Mazzin was no longer frozen in place. Exhausted, his gaze darted around, trying to chart an escape. After a moment, he slumped to the ground.

"I am of the blood; I have rights that surpass the rules of most Folk," the Goblin whined, with only a calculated touch of defiance. "I am of the House of Horshog! I call for justice and clemency—and mercy."

The King, the judge, and the executioner shook his head, a look of almost-sad resignation on his scarred face. "You gave no mercy, Mazzin of the Northern Kingdom. Therefore, royal blood or no, you are not entitled to receive mercy in return. Done is done."

The clouds dissipated, and the stars slowly reappeared in the night sky as the High King of Faerie put the Greencrystal and its thin chain in the back pocket of his jeans and bowed his head toward the whimpering Goblin sprawled on the ground in front of him.

In the next instant, Garrhyn shifted, and became a bright-hot whoosh of purging, golden fire that completely enveloped Mazzin and his final outraged screams, and reduced him to ashes.

A small night breeze cooled and then blew those ashes carelessly into the darkness.

Next, the glittering fire moved around the forest thicket where the duel had taken place, purging every trace of Mazzin's presence from earth and grass and tree. The Goblin's wooden scrying bowl and even the bottles that had held the wine were consumed by the pure, healing flame that was, in fact, the High King of Faerie.

His work completed, the gold fire cooled and faded, revealing an exhausted but somberly satisfied Garrhyn.

His throat and his hands were still bleeding a little from the wolfhound bites, and his body ached, head and chest felt bruised and tender but he wasn't in pain. With a silent smirk he decided that he was more tired in this moment than he had been in about four hundred years. Breathing deeply, he sat down and settled himself against a tree to rest.

He listened for a while as the trees and their Sprites began to wake themselves up; because Mazzin was ended, his forced quieting no longer held them. Garrhyn could hear the whispers of night birds returning to the sky, and the stealthy movements of other forest residents, too, as they scurried through the darkness.

He closed his eyes and let his mind drift in a peaceful haze of softened golden light, which gently faded as he fell asleep.

HALF AN HOUR after the dawn streaked pink and orange light over the forest where he slept against the tree, several things happened to Garrhyn all at the same time.

He was jolted awake by the loud, shrill scream of a female voice somewhere behind him. The scream coincided with a deep male voice that shouted:

"Your Grace! Dive to the dirt! *Left!*"

Groggy, Garrhyn dove to his left, and as he did, he felt a sharp, cold pain in the back of his right bicep. He was fully awake now, and he realized that he had been stabbed.

In the same instant, two bodies collided and rolled over him onto the ground several feet in front of him.

Despite the searing pain in his upper arm, he saw a tall, lean Wood Elf fighting a short, thick Bogle. He found himself being eased away from the fight by another Wood Elf, a pretty female, who was already pulling off his leather jacket so she could examine the ragged cut that was bleeding down his arm.

"Your Majesty," she said as she tore open his shirt to examine the damage, "I am Hazella. I will attend your wound. Dendrion, my husband," she indicated the Wood Elf ducking a punch from the Bogle, "will attend to your attacker."

As Hazella worked to stop the bleeding of Garrhyn's arm and anxiously glanced at her mate, Garrhyn watched the fight in something of a daze. The Bogle and the Wood Elf battled each other about ten feet away from where he sat now. Bodies were punched and slapped, clothes were torn, a boot flew across the clearing, and the two fighters rolled in the dirt, each trying to gain the upper hand.

At one point, the Bogle bent to the ground and reached for the dagger he'd used on Garrhyn, which had been knocked from his hand when Dendrion had first thrown himself at him. But the Wood Elf was faster than the Bogle, and scooped the dagger from the dirt and leveled it at his opponent.

Belatedly, Garrhyn recognized the dagger as one of his own, one that should have been retrieved along with the Greencrystal and the Queen's jewelry, from the museum in Glasgow. "Slole," Garrhyn muttered under his breath.

Hazella urged the King to slide further away from the fight; this he did without protest. When she was certain that he was settled and the bleeding had slowed down, she left the King and ran back into the trees, returning less than a minute later with some soft loam, which she pressed against the King's wound and bound it in place with a piece of cloth she tore from her skirt. He smiled his thanks, and hoped that she did not notice that he was starting to shiver.

In front of them, Slole heaved himself at the Wood Elf, and slammed him with his fists. The courageous Dendrion fought back, but was tiring.

"With respect, Your Majesty," Hazella murmured, "Please help Dendrion if you can..."

Struggling for the dagger Dendrion held above his head, Slole increased the intensity of the blows he delivered.

When Dendrion felt he could fight no more, he leaned out of Slole's way, and hurled the dagger as hard and as high as he could. It sailed through the air, and landed point-first into a nearby oak tree, far enough above a Bogle's head to be well out of reach.

Slole hit the Wood Elf hard, then bolted for the tree to try to regain the dagger.

Garrhyn's face was pale from shock, blood loss and pain, but he was awake and in command now. More exasperated than angry, he threw a wave of sparkling golden light at Slole and roared "You are not a very *nice* Bogle!" The surprised, not-nice Bogle was suddenly dragged ten feet straight up, then slammed repeatedly against a tree, and finally was left hanging in the air.

Helpless, Slole wriggled. But instead of looking frightened, he filled the early morning with low growls and barks as he glared down in angry defiance.

Hazella ran to Dendrion, helped him up, checked him for damage, then walked him to where Garrhyn sat scowling up at the Bogle.

"Sire," Dendrion bowed to his King.

"Dendrion," Garrhyn nodded in grateful acknowledgement.

The Wood Elves helped Garrhyn to rise and stand. "I owe you my life," he told them. "But before I do anything else, I must rid us of this unseemly creature."

With a small gesture from Garrhyn, Slole—who was still swearing and growling ominous threats—was lowered to within a foot of the ground. At the King's request, Hazella and Dendrion stepped back and moved away, beside the oak tree that held the King's dagger. With a few words of apology to the tree, in the Old Dryad tongue, Dendrion pulled the dagger from the tree's bark, and waited while the tree sealed its small wound.

Hazella and Dendrion then touched the tree's wound with loving fingers, whispered a blessing and their thanks, and stepped behind it.

The Bogle's shouted threats and insults got more vicious. "I should have given the Queen the punishment she deserved. If I had had only a few minutes more—"

Finally, the King spoke to the Bogle. "Enough," he said with a sigh.

Slole, annoyed that his feet were still too far from the ground, hissed at Garrhyn. "I nearly had you! Had I succeeded, Mazzin would have rewarded me well!"

"Mazzin has been ended."

"Untrue!" Slole countered, observing the King with critical eyes. "Mazzin has the Greencrystal, and he will defeat you."

Garrhyn pulled the Stone out of his pocket, waved it so Slole could see it, and returned it to his pocket without a word.

Slole blanched but said nothing, waiting to see what the King would do.

The King was not in the mood to do anything. The wound in his arm hurt, he was hungry, cold, thirsty, exhausted, and a little cranky. He turned and shot a glance at the Wood Elves; they were holding hands as they stood behind a tree, they now had their backs to him so they would not have to watch whatever was going to happen to the Bogle.

Garrhyn sighed again, and wondered if his next move would haunt him for the rest of his days—but he did it anyway.

He turned again and looked at Slole, who was still trying to get his feet to touch the ground while sputtering curses under his breath. When Slole noticed that the King was looking at him, he glowered and spat. "What will you do now, High King of Faerie? Demand royal justice and punish me for the Mischief? Perhaps. But know this: Arrendel was weak, and so are—"

The High King of Faerie flicked his fingers at Slole, and golden light flew at the Bogle. "Shut up. And *end.*"

With that, Garrhyn turned toward Hazella and Dendrion, leaving Slole flailing his arms and mouthing angry words while he began to fade into nothingness.

Walking toward the two Folk who had saved his life, Garrhyn realized that Slole's death was not going to haunt him after all. It was possible to believe now that everyone involved in the horrors of the Mischief had been dealt with. He would grieve for all of the victims of the madness, including his dear friend Emmel, and young Borril, too. There would be little or no sadness over the ending of Mazzin or Slole, even among their own people. Perhaps that was something about which Garrhyn could be sad, but it would not haunt him.

The King only barely made it to the place where Hazella and Dendrion waited, and then slumped to the ground, exhausted. "Let's rest a while longer," he told them.

"Your Grace, you need breakfast. I will find us food and drink," Hazella said, and at the King's nod, she hurried off into the woodland.

Dendrion sat down by Garrhyn, carefully arranging himself around his own cuts, bruises and aches.

"Again, I thank you, truly," Garrhyn said. "How did you come to be here when I had need of you?"

Dendrion smiled, even as he rubbed his sore jaw. "Trees talk. They are terrible gossips, of course, Your Grace, so it was not difficult to find you. When we first arrived, and saw that you were sleeping, we went to see friends who live in the pine grove beyond the hill, over there." He pointed, and winced, then smiled again. "When we returned, just after dawn, we saw the Bogle moving up behind you. But we did not know if he was friend or foe, so we waited. Then we saw that he meant you great harm."

Garrhyn let out a deep breath, and nodded. "Hazella's scream woke me, and your order to move out of the way saved my life. I must think of a practical and tangible way to show you both my gratitude for your quick thinking, your kindness...and your bruises."

Dendrion laughed. "Strange to be rewarded for things we were honored to be able to do, Your Grace. How could we not do all that might be required of us to come to the aid of our King?"

The King studied the Dryad beside him, and smiled. "Even so," he said softly.

As Dendrion handed the King his dagger, which Garrhyn slid into his boot, the Wood Elf said, "The Lady

Maggie also rewarded us. She is why we were here at all. She granted us permission to stand by you in the forest."

"She did what?" Garrhyn was mystified by this, then decided he was both confused and absolutely entertained by this inconceivable notion. "She did?"

Dendrion nodded, pride glowing in his green eyes. "We helped the Lady Maggie, and Swiftaine, too, with a small matter involving the care of the Lady's cats."

Intrigued, Garrhyn raised an eyebrow and grinned. "Tell me more."

By the time Hazella returned with a basket of bread, cheese, ale and fruit, Garrhyn knew as much about Maggie as Dendrion did.

three

IT WAS LATE morning when Swiftaine came in through the front door, scanning for Her Grace. A radio, which sat on the second shelf of a book case on the far wall of the living room, was tuned to a classical station for background atmosphere, playing a Liszt piano sonata.

The Spriggan noticed with surprise and pleasure that Arrendel was seated on a couch, covered with a blanket, a pillow behind his blond head. He looked pale still, but no longer seemed fragile. Swiftaine's heart swelled with gratitude; he covered his feelings with a barky little cough, and waited.

Thomas Lear sat on the opposite couch, a cup of coffee in hand. They had looked toward Swiftaine and nodded as he'd entered the house, but it struck him as he nodded back at them that theirs was a serious conversation, one that he should not interrupt.

Instead, he heard Callie's voice in the kitchen, so the Spriggan moved toward the sound of it, then waited in silence by the kitchen doorway, and watched.

The Queen and Maggie were putting the finishing touches on breakfast. Both women looked a little more rested and relaxed than the past two days might otherwise have allowed for, and Swiftaine was pleased to see it. Her Grace was buttering toast, while Maggie spooned hot scrambled eggs into a large serving bowl. A platter of fried bacon, a basket of fresh fruit and a bowl of applesauce were already on a large serving tray on the kitchen table.

"I am sorry that we haven't yet discovered the charm for keeping him Upworld permanently," Callie was telling Maggie. "We're going to keep looking. I know it exists, I just don't know where, yet. We'll find it."

Maggie nodded. "Right now, I'm grateful he's alive, and that he's already getting better. It's enough for now..."

"...*almost*." The women said the word simultaneously, in the same knowing tone, and laughed together.

Swiftaine made a show of stepping into the kitchen, and the women stopped laughing and looked at him, Callie most expectantly.

"What did you find out?" asked the Queen.

"The Dryads are celebrating; it's a noisy day in the woodland, Your Grace. The trees will be talking about this for three hundred years. His Grace has resolved all issues related to the Mischief. The offending Goblin is ended, as is his last dishonorable Bogle henchman."

Swiftaine's eyes were feasting on breakfast. He was hungry.

"...and...?" Callie prompted, knowing there was more.

"Pretty food!" Swiftaine said, eyeing it.

"The report?" Callie pressed.

"Oh. Yes. The King was injured, but has been attended to, by our friends Hazella and Dendrion, Maggie. All is well. His Grace has the Greencrystal in his possession, as well as one of his daggers, previously purloined by Mazzin. The King has made it known that he expects to arrive here sometime today, to see for himself that all is well before he returns to Faerie." His report delivered, Swiftaine looked with unveiled longing at the large tray that held breakfast, which Maggie was carrying to the living room.

Callie handed Swiftaine a second, smaller tray that was loaded down with napkins, silver flatware, salt, pepper, a full toast rack, and butter. "Thank you, Swiftaine, for your excellent report."

"I do enjoy listening to the trees and their Sprites gossiping, Your Grace," admitted the Spriggan. "And Upworld trees are much freer with their opinions than their cousins at home."

"Nevertheless," she said very quietly, "should I be concerned about his injury?"

"The trees were not, so I do not believe so, Your Grace. He was seen laughing with the Dryads who attend him. I am eager for His Grace's grand telling of this tale. Provided, of course," he winked at Callie now, and turned to take the tray out of the kitchen to the dining room, "that I do not starve to death before then..."

The group had their rather late breakfast together in the living room, so that Arrendel did not have to get up from the couch. Maggie sat beside him, and Thomas and Callie sat across from them on the opposite couch, the large coffee table between them covered with breakfast. It was a time to revel in small talk, and they did.

Swiftaine sat up on the bookshelf, beside the radio, upon which he had placed the tea saucer that held his breakfast. His long fingers twitched as he reached for the last bite of fried bacon and put it in his mouth. When he had finished eating his buttered toast, his fingers twitched some more, and found their way to the buttons on the radio, which he began to play with as unobtrusively as possible.

"Oh, don't say that—I can't believe you're not going to wait for the King, Callie." Maggie was saying. "You can't leave before he gets here."

Callie shrugged. "He is coming to see Arrendel, but I'm sure he's been eager to meet you. You don't need me here, and Thomas and I should be getting back. I left Zodiac and one of my most trusted councilors in charge, and it's time I let them get on with their business instead of having them deal with mine." The Queen grinned at Maggie. "I'm hoping to be permitted to visit you here anytime I'm in the neighborhood, though."

Maggie grinned back at her new friend. "I'd like that."

The radio station slid from classical music to a yodeling competition.

All eyes turned to Swiftaine, who failed to look innocent.

"Great Gods!" Callie groaned. "Find something else and then leave the radio alone, or switch it off, Swiftaine."

With a small pout, the Spriggan moved the tuning button scratchily across several other stations.

"Thank you for making breakfast, Ladies," said Arrendel. "It was very nice."

"Glad to hear it," Maggie said. "I was afraid I'd over-seasoned the eggs."

"They were great," Thomas replied.

"Tasty," Arrendel added.

"Except that we really can't," Swiftaine mumbled to himself, unaware that he'd been heard by everyone around the coffee table.

"You can't what?" Maggie wanted to know.

"Taste the food. Not very much," Swiftaine told her, and Callie and Arrendel both gasped.

"Swiftaine!" Arrendel chided.

Red-faced, Callie glowered at the Spriggan hard enough to make him wince. "Swiftaine, why I haven't locked you away in a very small box for a very long time is a mystery to me...but one that I may rectify within the hour..."

Maggie was looking at Arrendel in amazement bordering on hurt. "You can't taste the food I cook?"

Helpless, Arrendel looked back at her, then glanced at Callie for assistance.

"I'm sorry about that," Callie apologized. "Maggie, it's not your food, it's all Upworld food. The Fair Folk can't smell or taste most of it. It's not that the food is bad, it's that it doesn't taste or smell like like our food. Which is why uninformed Faeries who come Upworld can conceivably starve to death, even with all the mortal food

41

available around them. They don't recognize it as food, don't know they can eat it and be sustained by it."

"Wow..." Thomas whistled.

Maggie gaped at Arrendel, whose blue eyes reflected unhappiness when they met her. "So when you tell me how much you liked dinner, for example, you're not telling me that it was delicious...you're telling me that you appreciated that I did the work and made the meal and that you're glad your stomach is full?" Her sudden, understanding smile was soft and genuine.

"Something like that," he said, glowing with love for her.

"So..." Thomas was thinking about mortal food versus Faerie food now. "So that means that when I eat Upworld food when I'm in Elvenhome, the Folk doing the cooking can't taste it, or smell it?"

Callie was considering this. "In a way. We're aware of certain faint scents, and we know the difference between the thin aroma of mortal food when it's good and the thin odor of mortal food when it's bad. And of course we can see if something's not right." She turned to Thomas and put a hand on his arm. "It's why mortals should never eat Faerie food, Thomas. The differences between what you can eat what we can eat alter mortal chemistry, sometimes in ways we can't predict or recognize right away."

"Like Terena?" Thomas asked.

"Yes. Like Terena, for example," Callie conceded.

Thomas was still thinking. "Wait a minute...if you can't taste food up here, what about whisky, and other life-preserving alcoholic beverages?"

Arrendel shrugged. "We can't taste most of them the way you can. The aromas and flavors are too weak. *Subtle* might be a better word."

Thomas looked almost sad. "That's positively dismal!"

"We can appreciate some of the better Highland whiskies, and if we drink enough, we can sometimes experience some of the more pleasant side effects that you mortals do when you drink too much," Arrendel added.

Swiftaine piped in, almost absently, since he was no longer in trouble with the Queen. "But we have to drink a lot of it."

Shaking his head in sympathy, Thomas declared, "They must be devastated, even suicidal, in Craigellachie, guys."

Maggie asked Thomas, "What's in—"

Everyone else spoke at the same time. "The Macallan distillery."

The radio slid across a few more stations, scratching across the laughter and conversation. Callie growled at the twitching fingers tapping on the radio. "Swiftaine, if you don't take your long, hairy fingers away from those buttons, I'm going to—"

In immediate response, the Spriggan stuffed those long fingers under his backside and sat down on them hard, as a BBC Radio announcer continued his report and everyone sat wide-eyed and silent as they listened:

"...to the report of minor seismic activity, 3.4 on the Richter scale, in the greenwood forty kilometers south of Inverness, at 21:30 last night. There were also local reports of thunder and lightning storms, although no rain fell, and reports of light activity as well, although of course it is not the season for the Northern Lights. The best we can ascertain," said the announcer with a teasing smile in his voice, "is that last night, the Fair Folk had a devil of a *ceilidh*! In other news—"

Swiftaine snapped off the radio, and the power button with it. "Oops," he said.

The Fey and the two mortals in Maggie's living room laughed hard and long. And with the laughter came the halting, first steps of healing for each one of them.

After the breakfast dishes had been washed by none other than Thomas Lear, Rock Star and Sometime Houseboy, he dried his hands on a dish towel, then returned to the living room to join the others.

Before he could sit down on the couch beside Callie, she gave him a near-timid, apologetic look, followed by a sunny smile and said, "Why don't you get your guitar, sit out in the sunshine, and play some of your songs for Maggie?"

He was not at all certain that he wasn't being dismissed.

Maggie chuckled. "I think Callie and Arrendel need to talk, Thomas. Let's go." She leaned down and gave Arrendel a kiss, then stood up and teased Thomas toward the front door.

Thomas nodded, but he was still a little confused. "Okay," he said. "But there's no guitar. It's still at my place, at the castle."

"Actually, it's in the Fiat, on the back seat."

He asked before he thought. "Zodiac and I did not bring it when we came up from Queensgate. How did it...?"

Callie grinned. "Is that a question you want to own the answer to?" She winked at her Court Singer as he shook his head with conviction. "No, I didn't think so. Now go relax and enjoy yourselves for a while. I'll come out and join you later."

They waited until Thomas pulled the front door closed behind him, and Callie sighed as she turned toward Arrendel, who watched her with interest from his recumbent position on the couch.

"It can't be as bad as all that...can it?" he asked. "What did Swiftaine tell you about the King?"

Callie moved to Arrendel's couch, and fussed with the blanket and his pillow a bit before she sat on the floor beside him. "Swiftaine's been talking to the Wood Sprites. Mazzin and Slole are ended, and Garrhyn was injured, but not seriously. He's in the company of two Dryads, and is on his way here now. He will want to be reassured that you are well, and to meet the woman who captured your heart, Cousin." She reached for Arrendel's hand, and laid her head against his hip. "Oh, what am I going to do? I won't have anyone to talk to, once you're living here with

44

Maggie. There will be no one I can whine at, complain to, or just fret in front of."

"Have all of your Ladies vanished, or lost the power of gossip, or no longer feel the need to soothe, support, and comfort you? Great Gods! Toss them in the cellars until they behave!"

"Shut up. It's not the same, and you know it."

"I know. But I like it when you get prickly." He gave her hand an affectionate squeeze.

"From the time we were *weans*, Arrendel, you were the only person in the world who didn't care if I was a crown princess, and even now you never expect me to always be the High Queen. You take me just as I am, in ways that so few others do. How am I going to manage without you?"

Arrendel smiled, and gave Callie's hand another squeeze. "What has happened to you, Old Thing? The Mischief appears to have been handled by the King, and we can trust that all will be well again. What has you so unhappy?"

Callie closed her eyes, took a deep breath, and snuggled against her dearest friend. "I think I'm tired, every way there is to be tired."

"Very likely."

"This Mischief badly frightened me, Arrendel. And I do not get frightened."

She did not see the look in his eyes, but she could feel it. "We were *all* frightened by that Mischief," he reminded her.

"True enough," she conceded. "But I do not know when I have felt this much alone."

He touched her hair with his other hand, and stroked her head to comfort her. "Tell me."

"So much has happened in so short a time. Perhaps I have lost my way. Terena is gone, you were forced to act in my stead and had to do things that tore at your heart, things I should have been responsible for."

Arrendel lifted Callie's chin so she could face him. She opened her eyes, and he met her gaze with calm certainty. "You are not to blame because I had to do my duty as the Heir Apparent. Done is done, no matter who had to own the doing. Know that, and let it go."

He waited until she gave him a resigned nod, and then put her head back down against his hip. "What else?" he prodded.

"Thomas is wonderful, isn't he?" She didn't wait for Arrendel to reply to the rhetorical question. "He's smart, he's pretty to look at and listen to. He's also funny, and warm, and a very talented lover, too. He's a bit spoiled and moody and he doesn't seem to truly like himself, does he? But he's gifted, he's passionate, and in his way, his magic is strong. And the music...the music makes everything all right somehow. For himself, for me, for all of us, hey?"

Arrendel nodded. "Perhaps you should spend some time alone with Thomas and his guitar. He and his music will help you to not feel so sad."

She looked up at him then. "Am I so sad, then?"

"You are, Cousin. What else is troubling you?"

He knew, of course, but he also knew she needed to speak the words.

"Garrhyn. He's different." She waited for Arrendel to say something helpful. When he did not, she continued in almost a whisper. "I don't know what it is, exactly. But he has changed. Why is that, do you think?"

"The broad answer is, I believe, that life is change, and nearly everything and everyone we encounter changes us, right?" Arrendel considered his words, then spoke again. "The truer answer is that I don't know how Garrhyn has changed; we haven't talked much. For what it's worth, though, Cousin, I don't know yet how *I've* changed because of the Mischief, and other things, but I know I have. We have all changed, in our own small ways. We can't help it, it's the natural course of life. The Mischief surely changed us, continues to do so. Our friend Thomas Lear has changed us. You are happier than you have been a long while. The Folk thrive on his presence, his words and his music. He has brought his unique perceptions and humor and personality to our very steady, merry, comfortable way of life. I've been glad of my friendship with him..."

Callie sighed. "And Garrhyn? What of his changes? I don't think I understand them."

"And as for Garrhyn," Arrendel began, thinking as he spoke, "the King as well as the man, we can surely assume that in recent months he has had encounters and experiences enough to cause him to change as well, things that only he may know about. The loss of Terena was especially hard for him, of course. And he will not soon recover from having lost Emmel. There are things about the Mischief that must haunt him as the King; he feels responsibility because he wanted to get the Greencrystal back in the first place. Of late, timing and circumstance have put you and Garrhyn together more frequently than in many years, making opportunity for encounters. Some of those encounters have been positive, and have made small changes to your strained relationship. Is this not so?"

"Yes, it is so." Callie almost smiled. "We do not seem to bark at each other, and neither of us have gone up in flames." She wanted to tell him about her unexpected meeting with Garrhyn in the forest, but she was still thinking about it so chose not to share it yet. She had something else more firmly on her mind.

"Arrendel...I have a secret: I have fallen in love with Thomas Lear," Callie groaned. She did not often develop intense feelings for her Court Singers. There had only been a few mortals over the hundreds of years who had touched Callie's lonely heart. She looked at her cousin, expecting to see the shock of her secret on his face. It was not there.

"I know you are in love with Thomas," Arrendel told her, and the surprise on her face made him laugh. "And...what of Garrhyn?"

"Strange as it seems, somehow, I have begun to think that a small part of me might still be in love with him, too. It is unfortunate that I will likely be gone before he arrives here to see you. Or perhaps not. Still, the time I spent with him yesterday was in some ways a reminder of our beginning. " Callie put her head back down against her cousin's arm. "I find that I am overwhelmed by everything, and that is unsettling, since I am never overwhelmed by *anything*. Events do not affect me in this way. I am tired. I have too much on my mind. The Folk need me, and I need them. And because you are staying here with Maggie, I am feeling lost and alone—and very sorry for myself. By the gods, Arrendel, I don't want to be Queen today. Can we get somebody else to do it?"

"Poor Old Thing," Arrendel soothed her, his voice thick with sympathy and love. "Thomas isn't old enough, wise enough, or Fey enough to truly understand you, although he probably would like to be the person you'd rely on. And Garrhyn is too tied up himself to be a true friend to you right now, although he knows you and he once knew how to be what you needed. And, worst of all, your faithless cousin is abandoning you, out of reach, living *worlds* away..."

Callie bolted up, and made a face at him. "Oh, damn you, Arrendel, it's not so far away!" Callie shrugged, then, quite by surprise, laughed; Arrendel patted her on the arm and laughed with her. "I seem to be all over the chessboard today."

"I think you need a brief respite from everything, Old Thing, except maybe from Thomas Lear," he suggested. "Instead of getting to Queensgate and Elvenhome today, perhaps you should stay Upworld for a day or two longer. Give yourself time with Thomas and his music. Grant yourself a little distance from everything else. Rest, renew, and then go home, feeling stronger and more like the Queen that you are. It might help."

Callie considered this. "It might, at that." She reached up and gave Arrendel a hug and a kiss. "Thank you." She settled down, her back against the couch, Arrendel's arm still around her. "Now: what in the world are we going to do about *you*, Cousin?"

Maggie was seated on the porch swing when Thomas got there with his guitar. He put the case on the ground and sat down beside her.

"So," Maggie began, "now that we've survived the strangest junk in the world, and have lived to laugh another day, what's next for you?"

Thomas shrugged. "Callie and I go back to Elvenhome."

"No, I mean, after your year and a day, Thomas. What's next for you?"

He nodded, understanding now. "Oh. My plan is to get back to my life. I'll write songs, record a new album or two, or ten."

"You'll return and get busy, just like that?" Maggie asked.

"Sure. Musicians have taken time away from the industry before and have come back stronger than ever. That's what I'm aiming for."

She studied him. "After spending time in Faerie, do you think that that will be enough for you? After all you've seen, all you've experienced? Now that you know there's so much more than what you thought was real about the world?"

Considering this, his nod was slow. "Yes. Since I met Callie, my music is better. Maybe I care about it in a different, deeper way. I've always believed that everything is viable 'grist for the mill,' so it makes sense to me that all I will have learned and thought about and felt by the end of my year will show up in the music one way or another."

"Fair enough," Maggie told him. "You may be on to something, although I'd never thought about it the way you have. I realized four years ago, after I met Arrendel, that my writing would never be the same again. The fiction. The faerie tales, I mean." She looked toward the house. "How could anyone meet and come to know these amazing Folk, and remain unchanged?"

Thomas nodded his agreement, deciding not to admit that he hadn't quite considered this in the way Maggie had.

The look in her eyes was earnest. "I also wanted to tell you that of course I would never say anything about your presence here, or anyplace else. I am aware that you are Absent Without Leave from the world we know. Your disappearance was in the papers, of course. I'll keep the secret, without question."

Since she was Arrendel's Lady, it had never occurred to him that she would have taken any other position. He told her this with a wry grin.

"Before we leave today, I'm going to give you my home address and private phone numbers in Los Angeles. Seriously, Maggie, if you ever need anything from me, anything at all, I hope you'll call or write, or come find me."

She was touched by the sincerity on his face. "That's kind, Thomas. I was hoping we might arrange to stay in touch. Especially since we have people in common."

"Goddammit, this is so surreal, isn't it?" he blurted, surprised as the words came unbidden. "I mean, damn, we really, really hang out with *Faeries*. We poor mortals have been through some really strange shit."

"It was strange for them, too, Thomas," Maggie reminded him.

"True. But now that the bad stuff is over—I think it's over, don't you?—doesn't it all just mess with your head?"

"It does. I'm afraid it will for a long time. But it also reminds me about what's important."

She was quiet while Thomas thought about that for a minute or two. "You've got a point," he said. This, too, had not occurred to him, although it would have eventually, he hoped.

Thomas stopped the swing and bent down, then lifted his old friend from the guitar case.

Maggie's eyes widened in genuine delight. Her heart might have even skipped a beat. "You're really going to play something for me?"

Thomas Lear, Rock Star and Court Singer, winked at her. "By command of the High Queen of Faerie." He ran his fingers over the strings, and corrected the tuning. "What would you like to hear?"

She didn't need to think about it at all. "Would you play 'I Don't Think That I Can Love You'?"

She'd surprised him, and the fact that she had done so startled them both. Maggie did not know how to read the look on his face. "Thomas? Did I say something wrong?"

He recovered fast, and gave her one of his best smiles. "No. It's just that I haven't thought about that song in ages. It's one of my first songs, considered "B-side" material. It didn't get much air play, so I'm almost amazed you even know it. I haven't sung it in about five years, maybe more." He eyed her. "It's a sad one. Interesting choice, for a woman so obviously in love."

"Oh, shut up. It's a great song. The melody is heartbreaking and beautiful, the words are raw and so honest, and you sing it so well. It's one of my very favorite songs. I've loved it for a long time."

"Then here is," Thomas said, sliding into poet/musician/performer mode. "Just for you, Maggie."

I don't think that I can love you
I haven't got the heart;
I'm afraid of getting shattered,
too afraid to do my part
to make the magic happen
and to finish what I start.

I don't think that I can love you
but I wish I was strong enough to try.

I don't think that you can love me;

51

you ache for someone else's touch.
You dream of him on starless nights
and your need for him is such
that I don't think I can reach you
though I want to very much.

I don't think that you can love me
but I wish you could have tried.

I don't think we'll love each other.
The admission made us cry;
our lives are far too different
and it makes no sense to lie.
If we had met some other day,
and time hadn't passed us by...

I don't think we'll love each other
but I wish we knew how
I only wish we knew how
to have given it a try.
I don't think that I can love you
but I wish to God I was strong enough to try.

When the guitar was silent and still, Thomas took a deep, sad breath, glanced at Maggie, and saw that she was as moved by the performance of the song as he was. After a moment, they smiled at each other, and another unspoken bond was forged between them.

"More?" he asked, when she was ready.

"Are you kidding me?" Maggie laughed in amazement. "I've got *Thomas Lear* beside me with a guitar. Of *course* more!"

He chuckled, and began to play "Dangerous Blue Eyes."

After that, he played an unfinished song called "All My Heart Needs to Know," which he told Maggie he was writing to honor a friend who had died recently. Wide-eyed, Maggie nearly wept over the lyrics. Thomas almost did, too. He followed the sweet, sad song with a couple of happier ones, and then took a few more of her requests.

Maggie sat back, and let the music hold her for a while as she experienced Thomas Lear, live in concert, sitting beside her.

An hour or so later, Callie and Thomas said goodbye to Maggie, Arrendel and Swiftaine. The Spriggan disappeared in a spark of flying fur three seconds after he had somberly shaken hands with Thomas and had received thanks, as well as a warning to behave himself, from his Queen.

"Any message for the King?" Arrendel asked Callie as he rose carefully from the couch, watching Maggie and Thomas hug each other.

"Only that I shall return to Elvenhome in a day or two, on the advice of my best friend. Thank you for that." Callie kissed her cousin's cheek, and they put their arms around each other for a long hug. "Tell him I'm very proud of...that I'm glad he...oh, just greet him for me, and ask him to do something very nice for Boston and Zodiac and the others who have warded Elvenhome in our absence."

"I will," Arrendel assured her. "Be good to yourself, Old Thing. Give yourself time to think, and to breathe, all right?"

"I shall try. And *you*...you get well."

"That is the plan."

"I like your Maggie. She's made of strong, smart stuff. And she loves you, too. Although I can't imagine why."

Then Maggie and Callie hugged each other. Callie whispered a few words into Maggie's ear. She nodded, and whispered back.

Thomas and Arrendel shook hands, then hugged each other hard.

"Take it easy," Thomas told his friend. "Be happy."

"I shall do both," Arrendel said with a tired but wry smile as he sat down on the couch. "And I wish the same for you."

Thomas hated goodbyes more than almost anything. He'd long ago run out of cheery words to sail him through the process. "See you later," he managed, and with a nod of his head, followed Callie out the front door with a final wave and wink at Maggie.

Arrendel and Maggie were quiet for a long moment, watching as Callie and Thomas got into the car. The High Queen of Faerie turned the key in the ignition, and the Fiat came to life, purred for a moment, and then drove away.

Maggie held a piece of paper in her hand. On it, Thomas had written his address, his several private phone numbers, the name of his business manager, and the manager's phone number. After reading the information five or six times, she turned and looked at her exhausted but cheerful lover, and spoke the only word that could reasonably form itself in her own tired brain:

"Wow..."

The rest of the day had moved slowly and uneventfully, for which Maggie was grateful. She was relieved and exhausted, but she was also amazed, humbled, thrilled, still slightly awed, and mystified, too. She knew it would take her weeks to process all the things she'd seen, experienced, and felt over the past few days. She was of the opinion that very little could impress her now.

The early evening found her in her office, curled up in her favorite chair and reading Dickens, when she heard the knock on the front door. For a second, her heart stopped; she knew who it had to be. It wasn't that she'd forgotten that the encounter was going to occur, exactly. It was more like she'd put it out of her head, since she did not know how to think about it. Arrendel had told her that it was possible that they wouldn't see their guest for a day or so, depending on his injury and what else he had to do before he visited them. This thought allowed Maggie to mentally push the pending arrival out just that much further. In any event, she knew she was counting on Arrendel, or even Swiftaine, to deal with the awkward introductions.

But there it was again: the knock on the door.

Arrendel had gone upstairs some time ago to take a nap. Maggie didn't have a clue where Swiftaine was, but it was likely that the Spriggan was outside somewhere, or he'd be jumping around announcing that their visitor had finally arrived.

With an uneasy jolt to her stomach, she realized that she was going to have to answer the door herself. Trembling only a little, she got up out of her chair, dropped *Barnaby Rudge* in it, and hurried to the living room.

A quick, wistful glance at the staircase told her that Arrendel was asleep. She was on her own.

Maggie took a deep breath, and opened the front door.

Her first glance at the man who smiled at her from the other side of the screen door didn't match her reflexive, storytelling mental image of what the High King of Faerie should look like...until he spoke.

"You must be Maggie," he said, and the porch light above him revealed a fast flicker of kindness, humor, and almost tangible personal power that reversed her original opinion before it had had time to fully form. His smile was warm, genuine, and strong. He wore a circlet crown that had golden oak leaves on it. Maggie recognized at once that this had been the ransom demand for Arrendel.

Jolted by that thought, Maggie opened the screen door at once, bowed her head in respect, and welcomed His Grace into the cottage.

She offered him whisky, which he accepted with thanks. He was tired, and was grateful for her suggestion that they sit on the couches by the fireplace. He watched her lay a fire as they talked.

"I apologize for presuming on your hospitality, dear lady. I needed to know that Arrendel is improving."

"He is. I believe he is still asleep upstairs. We've had Naiad Healers in to help—"

"Bossy old crones," the King chuckled. "But they know what they're about."

"They seemed to," Maggie said. "Arrendel is already much better."

"Is Swiftaine about?" asked the King, looking around. "He's not often far from Arrendel, even when he is instructed otherwise."

Maggie shook her head. "I haven't seen him since the Queen left with Thomas, earlier this afternoon."

If the King's eyes clouded for a fraction of a second at the mention of his Queen and her Court Singer, Maggie chose to take little notice of it, and instead moved back to the subject of the Spriggan. "Swiftaine, Your Grace, saved my life, and Arrendel's, too. While I admit that before, I managed to somehow overlook his stronger, more creative qualities and had focused on the small ways that he can be...um...a *challenge* to deal with, I won't make that mistake again. He was, and is, wonderful, Your Grace, and I am grateful to know that he is around, somewhere."

Maggie put a match to the kindling and, once it caught flame, she stood up, dusted her hands off, and sat on the couch opposite the King. "We heard that you were injured. Is there anything I can do to help?"

He smiled, and she could see how very tired he was. "Thank you, but no. It was a nasty bit of business, but nothing to be concerned about."

"What happened?" Arrendel's voice came from the top of the stairs. The King turned to see his friend make his way down the staircase, and also noticed the look in Maggie's eyes as she watched him descend. "We heard that the Bogle Slole knifed you with your own dagger."

Slowly, Arrendel walked over to the couch where the King sat. The King rose, and they embraced.

"You worried me," he told Arrendel, his voice soft with emotion.

"You weren't the only one who was worried," Arrendel replied just as softly. "I thought I was done." They sat down together, each using an arm of the couch for support. "So what happened?"

The King sighed. "I was rudely awakened by getting stabbed." He pointed to his right arm with his left hand. "In the back. I'd been asleep against a tree at the time."

"It's been looked at?"

The King nodded, and smiled at Maggie across the coffee table. "Slole was interrupted by two friends of yours, Maggie. Two Wood Elves by the names of Hazella and Dendrion."

Maggie's eyes widened.

The King nodded. "And, according to them, I have you to thank for their being present when I was in danger."

Maggie's eyes widened more. "How?"

Beaming now, the King laughed. "Did you give them permission to attend me when I arrived to deal with Mazzin? They took you at your word, and not only watched over me when I slept, but managed to interfere with Slole just as he was about to stab me to death."

"Wow..." Maggie blurted.

"And your injury? A knife wound?" Arrendel frowned.

The King pulled himself out of his leather jacket, and showed Arrendel and Maggie the slash on the back of the right sleeve. "Hazella attended to the wound, stopped the bleeding, and put some forest loam on it. It will heal. I can be patient."

Maggie was thinking. "Your Grace, can you not simply heal the wound and be done with it?"

He gave Arrendel a side glance. "Your Lady is smart." He looked at Maggie with approval. "It's not quite that easy. There is a difference between making a thing happen, and the unmaking of a thing that has happened." To his amazement, he noticed that she was following this.

"There is danger in unmaking. If you don't know all that went into the making of a thing, the unmaking of it—"

"—has unforeseen complications?" Maggie finished his sentence.

"Just so," said the King. "I will let Nature take her course."

"Are you in pain?" Maggie wanted to know.

"It's not too bad," he told her. "The whisky is helpful."

"Would you like me to get you something else to make it feel better? Aspirin? A warm compress?"

The King grinned at Arrendel. "She seems to be quite handy to have around."

It didn't take long for Maggie to recognize that Arrendel and the King needed some time alone to talk. She excused herself and, grabbing a glass of water from the kitchen, retired to her office, closing the door behind her.

"Are you truly well, Your Grace?" Arrendel pressed.

"Are you?"

They both laughed.

Arrendel rose from the couch, got a crystal glass and the bottle of whisky that Maggie had opened for the King, and brought them to the coffee table. Once there, he sat down again, poured himself a drink, and refilled Garrhyn's glass.

"The Queen told me to thank you, and to express her pride in the work you did to end the Mischief," Arrendel began. "She seemed to need a small respite, so I suggested to her that she stay in Edinburgh and rest for a day or so before returning home. She agreed. She also said something about you making sure that everyone who is warding the castle and the Folk during the Royal Absence gets duly rewarded for their hard work."

Garrhyn nodded, but said nothing.

"She is tired and out of sorts, as we all are," Arrendel confessed.

"True enough. Did she tell you that she said the child's name? Our son's?"

Arrendel's mouth opened, and closed again.

"She did," Garrhyn explained, "when she approached Mazzin. Also, when she sent me some of her own power last night, so that I could defeat the damned Goblin. I don't know that she'd said his name too many times since..." his voice trailed off for a second. "And neither had I. She did it, though. Brave lass, that one, eh?"

"I think we've all been brave. We deserve another drink."

They sat silently for a long moment. Arrendel had a thought, and a huge grin spread on across his face. "Swiftaine told Maggie this morning that we can't taste mortal food."

"Oh?"

"Yes. He told her this during breakfast."

"No..."

"Yes!"

"And how did she take it, considering she's been feeding you all this time?"

"Quite well, actually. She has a good heart, and wicked sense of humor."

"An inspiring combination in a woman," laughed Garrhyn. "She seems to be quite taken with you."

"And I with her, Your Grace. I have loved her for the last four years, and have wanted no other."

"Seeing you together, I agree that there is every reason for you to wish to stay here with her, without interruption."

Arrendel's sigh was infused with sadness. "I appreciate that. But I have been unable to discover the charm that will allow me to stay permanently. The Queen has promised that she will keep looking, and of course I will keep looking. I thought I'd found it...but that is a harsh story. One for another time, perhaps."

Garrhyn eyed Arrendel, his gaze thoughtful. "It must chafe you, wanting to be here with the Lovely Maggie, and also wanting to be in Faerie."

Shrugging, Arrendel sighed again. "I am a royal prince of Faerie; my life has always belonged to the land and its Folk, and I am honored that it is so. I am physically tied to the land, just as you are. I do not truly have a choice about staying Upworld for long periods of time. Still, if I had two hearts, I'd keep one here, and one at home. As it is, I've chosen to give my one heart to Maggie. I can continue to divide my time between the woman I love, and the people I love." His face wore a faintly wry smile, but there was still that hint of sadness in it.

Garrhyn turned and faced his friend. "Arrendel, if I work the charm that will allow you stay here with Maggie without the need to return to Faerie to stay well and alive, would that please you?"

Arrendel's surprise made him speechless.

Garrhyn continued: "Before you say anything, have you considered what would happen if you could stay with Maggie permanently, and give up Faerie? Forgive my candor, but if you give up Faerie, and your life there, in exchange for a life here, with her, what will you do when she has ended, and you are forced to remain here for all time?"

Stunned to his core, Arrendel stared at his hands. "I would choose Maggie, and live with the consequences."

"And forever give up your life at home?"

"Yes," Arrendel whispered. "If that is the price."

"I see." Garrhyn attempted to stifle a growing grin, but gave up. "What would you say if I told you I've discovered the charm that will allow you to have both Maggie *and* Faerie?"

Arrendel's head jerked toward Garrhyn.

"While I was dealing with that old stoat Horshog in the Northern Kingdom, I paid a brief visit to his father's uncle, Riban of Northia, longtime dreamer and sometimes master of archaic Fey magic." The King's laughter was merry as he watched Arrendel's face begin to register a glimmer of understanding. "I told him about your problem. He spent a few hours researching the notion, and found what you have been looking for."

"He found it?"

Garrhyn nodded. "He did. Tested it, too."

The Water Faerie was struggling to grasp this information. "Tested?"

"Yes. On one of his cats."

There was an explosion of unsuccessfully suppressed giggling from the staircase. Garrhyn and Arrendel turned and were surprised to see Maggie, sitting on the stairs next to Swiftaine. Both the lady and the Spriggan were laughing helplessly.

Arrendel looked stunned, and said nothing. The King rose, and turned toward them, his face quite serious. "It is unwise to spy on private conversations of this nature, Maggie. It is both impolite, and often dangerous." He glared at Swiftaine, who squirmed and twitched before he evaporated from the room, leaving Maggie alone to answer to the King.

Maggie did not appear to feel humbled, or much threatened, by the King's ire or Arrendel's silence. She stood up, and walked over to where Arrendel sat.

"Your Grace, when Swiftaine popped into my office and told me that you were discussing...well, it involves me, too, and I wanted to hear everything you had to say, not just what you thought might be appropriate for mortal ears.

"Arrendel," she murmured as she stroked his shoulder in gentle supplication, "this is about us, our choices, not just yours alone." She looked at the King, her eyes searching his for understanding and acceptance. "I knew there was no danger of exposing you to things you might have concerns over, Your Grace. I've been writing Faerie tales for twenty-five years, and I know the difference between fancy and fact. I know that while you are present here, Arrendel would never address you by your True

61

Name, in case it could be overheard and thus make you potentially vulnerable."

Garrhyn stared at Maggie, his face unreadable.

"Has he in fact used your True Name since you arrived? Correct me, Your Grace, if I am wrong."

The King met her steady gaze, and then shook his head. "He did not. You are rude, and perhaps beyond your depth, Lady, but you are correct."

Maggie did not flinch, or look away as she faced the King, defiance flickering in her pale blue eyes. "I regret that you might not think well of me, Your Grace, but I can live with that. I have spent four years loving a Water Faerie, and, amazingly, been loved in return. I have shared my home, and sometimes my temper, with a Spriggan. I have watched my true love shift from the form I know, and change into water. And quite recently I have been in the unwilling company of bad Goblins, Bogles, Gnomes, a Phooka, and a Bodach. I have also been in the delightful company of Dryads, and exposed to gifted Naiad Healers—who disapprove of me, by the way. And I've been in the astonishing, delightful company of the High Queen of Faerie and an internationally-famous, mysterious, wonderful mortal rock-star musician. And now I am standing before the High King of Faerie!

"Do you seriously think I am going to use lightly, or with evil intent, the True Names of the two Folk with whom I've shared my life? I spent a good bit of time with the Queen over the last two days; I am unaware of her True Name, and am glad of it. I would never wish to be part of anything that caused harm, or any kind of wrong for the Folk.

"I wear a Dunnor's Bell, given to me by the man I love, and with whom I want to wake up every morning for the rest of my life.

"Now: if you know the charm that will grant Arrendel the greatest gift, to let him have both this life with me, and his life in Faerie, let's have it!"

Taking a deep, elongated breath, Garrhyn looked at Arrendel and shook his head. "I do not know whether to congratulate you or sympathize with you, my friend. She is quite... something, is she not?"

"At times, my King, words truly fail," Arrendel confessed, pride vying with hope in his dark blue eyes. He took Maggie's hand, kissed it, and fell in love with her all over again.

As she squeezed Arrendel's hand, Maggie swallowed a smile and got down to business. "Since that's settled, Gentlemen, let's discuss the charm. And before we get started, maybe we should talk about what happened to Riban's cat...?"

THE ACTUAL, PHYSICAL resolution of Arrendel's problem took less time to implement than either the imaginative Maggie or the amazed Arrendel himself could have dreamed possible.

The King stood silent beside Arrendel near the porch, observing as Swiftaine poured two buckets of loch water into a large metal container in the middle of the yard.

It was dark, but the full moon shone steady and bright, as if were granting her approval of the King's work.

The Spriggan took the now-empty buckets to the side of the cottage, turned one over and sat down on it, watching and twitching. After a hug and a long kiss from Arrendel, Maggie moved to the porch swing, and sat, reminding herself to stay quiet as she pulled her sweater tight against the night's chill.

The King walked to the metal container, looked up at the sky for a minute or so, and then smiled. He gestured to Arrendel, who crossed the yard to stand beside him. Arrendel then slid out of his slippers, and stood in the contained loch water.

Golden light shimmered around the King, then also embraced Arrendel and the water. Words were spoken that only Arrendel heard. Then a wild streak of solid golden light shot, bright and silent, from the King's circlet crown and into Arrendel's right eye.

Maggie gasped, but kept her promise and said nothing. Nor did she move. She peered over at Swiftaine, and saw that he had covered his face with his twitching fingers. She watched the Spriggan, until she decided that he was all right. When Maggie returned her attention to Arrendel and the King, they were already finished.

Arrendel had had to make some hard decisions, but he'd made them gladly. He could now live anywhere Upworld that he chose, for as long as he chose, without suffering ill effects, thinning or fading for lack of natural Faerie sustenance, light and water.

On the other hand, Faerie food was forbidden from now on—even when he chose to return to Faerie forever—but Arrendel made the sacrifice with courage, and smiled when Maggie insisted that the King make it possible for Arrendel to actually taste and enjoy mortal food in its stead. Delighted with her, the King flicked the adjustment into place, just to see her smile.

And all it cost the Water Faerie, really, was a change of eye color. Arrendel's eyes were still a vivid shade of deep blue; however, one eye now had something extra. Within it shining blueness, Arrendel's right eye had a permanent, distinct spray of golden flecks in it.

The charm was about the eye.

Using moonlight, his own golden magic, and the music of the night sky, the King had also created a small but strong protective patch for Arrendel's newly-changed eye. When Arrendel chose to return to Faerie by water, or by land through the portals like the one at Queensgate, his re-entry would only be successful if he wore the patch over his gold-flecked right eye for the entire journey homeward. Once in Faerie, he would have to keep his gold-flecked eye covered at all times, or he would be unable to return to his life Upworld.

"A patch: for protection, and for promise," the King said, in an even tone that rang of ritual.

"For protection, and for promise," Arrendel repeated, bowing his head. "Sire, dear my friend, you have given me the opportunity to live the lives my heart wants to live."

"Then be at peace, Arrendel, and live all of your lives."

The Water Faerie studied the King's face in the moonlight, then glanced across the yard at Maggie, who had remained obediently in place on the porch swing, her eyes glued to her lover. "A small change to my eye, and I can live the way I choose? Is it truly that simple, Your Grace?"

The High King of Faerie nodded. "Anything more complicated would border on the unnatural. But if I may suggest...?"

"Do."

"If I were you, I'd be certain to tell the lovely Maggie that she must kiss you several times each day to make the magic hold...lest you begin to fade."

The King winked, and Arrendel laughed.

"Sire, you are a sly romantic."

"Aye. Well, it stands to reason, all things as they are." And with that, the Sly Romantic winked, patted Arrendel's shoulder, and headed over to the swing to talk to Maggie.

The realization struck Arrendel hard as he watched the King gallantly kiss Maggie's hand: *He loves the Queen still, yet he is lost in his feelings, and she is confused in hers*. His heart ached for the King, and for his beloved cousin. It was at this moment that Arrendel found himself suddenly wishing that Thomas Lear's year and a day as Court Singer was at an end, so that Garrhyn might have a clearer path to begin again with his wife.

Although he was invited to stay the night, the King chose to make the journey to Elvenhome instead.

As he put his leather jacket back on and prepared to leave, he smiled at Maggie, and patted her dark curls with affection.

"Your hair is pretty, but it is far too short, Dear Lady," he teased. "I daresay there is not enough of it for Arrendel to take hold of in order to drag you across the room to have his way with you."

65

Giggling, Maggie replied tartly, "Your Majesty, I am afraid Arrendel would not have to drag me across the room to have his way with me. I think he would have to *race* me." She shrugged with feigned innocence and winked at him.

Zipping up his jacket, the King met Arrendel's eyes over Maggie's head. *You have chosen exceptionally well,* he whispered into Arrendel's mind. *She is a treasure. You have my blessing, my friend. Be happy.*

The blond Water Faerie, formerly the Heir Apparent to the High Throne of Faerie, bowed his head, and ritually touched his fingers to his forehead and his heart. Then he smiled at his King as Maggie turned and moved to stand beside him.

They stood together near the front door and said their goodbyes.

"You scared the hell out of Swiftaine," Maggie pointed out. "Poor Spriggan. He's a worrier where Arrendel is concerned."

"Say goodbye to him for me. Send him back if he becomes too much of an interruption."

Maggie nodded with a solemn smile. "We will, Your Grace."

"Travel safely," Arrendel said.

Catching a glimpse of the golden flecks in Arrendel's eye, Maggie told the King, "You know, they kind of look like stars. I like it!"

"We are relieved to hear it," Arrendel teased her. "If you didn't like it, the King would never hear the end of it!"

The King opened his arms, and Maggie moved into them and gave him a hug. "Thank you for everything you did, for all of us. Thank you." She leaned up on her tiptoes, and kissed him on his left cheek. "Meeting you has been the stuff of true faerie tales, Your Grace. I may never recover."

She backed away slowly, and bowed.

Something occurred to the King. The words came before he had time to consider them: "Does the scar truly not frighten you, then?"

Maggie was baffled. She looked carefully at him, then at Arrendel, and back at the King again, her confusion evident on her face and in her voice. "What scar?"

The King and Arrendel exchanged a strange, intense look that Maggie noticed but could not understand. She recognized that an important question was being asked, and answered. She could not, however, gauge anything about it except its importance to them, and the unspoken sense of confusion around it. Both men looked at her with something she could not read in their eyes, and then the High King of Faerie wished them a good night, and with a nod of his dark head, vanished.

The irony was not wasted on Garrhyn. Two of the most remarkable mortal women he had ever met had crossed his path in the same twelvemonth, and both were loosely connected to Thomas Lear.

He pulled his circlet from his hair, and studied it absently, tracing his finger over the boldly-fashioned oak leaves that all but covered the tiny, encircled willow tree charm at the center of the design. Oak was the sigil of his house, willow the symbol of true Fey kingship: strength and indestructability through willing flexibility. He raised the circlet to his lips, and gently kissed the willow charm, thinking fondly of Susannah for a brief moment, and wishing her well, wherever her road might take her.

He shook his head at the wonder of Susannah and Maggie. These women had accepted him as he was, without fear or pity, and had, each in her unique way, brought a small but steadfast shimmer of light and hope into his dismal, empty soul.

It struck him as ironic that neither of these mortal women was alarmed by the evil look of the ugly, long, ragged scar on his face. It confused him and perhaps even frightened him a little that somehow Maggie hadn't seen it at all, as if it hadn't been there. Was the scar not there when she looked at him?

He lifted his hand and ran his fingertips along the length of it. It was there, but she had not seen it. What did this all mean? He did not know if he could bear to think about it, mystifyingly ironic or not.

And yet the further irony was that although Thomas Lear was the incidental catalyst for Garrhyn's fateful and happy encounters with both Susannah and Maggie, the only woman that he truly wanted—and needed, he admitted to himself without a menacing scowl—was the woman who had left for Edinburgh with Thomas Lear.

No, the irony of it all was not wasted on Garrhyn, the High King of Faerie.

Nor was the hollow pain of it.

four

AS THE SUN began to set in earnest on that day, Callie drove the pearl-gray Fiat, with the small silver bells on the steering wheel, south on the A90 into the heart of Edinburgh.

They had spoken little during the trip southward from the Highlands; both were weary almost beyond reckoning. There had been little need for words.

Thomas stretched in the seat beside her.

His subtle movement drew Callie from her own thoughts. She glanced at him and smiled softly, the exhaustion caused by yesterday's strenuous adventure making her face all the more beautiful to him in the fading light.

"Long day," Thomas murmured, touching Callie's cheek with affection. "Correction: long *days*."

"True," she replied, eyes back on the road. "I am ready for some unpeopled, deadly tedium, aren't you? Yes, tedium and a great deal of quiet are quite appealing. Still, I would almost give up a portion of the Southern Kingdoms for a long, hot bath..." Her eyes glittered in amusement and she laughed tiredly. "The good news is that I don't have to. We're nearly there."

He was looking forward to going back to Edinburgh, and to seeing her house. At first he'd been surprised and a little confused about the fact that she owned a house in the city, and that they were going there instead of heading directly back to Elvenhome, as he'd assumed they would.

Ten minutes into their trip, he'd asked her about it. "You have a real house there?"

"Yes."

"How long have you had it?"

"Truly? Only about a hundred years, maybe a little less," she said with a grin. "Why?"

He frowned. "You had a house in Edinburgh, but we spent our first night together up on Calton Hill...and it was damned cold! So..."

Callie knew where this was going, and she chuckled while she waited for him to catch up. "Ask the question you want to ask, Thomas."

"Why in the world did we spend the entire night outside in the cold when you had a house? Does it have heat and plumbing and electricity?"

"It does."

"Then why, Callie? That's just weird."

"It may be 'weird,' but it's the way my encounter with a Court Singer begins: the first touches happen outside. It's a tradition, begun forever ago with The Rhymer, and I like it."

Thomas considered this then, unable to find any real fault with it, shrugged and let it go. "Still, it was *October*, Callie."

"Did I not keep you warm enough that night, Thomas Lear?"

He loved it when she giggled like that.

The Fiat, bells jingling, drove to Charlotte Square. It was after working hours, so the houses in the Square, many of which served as offices for some of Edinburgh's wealthiest businesses and various political and international agency headquarters, were closed for the day, their windows dark and quiet. There were cars parked

70

around the gated garden at the center of the Square, but the Square itself was deserted.

Callie pulled the Fiat up to the curb in front her house, and turned the motor off. She took a deep breath, and let it out in with a slow, contented sigh. "Welcome home, Thomas...for the next day or so, anyway."

Number 12 Charlotte Square stood in elegant dignity at the end of a row of similarly-dignified attached Georgian three-story houses. Callie and Thomas got out of the car. Two wrought-iron street lamps that stood on either side of the staircase leading up to the front door woke and glimmered in tandem, illuminating the six steps for the High Queen and her Court Singer.

Callie inclined her head toward the lamps in acknowledgement. "Thank you," she said.

Carrying his guitar case, Thomas couldn't decide if he was too well-acquainted with the way things happened around Callie to be at all surprised by this, or if he was just too tired to care. He settled on a wholly-unconcerned combination of the two as he and Callie walked up the steps to the front door of Number 12.

Once there, he waited, expecting her to put a key in the lock so they could go in. It took him a moment to realize that there was no door lock in evidence anywhere. He caught Callie's eye, and frowned in passive bewilderment.

"Thomas, there are keys, and then, there are *keys*." She winked at him, and made a delicate flicking motion with her thumb and forefinger. "*Twelve blessings, open to me*," Callie informed the heavily-carved oak door, which opened inward at once.

It did not perplex Thomas Lear in the slightest that, as they entered the house and closed the door behind them, there was welcoming heat and light and the smell of dinner cooking.

The next morning, Callie sent the HobGoblin kitchen staff back to Elvenhome with her sincere thanks for filling the larder and the refrigerator, and for preparing a few extra meals. Privacy restored, the High Queen and her Court Singer enjoyed lazy, uncomplicated time together.

After a long, lingering bath in the sunken tub in the master bathroom, they slid into clean clothes (brought by the staff, at Zodiac's request) and talked about Arrendel and Maggie.

"I didn't know if I would like her, but Arrendel would have been unhappy if I hadn't..."

"Imagine your surprise..." Thomas teased her. "She's adorable. And smart."

"And she loves him. I have rarely seen him this happy." She looked as though she were about to say something more, but changed her mind.

"Something wrong?" he asked.

She looked at him as if he had two heads, then realized what he was asking, and laughed. "Oh, no...it is only that I was about to start thinking about not seeing him at the Castle, but I refuse to fuss about anything today." Callie took Thomas' hand as they walked down the staircase. "Today I may have to remind myself that Change is a good thing. Tomorrow I can embrace it with my usual enthusiasm."

He squeezed her hand, and she squeezed his in return.

She took great pleasure in giving him a tour of the house; she loved the place. It was a three-story home, classic Robert Adam, built around 1820. Callie showed Thomas what had once been the servants' quarters, the spacious kitchen which took up nearly all of the bottom level of the house, and the sunny upstairs salon, across from the huge bedroom where they'd slept the night before.

"It doesn't seem this big from the outside," Thomas remarked as he admired the wall paper. It was in perfect condition, although he suspected it was original.

"No, it doesn't. And if there have been a few changes made to the house since I acquired it, those changes are not visible from the outside, either."

Thomas nodded his understanding. "It's a great house."

Callie was tugging on Thomas' sleeve, moving them playfully down the hall. "Any interest in a late breakfast? Your favorite Elvenhome cook, Lana Turner," and here Callie rolled her eyes in mock exasperation, "Lana Turner prepared everything especially for you before I sent her home with the rest of the Folk."

"I'm all about it! Let's eat!"

They entered the beautiful dining room and made their way to the sideboard. Thomas was not surprised in the least that the coffee was still hot, as were the eggs, the bacon, the potatoes, the haggis, and the toast.

Two places were set at the large, round mahogany table, and there were fresh daisies, miniature sun flowers, and apple blossoms in a large crystal vase at the table's center. A copy of *The Scotsman* sat beside the vase; they read it while they ate. Thomas lost himself in the news, and attempted to unravel the mysteries of Scottish football. Callie glanced through the arts and entertainment section, looking for interesting book reviews.

When she saw it, she stared at it blankly, her hands trembling. She was stunned by her reaction, and even more stunned by the timing. *All is Timing and Energy,* she reminded herself, *and, when all is said and done, all about choices, too...*

After a long moment, she took a steady breath, and reassured herself that Thomas had been so busy groaning over his lack of knowledge about football that he hadn't noticed that the world had, in fact, changed a wee bit more.

Later on, they sat in the drawing room, content to share the space and entertain their own thoughts.

He replaced his B string, tuned it, and then played his guitar.

He could tell that she had slept well and peacefully last night, her dreams gentle as he'd held her in his arms and relaxed himself into her warmth. She looked rested, but he knew from wading through his own thoughts that the tension of Arrendel's torture, abduction, the rescue and all that followed it would take them both some distance and time before it eased away and faded into the shadows of memory. He was glad to see that the slice across her chin was healing quickly, though.

Yet as his fingers moved on the strings, he noticed something unsettling that he hadn't noticed before. There was a subtle sense of restlessness about her this afternoon that he would never have associated with the Callie he knew.

On the surface, she was tranquil enough. Seated in the overstuffed chair by the windows, she appeared to be focused on the brightly-colored flowers she was stitching on soft Irish linen. He knew she found her needlework soothing and meditative, that she loved the mechanics as well as the energy of it. Thomas had seen Callie relax with her needlework many times before. This did not look right somehow.

From where he was sitting, it didn't seem as though she was enjoying her favorite solitary diversion. Her mind was working hard behind her lovely brown eyes, and her hands moved perhaps too quickly for the activity to be a leisurely one.

What was she thinking?

He understood that she had a lot to think about. His own head was filled with images that would take him a long while to process. He knew that she had spent time with ScarF, and understood that it had cost her something, but he did not want to ask her about it. He also knew that Callie's parting from Guardian/Arrendel (Thomas was still mentally juggling his friend's True Name but he almost had it down) was upsetting her, too, although they both knew she'd certainly see her cousin again.

There was something that had Callie visibly agitated. Thomas wondered: *If I stopped playing the guitar right now, would she notice?* Her face was serene. She was pulling and pushing the silk-threaded needle through the linen in a swift, easy, perfect rhythm, but there was a glimmer of her inner turbulence rippling just inside the boundaries of his own awareness. The notion made him squirm.

It finally struck Thomas that she was not looking at her hands or the needlework at all while she worked, had not looked at them for some time.

He put down the guitar, stared at her, and waited.

She did not notice that the music had stopped.

"Callie?"

It took her a moment to recognize that he had spoken. She flashed him a tiny smile.

"Yes?"

"What is it?"

"What is *what*?"

He was on uneasy emotional ground, but he didn't care much; he wanted to help her, and perhaps he could, if he understood the problem. "What's wrong? You've been 'off' all afternoon. Has something else happened that we need to worry about?"

She looked at him, at the concern in his eyes, and her smile grew and brightened her face. "Oh, Thomas, you look so serious!" she chuckled.

He was confused now. "You seem so...I don't know...on edge and I..." he shrugged.

"I'm sorry, Thomas. I was thinking about an old friend." She hesitated for only the space of a long heartbeat, and then dropped her needlework into the chair beside her, stood and moved to Thomas' couch and sat close beside him. "I saw something in the newspaper this morning, and I want you to know about it."

Thomas nodded. "Okay."

"I saw in *The Scotsman* that a dear friend happens to be here, in Edinburgh. I haven't seen him in a very long time. To be truthful, I haven't thought about him, or our friendship, for years."

Thomas touched her shoulder. "And you want to see him. Why don't you, then?"

"At first I didn't consider it." Callie put her hand over Thomas', on her shoulder, and squeezed it. "I didn't think I wanted to see him. But he's been on my mind, and I now I think I'd like to...to say hello and see how he's been getting on."

"Then you should see him. Where is he?"

"He's performing at one of the local pubs tonight. It's about a fifteen-minute walk from here."

Thomas' eyebrows lifted as a new thought smacked him in the back of the head. "Performing?"

Callie nodded and said nothing, searching his eyes for understanding.

"You saw something in the paper. Your friend is performing tonight." It wasn't that hard to put together. "Your friend is a musician."

Callie nodded again.

Thomas didn't know whether to be suspicious or genuinely amused. To cover both possibilities, he forced a smile. "Is this a 'close, personal friend,' Callie?"

Recognizing his thin ice, she laughed warmly and melted it, to save him from drowning in the wrong emotion. "It's more than fair to say that," she told him. "He was my Court Singer some years ago. My last one."

"And he's *here*?" Thomas blurted, fitting the puzzle together too many pieces at a time.

Callie watched him work at it, and slowed him down. "Yes. He lives just outside of Glasgow, or did, when I knew him. I haven't seen him since he left Elvenhome."

Thomas struggled to get his head around the idea that there was a living Court Singer...his predecessor! For some reason, he'd assumed that Callie's Court Singers were spaced in some way that made it impossible for two to exist at the same time. He never thought...

76

Callie placed a soft hand on either side of his face. "Thomas, I do not want this to trouble you. I will not see him, if my seeing him will cause you discomfort."

He looked into her eyes, knew that she meant what she said, and suddenly felt foolish. He made a couple of lame attempts to back-pedal, then told her the truth. "I never thought about other Court Singers, other than the famous ones. Maybe I didn't think of them as real people. I didn't think anyone would still be alive...I mean—" he faltered, feeling awkward and somehow ashamed.

She rescued him with the facts. "He—the last Court Singer—arrived in Elvenhome in 1950. He was twenty-five, he spent a year and a day with me, and afterward, he returned to his life." She gave Thomas a minute to absorb this information, then continued. "He is a musician, a singer and songwriter. You were aware I have a weakness for the type?" she teased, and was rewarded with the beginnings of her lover's uneasy smile. "Oh, Thomas, don't look so torn. I do not have to see him. It is a small thing, not deserving of such a look!" She punctuated this with a kiss.

Thomas was doing the math, and hoping he didn't sound petty. "So he's fifty now?"

Callie sighed. She acknowledged to herself that she had made the wrong decision in mentioning this at all, let alone considering it. "He would be fifty," she conceded.

A new thought burst into Thomas' mind, and he sat back and gaped at Callie, too many possibilities crowding him. "Would I know him?"

Callie shrugged. "I don't know, Thomas." With a serenity she did not feel, she met his gaze, then sighed again. *Done is done*, she thought darkly. "His name is Michael MacAllistair."

Thomas had been in the music business for long enough to recognize just about everyone who'd made any kind of mark.

"Well?" Callie asked after a moment. "Do you know him?"

Thomas shook his head. "Never met him. I've heard of him, though, of course. Originally folk music, then some good rock and roll, some traditional but mostly contemporary Celtic, and some history-based stuff too, that too many people didn't know what to make of, I think. Never hit it huge in the States, but still made some good noise ten years ago, did a couple of U.S. tours. He was, at one time, probably one of the top thirty living guitarists in the world."

Callie nodded. "That's Michael."

Thomas took her hand. "And he's here?"

"Yes."

"And you'd like to see him?"

Callie bit her lip, and told Thomas the truth. "Yes."

Instantly, jump-started from absolutely nowhere, The Monster In Thomas Lear's Head resurrected and roared to life with an outraged insecurity that Thomas would rather have died than have to admit to. He felt his hands clench possessively around Callie's, and then hoped that she hadn't noticed.

Of course she'd noticed, and she surprised him when her grip tightened fiercely, matching his own. "Thomas, hear me. It has nothing to do with you, or with what we have now," Callie began. "It has to do with the notion that the Mischief, from the very beginning, has unsettled me. I have tasted some bitter failure of late and, oh, success too, but I fear I have lost my balance. I did not wish to confess it aloud, but I find that Arrendel was right: perhaps I am not ready to return to Elvenhome. Certainly not when so much is required of me, and I feel I have nothing left to give the Folk." Her eyes filled with liquid pain, but she did not hide her tears from him, either. "When I saw Michael's name and photograph in the paper this morning I thought that perhaps a small thread of my own history, spending a familiar moment with someone I knew long ago, would help me to regain a little of what was lost." Callie struggled to compose herself, and she tried to smile at him around her pain. "But High Queens do not put their wishes above the wishes of others; it does not serve. And if you, Thomas, could be made unhappy by my talking with Michael, then of course I shall not do it."

Listening to her, watching her face, and feeling the truth of her resolve was too much for him. He told the Monster In His Head to fuck off, and put his arms around his Queen. "What time is the show?"

Thomas didn't anticipate her response. Her words buried the Monster, took Thomas' breath away and melted, then broke, then revived his heart in the same few seconds.

"Seven-thirty," she whispered into his ear. "Are you coming with me?"

In the drawing room, as he worked on the song about Terena, Thomas' mind kept spinning over the reality of Callie and her previous Court Singer. While it was true that he had mixed feelings about the whole Michael MacAllistair thing, he recognized that he was looking forward to seeing the man perform live. Promising himself that he would trust Callie, and keep his head on straight, he went back to work on the sad, wistful lyric.

Out in the hall, by the dining room, Thomas thought he heard Callie talking with someone. *Likely herself*, he mused while he played a little of the haunting melody on his guitar.

Wait a minute...no, he was sure he heard a gruff, small voice responding to Callie's own. Someone else was here in the house. Intrigued, Thomas moved with a touch of stealth toward the drawing room door, and strained to hear what was being said.

"Will there be anything else, Your Grace?" asked that gruff, small voice, which, it turned out, belonged to a grizzled-looking male Pixie. When Thomas peeked into the hall, he saw that Callie's back was to him, but he could see the Pixie reach up and hand her a small envelope. She in turn gave him some shiny gold coins, which thrilled him.

"For my new gray hat!" he laughed, as he bowed to his Queen.

"Many thanks for managing the errand, Dear One," Callie told him.

With a deeper bow, the Pixie, coins in hand, evaporated from the hall with a satisfying pop.

Chuckling, Callie fanned herself with the small envelope. Without turning around, she asked merrily, "Yes, Thomas?"

He was busted. "Wow...do you have Folk planted everywhere? Good work."

Callie spun around and faced him, waving the envelope, a look of satisfaction crowding out her reflex to tease him. "We need tickets to get into the performance, Thomas."

"Oh," he muttered. "I knew that..."

At six forty-five, Callie walked back into the drawing room, where Thomas sat reading a book. Dressed in a midi-length brown skirt, black boots, a white blouse and a long, burnt-umber cardigan, she looked fabulous. Her lush, long brown hair was delicately pulled back by two small, ivory combs. She wore round silver earrings; the elegant points of her long ears were lost purposefully in her hair. She smiled at Thomas, and tried to see what he was reading.

"Burns," he replied to her unasked question. "There are some great lines here, but I can't make heads or tails of too many of the words so I haven't got a clue what the hell he's saying. Damn, Callie, it could be just about anything! I never thought about this being a foreign language!"

Callie chuckled. "But you're reading it."

"Yeah," Thomas grinned. "Don't ask me why."

"I wouldn't dream of it." She crossed the room, and stood by the tall windows overlooking the Square, and looked out the window. Then she turned to face him, her face wearing something of a determined smile. "We should get ready to leave for the concert," Callie recommended.

Thomas put the book of poetry down on the sofa beside him. "I'm ready," he said.

"You're *almost* ready, Thomas. There are a few things we need to take care of before we can go."

He watched her move to the small writing desk by the fireplace. Sitting down, she opened the center drawer of the desk and lifted a piece of cream-colored parchment from it then closed it again, all in one fluid motion. From the top left-hand drawer, she extracted a long, white quill and a pot of ink. These she placed on the desk in front of her, beside the parchment.

First dipping quill into ink, biting her bottom lip, Callie held the quill poised over the parchment. When she was ready, she touched the quill to the parchment. The sound of the quill flying across the paper was enough to move Thomas from his position on the sofa toward Callie at the writing desk. He thought she must be drawing something rather than writing, and he was curious.

He came up behind her as she was finishing up. "Just another moment," she murmured. One fast flash and flourish of the quill; Thomas saw over her shoulder that Callie had in fact written a note, addressed to "M." and signed "D." Seconds before he could get close enough to read the contents of the note in Callie's elongated, graceful handwriting, she placed the quill beside the ink pot on the desk and said, "Stand back a little, Thomas," which he did at once.

She whispered something he could not make out, then lifted her right hand over the note. "Go," she commanded the parchment. It went, in a small burst of green light.

"Well, that's done," Callie said, as much to Thomas as to herself as she turned to face him.

"What was that?" Thomas wanted to know.

"Well, I have to let Michael know we're coming. It's only courteous." She stood up and studied Thomas from head to toe with a critical eye.

"What? I took a bath, washed my hair, and I shaved. Am I not presentable?"

81

She laughed. "Of course you are. You look wonderful." She pursed her lips and stared at his face. "The problem is that you look like Thomas Lear."

Before he could ask, he understood. "Right. And no one has seen me for a while, so it might get tricky if I get recognized."

Callie nodded. "In order for you to go with me to see Michael perform, I need your permission to make you...less noticeable."

"I usually just put on a hat and dark sunglasses when I want to sneak into places," Thomas offered. "But that's not going to work, is it?"

"No," Callie grinned. "I was thinking of something a bit more direct."

"What are you going to do?"

She put her hand on his arm. "Nothing drastic. I would like to put a small glamour on you. You will still look like you to you, but when anyone else looks at you, they will not have any reason to connect 'Thomas Lear' with what they see."

She gave Thomas a minute to let it sink in. "So it's me, but no one will *know* it's me?" he asked, not sure he was comfortable with it.

"That's correct." Callie nodded when Thomas frowned. "With your permission...?"

"You'll make sure that you lift the thing so that when I'm back in LA..."

Callie laughed now. "Don't worry, after tonight, you'll be your own recognizable, everyone-knows-your-face, famous and quite handsome Thomas Lear, Rock Star. I promise."

He narrowed his eyes at her. "When you laugh like that, you're not very encouraging, you know, Callie. Wait a minute, hold on—will *you* still recognize me?"

"Of course. I'll know it's you. You'll be the unidentified man hanging out with the High Queen of Faerie," she said with a playful giggle.

82

"Very funny, Your Grace," glowered Thomas.

She stifled her giggling, cleared her throat, and looked at him, one eyebrow raised in the question.

"Yes," he grumbled good-naturedly enough. "Let's get the show on the road and—"

Before Thomas could finish his sentence, a puff of thin green smoke, scented with earth and rain, whiffed into his face and then vanished. "That's it? Well...did it work?" he asked.

"I'm assuming that's a rhetorical question," she sniffed. "Let's go."

They walked together to the front door. As they passed the mirrored hall tree in the entryway, Thomas stopped and took a good look. He recognized the man who looked back at him, and shrugged. "Good-looking guy," Thomas winked at Callie with a wry grin. "But who the hell *is* he?"

"Oh, someone I picked up, once upon a time," Callie retorted.

Thomas kissed the top of her head. "Right. Very, very funny."

They walked through the front door and out into the evening. Callie pulled the heavy door to Number 12 Charlotte Square closed behind her, and spoke to the lock: "*Twelve blessings, hold fast.*" The oak door bolted itself. She beamed at Thomas. "Good. Let's go listen to some music."

She slid her hand into Thomas', and they walked down the stairs and into the evening.

"Callie?" Thomas asked tentatively after they'd walked half a block.

Her mind was somewhere else. "Yes?"

"Who's 'D.'?"

"Who?" For a second she didn't know what he was talking about.

"'D.' You signed the note with a 'D.'"

"Oh that." She gave him a small but very warm smile. "D is for Delia. That's what Michael named me."

THE ABBOTSFORD, ON Rose Street, was a local bar famous for its hundreds of varieties of excellent single malt. It had a restaurant above it, also called The Abbotsford and, tonight, dining tables had been removed to make room for the concert. A small stage had been erected, and there was a respectable lighting and sound system in place for the show.

Thomas and Callie entered the Abbotsford, got a pint and a glass of single malt respectively, and then walked up the stairs.

Although it was a smallish venue, it had definite possibilities, Thomas told Callie as they took their seats in the third row, center, joining the eager audience.

For the first time in more than a decade, Thomas sat in a crowded public place without anyone recognizing him. No one stared, pointed, or approached him. Not a soul was aware that they were breathing the same air as Thomas Lear, Rock Star.

It was a strange feeling. He was not entirely sure he liked it.

This thought made him smirk at himself the instant he realized he would never say such a stupid thing to Callie.

Callie was looking around. Maybe, Thomas thought, she was trying to catch a pre-performance glimpse of Michael MacAllistair.

"Twenty-five years is a long time for us mortals," he reminded her, in an attempt to be helpful. "He's likely to have changed, maybe a lot."

"Hmmm..." Callie said, as though this hadn't occurred to her yet. "Even if I didn't recognize him in the crowd, he'll recognize me soon enough. He won't be able to help it."

She was beautiful tonight, of course, but she wasn't dressed as the High Queen of Faerie. He raised an eyebrow. "Really? Why?"

Callie turned to Thomas and, leaning in close, whispered in his ear. "Don't you know? When we're

Upworld, and in a darkened space, we Faeries can, at will...*glow in the dark*." She crossed her eyes and made a face at him. "So much for your Master's degree in Medieval Literature." Snorting with a quiet laugh, she kissed him on the cheek.

"You are a bad, bad Faerie," he grumbled; she'd had him for a second, and they both knew it. A heartbeat later, he laughed with her as he noticed that, in this moment, she was noticeably more relaxed, more carefree, and happier than she'd been since she'd come back from her Royal Progress across the kingdoms. That seemed like forever ago, and Thomas understood that it probably felt even longer than that for Callie.

He was glad they had this date tonight to hear her previous Court Singer play and sing. He reaffirmed to himself that he was looking forward to the whole experience.

He repeated this in his head for a few minutes, until the overhead lights dimmed, and a small, frail ray of spotlight began to grow warm and inviting on the stage.

"Time to make some music..." Thomas whispered for his own benefit, mentally wishing the guy a good show.

The sound of growing applause heralded the arrival of the musician who had, once upon a time, spent a year and a day with the woman now seated beside Thomas Lear. Guitar in one hand, and a pint of ale in the other, Michael MacAllistair took the stage.

His longish hair had more gray than light brown in it. Dressed in jeans, a blue suede shirt and runners, his blue eyes skimmed the audience, drawing them in. He had a strong chin, and a mouth designed for grinning. "I thought I'd come by the old Abbotsford and play a bit tonight...didn't know if you'd be here or not, but as usual, I didn't mind much. See, I needed a pint..." he said with a sly shrug, eliciting a laugh of familiarity from the audience. He took a long sip of his ale, put it down on one of the two barstools that sat on the stage behind him and then, with an easy grace, he began to play.

Michael sang in a rich baritone. His first song was one that was an obvious audience favorite; at the chorus, they sang along. At first Thomas thought it was a strange little song about a farmer extolling the virtues of his beloved wife or lady love...but the punch line of the tale was that the farmer was praising his favorite Highland cow.

"Might have worked better if she were a sheep," Thomas muttered under his breath.

"Now, now..." Callie chuckled. "He's just warming up. You'll like a lot of his songs."

When the laughter and applause died down, Michael sat on one of the bar stools, took another sip of his ale, and spoke to the audience, several of whom were calling "Hello, Michael!"

"It's good to see that you remember *my* branch of Clan MacAllistair's family anthem," he told them, and there was more laughter.

He waited a beat, then Michael's tone moved from the playful to something far more intimate. "It's been a good while since I've been back to Edinburgh. Let me tell you how I've been spending my time."

And with that, something in the air almost shimmered around the musician in the spotlight as he moved his audience into MacAllistair magic.

Three songs later, Callie nudged Thomas, who was studiously watching Michael play a particularly complex riff. "Told you."

Never taking his eyes from Michael's hands, Thomas nodded. "You did. He's amazing." Genuinely thrilled by what he was seeing, Thomas had no difficulty in acknowledging to himself that Michael was a far better guitarist than he himself was. But it didn't matter a damn; he was as mesmerized by the performance as everyone else in the place, and he was having a great time. He'd almost forgotten what it was like to be around other serious musicians. This realization was a surprise, although of course he did enjoy the Fey musicians he'd met at Elvenhome. Still, Michael MacAllistair was the first

86

great guitarist he'd seen and heard in more than six months, and Thomas wanted more.

Callie smiled to herself, and returned her attention to the man on the stage. This had been a good idea after all.

Twenty minutes later, as Michael left the stage for a "wee ale break," one of the Abbotsford staff handed Callie a folded piece of paper, bent and whispered in her ear, nodded his head directionally, and moved away.

Callie read the note. She smiled sweetly as she passed it to Thomas. "Ever been backstage at a concert, Thomas?" She laughed when she saw the variety of reactions on his face before he grinned. "Let's go and say hello to Michael."

There wasn't exactly a dressing room; it was one of the oversized storage rooms for the restaurant, located in the basement. Still, it was well-lit, had a strategically-placed mirror and a serviceable table and four or five chairs among the mountains of boxes, cases of wine and single malt, stray furniture, and pantry items that crowded the space.

A somewhat restless Michael MacAllistair sat at the table, drinking another pint and changing a guitar string, and also considered changing his shirt.

Callie knocked once on the door, and walked in, Thomas following close behind. Michael was on his feet as they entered. His eyes lit up at the sight of the High Queen of Faerie; he searched her face almost hungrily. All else forgotten, he strode over to her.

"Delia!"

"Hello, Michael."

They embraced.

"A rather spontaneous visit," Callie began. "But it was a good idea – you're..."

Michael's rush of words in her ear interrupted her welcome. "I've dreamt of this, over and over, and here you are!" He hugged her close.

"Not for long if you crush the wind out of me," Callie said with a wry smile, elegantly extricating herself without hurting Michael's feelings.

Michael let go of her only so he could look at her some more. "I've been trying to think of what to say ever since I got your note, even when I was in front of the audience...but everything just..." he shook his head, a look of confusion and merriment blending in his eyes. "It doesn't matter. It's grand to see you! How are you? My God, you haven't aged a day! Even knowing that you wouldn't have doesn't lessen the wonder of it..." He stopped for a second, and regrouped. "Of course, I've changed a little, no?"

Callie's eyes glimmered with approval. "I'd say the years have not been unkind to you. And the music is, as always, perfect in every way." Reaching behind her, she literally pulled Thomas into the conversation. "Michael, my dear, I'd like you meet someone you have much in common with. This is the present Court Singer of Elvenhome. His name is...Tom."

Fair Folk do not lie; however, they have been known to abbreviate on the spot, when necessary.

Thomas bristled at this, but kept his irritation well-masked and his mouth shut. He had never tolerated being called "Tom," and "Tommy" was entirely out of the question. He'd been Thomas even as a child, and had always preferred it. No one important to him had ever called him anything else.

Callie knew he was annoyed, and she touched his arm to remind him of why she'd had to do it. A glance or two between them, his arched and hers soothing, settled the matter in an instant, and he relaxed.

"Good to meet you, Tom," Michael said.

"You, too," replied Thomas, shaking Michael's offered hand.

"He's a musician, Delia, not one of your sad, drunken poets. I can tell by his hand he plays guitar." Michael focused on Thomas only peripherally, but he was trying. "She's soft in the head for poets, you know, but she's wild

88

for guitar players, so you're probably in good shape. And if you are a poet, too, then well done! She's likely mad for you. Weird, though, meeting another Court Singer, aye?"

"Yeah," Thomas admitted.

"For me, too." Michael made a face at Callie. "She's a handful, this one. The stories I could tell you..."

"Stop it," Callie told him, but she couldn't frown at him. She was delighted to see him, more than she'd expected. "You should attempt to behave yourself. The change would do you good."

Michael laughed and waved her comment away. "How long are you here...in the city? Do you have time to—?"

Callie shook her head. "We're leaving tomorrow."

"Tomorrow! Is it a must?"

"I'm afraid so."

Michael tried to not look disappointed. "Ah well. There are a handful of things I'd dearly like to discuss with you sometime, Your Grace," he said.

"I was thinking that, too. It has been a long time, Michael."

There was a brisk knock at the door. A male voice announced: "Five minutes, Michael!"

Thomas saw the flicker of sadness in Callie's eyes, and felt sorry for her. Then he had an idea. He touched her shoulder. "Why don't you guys have dinner after the show, and I'll see you at the house when you're done?"

Callie studied his eyes. "Truly?"

"Sure," Thomas said.

With a grateful smile at Thomas, Michael told Callie, "Let's meet here right after, then. I'll need to chat up some people, sign autographs and hit on a young lass or two, but I'll be done in about five minutes."

Thomas and Michael laughed. They knew how that was.

"Musicians!" Callie groaned.

"Let's go," Thomas all but pulled her toward the door. "He's got to be on stage in four minutes, and he hasn't finished changing his D string." Waving, he smiled at Michael. "Have a good rest of the show. I'm looking forward to it!"

As they hurried back to their seats, Callie asked Thomas, "Are you certain about dinner?"

"What?"

"Dinner. With Michael. Are you sure about it? You don't object?"

"I don't object." He didn't, actually.

"You can come, too," she said. "In fact, you should come. You two would have a lot to talk about."

"That's the point. He wants to talk with *you*. You haven't seen him in a long, long time. You don't need me there."

"What if I did?"

"You don't."

Seated now, she studied him, and sighed. "And you're all right with this, and you're all right about going back to the house without me?"

"I remember how to get there, and I remember the key for getting inside. Callie, it's fine. I've got my guitar, I'm pretty sure I can occupy myself until you get home. It's not a big deal." He meant it.

"Do you mean it?" she asked anyway.

"I mean it. Jesus, Your Grace, go spend time catching up with your old friend, and I'll see you at bedtime. Yes?"

"Yes."

It was settled; she'd have dinner with Michael, and he'd go back to the house and spend a quiet evening alone. He would appreciate the temporary solitude. Given the circumstances, it was the exact right call. The happiness in her gaze confirmed it.

And the minute Michael MacAllistair returned to the stage, Thomas' (mostly) unselfish, (largely) magnanimous gesture began to slowly eat at him.

The second half of Michael's concert was filled with a variety of songs he'd written in the early years of his career. Thomas was pleased that he recognized two of them, and even sang the chorus of one with the rest of the audience. He was having fun tonight. On the other hand, he was beginning to regret that he wouldn't have a chance to talk with Michael about guitars and poetry and music and...

Almost before Thomas realized it, the show was over. At nine-thirty, the audience was on its feet, stomping and shouting, cheering and applauding. Michael bowed, waved, raised his empty glass, and moved from the stage and into the welcoming crowd, talking and laughing with people as he headed downstairs to the bar.

A few minutes later, Thomas and Callie came down the stairs, too, headed for the front door.

Once outside in the cool night air, he turned to her and grinned. "You were right. He's very good." He squeezed her hand. "Thanks."

Callie was enjoying the evening breeze. The Abbotsford had perhaps gotten too crowded for her, but she was smiling as she breathed deeply with her eyes closed. "Are you certain you won't come with me for dinner?"

He snorted. "I thought we were finished with that."

She opened her eyes and studied him. "Me too. But I can't help wondering if you're going to want to change your mind by the time you get back to the house."

"I won't."

"Are you going to take a cab back?"

"No need. It's not a long walk."

She gazed into the depths of his eyes, and did not see what she was looking for. Wishing that she could show him her heart, and knowing that this was not the place or time, she leaned into him for a long, lingering kiss. "I'll see you later, then," she said, caressing the side of his face.

"Have fun, Your Grace," Thomas told her.

Nodding, Her Grace turned and, with a last affectionate look over her shoulder at her current Court Singer, walked back into the bar.

Thomas confirmed his bearings, then began to walk toward Callie's house in Charlotte Square.

He *wanted* her to have a good time at dinner with Michael MacAllistair, he reminded himself. The past few days had been terrible for everyone, but especially for Callie. She needed a breath of fresh air, and a little distance from all the craziness. Arrendel had hinted at this when they'd talked privately; the Water Faerie's great concern for his cousin the Queen had been realistic and undeniable. If Callie needed to have dinner and conversation with a friend from her past, Thomas was all for it. Of course he wanted her to have a good time.

But not too much of a good time.

He had walked less than a block when he felt the first flicker of irritation spark into a hot burst of pent-up anger. She was having dinner with Michael MacAllistair!

Old friend my ass, whispered The Monster In His Head, making a second spontaneous appearance today.

Thomas Lear found himself recounting the situation to the one layer of himself that should have stayed asleep and benign. Since he'd mellowed considerably during his time in Elvenhome, Thomas might have, under other circumstances, wondered what had suddenly awakened the Monster. This time he did not. Anger took over.

She had made the wrong choice, he fumed. He had been gracious and sweet, helpful and supportive in suggesting that Callie and Michael go eat and talk about old times. He'd even meant it, in the moment, he really had. She was supposed to have been delighted, and a little turned on, too, by his unselfishness and his altruistic generosity. And then she was supposed to gracefully turn it down, give Michael a friendly peck on the cheek, and come home with her Court Singer. The *present* one.

Thomas was uncertain about where it had all gone wrong, but it had gone to hell, and he did not like it.

Who the fuck did she think she was toying with? The Monster howled at him. *You don't need this shit. You're Thomas Lear!*

"I don't need this shit," Thomas repeated under his breath with a bitter, heated growl.

Screw it. Go home.

The thought made him stop abruptly in the middle of the road he was crossing. A car slammed on its brakes and its driver leaned on the horn and shouted at him, but he didn't really hear it. He got to the other side of the street, and stood on the corner as he considered this new idea.

Show her. Walking away is the only way to show her. She can't treat you like this.

He was Upworld. In Edinburgh. He could get on the phone and call Stan or Jack or even Myra, have them wire him some money or arrange for his ticket (his wallet was in a drawer in his bedroom at Elvenhome Castle), and he could get a taxi to take him to the airport and catch the next plane to Los Angeles. He'd only been away for about six months, give or take. He could go back to his life on his own terms. Callie wanted to play with Michael instead? That was fine by him.

Thomas Lear, Rock Star, would be the very first Court Singer who told the High Queen of Faerie to go fuck herself. He would totally shatter the Rhymer myth, and he would be justified in doing so. It would be Callie's fault; she had forced his hand, and she could remember that forever.

He started walking again, laying out his plan in a fury, when he heard footsteps half a block behind him. He peered over his shoulder and let out a surprised gasp.

A Troll was following him in the dark, his lumbering gait all but heralding that he belonged to Faerie. Dressed in jeans, a blue jacket and heavy boots, the Troll pretended that he wasn't trailing Thomas at all. He was huge, well over six feet tall, and husky. Thomas could outrun him, he was sure of that. He wondered how Callie had arranged for him to be tailed, and when she'd done it. There wouldn't have been any reason for it.

She was decisive, quick about doing things when she made up her mind to do them. But this? Seriously?

He's definitely Fey, hissed The Monster derisively. *She has quite the network of guardians to keep an eye on you. Best to get back to LA and forget this waste of time.*

Guardians?

Thomas' thoughts flew to Arrendel, the friend he'd called *Guardian.* The Monster had inadvertently slowed down Thomas' anger. He knew that The Monster was part of his own headspace, and having one of his darker sides accidentally call in the light that was Arrendel almost—but not quite—made him smile. *Damn, I am really fucked up,* he groaned to himself, and deliberately slammed the door shut on The Monster for the moment.

He was home; there was Charlotte Square, and Callie's house was waiting for him. He'd get there, sit down, and then decide what to do. After all, his anger rekindling at the thought, he had the rest of the night alone to think about it.

He quickened his pace. The Troll behind him moved faster.

Thomas arrived at the front steps that led to Callie's front door. But instead of rushing to the door and speaking the door key that would let him in, he sat on the steps and waited for the Troll to approach.

The Troll hurried along the pavement, and did not slow down as he neared the well-lit steps where Thomas sat.

In fact, when the Troll reached Thomas, he didn't do more than glance at him as he strode by.

Thomas was confused. "Wait—" he called, only a little nervous.

The Troll stopped, and turned back to look at Thomas. "Me?" he asked.

"Did she order you to follow me home?"

"Who? What? No, man, I'm not following you. I'm late." And with that, the Troll hurried off.

94

Thomas watched him bolt down the street, move past the gated garden in the middle of the Square, and turn a corner.

Mystified, he stood up, and moved to the front door. What if the Troll hadn't been a Troll at all? What if he'd just been a big guy, walking behind Thomas? Maybe Callie had told the Troll to make sure he got to the house, but he wasn't allowed to leave, because the Troll would be watching...

"Fuck it," Thomas muttered, then addressed the front door roughly. "*Twelve blessings, open to me.*"

The door opened, and Thomas went inside, taking his irritation, his anger, his hurt feelings, his annoyance, his Monster, his frenzied escape plan, and an unexpected degree of sudden exhaustion with him.

As he closed the door behind him and switched on a light, the only thing he was sure about was that he wanted something to eat. He also wanted a bottle of whisky.

five

"I THOUGHT IT would be quieter, private, and we could really talk," said Michael, by way of explanation, as he held open the cab door for Delia and she stepped in. During the ride, they spoke of the weather, the concert, and the steak dinner Michael would prepare for them tonight. The cab sped through the darkness.

Shortly thereafter, Michael and Delia arrived at a pretty Victorian-styled house in Edinburgh's Morningside district. The home belonged to a friend of Michael's, who had offered it for the weekend he was in town.

Once inside, Michael propped his guitar case against a wall, helped Delia out of her long cardigan, removed his jacket, hung both up, and moved toward a cabinet to get some whisky.

"Are you hungry?" he asked.

"More or less," Delia said. She pulled off her boots, wriggled her toes, and settled herself comfortably on a plush green sofa.

Michael brought the drinks. "Now there's a familiar sight, if ever there was one," he whistled, looking at her. "The Queen curled up like a sun-dappled cat in a summer garden."

He sat beside her, handed her the glass of whisky, and tried not to tremble as his eyes feasted on the face he had loved more than any other.

"The note I sent, Michael. I hope it didn't shock you too much."

Michael laughed. "Shock me? I was just taking my guitar out of the case in that storage room at the bar, and when your note popped onto the table in front of me, I damn near wet myself! A crazy, unimaginable dream comes true out of nowhere, and suddenly my willie has no idea what to do!"

She frowned, more at herself than at her old friend. "I know it was selfish of me. I saw your face in the newspaper..."

"I'm delighted that you did, delighted," he told her. "So, Darling Delia, talk to me. Tell me what this is about."

Delia took a long sip of her whisky. "The note—"

"The note," he cut her off with a knowing look, "says that you're in Edinburgh. It also says that you wanted to talk about the old days, gentler days, and that you've got a friend with you. Lady Lass, what's been going on that the 'old days' are more interesting to you than the ones you're living now? If you taught me nothing else during my year and a day, you made sure I learned that!"

Only Michael McAllistair had ever called her "Lady Lass," and Delia's heart, desperate for a safe and familiar harbor, skipped a beat, then relaxed. Her eyes sparkled, she took a deep breath, and considered which bits of the last twenty-five years she might share with him.

Watching her eyes, Michael saw that she had decided to tell him nothing about what was bothering her. He wondered if Tom had anything to do with her unhappiness, then ruled it out. Delia's troubles were private ones, they had to be. He knew her to be a lady of great personal power, and grace, wisdom and humor. She was all that and so much more: she was the High Queen of Faerie.

She was also a lady with too much on her mind and, Michael realized, nowhere to share it. Not even with him. If he felt badly about that, he ignored it, and focused on his former lover and beloved Queen.

97

"Here's an idea. How about I start the dinner, and you come and tell me how The Berries are faring?"

The look on Delia's face proved that he'd made the right call. She tucked her troubles away, whatever they were, and followed him into the kitchen.

"The Berries," the collective name Michael had given the Queen's Ladies when he was the new Court Singer in Elvenhome, were happy and thriving and busy, Delia said. Michael grinned as he worked and she told random, funny tales about the loves and other escapades of "Cranberry", "Strawberry", "Raspberry", "Blueberry", "Loganberry", "Gooseberry" and her merry compulsion to collect and wear tall, pink pointy hats, "Blackberry" and "Mrs. Pomegranate".

Laughing, Delia helped cut up lettuce and tomatoes for salad. She hadn't thought of her Ladies as The Berries for ages. This felt good, and so distant from the strain of recent events. She recognized that she was wrapping herself in the safety of emotional distance from the Mischief and everything that it had touched. Separated from it all for a single evening, with someone who held a tiny but sweet piece of her history, was *wonderful*.

"Oh, Lady Lass?" Michael gently interrupted her mental digression. "You were off somewhere, so you didn't hear me. I asked about your cousin, you know, dear "Cousin Angus." Long blond hair? Tall? Great swimmer?"

Delia's genuine, merry laughter filled the kitchen.

After the meal, they sat together on the sofa in the living room, and drank wine.

"You said you had 'a handful' of things to talk with me about, back at The Abbotsford," Delia said.

Michael nodded. "I did say that. Here's one of them: Have you ever asked any of the Folk to watch me, or maybe see what I was up to from time to time?"

Sipping her wine, Delia's eyes met his, but she said nothing.

"I've wondered about it, every once in a while." When he realized she wasn't answering, he continued. "About a year after I left Elvenhome, I was sitting in a pub in Glasgow, and a man who could easily have passed for a young Dwarf watched me the whole time I was there. I smiled at him, even waved him over to my table, but he only sat and stared."

"Really?"

"Really. And once about every five years or so, I've found myself looking at someone who looks quite Fey. One was Dwarfish, two were likely Elfish, once the watcher absolutely had to have been a Goblin hidden behind a bad glamour. Anyway, they'd be looking back at me."

"What happened after that?"

Michael frowned. "Nothing. Not a bloody thing. They watched me for a while, and then they stopped watching me, and then they went away."

"Did they *pop* away?"

"No. They just walked away, or they were gone the next time I happened to look over at them." He poured more wine into both of their glasses. "Your Folk, Your Grace?"

"No," Delia chuckled. "I don't set spies and watchers on my Court Singers. If I did, though, I daresay they'd be a lot more social. They'd want to have a drink with you. The Folk loved having you with us that year, Michael."

"Hmmm. Well, now I know." He did not sound convinced, and his tone amused them both.

"Now you know."

"Not Fey spies from my Queen?"

"No."

Michael drank his glass empty. "Damn."

They talked about Michael's music, and when she asked, he played a couple of his old songs, and then a couple of new ones for her. Delia was enchanted.

99

When he finished singing, as he leaned forward to lay the guitar down, he reached for Delia, and kissed her.

After a long moment, he released her, brushed her hair away from her eyes with trembling fingertips, and searched her eyes. "Is it too much to hope for," he asked softly, "to entertain the notion that you might be willing to stay for breakfast? If for nothing else, Delia, maybe for 'Old Times' Sake', as they say?"

"I won't be staying for breakfast, my dear," Delia's voice was kind but her message was firm.

"Well, you can't blame a man for trying..." He winked at her, trying to make a tease out of it. "You're sure, are you?"

"I'm sure."

He sighed, theatrically enough to make her grin. "Well then, I guess you'd better tell me a tale of the Folk I haven't heard before, so I can write a new song. Something to distract me from meditating upon your loveliness."

"I know just the one," Delia assured him, and they each settled comfortably on the couch as she began the tale.

Later, they were laughing about previous Court Singers. Michael knew many of the stories, but they were great fun to hear again. He threw in a couple of funny anecdotes about some of the women he'd known since he'd left Elvenhome. The wine flowed as freely as their laughter.

"You're staring at me, Michael," Delia pointed out when they were catching their breath, "and studying me like you haven't seen me before. I own that it was selfish; was it also a mistake for me to step into your evening this way? Have I caused harm?"

Michael shook his head. "Oh no, no, no, Your Grace, it was not a mistake, no harm done. And if it was selfish on your part, that's all the better." He winked at her. "So I won't have to feel selfish alone." He beamed a knowing smile at her. "Don't you see, Delia? You wanted to see me, you wanted to, or *needed* to, talk and laugh with me the way we did a long time ago.

"This makes me the only Court Singer you've come back to spend time with, right?"

The Fair Folk do not lie; however, they have been known to reshuffle the decks of conversation away from the suit of hearts.

Delia smiled. "I was already in Edinburgh, Michael. But I did want to see you." *It's true,* she thought. *I needed the ear of an old friend to help me remember happy hours and forget sad ones.*

"Then the magic is still here for you, as it has always been for me. Delia, I've never loved anyone else, not in all these years. I've foolishly imagined that you really did have some of the Folk look me up every so often, and tell you what I've been doing. I've hoped that I've made you proud, and that you'd miss me a bit. And now that you've come back—"

"I'm not 'back,' I'm simply here just now." Delia took Michael's hand, and looked deeply into his eyes. "My sweet man. On occasion, I've regretted giving you the choice to remember your time with me..."

"I have never regretted it."

"That may be, Michael, but you also did not move on with your life the way you planned to once you left Elvenhome. I feel sad about that."

"Don't."

"I do."

"I've been more or less content, sometimes happy. The music is a wonderful lover, of course, and has always been the best part of my world. I've done more than I ever thought I could, or would, and I have you to thank for that." He took a sip of wine and continued. "There honestly have been women. I've not always been alone and miserable while I've thought about you, and remembered."

She sighed. "But you did not move on to the dreams you dreamed then, or find the love you deserve."

His eyes were serious as he met her gaze. "Because I'd already found her, and loved her. I still do love you, Delia. You coming back to me is what I've dreamed of and wished for and written about. You're in most every serious song I sing. We were good together, happy, weren't we? Now that you're here, we could begin again, and let the song go on and on..."

Watching him, she wondered what she could say that would be both kind and useful to him. It had been his choice to remember their time; she had granted it despite her reservations.

In a flash, she knew she would never offer Thomas Lear the same option.

Michael had been studying her, waiting for a response. He was trying to look casual and loving without crowding her with the intensity they both knew he was feeling. "So?" he said, as lightly as he could manage.

"You are wonderful," Delia said, blessing him with a radiant smile. "I love so many things about you. We had a blissful year and a day, Michael. Neither of us have ever forgotten it."

"Well then," he interjected.

"Wait," she said, placing her fingertips gently on his mouth. "I do love you, but I am not in love with you. We both know that I never was. You know the difference. I have never believed that there is only ever one person who can hold our hearts, Michael. If that were so, then when we lose that one person, we would wither and die from the pain of the loss...but we don't. We go on, if we choose to. And sometimes when we haven't chosen to. We go on—and when it's time, we find someone new to love, and to trust with the holding of our hearts. This is one of the ways of love."

"I love you, Delia." His eyes were filling with a hopelessness he could not quite accept.

"And I love you, Michael," she told him firmly. "You will always be precious to me, especially for sharing this evening with me, when I needed respite.

"In gratitude, I can offer you a gift, one that you richly deserve."

He had looked away. He looked back at her, his gaze wistful.

"I can erase your memories of Elvenhome, and of me, so that you can find someone to share your love, your life, your music, all of it."

"I'd lose my memories of you?" he asked, wide-eyed.

Delia nodded.

"No!" he cried. "No, don't take them away. Please. I will learn to make myself available to love someday, but don't withdraw my beloved Muse, Delia, I beg you."

She bit her lip, considering the repercussions of her planned action.

"Delia, please," he repeated.

"Very well," conceded the High Queen of Faerie. "You may keep your memories, my dearest Michael; they will remain yours to do with as you will. And to help you on your quest for the next lady to whom you will give your heart for safekeeping, I will tell you something that may help you step away from your feelings for me. It's a secret that is a surprise to me, one that I shared with 'Cousin Angus' only yesterday."

Intrigued, Michael poured the last of the wine into their glasses, and waited.

Delia took a deep breath, then told him. "Once upon a time, as you know, I joyfully gave my whole heart to a King. When he could no longer hold it, because he had lost his own, I took my empty heart back, and kept it in a safe but lonely place while I moved through my days and years, centuries without it. I have cared for so many others, you among them, my dear. But that was loving, not living in love. There is a difference, and you know it well.

"Here is the secret: Michael, my heart is no longer resting in its safe place. My heart is full, and I have given it to someone I can trust will hold it, and who will trust me with the holding of his. I am in love, with a mortal, and I am very happy."

He struggled to find his balance. "A mortal?" *Not me,* his heart wailed in pain, but he valiantly ignored it for now.

"Yes," she said, marveling as much at her open admission as at the dancing of her emotions.

It didn't take him more than a few seconds, even though his own heart ached. "Your Court Singer, is it? Tom?"

"Thomas," Callie said, with a giddy smile. "You might have heard of him. He's Thomas Lear."

"Thomas LEAR?" Michael thought about this. "The man I met tonight?"

Callie nodded.

"Really? He didn't look much like Thomas Lear, Delia." A thought occurred to Michael. "Oh. You covered him in one of your glamours."

Callie nodded again, still smiling.

"Well then, Delia's in love, at long last. I'm glad for you!" He tried to smile, and let out a long, slow breath. "Lucky man," he offered, although his heart was heavy.

IT WAS NOT long after that, around three-thirty in the morning, when Callie popped without a sound into her darkened bedroom in the house in Charlotte Square. She was tired, but in a happy, peaceful mood. She'd hugged Michael goodbye, even kissed him fondly, thanked him for the evening, and she truly wished him much happiness for all of his days.

With a hushed sigh, she pulled her long cardigan off, tossed it onto the back of a chair, and looked at the bed.

Thomas wasn't in it.

He was sitting on the floor beside the bed, drinking in the dark. His back was against the wall, and he held a glass upside down in his hand. Two empty whisky bottles lay on the floor beside him.

Even before Callie turned the light on, she knew he was glowering at her.

104

"Did you make it with him?" Squinting in the sudden brightness, Thomas growled menacingly as his eyes scanned her. "You did, didn't you?"

The wave of drunken anger that he shot at her caught her off-guard. "Thomas? What's amiss?"

He glared. "What's 'amiss'? I'll tell you what's amiss, Your Grace. It's nearly four in the morning. You've spent the night with an old lover, and left me here alone to do nothing but think about that. After all we've been through this week alone, I can't believe you'd fuck your old Court Singer. But you did, didn't you? You did, and to hell with everything else, right?"

Callie looked at him, forcing herself to remain calm. It took her a moment to respond. She weighed her options to see how she would play this particular game. When she did speak, she was quiet and kind. "You are tired, Thomas, and you are drunk. Your feelings are hurt; I understand that. You should get into bed, and sleep. All will look different to you in the morning."

He staggered to his feet, dropping the empty glass onto the carpet as he moved. "That's no answer. You fucked him!"

She was tired, but she held on to her temper. "Whether or not I gave myself to Michael MacAllistair is not the point."

He interrupted her as he sat unsteadily on the bed, his anger boiling. "It *is* the point, and you know it!"

The game was evident, but Callie was not inclined to play it now. Over the centuries, she had known many mortals. She had been intimate with enough of them to be well acquainted with the vagaries of mortal emotion when sex, jealousy and too much alcohol filled a moment. *And not just mortal emotion*, she reminded herself with a sigh, then let that sad thought go as she focused on Thomas.

She cut to the chase, knowing before she said anything that it would do no good. They were going to have to play this all the way out. She sighed. "I did not share myself with Michael. We ate dinner, drank a bit together, and talked. And then I came home."

105

His beautiful brown eyes were smoldering. "I don't believe you," he snapped.

"Of course you don't," she conceded, her exasperation growing despite her best efforts to be patient with him. "You can't, right now. Just accept that what I said is true, and go to sleep."

He rose from the bed, and stood to face her. "I thought that what we have together is important to you. You've always acted like it is. I don't need this shit, Callie, and I won't just take it. Nobody cheats on me! Nobody!"

She should have reminded herself that she loved him, and that he was only drunk and slightly ridiculous in his anger. But she'd had a long day, plus weeks of worry, grief and strain, and she had had enough of this craziness. "Oh, shut up," she said quietly, and left the room.

Callie walked down the hall toward the staircase, deciding to return to the comfort of her needlework in the drawing room. It was not a surprise that Thomas followed her, several paces behind, shouting.

"Do you want to replace me with him? Maybe you should, and I can get the hell out of here!"

She kept walking, turned on a light switch as she passed it, and moved down the stairs quickly to put distance between them. "I did not give myself to Michael, although he wanted me to. I needed a friend, someone who knew nothing of the Mischief. We talked. Now let it be, Thomas."

Callie turned the lights on in the drawing room as she entered it. Thomas came down the stairs and followed her.

"How could you have chosen to spend time talking to him, then, when you had me? You sent me home alone. Your spy made sure I got here, and that's fine, just fine, Callie—but you sent me home and..."

She whirled to face him. "Your anger has made you thick-headed! You were the one who suggested that I have dinner with Michael! You declined my several sincere offers to have you join us! You insisted that we should have time to talk alone!" So great was her frustration that she wanted to scream at him. Instead, she went cold and quiet, and she saw quite clearly that Thomas was feeding his drunken rage with his own private bitterness, much the way Garrhyn, once upon a time, had fed his own. "This was *your* doing," Callie told Thomas. "Yours."

He took a furious step toward her. "I thought you were going to decline the suggestion, enjoy the rest of the concert, say goodbye to him, and come home with me!"

Yes, I know you did, you fool, she thought. *And I should have done it your way, but I needed an old friend, if only for a little while.* She kept her voice steady. "And you could feel generous and unselfish and reasonable."

He didn't know what to say to that, since she'd called it exactly right. Blushing, he was a little ashamed of himself, but he couldn't think about that now.

"Go to bed, Thomas. I was not intimate with Michael, and there's an end to it. Please."

He was too drunk, too angry, and too tired to consider the possibility that she was telling the truth. *She is too beautiful, too calm, and too much the High Queen of Faerie to not take and be taken by anyone she chooses*, he told himself. Michael was handsome, talented, and a comfortable part of her past. She had had need of Michael tonight, not Thomas.

It was unthinkable.

How could she choose the admittedly aging, local musician over Thomas Lear, Rock Star?

You don't need this shit, the Monster In His Head whispered helpfully. *If she doesn't need you, you don't want her. Tell her!*

Callie tried one last time. "Thomas, my dear, you are exhausted. Go up to bed, and we will sort it all out in the daylight."

He had had enough. "Fuck this, Callie. Fuck it! I'm going home. To L.A."

She sat down on in a chair and looked over at him. "You cannot. Done is done."

Thomas ran his fingers through his hair, planning his departure as he tried to wake himself up. "Bullshit. I can get to the airport. I can make a couple of calls and have a ticket waiting for me when I get there. I'm going back to L.A."

"Unfortunately, every road you take—whether it's to the airport, or to a train station, or a walk into the center of Edinburgh – every road you take will lead you only to the woodland behind Queensgate," she explained. "Done is done, Thomas, and neither you nor I can undo it."

"Bullshit!" he barked.

"You were aware of this from the very beginning. It was the price you paid—"

"I might try it anyway," he pointed out, the look on his face as petulant as the tone of his voice.

"As you choose," she said wearily.

"I will!"

"Again, as you choose. But done is done."

"Maybe. And maybe not," Thomas countered. He moved past where Callie sat and, picking up his guitar from where it rested against the couch, bent down and placed it in its case. Snapping the case closed, he snarled at the High Queen of Faerie.

"The thing that pisses me off more than anything else is the knowledge that, despite any feelings I might have had for you, you were just using me the way you've used the rest of your Court Singers, from the very beginning." Standing up, he shook his head at her. "Could be that your King ScarF was on to something when he stepped away from you. You've displaced him with Court Singers, over and over again, and maybe you just can't get it right. But I've had enough of this. You don't get to use me anymore, Your Grace!"

He was looking right at her, but he wasn't sure that he actually saw Callie stand up and take two steps toward him.

"Thomas Lear," she hissed, her brown eyes blazing, *"YOU WILL BE SILENT!"*

When he thought about it later, he couldn't have said whether, in her fury and his alcohol-twisted mind, Callie had gotten inexplicably larger, or somehow brighter. All he knew was that she suddenly seemed to fill the entire space in the room. Her angry presence, and the unmistakable threat of fire behind it, appeared capable of burning up all the breathable air around him. He was aware that when she narrowed her fury-filled eyes and ordered him to silence, he'd had no thought of anything except instant, unquestioning obedience.

Although he was angry, too, and he had a few more provocative things to say to her, he shut his mouth. Despite his mental dizziness, he marveled at the knowledge that he had no choice. He may even have bowed his drunken head in submission while he wondered how they'd gotten to this terrible, shameful place.

Despite the ferocity of the expression of her wrath, she was, he noticed all over again, incredibly, unimaginably beautiful. Even the sadness he saw revealed in her eyes was glorious in its way. It surprised him, somehow, that he had contributed to that sadness.

He wanted to say something to make the moment better, but he was fully wrapped in silence, and could not reach for words. He had too many feelings that he could not sort through fast enough to decide what to say to her. She looked powerfully feral, angry, hurt and, for only the second time since he'd met her, entirely dangerous.

What startled him more than anything else was that she was also entirely closed to him.

After a few long minutes, the frenzied energy around them dissipated into an uneasy stillness. All was as it was before, except that it wasn't, really. They had changed.

Moving back to the chair she'd occupied, Callie sat down heavily, and took a few deep breaths. Then, her eyes shining with sadness, she said, "Do not assume that I am invulnerable to emotional pain simply because I am not mortal. Pain is pain."

He should have apologized, for all of it. He could have saved the moment if he had simply taken responsibility for this insanity.

But he didn't. He thought about his life, his mistakes, his failures, and the heady lies (no, the fiction, the *fiction*) he'd created about himself and sold to the world to explain himself and make himself appear to be worthy of his music. He had despised himself before, and often, but never like this.

Thomas Lear, Self-serving Bastard, met Callie's unhappy gaze and frowned.

"Are we finished with this?" Her question was dripping with misery.

He found his words, and pushed them out; they were as true as they were unkind. "Yes, we're finished with this. And right now, I hate you as much as I hate myself."

Thomas turned and went up the stairs to bed.

THOMAS WOKE, WITH a hangover that could have toppled Edinburgh Castle from The Rock.

Despite the eager sunlight that seeped in around the closed curtains, he went back to sleep, in self-defense.

When he woke again, the daylight was shadowed and quiet. He made several half-hearted, tentative moves, to see if his pounding head and queasy stomach would let him get out of bed. It took some convincing, but he managed it.

After visiting the bathroom and pulling on his clothes, he made his way down the staircase, looking around for Callie.

She'd been right, of course, and he'd been wrong and stupid and mean. He had to fix what he'd messed up last night. He wasn't sure about everything that had happened, and was even less clear about everything he'd said, but he was going to own all of it, apologize, and make it up to her.

Because his head hurt, he walked carefully into the drawing room, hoping to find her working on her needlepoint. The clock on the mantel chimed. He was stunned that it was five p.m.

Someone was sitting in the chair by the windows, as he'd imagined she might be.

It wasn't Callie. It was Zodiac.

Thomas closed his eyes for a moment to reset his bearings. When he opened them again, Zodiac was standing up, a faint hint of resignation in his eyes.

"What am I doing here?" Zodiac prompted Thomas. "I am here to take you back to Elvenhome."

"Where's—?"

"Her Grace has returned to the castle. She did not feel that she could stay away from the Folk any longer, and she did not wish to wake you."

Or she did not wish to see me, Thomas thought guiltily. He looked at his friend. "Did she say..."

Zodiac frowned. "It was apparent that she was displeased, but she did not choose to confide in me. For which I find I am grateful."

Thomas groaned, as much from dismay and regret as from the hangover.

"You look completely terrible, Thomas, whether you earned it or not. Would you like me to get you something to eat or drink?"

Thomas blanched. "God, no..."

"Very well," said Zodiac. "In that case, let us get going. I took the liberty of putting your guitar and a few other things in the car. The sooner we start, the sooner we shall make Queensgate."

Zodiac headed for the front door at a brisk pace.

In a daze, Thomas tried to catch up with what was happening.

The front door was opened. After a moment, Zodiac called "Come on, Thomas!"

The ride from Queensgate to Maggie's cottage in the Highlands had been filled with lively conversation; Zodiac and Thomas had talked throughout the entire trip.

111

Tonight's return journey from Edinburgh to Queensgate was altogether different. Zodiac recognized that Thomas not only felt like hell, but that the Court Singer had wrapped himself in dark, private thoughts that he was not inclined to share. He stared out the passenger side window, oblivious to everything but the unnerving, constant clash of his own emotions.

At first, Thomas had seemed to be upset, frustrated, unhappy, and a little guilty, which, Zodiac conceded silently, was most likely the appropriate combination for whatever had occurred between the Court Singer and Her Grace. But eventually, Zodiac sensed that those feelings were being joined by darker ones; Thomas seemed both angry and depressed, tense and restless, bitter and lonely. The depths of the changes to Thomas' emotional climate made Zodiac press the Fiat's accelerator a little harder. Things did not feel right. It would be best to get Thomas back to the castle as soon as possible so that Her Grace and her Court Singer could sort things out and set everything back into a merry balance.

Several times, as the Fiat drove in the twilight, the Queen's Lord High Chamberlain attempted to talk with his friend. "Do you want to stop for food or coffee, perhaps?"

Without a word, Thomas shook his head and kept his eyes on the road ahead.

Later, Zodiac said, "Is there anything I can do to help? If you want to talk about it…"

"No. Thank you," Thomas muttered.

A while later, as he thought about it, Thomas had a useful thought about Zodiac's offer. "You know," he began, "there is something."

"Good," Zodiac replied, relieved that Thomas was making some progress toward returning to himself. "What can I do?"

"When we get back, I want to read everything about Thomas the Rhymer. Factual stuff, poetry, histories, all the tales you've got. I want to know all about him. I know

112

some stuff from the literature I've read before, and from what Her Grace has shared with me. But I want more. All the information I can get my hands on from the Library, and anyplace else you can think of. Maybe I can talk to some of the Folk who knew him? Can you help me with that?"

This is encouraging, Zodiac thought. "With pleasure," he said. "Are you going to write a song about The Rhymer? That would be a marvel of a thing!"

Thomas looked out of the passenger window again, his face unreadable. "It sure would."

The Court Singer doubted that there would be a song in it. This was more of a personal fact-finding exercise. Thomas decided that he wanted to know The Rhymer's full story, all the nuances, so he could see what might be in store for Thomas Lear. Callie had said once that she didn't ever confuse him with The Rhymer, but Thomas wasn't so sure about that.

The current Court Singer wanted to know everything there was to know about the first Court Singer. And once he did, maybe he would write that song. And if the song could smack Callie's feelings around a little bit, so that she'd be as miserable as he felt now, maybe that was okay too.

six

Once upon a time, a handsome and powerful High King fell completely in love with a beautiful Princess, the only daughter of a lesser King who lived at the farthest end of his Kingdom.

Almost at once, the High King and the Princess found that they had much to talk about. In time they discovered how well they could speak to each other without words. They shared a deep love for the land of Faerie and its people. She told him stories that made him think; he told her stories that made her laugh.

It did not take long for the Princess to fall in love with the High King. He was handsome and strong, gentle and just; she knew she wanted to be with him always.

In a fragrant garden on a summer morning, the High King asked the Princess to marry him and share his life, his love, and his kingdom forever. She promised to be his wife and to stay with him until the end of their time.

So great was their love that, even at its beginning, they each knew that they would always be in love, and would always be happy together.

All the Folk of Faerie were invited to celebrate the Great Marriage and attend a merry feast in honor of the royal couple's love and happiness.

In the days before the ceremony, the Princess made final preparations to move to the castle at Elvenhome and take her place as High Queen of her people and as the loving and beloved wife of the High King. At the same time, the King stood in his Tower Room, gazed out of the windows and tried to think of the perfect bridegift for the woman he already loved more than life.

He wanted to give her something special enough to last through the fullness of the long and happy years they would spend together. It had to be something that would always make her smile, something that would forever call him to her mind and heart when she saw it.

It took him the better part of a full day to decide what to make for her. It was perfect, and he smiled when he thought about how much it would please her.

And then he flexed his fingers, formed a clear image in his mind, and went to work.

The night before the wedding, the King and his Princess walked hand in hand through the King's favorite garden in the vast castle of Elvenhome.

115

The moon was full of light and song, and the stars danced merrily, rising and falling to the music only stars can hear.

And at midnight, under that brightly-glowing moon and the swirling stars, the King and his beloved shyly exchanged gifts, created for each other by their own hands.

He could not wait for her to see what he had made, so asked her to open her bridegift first.

Now, everyone knows how much the Fair Folk love music; they can sense it in every theme and element of their lives. They hear melody in sunshine and moonlight, they can taste it in the rain and touch it on the trees. Every faerie has his or her own inner song; as a race, their absolute delight in music is as boundless as laughter. Some say that faeries can see music.

And of all the Folk the High King had ever met, the beautiful woman who stood beside him in his garden this night loved music more than anyone else. It was as though he could hear a gentle, rhythmic cadence in her, the soft suggestion of an as yet unsung song as she smiled at him in the moonlight.

He placed a small box, wrapped in the glow of a rainbow, into her lovely hands.

At his urging, she opened the box, and emptied its contents carefully into her hand. The moon shone brightly on the gift. The King beamed as the Princess gasped in delight.

Standing upright on her palm was an exquisite, perfectly-formed golden harp, no more than ten centimeters in height. It had a silken red ribbon around its arm that carried a private message for her eyes alone. She read it and smiled softly.

Then the harp trembled into wakefulness and began to sing, a sweet refrain from the depths of the King's soul that he had not shared with anyone before. Like their love, his music flowed joyously into her heart for a lifetime of safekeeping.

"I give you 'Moonsong,' and with it, the gift of myself," he whispered to her, his chin trembling. She looked up into his face with happy tears in her eyes, and kissed him.

Later, under the same moon and stars, the King opened his gift from the Princess. In a tiny round box, she had placed a golden chain, from which hung a handsome golden charm in the shape of a harp.

He removed it from the box, and studied it admiringly; it was very like the harp he had just given his bride. She took it from him and fastened it around his neck. His eyes widened in surprise and pleasure as the small harp charm, which now rested flat against his chest and above his heart, played sweet music that hinted at the harmonies that he knew danced inside the mind and soul of his Princess, soon to be his Queen. It was a glowing song that only the two of them could hear.

"How did you know?" he asked, overcome with the wonder of her.

"The same way you did, I suppose," she answered, smiling at him with love in her eyes.

He took her into his arms and kissed her again, then murmured something that made her laugh. When the King asked her to dance with him, the Princess placed the harp called 'Moonsong' on the ground a little distance away, and took the King's hand. Moonsong played sweetly as the High King and his bride danced together in the sparkling moonlight.

Above them, the stars smiled.

CARRYING A STURDY basket laden with food and wine, Lavender thought about Thomas as she moved through the corridor. She wondered if she should wait another day, let the present opportunity fall away yet again, and bide her time until he was not so angry and unhappy.

No, she determined, with a decisive lift of her chin, *the timing is perfect. I can make this work.*

It was true that he had been in a foul temper since he had returned from Upworld. He had also been solitary and withdrawn. As far as she knew, Thomas hadn't spoken to anyone but Zodiac. All the Ladies were concerned about him; they were as interested in his well-being as they were in the gossip about him. Lavender had tried to consider a way to charm information from Zodiac, but she knew that if the Queen's High Chamberlain was confiding in anyone at all, it was Her Grace.

Still, the things that Her Grace did *not* tell the Ladies held tantalizing hints of what had happened in Edinburgh. No one seemed to know the specifics. Her Grace only said that she had spent time with former Court Singer Michael MacAllistair. It was not a surprise that Thomas might be raw and angry about it. Like many mortals, he both did and did not feel the same way about physical play as the Folk did, and this paradox, Her Grace had explained to the Ladies long ago, preyed on his mind.

There was much talk all over the castle, for the Fair Folk love gossip. Everyone knew what had happened to Lord Arrendel, and now everyone knew about Lord Arrendel's Lady Maggie. Thomas was being heralded as a brave if reluctant hero. Yet Thomas didn't want thanks from any of them. He had stayed alone in his apartments, and avoided everyone.

Including Her Grace.

The Lord High Chamberlain had arranged for Thomas' meals to be delivered by HobGoblins from the Kitchens. Iris told the Ladies that she had heard that Thomas had appropriately thanked whoever had brought each meal, but apart from that, it appeared that he had not spoken with anyone save Zodiac, and even those conversations were brief.

More shocking were the rumblings that Her Grace and Thomas had not spent any time together since Thomas' return with Zodiac, a week ago. Her Grace seemed content to let Thomas work his unhappiness out on his own. She no longer seemed irritable about whatever had passed between them. She had reassured her Ladies that Thomas would move through his dark time in his own way, and when he was ready, all would be well again.

Where Her Grace was willing to be patient and give Thomas the time he needed to find his voice again, Lavender discovered that she was not.

Yes, the time was ripe; she had to be sure she did everything right. She didn't mind his supposed black mood at all. In fact, Lavender rather liked him angry, sullen, and quiet. She had seen him walk down this same hall when he had returned from Upworld. She had wanted to welcome him home, and to have him see that she had waited to greet him, but he had not noticed her. There had been something erotic and inviting about the dangerous look in his dark eyes; the untapped, unspoken anger, hurt and jealousy she could read in their brown depths made her shiver with wanting him. He was a man who understood the power of his own bitterness, and he knew how to make the most of it. She could conjure an image of him at this very moment, writing a pain-filled song of wrenching betrayal by a careless Queen. Lavender longed to hear it, and to watch the pain play on his face as he sang. He was always so open and alive when he sang his songs, which was one of the reasons anyone who heard him sing could feel whatever he was feeling right along with him. It was exciting in a way she barely understood, but she wanted to taste it with him, again and again.

The fact that Thomas could be jealous and emotional about Callie's playfulness with the handsome Michael made Lavender want Thomas and his oversensitive, evocative passions even more.

That the Queen had pushed him too far was as clear as a summer sky to Lavender, and she knew she could easily use Her Grace's mistake to win Thomas for herself. He would grow to love her as much as she loved him, she was certain of that. She was only going to help the process along a little. There could be no harm in that.

Or at least, not very much harm.

She moved purposefully toward his door, the heavy basket over her arm seeming suddenly much lighter. Her time had come, at long last.

She could almost feel Thomas' hands and mouth on her face. She told herself that despite all the wanting and needing and waiting she'd done since he had named her "Lavender," she would not have to wait any longer. Tail twitching happily behind her, Lavender quickened her step, her eyes radiant with love and desire.

She knew without a single doubt that having him love her would be worth anything she had to do to make it happen.

THE COFFEE TABLE in Thomas' sitting room was covered with stacks of books, scrolls, and notes all related to The Rhymer. Zodiac had been as good as his word, and had located and delivered as much documentation as Thomas could read in a month. He'd even provided Thomas with a list of the Folk who still lived in the castle or in the village who had met The Rhymer, and who would answer any questions Thomas might want to ask them. Thomas had read several of the books, but hadn't found anything remarkable yet.

In a bleak mood, Thomas distractedly played his guitar, attempting without success to push Callie out of his mind. There was a small stack of paper and a pen on the dining table, beside which he sat; he had been writing poetry. Rather, he'd been *trying* to write poetry. The lines systematically scratched through every word on several pages announced the fact that the writing was not going well. This additional failure did nothing to improve his miserable frame of mind.

He was no longer angry with Callie, although it had taken him a couple of days to get to that point. Now he was merely annoyed that she'd been so generous about everything. His bitterness was aimed at himself, for having acted like a jackass, and for having set up the stupid situation in the first place.

This alone would have been little enough to deal with and move beyond to regain his balance, but there was much more troubling the Court Singer. He was not writing well, despite his need to spill his self-induced torments onto paper and into music. Guilt and sleepless exhaustion blended with frustration, unnerving vulnerability and a small collection of old and familiar personal demons. He was trapped in his head with himself, and after a week of self-imposed, blindingly dark solitude, he had all but strangled the parts of himself that he liked best.

He was badly confused, too. He was used to his own bleak moods; they were part of him. They often had been the strange but fertile breeding ground for some of the best songs of his generation. He'd get down and deep in the mire of his internal mud, and in his darkness, he'd eventually encounter the light that ultimately evolved into the music of Thomas Lear.

That he couldn't write, or even think with much clarity, and was perpetually drug-free (if not always sober), only added to the overall impossibility of his current situation, pulled him deeper into himself and, paradoxically, farther away from his music and everyone he knew.

He'd tried to hide in the books he was reading, but he couldn't concentrate. He tried eating too much, and then not eating enough, to see if he could shake things up a bit and find his footing. He considered asking for Orchid, his favorite of the Queen's Ladies, in the vague hope that he could recalibrate himself by listening to the sweet Selkie talk about easy things, and thus make room for the catharsis he would need to find his way back to himself. He did not believe that he could find it on his own this time. Eventually the notion of exposing Orchid to his dismal, dangerous mood left him feeling numb and a little sick. He admitted to himself that perhaps the only thing standing in the way of his being happy and well and finding his music again was to travel through the dark side of Thomas Lear, and he hated himself for it.

As he sat there and played, he sighed. The music that came somewhat haltingly from the guitar was beautiful in its way, but to Thomas it sounded clumsy and forced. Disgusted, he almost considered calling for Zodiac and asking for a couple more bottles of whisky. He had done this two or three times since he'd come back. Thomas Lear, Train Wreck, wanted to get—and stay—drunk for a while.

When the knock on the door came, he groaned, only barely containing a peevish shout. He knew it was not Zodiac. He was not in the mood for spontaneous conversation of any kind. He glared at the door and willed whoever was on the other side of it to go away and leave him alone. He knew it would not be Callie, either, and even though he did not want to see her, he wanted to see anyone else even less.

The knock came again, louder and more insistent this time. Thomas sighed. Resigned to dealing very briefly with his intruder, he put down the guitar, ran a hand through his hair in frustration, and got up and opened the door.

Lavender stood there, carrying a big basket of food, smiling up at him. Her bright blue eyes met his easily, glittering with flirtation. "Hello, Thomas. I've brought you a picnic! Are you hungry?" She looked at him, eyes filled with expectation.

Damn, the food smelled good. Was he hungry? He didn't know. He didn't care. He was fairly sure that he'd had a burger and salad earlier today, or had that been late last night? He hadn't kept track of meals. He knew Zodiac would not let him go too long without eating. Each person who had delivered his meals this week had done so swiftly (probably in self-defense), with a fast murmur of the blessing *Eat and drink, free from care...* before escaping from his glowering presence. The whole thing might have been almost funny, if he'd been in a different frame of mind.

He didn't care about that right now; he only wanted to be left alone. He frowned at Lavender, hoping she'd go away so he wouldn't have to break his bitter, self-enforced silence.

She didn't take the hint.

He wanted her to walk away, but she stood there looking up at him. She didn't deserve the intensity of his misery. Treating her badly because he was in a vile mood would not solve anything. It would only make matters worse if he hurt her feelings.

What the hell, maybe she'd just leave the food and then go. Mouth clamped shut, eyes narrowed, he moved out of the doorway so she could bring her basket in.

As she walked past him, he found himself, as usual, glancing at her backside. Although it was not readily discernible through the back of her gown, her tail still fascinated him; he hadn't decided yet whether he found it erotic or repulsive. In every other respect, he supposed, she looked as human as Callie did, Callie's delicious long and pointed sexy ears notwithstanding. Lavender's ears were tiny, and only a little pointed. She wore small golden earrings in them that caught the light of her long blonde hair. But her tail! The few times Thomas had seen Lavender in breeches, her tail was plainly visible; it stuck out of a specially-designed hole. He had never seen the place where the tail sprouted from her bare skin, and he had wondered about it, quite a few times, in passing. *Either very creepy*, he mused, *or very, very beautiful.*

Startled, he realized that she was talking to him, and that he hadn't even pretended to listen. He looked over at her, wondering if he could make himself speak at least enough to apologize.

She was taking food out of the basket, and putting it on the dining table. Everything smelled fantastic. He'd let her talk for a while, and then she'd go away, and he'd eat something. Maybe he was hungry after all.

"At first I thought I wanted to take you out to the lochside for a picnic," she was chirping, her voice merry, "then of course I remembered that if you leave your rooms, you can't speak. And while I'd love to sit in the sun and charm you all day with my own chatter," she laughed now, a light and airy sound that seemed to cheer the moment a little, displace some small measure of his bleak mood, "I'd much prefer that we could both talk. So I hope you don't mind if we eat here, Thomas…"

He hadn't shaken off his anger and depression, and didn't want to. He had worn it tight around himself for more than a week, and it was becoming a second skin. Food or not, he wanted her to go away.

Working to keep the low growl out of his voice, he tilted his head toward the door, indicating that she should leave the food and go. "Lavender, I'm not good company right now."

"I know it. But I was hoping that if you had a distraction or two, you would begin to feel better." She kept her eyes on the deep basket she was unpacking, but she did not hide the smile in her voice. "I have other distractions in mind, if you are not hungry. For food, that is."

His eyes opened wide in surprise as a notable portion of his irritability threatened to dissipate at once in the face of her unexpected invitation.

She didn't turn around, only continued to put food on the table. "The way you are staring at me, one would think that you were surprised, Thomas," she said, with a laugh. "You cannot be unaware that I find you beautiful and desirable."

He couldn't think of a single thing to say. She laughed again, and turned to face him.

"Everyone knows you have only had eyes for our Queen since you first arrived; the enchantment you were under then was her own. Perhaps you are in the thrall of that enchantment still. It does not matter. You are not tied to the Queen, except when she commands it." Lavender eyed him seductively. "And she is not in the castle."

This was, of course, news to Thomas. "Not here?" his voice sounded dull and empty.

"No."

He hated himself for asking, cringing as the words passed his lips, but he couldn't help it. "Where did she go?"

"She is riding in the wood with some of the Court. They left hours ago, and will not be back until dinner. She said she wanted to stretch some of her muscles." The basket was empty now and Lavender placed it on the floor beside the table. There was a veritable feast in front of him.

Lavender turned to Thomas with a suggestive smirk. "The Queen has not had enough *exercise* of late, as you would know better than anyone else." The blonde Elf giggled.

Thomas winced, and forced himself to breathe. Lavender watched him struggle for a moment, then she said, "Do you know, I have not seen the Court Singer's garden for many years, and it truly was one of my favorite places in Elvenhome. Would you show me?"

"Now?" he asked, attempting to hide his confusion. The bleak mood that had started to move away was back again, full-forced and blinding.

"Now," she replied.

He wanted her to go away. He felt sick; at the mere mention of Callie, anger and betrayal and other things that he couldn't immediately identify swirled around inside him. Lavender had to see that he didn't want to do this, she *had* to. But she didn't, and he did not want to make things worse by mistreating her. Perhaps if he just showed her the damned garden and then calmed down enough to ask her to leave, it would be all right.

Oblivious to his feelings, she chattered at him she led him toward his bedroom, which she ignored as they passed through it. She opened, then walked through, the double glass doors that took them out into the gardens.

"It is still lovely out here," she said, appreciating the flower-scented air. "I have always been especially drawn to this place, it is so beautiful. When I was a little Elf I would come here and talk to the trees and the flowers. I even spoke to the stones in the garden walls!"

Thomas did not bother to pretend to be interested. He wanted her to leave him alone. Once she was gone, he would get his hands on some whisky and drink himself hopelessly blind, deaf and numb, even if he had to force himself to talk to Zodiac in order to do it.

He cringed as he glanced at Lavender. She was still babbling away, happy and glowing as she took in the serene beauty of the garden. "...because my mother's family were Dryads, of course! Oh, look!" she gasped, and ran over to the ancient rowan tree and hugged it with affection. "Hello, Father Rowan! You look well!" She gave the bark a kiss, patted the tree, and looked back at Thomas. "Is there still a sea of blue columbine? It has been such a long while since I have walked here."

Thomas pointed to a spot approximately thirty feet behind the rowan tree. "It's back over there," he mumbled.

Lavender dashed down to the columbine bed. "Oh, Thomas, it is so much larger than I remember!"

Thomas moved until he stood stiffly beside her; it was all he could do to keep from pacing. "I like the wildness of it," he pushed the words out in what passed for a tired reply. "It seems so free, in its way a lot like Faerie."

"Yes, it is indeed very much like Faerie," she echoed, nodding her head. "Freedom is the most important thing to us, it is in the air we breathe, the food we eat. It is our way. We are forever free to do as we please, in every aspect of our lives."

"Great work if you can get it," he muttered under his breath.

"What?" she asked.

"Forget it," he said.

126

She turned to him, then, and put a small hand on his arm. "Oh, Thomas, you do not need to be so unhappy!"

At any other time, the look of sympathetic despair in her eyes would almost have made him laugh. Instead he made a sound like a cross between an angry croak and a sob. "I don't?" he scowled, bitterness rolling over him. "You know what happened in Edinburgh. I'd imagine everyone does."

She looked at him solemnly. "I know that you were hurt by it, and that you are still hurt by it." She squeezed his arm. "I would like to help you to feel better."

He looked at the small hand on his arm, then met her steady gaze and studied her eyes as a spontaneous, spiteful—but intensely sexual—impulse took hold of him.

He'd had this particular sexual thought before, of course, but had never acted on it, even though he understood that Callie had no objection if he wanted to share himself with anyone else, provided he serviced her when requested. The openness of the Fey perspective on sex, he thought wryly, had somehow closed the door a little on the way he had always greedily dealt with it before Elvenhome.

For reasons he hadn't bothered to examine, Callie had been all that he'd needed or wanted since his first arrival in Faerie. He'd had moments when he wondered what it would be like to fuck Juniper, with her long limbs and her obvious physical strength, and the daring wisp of danger around her. And every so often he'd seen a beautiful guest at a feast, and had been duly aroused. There was no denying that the tiny, perfectly-made, purple-skinned, purple-haired, purple-winged Sylph he'd named Violet was unbelievably (and somewhat alarmingly) erotic; he'd had one or two rather spectacular wet dreams about her. All that aside, Thomas' sexual desire had focused itself exclusively on Callie. He had simply ignored any other temptation.

Looking at Lavender beside him, he chose not to ignore this one.

Reassured by his silence, and aroused by the sullen spark in his eyes, she inched closer to him. "If you want me, I am here. I want you, and want to give you pleasure."

He did not breathe.

"As Her Grace is not at the castle, she will not be looking for you, even if all were well between you. And unless she commands your presence, you are free to do as you will, with whom you will." Lavender's voice slid into silkiness as she gave him a sweetly provocative sideways glance. "Do you not want me, even a little, Thomas?"

She raised herself up on the tips of her toes, held on to his arm, and kissed him on the mouth. The soft touch of her lips surprised him; he had not considered that he would actually want any woman but Callie while he lived in Elvenhome. But Lavender was here, sliding her sweet tongue into his lonely mouth, pressing herself against him. He felt his blood flow potently for the first time since Edinburgh. The cloying tightness he had been carrying in his chest and shoulders began to relax. He was breathing more easily.

Lavender's hand moved along his hip. He closed his eyes, deepened the kiss, and pulled her closer.

Later, she took Thomas' hand and led him to an oak tree that stood on the far side of the columbine bed. A tall oak shaded a small patch of soft, sweet-smelling grass. Leaning against the tree, Lavender put her arms around Thomas and kissed him again. The hungry urgency of the kiss and the press of her hands on him set his body deliciously on fire. Thomas Lear let himself burn, with a vengeance.

Layering hot kisses on her lips, face and throat, he cupped her right breast with one hand while deftly unlacing the back of her gown with the other. She smelled of sage and fireweed honey. The rich, smooth touch of her skin reminded him of the exquisite velvet jacket he'd been gifted with after his first Faerie Court feast.

The blend of the sensations she aroused in him made him ache with wanting. It was all he could do to not explode from the heady intensity of it. He took several deep breaths, eased her hands from him, and pulled away from her only far enough to help her step out of her gown, which had slipped from her shoulders and was now down around her feet.

She helped him pull his tunic off over his head. She kissed his nipples, and ran her tongue over them, making him groan in anticipation. Then she slowly, slowly unlaced his breeches, taking her time pulling them over his stiff cock, and removed them.

Her breath was warm and sweet against his ear. "Thomas, have you ever made love to a lady with a tail?" Her back was against the tree; in his growing arousal, he'd forgotten for a moment that she had one.

"No, I haven't. At least, not yet..." he chuckled, and so did she.

"All you need to know is that you cannot hurt my tail. It is much stronger than it looks. And it is extremely sensitive at the base where it attaches to my body. You can touch it," she concluded with a provocative shiver, "as much as you want to."

"I'll keep that in mind," Thomas said, and they both laughed as he kissed her, edging her back against the oak. He knelt, then, and ran hands and mouth over her legs, and up the insides of her thighs. She caressed his face and neck with her left hand as she swayed a little against him. Only then did he turn her against the tree, and, letting his left hand play at the intersection of her thighs, he ran his right hand over her small, perfect backside.

And then he saw her tail.

It was the same pretty blonde color as the hair on her head. It was more like a cow's tail than a horse's, and thinner than he'd expected, with an end that tapered out into wispy, fine blonde strands. It began just below the hip line, and it hung almost to the ground behind her. There were bright blue beads braided into it that perfectly matched the cornflower blue color of her eyes.

He wanted to touch it, but when he reached out his hand, he hesitated.

"Do not be afraid to touch me, Thomas," Lavender whispered, rocking herself firmly against his left hand and supporting herself with her hand on his shoulder.

Thus encouraged, Thomas touched and then stroked Lavender's tail. It was very beautiful and soft, not coarse as he'd imagined it would be. It, too, smelled of fireweed honey. He leaned into her, and experimentally touched the base, where tail met torso.

Left hand still busy, Thomas bent down and ran his tongue along the tail's base. Lavender moaned, stiffened, then writhed against him in her pleasure.

He caught her in his arms, and they lay down together in the sweet grass. There he took her into his arms and lost himself, and much of his pent-up misery, in her.

There was little if any talking; the communication they shared was touch and movement, sighs and smiles. And after a time, once they were both well satisfied, she held him against her breasts, and he finally slept.

The fragrance of fireweed honey, mingled with the heady perfume of musky sex, woke Thomas. Lavender's soft tail, held casually in her hand, was trailing down his body, from face to groin. It tickled.

"Are you awake, Love?" Lavender said as she nibbled on his neck.

"Parts of me seem to be more awake than others," he told her with a smile as he opened his eyes and then winked at her.

She giggled as she edged her hand down his chest and over his belly. He sighed contentedly, and played with the smooth blue beads as he felt his arousal build again.

LATER, THEY LAY together in the grass, sprawled across each other. The quiet of the moment was suddenly interrupted by the very loud and demanding growl of Thomas' stomach.

Lavender's smirk was sweet, and she kissed his belly, since she was already resting her head on it. "You are hungry. But for food, this time."

He brushed the top of her head with his hand. "It's been a while since I've eaten. And since there's a picnic inside..."

"Am I not clever?" she teased him. "I have thought of everything you need to satisfy you today."

He sat up and kissed her, then stood up, and walked over to collect their clothing. When he returned to her, she was on her feet, arching her back and stretching her body rather prettily.

He raised an eyebrow. "If you keep that up, I'll probably starve to death."

They dressed, and headed for the garden doors that led back into Thomas' apartments and the waiting picnic.

He was ravenous, and close to fainting with hunger after the physical workout he'd had with Lavender. The table was as they'd left it. He saw fruit and fowl and wine and freshly-baked bread and cheese. Everything looked and smelled marvelous. He barely knew where to begin. Since it was closest to his hand, he reached for the loaf of bread first, broke off a piece of the end, and popped it into his mouth. "I wasn't ready for all of this when you first came to the door, but I am now." He approved of his much-better mood, and wondered how long it would last before the depression descended again.

"Do you see how well I can take care of you?" she asked, watching for his approval as she handed him a goblet of wine.

He cut a roasted chicken into four large pieces. "You've thought of everything." He smiled. "Nice job," he added, pushing more food into his mouth while he filled his plate.

Finally sitting in one of the armchairs with a full plate on his lap, Thomas ate with more enthusiasm than he had since his fight with Callie.

He had devoured two large pieces of the chicken and a pear, most of a loaf of bread, and almost a quarter of a pie before it occurred to him that something was missing.

He looked down at Lavender. She was seated on the floor next to his chair, nibbling on a slice of bread loaded with honey, a blissful flush on her face. Thomas smiled at her, but the nagging thought returned, louder in his head this time. He couldn't place it, and he stopped in mid-bite to think. Something was wrong, and he had a momentary bad feeling about whatever it was that he could not recall.

He relaxed again as it came to him in a pleasant flash of memory.

"No ritual blessing?" he asked after he swallowed another mouthful of the bread, taunting her with feigned shock and horror. "When food is brought to me, no matter who brings it, I am generally told where it has come from. And there's always the final blessing: *Eat and drink, free from care...* It used to annoy me a little, because it happened at every meal, but I'm used to it, and I kind of like it."

Lavender finished chewing. "Not this time," she pointed out, refilling his wine goblet and handing it to him in a smooth motion. "In the garden, you danced with me in so many nice ways that I can barely think at all. You will know about your food later."

"Fair enough," he said, smiling as he drank. "That's assuming there's any food left for you to tell me about. I'm a bottomless pit at the moment. Would you hand me that apple, please? And the cheese?"

Lavender watched with barely concealed triumph as Thomas bit into the apple, chewed and swallowed, and chased it with some cheese and more wine.

"This is a really good apple," he told her, taking another bite. "It's killer! Doesn't taste like any I ever had. It's much more exotic, delicious. Where's it from?"

Faerie Folk do not lie; but, just like mortals, they can sidestep the truth easily enough, and do so when it suits them. "It has come from the same place as the bread and the chicken and the sweets and the wine," Lavender assured him daintily, playing with the beads in her tail.

"Some exotic place, then," Thomas mused. "Portugal? Italy?"

"Someplace you might think exotic, certainly." She ran her tongue over her lips to tease him. "Finish your apple, Thomas, so you will perhaps have the strength to finish me!" *And you will be mine for as long as your life lasts*, she added to herself, happy as she smiled at the other three apples she'd placed in a large bowl on the dining table.

"It's a deal," he said, and took a couple of quick bites from the apple.

He had just washed it all down with more wine when, without warning, Callie burst into the room in a formidable blaze of hurricane fury. If she saw Thomas at all, it didn't show on her face. She had eyes only for Lavender, who was at that moment preparing to refill Thomas' empty wine goblet.

Brown eyes flashing with ominous power, Callie looked dangerous. "What have you done?" she demanded.

Lavender froze. She met Callie's fierce stare and tried to form words, but failed in the attempt.

Rage and destruction crackled as Callie spoke very slowly, as if she were struggling to force her words out around her fury: "Speak to me *now*, Lavender. I command it. What have you done?"

"I gave him food. He has eaten it. He will be yours as long as you will it, up until the end of his year and a day. And then, since he cannot ever leave Faerie, he will be mine." She looked desperately at Callie, begging her to understand. "I will make him happy. I will never hurt him. I will give myself only to him, and he will be mine, always!"

Startled and confused by Callie's unexpected presence, and alarmed by the malevolent storm he saw on her face, Thomas was only vaguely aware of what was happening, but the reality was slowly dawning on him. "Food. You brought the picnic. You gave me *Faerie food*???" He gaped at Lavender in utter disbelief. He leaped to his feet as if he

133

could physically move himself away from the shock of what was happening.

In an immediate effort to reassure him, Lavender took a step in his direction, but was halted at once by a murderous look from Callie. The blonde Elf froze, but addressed Thomas, her voice pleading. "Sweet Thomas, I only wanted to keep you with me. Her Grace will be forced to abandon you for breaking faith with her, and even if she still wants you for the rest of the year, after that, you can still be mine. I will treat you well, always. We can be to each other what we have been today." She would have smiled reassurance at him then, but Callie's fiery glower stopped her from doing anything at all.

Thomas was frightened, and growing more agitated by the moment. Helpless, he looked at Callie for answers. He couldn't think, he couldn't move. He wasn't sure he could breathe.

The urgent, sharp tone in Callie's voice pierced his attention. "Thomas, how long ago did you eat?" He looked at her numbly. "Thomas!" she demanded. "When did you first eat this food?"

He struggled to answer her through a fog of growing horror. "Twenty minutes ago, a half-hour at most. No more than that."

Callie let out a deep breath in a rush. "Good," she said, biting her lip. In the next instant her right hand made a forceful, blunt gesture in the air that produced a pulsing gleam of green light, and almost before her hand stopped moving, Thomas' belly cramped violently, his body jerked, heaved, and he vomited. Then he fell to his hands and knees on the floor, retching convulsively, bringing up the Faerie food he had consumed.

"Zodiac," Callie said in a steady voice that held a firm command.

In a flash, the Lord High Chamberlain appeared beside her. "My Queen?"

"Take care of Thomas."

Zodiac bent down to aid Thomas. Still on his hands and knees, he was pale and shaking, gasping for breath as

134

another staggering wave of nausea hit him hard. "Oh, shit, here it comes again..."

Zodiac grabbed a big bowl from the table, dumped the three apples it held, and got it to Thomas just in time. One apple rolled far under the dining table, another sailed across the floor toward the music cabinet, and the other made it all the way to the windows, where it rested only barely visible beneath the heavy draperies.

Callie, eyeing her Court Singer with a good deal of sympathy, took several steps toward Lavender, caught her by the hand, and drew her through Thomas' bedroom door toward the garden. "We will talk outside," Callie said in a steely voice, leaving Thomas, still vomiting miserably, in Zodiac's care.

seven

OUT IN THE garden, the royal rage softened into compassion as Callie looked into Lavender's eyes and read the truth in them. "Why did you think this was a good thing to do?" Callie demanded with far more sadness than anger.

Lavender looked down, unable to maintain eye contact with her Queen. "I wanted him. It was my turn to have the mortal lover if you did not want him. My turn."

Callie's voice softened. "But I did not cast Thomas aside, nor do I mean to. Surely you know that."

"But he was so unhappy about Edinburgh..." Lavender began, her voice pleading.

"That is not your concern, Lavender," said the Queen, more sharply than she meant to.

Lavender trembled at the Queen's tone, but stood her ground. "Nevertheless, Thomas was hurt by it, enough to pull away from you, from all of us, Your Grace. I wanted to ease his hurt, and so I did."

"You also wanted him for yourself." The Queen's eyes narrowed.

"I did. And I do."

Through the open garden doors of Thomas' bedroom, they could still hear his violent retching. "Holy Mother of God..." Thomas groaned, and threw up again. Zodiac's voice made quiet, comforting sounds, indecipherable in the distance. Then all was still for a few moments, after which Thomas moaned "Oh, Christ...there's more coming up..." just before the vomiting resumed.

Callie sighed. Poor Thomas. And poor Lavender, too, who had quickly glanced back at the open garden door, visibly aching to help Thomas.

Callie stared into Lavender's unhappy blue eyes, willing her blonde, sweet Lady to understand the enormity of the wrong she'd done to Thomas, and the wrong she had done to herself. "Can you see that what you did was damaging to him? That you would chose *for* him, and trick him into breaking faith with our laws, to force him to stay in Faerie, is not the act of one who loves. It is the act of one who needs to possess."

"I want him to stay! I love him!" Lavender cried.

"You very well may. He is a man who attracts many facets of love, everywhere he goes; it is one of his gifts. But do you see that you did not treat him with love?"

Lavender shook her head, and tears began to slip down her cheeks. "I gave myself to him in love. And he took me in love," she insisted, but her resolve was weakening.

"That is as may be. But that is not the event that gives me sadness. You did not show love when you forced possession. Please tell me that you can see that."

Lavender considered Callie's words. More tears streaked down her troubled face. "Will *he* understand that I did it for love? He must!" she said in a whisper that had more desperation than hope in it.

Callie sighed to herself; this was not going well. "In time he may. But right now he is going to be angry with you for tricking him and putting him at risk, and he is going to be angry with me for forcing the food out of him. I think we have both frightened him, and we are each going to have to answer for it."

The terrible sounds of retching had stopped. Perhaps the worst of it was over, then. Callie hoped so.

An immeasurable depth of grief, tinged with remorse and longing for Thomas, coupled with a sudden vast

137

emptiness for simultaneously angering Callie and causing such harm, had all but shattered the normally light-hearted Lavender. "Are you going to punish me, Your Grace?" she asked, her voice miserable.

"Punish you?" Taking Lavender's shaking hands in her own, Callie gave her the kindest of smiles. "Not I," she said, her words genuine and true. "Oftentimes understanding the Why of a matter is more important than seeing the What; it is the Why that changes the color of the What. I want you to consider *what* you have done, in truth, and the real reason behind *why* you have done it. And when you can own that, you will begin to learn to love without tricks and the desire for possession. And together, you and I will work to give you what you feel will best serve you. Agreed?"

Humbled, Lavender knelt at Callie's feet. "I suppose I have a lot of thinking to do, Your Grace," she wept.

"Go in peace. And come to me when you can hold the truth of it in your hands."

Rising obediently, Lavender met the gentleness in Callie's eyes, and tried to smile. She flashed her eyes toward Thomas' bedroom door. "Should I...?"

Shaking her head, Callie put a hand on Lavender's shoulder. "I think that would be a bad idea. Walk back through the garden instead."

"But, please, Your Grace, I would like to tell him..."

Callie shook her head again, this time with firmness. "You can tell him later. Go now." Lavender dropped a deep curtsy, wiped her running face and nose on her sleeve, and gave Callie a weak but trusting smile. Then, shrouded now in painful sadness, she turned and walked away through the garden, back toward Callie's apartments.

Callie's eyes filled then, and a shining, solitary tear rolled down her cheek as she watched Lavender move out of sight. "Learning is often so painful, Sonorielle," she whispered. "And Love, in all of its aspects, can sometimes be a hurtful teacher, with far too many lessons to impart. Do any of us ever get all of it right, I wonder?" She brushed the tear away with the back of one hand, and smiled a little sadly. "How can we truly come to terms with all that Love teaches, when we are so much less ourselves if we have to live without it?"

The High Queen of Faerie, Defender of Elvenhome, took a deep breath and abandoned further consideration of the nature of love. She did not want to think about anything at all. She worked to clear her mind, but it was not easy. She was shaking from the emotional exertion that had begun well before this day's unhappy misadventure. She saw again the drunken, angry, devastated look in Thomas' eyes when they'd fought about Michael MacAllistair eight days ago, and then that mental trigger brought to mind everything that had happened: the Mischief, the hells that Arrendel had endured, her encounters with Garrhyn, all of it.

Callie missed Thomas, and would have told him so long before now, had she not understood that he had wanted and perhaps needed his private wounds to bleed and fester before he would choose to allow them heal and then let them go. She was sorry for his hurt, but knew that it was his to do with as he pleased. He had chosen to pull away from her, from everyone, and to suffer. It had not been her own choice, yet she had honored his.

And by doing so, she had unwittingly helped to set the stage for what had happened to him today. She shook her head, not wanting to own the truth of this but feeling a heavily-weighted responsibility nevertheless.

A sob escaped her. To steady herself, she spent a quarter of an hour walking alone in Thomas' garden under the late-afternoon sun, arms wrapped tightly around herself for comfort she could not find.

When she felt centered again, she walked toward the doors of Thomas' bedroom. As she approached, she saw two young Dwarfs, pages who served Zodiac, wheeling a soaking-tub out the door. It sloshed as they moved it away. Two other pages were finishing up cleaning in the living room. The four left without a word, and closed the door behind them.

Zodiac sat in the chair opposite Thomas' bed, facing the open garden doors. He nodded at Callie when she stood in the doorway; everything was all right. She moved into the quiet bedroom.

Thomas was curled into a tight ball in the center of the bed, eyes closed, his bare back to the garden doors. When his Queen entered, Zodiac rose from the chair and gave her a respectful bow. She smiled her gratitude, and made a small dismissive gesture with her hand. He vanished at once, leaving her alone with Thomas.

Callie stood for some minutes and watched the muscles in Thomas' back move as he breathed. His hair was slightly damp from the bath. The slick sheen of sickness had been washed away; he smelled of fresh rosemary. He was covered to the waist with a sheet. She knew he wasn't fully asleep. She also knew he didn't want to talk now, but that he would, if she waited long enough. She moved, silent and calm, to the chair Zodiac had vacated, and sat down, studying Thomas as he rested.

When he opened his eyes, perhaps a half-hour later, she was still watching him.

"Come to view what's left of the corpse, Your Grace?" Thomas murmured tiredly. He was pale, and he trembled a little when he shifted his body so that he could look at her.

Callie gave him a slight smile. "I suspect there's a little life left in you yet." He frowned at her. "All right, perhaps not very *much* life left. Enough to plan the wake?"

The corners of his mouth twitched, but the smile that usually followed the twitch didn't come this time. He found that he didn't know what to say to her. So much had happened today, and he'd taken too many wrong turns since Edinburgh, too much time alone with his black moods and his regrets, and he did not think he had the heart to tell her what was on his mind. He tried and failed to open the conversation.

She did it, instead. "I'm very sorry I had to deal with the food problem the way I did, Thomas, but there was no time to do anything else. I know it was unpleasant for you. I apologize, most sincerely."

He gave her a wry, humorless look. "It was a nice trick," he told her, attempting to sound casual but missing the mark. He whined a little instead. "Next time, just kill me straight out."

"If there ever is a next time, I'll try to keep that in mind," she replied, trying not to smile.

There was a faint glimmer of embarrassment in his voice. "I'm afraid I made a hell of a mess. You could have at least given me a chance to get to the privy, and then Zodiac wouldn't have had to...he helped me with the bath, but—"

She reached across the bed and took his hand, which was still clenched in as close to a fist as his weakened body could manage. "Let it go, Thomas. It's over now, and the important thing is that I'm fairly certain you don't have any Faerie food in you now."

He smiled then, a small one that stayed on his face for a few seconds before it faded. "Callie, I'm 'fairly certain' that not only do I not have any Faerie food in me, I'm probably missing a couple of vital organs. And I don't think my stomach will be on speaking terms with me anytime soon." He shuddered at the memory. "I don't think I've ever been that miserable and pathetic, even when I got sick on booze and chemicals. God...everything hurts. It did occur to me that today could be payment for the drug and alcohol detox Elvenhome and Faerie water spared me from when I first got here. I've never forgotten about it, but right now, I feel like I'm doing my detox, like it or not. I feel fucking terrible."

"Don't worry," she assured him with a grin she couldn't help, "I can promise you you'll feel even worse tomorrow."

He groaned, but it was only half-hearted. He gazed at her hand holding his, and relaxed a little, unable to keep his thumb from moving gently over hers.

She waited until he met her eyes again. "We have some things to talk about. We can wait until the day after tomorrow if you'd like."

He shrugged, closing his eyes. "Am I really going to feel worse tomorrow?"

She nodded, and sighed sympathetically. The sound of it almost made him chuckle. He opened one eye to look at her. "You can count on it, I'm afraid," she said. "Your muscles are going to give you grief, and you're not going to be at all happy when your stomach decides it's finally hungry again. It'll be hard for a few days, but tomorrow will be the tough one. The mortal body absorbs Faerie food differently than the food normally consumed by mortals. I'm certain we got most of your personal Faerie feast out of you, Thomas, but it's probable that your body had already begun processing some of what you ate. It'll be all right, it will only be unpleasant for a day or two, until the wrong food's all the way out of your system."

He was not convinced that there could possibly be any food of any kind left in any part of his body, but he didn't have the energy to think about that, much less argue the point. "I guess we should talk now, then."

Callie let go of his hand, and sat up straight in the chair. "Shall I start, or do you want to?"

He thought it over and mumbled, "I guess I will."

She waited as he moved again. He winced while he found a more comfortable position. When he was ready, he pulled out his anger and his frustration and his pain and his love and his fear, and showed them all to her with an honesty sharp enough to slice his aching heart into worthless ribbon.

"I hardly know where to start. So much has happened," he began. He looked at her, his eyes almost begging her to understand the words he was not sure he could say. "I played...no, I *had sex* with Lavender today. Several times."

Her face and voice radiated a kindness that could have destroyed him in his misery, but somehow it did not. "That

142

is not an issue between us, Thomas. You are free to share your body wherever you please. You know that."

"That's not it," he said, sadness clouding his tone. "I did it for the wrong reasons. You know it and I know it. She's pretty and—"

"And she wanted you," she interrupted him, quietly. "Remember that. She's wanted you from the very beginning."

"That's not it," he repeated. "I played with her because I wanted to hurt you. I know that, from your perspective, the sex itself is not the point, even though I think it is." He looked at her, sorrow shining in his eyes. "I wanted you to feel as bad about my taking Lavender today as I did about you spending the night with MacAllistair and sending me back to the house alone. You said you didn't fuck him, and I didn't want to believe you, and I couldn't figure out why. I've been angry and bitter and resentful. I've been unable to write or sing, or, God, even think clearly. Before I decided to touch her today I knew I wanted you to be jealous, to promise me you'd never look at another man, and to keep that promise."

He waited for her to interrupt him, to protest, but she simply watched him in silence as he continued. "I used her, like I've always used women. I would have used anyone today, I know that. She was the one who happened to be here, she was more than willing, and that made her convenient." He lowered his eyes in genuine shame. "I used to think that my love for you was just the result of the enchantment from the night on Calton Hill. I don't think that's all there is to this, though, Callie. I think I'm in love with you. But if I was genuinely in love with you, the way I've always believed that real love *should* be, I would never have been willing to hurt you just because I'd been hurt. I failed you, and I'm sorry. I am such a stupid fucking jackass. I admit I'm angry and jealous of your Michael MacAllistair, but I'll deal with that. I was willing to hurt you and, God help me, I liked the thought of hurting you. That's not love."

He didn't look at her, so he couldn't see that she was beaming at him. He looked up at her when he heard the unmasked pride in her voice. "Oh, Thomas...I suspect there is hope for you yet. Love can be such a hard taskmaster, but the lessons sometimes appear to be worth the trouble." He didn't understand. "I had a talk with Lavender while you were," she made a dismissive gesture "otherwise occupied. She believes she is in love with you, and is now pondering why removing choices from the one you love, and instead attempting to possess that person, is not for the best, for anyone. Love is teaching Lavender some difficult lessons as well."

Her face grew serious. "She is sorry that she deceived you. She decided some time ago that she wanted you. I failed to notice how much, until it was almost too late. For that also, I apologize. She chose to keep you the only way she believed she could, but she was wrong. Fortunately, there was no permanent damage done, and I shall make certain that nothing like this happens to you again. Lavender is going to deal with the consequences of her actions. She will come to you at some time in the future and ask your forgiveness. I hope you will hear her."

"How could I not? What I did to both of you was far worse than what she did to me. At least her motivation was a hell of a lot more honest than mine was." He looked up at her. "Do *you* forgive me, Callie, for being willing to hurt you?"

"There is nothing for me to forgive. You did nothing terrible to me, Thomas. You did it to yourself. You were hurt, you drank with your demons, you were angry, and you suffered. Forgive yourself, and then move away from it in peace. It doesn't have to matter."

"It does matter," he said, bitterness burning in his mouth. "I was more than willing to hurt you. I wanted you to be unhappy. That's not love, Callie, that's...that's monstrous."

"Then move forward, and do not behave like a monster any longer—to me, to yourself, to anyone."

"It's not that simple," he snapped, making a face when a back muscle cramped painfully.

"Yes it is," she returned. "Think about it: you have only to treat yourself kindly. When your feelings were hurt about Michael, you should have treated yourself with kindness, not anger. Had you done so, you would never have gotten around to being truly angry with me. And your joining with Lavender could have been a happy encounter that you might have chosen to continue."

"You're insane," he muttered under his breath.

"What?" she asked lightly, even though she'd heard him.

He sighed and ran his hand through his hair. "Nothing."

"That's what I thought you said," she chuckled.

"One more thing," he said, choking a bit, for the words were difficult. His eyes searched her face. "I cannot believe I said that shit about you and the King and being used. I was angry and drunk and stupid, but that's no excuse. I'm sorry, Callie, really. I keep hearing the words in my head, and I was such a..." He groaned, embarrassed.

Callie shrugged, by way of apology. "I lost my temper, Thomas. I'm sorry I forced the silence on you."

"Well, you were right to shut me the hell up. I get that now. I crossed a line, and I was unkind." He frowned as he remembered what he'd said to her, and the bitter rage behind those words. A thought occurred to him, and his mouth turned up in the beginnings of a hopeful smile. He couldn't help it. "When you silenced me, I wasn't quite done. I still had a few more particularly dumb-ass things to say to you."

"Thomas, I am most certain that you did." Suddenly Callie giggled, and he found himself laughing with her.

"You were up front about the boundaries of our relationship from the beginning, and haven't changed the rules at all." He took her hand. "Can you forgive me for being such a self-absorbed bastard? I was wrong, about so many things, then compounded the wrong by wallowing in it. I seem to do that, although it always surprises me when I realize that's what I'm doing...but can you forgive me for wanting to make you as miserable as I made myself?"

"Of course I can," she answered, leaving him no room to doubt her. "Thank you for considering my feelings."

He settled deeper into the covers and felt himself begin to relax. He sighed again, but it was a sigh of emotional release, and he very nearly smiled at her. "That's it for me."

"Which makes it my turn," Callie told him. "First, let me again apologize for the harsh and hasty treatment you received at my hands after you ate the food." He started to protest, but she raised her hand to silence him. "I know that it needed to be done, and quickly. I am not sorry for the doing of the thing, but I do regret that it was so hard on you. I will also regret it tomorrow, when you feel so much more terrible. It is a fault of mine: I respond with admirable speed when there is urgency, but I seem to have a history of not responding *thoughtfully*."

Both Thomas and Callie were thinking of the High King, and the long-ago tale of the water goblet. Each of them let the images go as quickly as they'd caught them.

"I reacted, and solved the problem, but perhaps a few moments of calm thought before I acted might have been wise."

He shrugged, and winced at the effort as his irritable muscles rebelled. "It's all right, Callie. Like you said before, it's over now."

"And I'm forgiven?"

He gave her a ready smile. "Of course you are. And thank you, for taking care of it...which reminds me. I know that if you hadn't dealt with the situation, I would have never been able to leave Elvenhome. But did Lavender say something like my eating the food was 'breaking faith' with you?"

"I believe she meant that even if you ate the food by her hand rather than by your own choice, in defiance of your obligations, I would have had to accept that as a rejection and a betrayal by you, and would cast you aside

146

as a matter of course. Then, by her reckoning, you could be happy to stay with her for the rest of your life."

"And breaking faith with you...?" he asked, trying to understand.

"You couldn't break faith with me, Thomas. It has nothing to do with the original enchantment. Oh, I know you've broken faith with yourself, time and again, you've told me so. But it won't happen with me."

"Why not?"

"Because I'm holding on to my end of the bargain with both hands, and I won't let it break."

He successfully kept his eyes from welling up with tears, but only just.

"Now," she said, "let me tell you about Edinburgh." She met his eyes and held them; he could not look away. "First of all, you never gave me the chance to thank you for your help in saving Arrendel's life."

"You could have managed that yourself," Thomas told her. The truth didn't hurt him a bit.

"Perhaps," she admitted. "But your presence made everything easier for me. And the fact that you were able to get him back to Maggie's cottage without me saved us time and reduced the risk of being seen. It would have been far more difficult without you there. And I thank you, from the depths of my heart."

"You're welcome," he murmured.

"As for my choice to spend the evening with Michael MacAllistair," she continued, "I admit the timing wasn't the best, still I needed some fresh air in my soul. The ordeal with Arrendel and Maggie was harder on me than I could admit even to myself. And when I saw that Michael was close by, I was suddenly a little lonely for him, lonely for another time. When you said that you'd go to the concert with me..." her voice faded, but returned a little stronger. "But you couldn't have known how very much I needed his familiar face. I didn't know it fully myself, not right away. It was selfish of me, and unfair, too, since I knew how it might make you feel. I put myself first, and I shouldn't have. Sending you back to Number 12 served me in the moment." She looked him directly in the eyes. "I swear to you, Thomas, that although he asked me to, I did not give myself to him. That is the truth that I should have made clear to you that night."

"You don't lie, Callie." He squeezed her hand in firm punctuation.

She nodded, continuing. "I didn't want to hurt you. Nevertheless, I knew you'd be wounded no matter what I did. I could see it in your face. And when he said that he had some things he wanted to talk about...well, he did. I think I was able to help him a little, which matters to me."

Thomas frowned. "I should have trusted you to be true to your nature, and gone back to Number 12 and gone to bed. It wasn't like I wasn't exhausted, or like you weren't going to come back to the house, no matter what had happened. I knew we were coming back here."

Callie let out a slow breath. "But it didn't work out that way. You had feelings, and Michael had feelings, and I had feelings, and they did not mix well at all, did they? I don't often put my own needs before everyone else's, but I did this time. And as a result, Michael was hurt, and so were you."

Thomas' eyebrow shot up. "He was hurt? MacAllistair?"

She looked at him in amazement. "You didn't know that?"

"How could I? I didn't let you tell me anything, remember?"

She shook her head in wonder. "How could you not have known that? Michael's as mortal as you are. He's a poet and musician, as you are. And he was enchanted as you were. He had to watch me choose to leave him to return to you. Like you, he has regrets from his past that he is helpless to change. And although he had nearly convinced himself that he might have me near him again, he had to relinquish those feelings and let me go."

"And then you came back to me."

"Of course I did. There was never any question of that." She reached over and took his hand again, and squeezed it. "I told him I was in love with you."

Thomas stared at her. "You what?"

"You heard me," she chuckled. "I love you, Thomas Lear. I love you very much."

He kissed her hand. "Oh, God, Callie..."

After a moment, he released her hand, and tried to find words for her, but he had too many and couldn't get close to the ones he most wanted.

She rose from the chair, stood, and unfastened the back of her gown. Moments later, it was hanging over the chair, and she was standing before him in her ivory lace shift. With a look of contentment, she sat on the bed and, her smile glowing, she touched his face, and kissed it. Without a word, she lay down beside him, put her arms around him, and held him.

Reflexively, he wrapped himself around her, but his voice held small, tired seeds of doubt. "You're staying here tonight? Despite everything?"

Her only response was to hold him tighter.

"Callie?" he persisted. "I don't think I can manage make-up sex."

"You're not in a position to take me tonight, Thomas. You don't have the energy, nor will your muscles wish to cooperate. You've been trying not to let me see how very sore and fragile you are at present, but I have noticed."

"Oh, have you?" he kissed the side of her face, and she elbowed him delicately in the ribs until he gasped at the muscle pain. "You're a hard woman, Callie," he said, loving her.

She breathed him in. "And you smell wonderful, which is something of an achievement considering where this day took you."

"Why, thanks very much," he said, rolling his eyes.

"Quite so," she murmured. "I simply want to lie here in your arms, hold you, and fall asleep knowing that you're

149

well and safe from harm. I want to dream of you, and wake up and see you smile...or try to." She frowned then, looking into his eyes. "Thomas, you really are going to feel bad in the morning. I'm going to be here with you, to keep you company."

He couldn't resist a smile. "Will that make me feel better?"

"Not in the least. But you won't be miserable all alone."

"Oh," he chuckled. "That's comforting. Remind me of that tomorrow, will you?"

They lay together in the gathering dusk, not talking.

After a long time, he broke the sweet silence. "Callie?"

"Hmmmm?"

"When you came dashing into the place like John Wayne and the Marines after I'd eaten the Faerie food...?"

"Yes?"

"How did you know? How did you know Lavender had brought me *Faerie food*?"

She was quiet for a moment. The bedroom was now dark enough that he could not see her face clearly.

"Callie? Tell me."

She sighed. "I had an uncomfortable sense that something was wrong, from the moment I left the castle for my ride in the woodlands. The sense of that 'something wrong' wouldn't leave me. When I discovered that Lavender had not accompanied us, knowing how she loves to ride in the wood and rarely misses an opportunity to do so, I had an idea that she might be acting on some misguided mission. I came to see for myself."

Thomas snorted in disbelief. "That's a pretty flimsy explanation, Your Grace," he chided.

She gave his knee a tiny kick with her foot, and was gratified when he inhaled sharply. "You think so?"

"Yes," he said. "That's just lame, Callie. You're going to have to do better than that."

"Am I?" she countered.

150

"You are," he snickered. "You expect me to believe that you came back from your ride, came straight down the corridor to my door because Lavender *might* have been in here with me, and you suddenly just *knew* that she'd fed me Faerie food?"

He could feel her smile, even in the darkness. "Yes."

"Oh yeah?"

She spoke slowly, with an exaggerated patience, as though he were a small and mildly stupid child. "Thomas, when I got to your door, all I could smell was Faerie food. It was obvious what had happened. I didn't know you'd joined with her. You could have been singing for her or playing chess with her, for all it mattered. But when I smelled the food halfway down the corridor..."

He interrupted her with a snort. "You could smell that the food was Faerie and not from Upworld? Oh, come on, Callie!"

"Did you forget the conversation we had with Maggie about the breakfast she'd made for us? Mortal food has no distinct aroma to us, while Faerie food is very aromatic, and is nearly as intoxicating to us as it is to a mortal's sense of smell. Surely you've noticed that when you eat your Upworld meals with the Court in the Great Hall? Remember I told you about this before. It's why some Fair Folk who find themselves Upworld starve; the uninitiated don't recognize Upworld food as food because they can't smell it or truly taste it, so they don't know to eat it for sustenance." She huffed. "I first smelled your Fey feast at the far end of the corridor, and flew down here like an arrow shot from a badly-strung bow."

"Wow," he conceded. It struck him that had Lavender's picnic happened at any place other than in his rooms, Callie would not have been able to smell it, and so could not have saved him. He knew with a certainty that she would never have intruded on any of his activities without cause. Thank God she had smelled the food! Because of the obligation she had laid on him that speech could only happen out of her presence if he was in his own space, she had in fact kept him safe, as she had promised. His aching muscles and frail stomach reminded him that

151

her actions today had kept him safe twice. And what was more, not only had they cleared the air about Edinburgh and MacAllistair, but she was in love with him. She *loved* him!

Could it be that he, at last, was holding the love he'd been searching for all his life? He was beginning to think so; she was here, she was his, and he knew that he was hers. He was ridiculously elated and, he thought with a glimmer of amusement, he might die of it. But he'd die happy, now.

He felt a peace and a clarity he had nearly forgotten existed. It had been a long time since he'd felt this safe and satisfied. He felt himself coming back to himself, and the awareness of this was so joyful that he could hardly bear it.

In that moment, the flicker of a hint of an elusive melody line radiated through him. A flash of lyric danced across his soul. Words and music blended in him, and he began to remember who he was again, the very best version of himself.

Almost giddy, Thomas started to laugh, although it hurt his damaged muscles and made his bruised stomach twinge in tense warning.

"What's funny?" she asked, sensing a change in him.

He gave her a hug and a quick kiss in the dark. "I'm happy. And free. There's a song or two in me again, Callie. I think I can write them, now."

She settled herself in the shelter of his arms. "My Love, I never doubted it."

CALLIE HAD BEEN right about how terrible Thomas felt the next morning. He woke from a deep sleep with a start, his stomach raging at him, lightning-bolt cramps nearly taking his breath away. He was careful as he extricated himself from Callie's warm, sleeping body, but she woke at once at his movement and the subsequent groan that slipped past his lips when he sat up and hurriedly made for the privy without a word.

He didn't look or feel any better when he came out than he had when he went in. He got back into bed beside her and tried not to stir.

Callie brushed a damp curl from his forehead as she sat up beside him. "I'm so sorry, Thomas. It's small consolation, but you'll feel better later on today." Their eyes met, his with physical discomfort and associated irritability held only barely in check, and hers with an unmistakable shine of amusement despite the sympathy in her voice. "Once you've eaten."

He slammed his eyes shut and his face paled. "Oh, no...no food, Callie," he whined. He didn't care that he sounded pathetic.

"No food," she echoed, "or, at least, not until you're ready."

If his eyes had been open, he would have glared at her. He felt terrible, as promised. The torn, strained muscles in his chest, belly and back ached, and his stomach felt bruised and burned. His head hurt, and his eyes refused to focus. The cramps that ran riot through his guts forced him to clench his teeth, leaving him tense, trembling and drenched with sweat.

Callie got out of bed, moved to the dresser, and dropped a thick cloth into a bowl sitting on top of it. Into the bowl she poured water from a crystal ewer, and soaked the cloth. From the bed, Thomas watched her wring the cloth out. The excess drops hitting the water made a silvery sound that he found almost comforting.

Cloth in hand, she walked back to the bed, sat down beside him, and began to bathe his pale face.

"That feels good," he murmured, watching her as she caressed his cheek.

"It's the least I can do," she told him. "I am sorry about—"

He grimaced as a sharp cramp shot a harsh spasm across his belly. "It's all right."

She looked at him dubiously.

"No, it *is* all right, Callie," he assured her. "You did what had to be done. I accept that, and am grateful for it. Well, for most of it," he amended. "It's Detoxification Day, with my name all over it. It probably won't kill me, and will be over at some point."

"Well, it will be over a little while after you've eaten," she reminded him with a slight twitch of her mouth.

"Okay," he said with resignation, "although the idea of eating doesn't appeal to me at all."

She barely suppressed a chuckle. "It won't, not in the slightest. But you're going to have to do it today." He shot her a look that was a sorry cross between despair and grave aversion.

She giggled. "Oh, Thomas, you look so wretched, but you're absolutely adorable!"

He was not amused. Testy now, he scowled at her. "If you're going to laugh at me, you can just—"

She lifted an eyebrow in challenge. "Just what?" she asked evenly, with a touch of amused ire.

Another cramp burned through his belly, making him shudder; he breathed through it. When it was over, his frown was weak, and he touched his lower lip with his finger. "Just...bend down here and maybe...give me a kiss?"

Taking his hand, Callie smiled at him. "Well, perhaps just one..."

eight

IT WAS MID-AFTERNOON, four days later. The Queen and some of her Ladies were sunning themselves on stone benches in the open courtyard near the south end of the castle. A small gathering of tall goldenfruit trees on one side of the yard provided partial shade, but the Ladies were sitting in the dazzling sunlight, chatting.

Juniper was cutting flowers from a small, fragrant garden that was contained against one wall of the courtyard. Beside her, Dahlia pulled petals from those flowers for one of her special compounds of fragrant potpourri. Juniper looked over at the Queen and asked, "And Thomas is faring better now, Your Grace?"

Callie nodded, smiling as she looked up from her needlework. "He is. He has had a terrible week, I'm afraid, but done is done. He will suffer no lasting effects from his food adventure."

"Is it true that he refused to eat anything at all the entire first day?" asked Carnation, who had missed the entire event because she had been visiting her family in Elvenwood, in the westland of Faerie, and had only just returned.

"Unfortunately, yes," Callie admitted.

Carnation frowned. "But did that not make him feel that much worse when he finally did?" she asked with some concern.

"Yes," said Callie. "He did not wish to eat, because he felt so terrible. He wouldn't listen when I told him that it would be much better for him to eat before he got hungry. But he waited until he was very hungry, when he woke on the second morning..."

The Ladies gasped in collective horror. Several of them murmured sympathetically.

"So when he finally ate," Carnation guessed, "it did not go well, did it, Your Grace?"

Callie shook her head, and bit her lip. "Not really, no," she replied, with a twinkle in her eye.

"Poor man," Iris sighed. "I should imagine his poor stomach went into fits."

The Queen nodded and put down her needlework. "I explained carefully what would happen. Still, he had to have it his own way." She smiled, her affection for Thomas brimming as she thought about him. "He has paid for it, too, I am sorry to say. A very stubborn man, our Court Singer. Fortunately for all of us, he is back to his Courtly self, perhaps only slightly humbled, and not too much worse for the wear."

Carnation's relief was written in her eyes. "I am very glad, Your Grace."

"I am, too." Had any of the Ladies been looking at Callie's face, they would have found it as unreadable as it was beautiful. "I am, too," she repeated in almost a whisper.

"And what of Lavender, Your Grace?" Orchid, seated on the bench beside Callie, murmured with shy hesitation. "Is she—?"

Callie looked around at the attendant Ladies, rested her eyes on each of them kindly before she spoke. "Lavender is well. She is confined to her chamber by her own choice, not mine. My only demand of her is that she considers what she did, and that she learns from it in a way that best serves her."

Orchid's eyes were wistful as she told the Queen, "I have been speaking with her each day, Your Grace. She is less unhappy than she first was. I know that she regrets..."

Callie patted the kind-hearted Selkie on the arm comfortingly. "Dear One, do not fret. I am glad she has had you to talk with. I would have gone to her myself, but she's been somewhat diffident with me since the incident, and I did not wish to make her more uneasy. She knows I will be glad to see her when she is ready."

Rose spoke up, poking the tip of her tall pink hat into the air as her head moved. "But are you not angry with Lavender for what she did? It was grossly disloyal, Your Grace. Forgive me for saying so, but it was." She looked around at the other Ladies before she continued. "I do not think she meant it to happen the way it did, not truly, but she did connive to steal your Court Singer from you, and she did it by treachery." Rose looked clearly perplexed and defensive. The tension of the Ladies blended as they each focused on Callie's face, searching for solid ground.

"I would say it was more trickery than treachery; a Queen must know the difference." Callie's smile was placid, her tone reassuring them that she was not angry with Lavender nor, for that matter, at the views expressed by her Ladies. "Lavender saw something, someone she wanted, and she anticipated events to occur in a specific way. When they did not, she took matters into her own hands. I do not fault her for her feelings; we all know what it is like to believe we are in love despite challenging obstacles. She allowed herself to be blinded by her feelings, though, and she acted from that blindness, and could have caused terrible harm. She made a mistake, my dears, but it is never wrong to make mistakes. It is only wrong to not learn from them."

Rose smiled a little then, relieved. "Has Thomas forgiven her?"

"To my knowledge," Callie answered, "she has not spoken directly with him. I know from conversation with him that he bears her no ill will."

"He is a very understanding man," observed Juniper with a smirk.

"Sometimes," Callie replied with a chuckle, and the others joined her in the laugh.

"What will happen to Lavender now?" blurted Dahlia, desperation evident in her voice.

"That, too, will be her choice, I dare say. When she has decided, she will share her mind with me."

"I miss her, Your Grace," Dahlia said, her eyes mirroring her sadness.

"So do I," Callie admitted.

Violet flew out of a nearby entryway and moved toward them, dancing through the air above the sunny courtyard. She smiled as she fluttered to the Queen, and whispered in Callie's ear for a long moment. Callie nodded her head as she listened, and then winked at the Ladies, who were all watching.

"We may have Lavender back among us soon. She has asked to see me."

LAVENDER DID NOT wish to meet with Her Grace in casual circumstances, although Callie herself would have preferred it that way. The Queen knew that Lavender's choice of a formal meeting indicated Lavender's serious consideration of the matter between them. Callie only hoped that the requested formality didn't herald anything else.

At the appointed time, Callie sat in her Presence Chamber on the Queen's Throne, high on the dais at the far end of the long room. Two guards stood on either side of the doorway through which Lavender would enter at any moment; otherwise, the Chamber was empty. Callie did not feel that Lavender should have to speak her mind and heart in front of an opinionated, entertainment-hungry Fey audience, or even the Queen's Ladies, who of course knew her well.

Callie smoothed her skirts and plucked fussily at her sleeves. She was wearing a shimmering purple gown, the rich hue a single shade beyond lilac. Callie trusted that when her friend entered, she would be cheered by the

158

sight of the Queen's near-lavender gown, and would recognize support and affection before she began to speak.

Tapping her fingers on the arm of the Throne, Callie warned herself for the third time in five minutes not to anticipate Lavender's conversation. She knew she must let Lavender deal with her own issues in her own way; anything less would be unreasonable and unfair. Callie would not stand in the way of Lavender's movement toward healing and learning, even if it was momentarily uncomfortable for the Queen.

There was a flurry of motion as the far doors of the Presence Chamber opened and Lavender, dressed in a gown of delicate peach-colored silk, entered and slowly walked the length of the room toward Callie.

At a nod from the Queen, the two guards turned and exited, closing the double doors behind them.

The two women were alone.

Callie rose to her feet, and stood with the backs of her legs pressed hard against the Throne. She watched as Lavender came toward her.

Lavender moved up to the dais upon which the Queen's Throne stood. When she reached it, she bowed her blonde head, and then knelt at the bottom step. She remained there, unmoving, until Callie offered carefully, "I am here. What is your will? Shall we sit in a window seat and watch the world sail by as we talk?"

Lavender did not look up. Message received, Callie closed her eyes and took a steadying breath. "I command you to look at me."

Slowly, Lavender lifted her head and met her Queen's gaze.

"It appears that you would approach me with the Throne standing between, beside and above the bond of our friendship. Is this the case?"

Lavender nodded, her sad eyes fixed on Callie's.

Sighing, Callie forced herself to sit and settle her body deeply against the back of the Throne. "Very well. So shall it be." She let her arms rest on the carved oak arms, and said in a subdued voice that still carried an air of regal command: "I bid you rise from your knees, and stand before your Queen. Speak your heart."

Lavender rose obediently, and held her hands out in front of her in honest supplication.

"Your Grace," Lavender began, her eyes calm but her voice quavering with melancholy rather than fear, "I have committed a great wrong to you, to Thomas Lear, and to the rest of the Court. I humbly beg your forgiveness for attempting to take from you by deceit that which was not mine to take. I have sent a letter to Thomas, begging his forgiveness for my actions. And I shall make whatever amends Your Grace finds appropriate to atone for my actions." Lavender lowered her eyes, and stared at the tip of her tail, which was twitching above the hem of her gown by her left foot.

Callie cleared her throat. "I am the High Queen of Faerie. I forgive you freely for your actions. I accept your acknowledgement of the wrong done to Thomas Lear. I know that he will gladly see you and tell you himself that he harbors no ill will."

The Queen had a bad feeling in the pit of her stomach. She kept speaking with a calm kindness, all the while wishing that she was locked in her Tower Room with her embroidery instead of looking down at her friend, facing what surely had to come next.

Callie pressed on. "What was done is done, it is over, all is forgiven. If Thomas is not angry, no one else has the right to be, and there's an end to it. Surely the greatest wrong committed that I can perceive is the wrong you did to yourself. Have you granted yourself the courtesy of understanding that love is not easy, and that giving love to yourself and to others is the key to receiving love in return? That once you fit into the circle of that love, it is the constant refreshing and giving of love that keeps the circle strong and true?"

Lavender's voice was small but audible. There was a layer of undeniable self-bitterness in it that she made no attempt to hide. "I wanted him, I was unwilling to wait, I took him. I lied to myself about my motives. I put him at risk. I defied your wishes, and I convinced myself that my actions were just." She looked up, and the sheer misery in her eyes broke Callie's heart. "I put myself above all, and told myself it was right to have what I wanted, with no thought of the cost. It is unforgivable, and I can find no peace." Lavender's chin trembled, and she touched it with her hand to calm it. "In my folly, I even forgot how much I love and honor my Queen," she whispered.

Callie bit her lip hard and studied Lavender's face. "What may I do to ease you?"

Lavender's eyes were filled with tears. "I would like you to release me from the honor of the Queen's service," she whispered.

"But why?" Callie groaned, although she already understood.

"I would not wish to be in the company of anyone who had committed the offenses that I have, and I do not wish that energy to hover around my Queen," Lavender replied, tears finally spilling.

Callie's voice was strangling in her throat. "What would you have me do?" she choked.

"Send me away."

"After three centuries of loving service? For a single, selfish mistake? Never!" Callie snapped in horror.

"I was wrong, Your Grace," Lavender reminded her.

"And you will learn from your mistake, and you will not do it again," Callie insisted.

"That is the trouble, Your Grace, do you not see? I do not know that I would not do it, or something like it, the next time. I can see my mistakes, my wrongs, but I cannot know that I will not repeat them, and for the same reasons. I am what I am, Your Grace. You must send me away."

Callie clenched the arms of the Throne so tightly with her hands and arms that her head began to ache from the strain. "I will never send you away. Banishment is not an option, my friend."

The women stared at each other wretchedly.

"You deny me my deserved punishment, my banishment from Court and your immediate service?" Lavender wept.

"I do deny it," Callie replied, her brown eyes narrowed, refusing to cry.

There was a long and jagged silence between them.

Callie endured it for as long as she could, and finally surrendered to the inevitable. 'You have an alternate proposition?"

"I do, Your Grace," came the somber answer.

Not trusting herself to speak, Callie nodded at Lavender instead.

Lavender took a deep breath and then spilled it out. "I have thought about it, Your Grace. I find I am weary of life at Court. I yearn for quiet, and for time to consider the True nature of things. I do love Thomas Lear, Your Grace, but I think I love myself too...while at the same time, I do not seem to love myself at all. I do not wish to stay where I am, but I have no wish to leave Elvenhome or to be too far separated from Your Grace..." The flow of Lavender's words trickled away.

"And...?" Callie prompted sadly.

Lavender stood up a little straighter. "And...I think I would like to be a tree for a while."

Callie sighed. "For how long?"

"I was thinking that a hundred years or so might be right. I have many things to think about, Your Grace."

"And you have already decided what kind of tree, and you also have chosen a location, have you not," Callie said. It was not a question.

Lavender nodded, and a small smile began to form on her face. "Yes, Your Grace. I should like to be a tree, an oak, and I would like to live in the garden behind the Court Singer's apartments. Oh, not for Thomas, especially," Lavender hastened to assure the Queen, and she was telling the truth, "but because I love that garden and would enjoy watching over that immense sea of columbine." Her blue eyes sparkled happily at the thought. "I could also learn much from Father Rowan for the next century, Your Grace, if he would not object to my company."

Callie eyed Lavender. "This what you would ask of me? It is what you want?"

Lavender nodded.

"When?"

Lavender answered without hesitation: "Soon. At once. Tonight."

"Would you like to celebrate your decision with a great feast? We could throw you a party, one that will keep you smiling for many long years." Callie wondered if Lavender could see that she was stalling.

"No feast, Your Grace, please. I'd like to go quietly. I'd rather not say goodbye to anyone. I'd rather they find out afterward. Then they could come to see me as they chose. I would like to do it tonight. Please?"

Lavender's gaze was steady and determined. Callie felt trapped. "You will make certain to let me, let *anyone*, know when you wish to resume your life among us in your natural form?"

Lavender's nod was serene.

There was nothing else Callie could do, and they both knew it. "Very well," she said. "I grant your petition." Then Callie's voice took on the color of command, and there was a hint of green magic in the air. "You shall meet me in the garden behind the apartments of the Court Singer at midnight. And when our work is done, I shall leave the garden, and you shall stay in it for the next hundred years...or until such time as you choose to return to us."

"Thank you, Your Grace." Lavender smiled up at the Queen.

Callie raised her hand in reluctant benediction. "Be well, live long, and live happily, my dear friend," she breathed. At Lavender's grateful nod, Callie stood, walked down the dais steps, embraced Lavender with a tender finality, and then walked alone through the doors to the right of the dais. Lavender lifted her head with dignity, then turned to walk back through the Presence Chamber and out the main doors through which she'd come.

In the anteroom behind the Presence Chamber, an unhappy Callie leaned her aching head against a cool, soothing stone wall and willed herself to stillness.

IN THE MINUTES before midnight, under a dim and starless sky, Callie waited alone in the now candle-lit gardens behind Thomas' apartments and wondered if there had been a way she could have avoided the present situation. It was not that Lavender was at all unhappy at the prospect of stepping away from Court life. If anything, she appeared to be more content than she'd been in years, and Callie knew it. And yet, Callie worried that the deeply quiet life Lavender had chosen for herself might prove to be much too subdued and silent for the playful and gregarious Elf.

She sighed, and shivered in the night's chill, rubbing her arms warm with her hands. The large tapers flickered, lighting the garden with a delicate glow from various levels on the ground, in the trees, and on the bench. Gazing at loveliness of the light, the trees, and flowers, she still found it difficult to smile as she considered the work before her. Done was done: Lavender had made her decision, and Callie was bound to honor her choice. *So be it*, Callie muttered to herself. *So it must be, but I don't have to like it.*

A soft, solitary rustling coming toward her from behind signaled Lavender's arrival. Callie took a deep breath, prepared herself, and put a bright smile on her face to mask her troubled heart as Lavender approached her Queen, and bowed.

When Lavender met Callie's gaze, there was such a look of love and trust in the Elf's blue eyes that Callie nearly cried out in despair.

"I am so happy, Your Grace," Lavender said with a smile. "Thank you for your forgiveness, and for granting me this precious gift."

Callie nodded, unable to speak. When she could at last master her voice, she said "Show me where you wish to live."

Lavender led Callie to a spot fifteen feet from the venerable rowan who warded the garden. "Here," she told Callie.

Callie looked around, mentally measuring the ground. "I think you'll want to be a bit farther away from him," she advised. "You do not want to tangle your roots with his, do you?" She put her arm around Lavender's shoulder, and edged her several yards further from the rowan. "Here. Is this all right?"

After examining the spot from every possible angle, Lavender nodded. "This is perfect, Your Grace."

Callie gave Lavender a long embrace, released her, and then took a few steps back. "Are you ready?"

Lavender nodded again.

"I have told no one about this. Are you certain that you do not want to take the time to tell your friends what you are doing, so you can say your farewells?"

Lavender nodded again. "It is for the best, Your Grace. Some of them are troubled and unsettled by my behavior, and rightly so. They will come and see me when they will. You will tell them that I am here, won't you?"

"Of course I will."

There were no more words to say. Callie wrapped herself tightly in the silence, wishing it could last.

Finally Lavender spoke up. "Your Grace?"

Callie looked down at her hands, and then faced Lavender. "Oh, all right. Let's get this done."

Lavender bowed to her Queen one last time, smiled merrily and blew Callie a comical kiss. "I will see you later, Your Grace."

"Stand still," Callie ordered.

Raising her hands high above her head, then extending her arms wide and arching them toward the ground, Callie whispered in a low voice, "Elf to Oak until

Oak longs to be Elf once more. Rest easy, be well, grow strong, breathe free, and find the music of your heart in your own time." A flood of green light sprang from Callie's outstretched hands. When the light grew fire-bright, Callie pointed both hands at Lavender. The smiling blonde Elf was engulfed in the warm green flame.

And then she was gone.

In her place stood a young, hardy, and actually quite pretty oak tree.

Callie inhaled, taking in a raspy breath that sounded like a sob, but her eyes were dry. She walked over to the tree, and put her hand on the bark, patting it with unspeakable tenderness.

The oak was warm.

"I mean it, Sonorielle," Callie informed the new oak, cherishing Lavender's True Name in the quiet darkness, "when you are ready to return, let one of the Sprites know, and you and I shall walk out of this garden together."

She stood with her hand resting on the bark for some time. Then she moved through the garden and ritually extinguished each of the candles, knowing that Zodiac would send someone to remove them before dawn.

When she was at last chilled to the point of genuine discomfort, she walked, exhausted, toward Thomas' apartments. Light was shining through the double doors that led into his bedroom. Callie knocked on the glass.

In a moment, Thomas came to the door, and let her in at once. "Callie? What—?"

She gave him a weak smile; it was the only one she had left in her tonight. "I saw the light and..."

Closing the doors, he drew her into an embrace. "God, you're frozen! Come here, let me..." He pulled her against him, and rubbed warmth into her arms and back. "What are you doing outside at this hour? I thought you were working late tonight with Queen Stuff."

Her shaky smile crumbled a little more at the truth of it. "I *was* doing Queen Stuff," she admitted. "I'm finished now."

166

The tone in her voice made him draw back and look at her. "Are you all right? You look a little beaten up around the edges."

"I'm well," she replied, trying to sidestep her sadness and distress. "It's been a long, long day." She searched his face. "Have I interrupted anything?"

He grinned and put his arms around her again, holding her protectively, tighter still when she suddenly threw her arms around him and held on hard. "I was working on a new song," he told her, covering his surprise at the tense desperation he felt in her. "And you are *not* an interruption."

He waited a long minute, simply holding her close, before he asked, "Are you going to tell me about it?"

She nodded against his shoulder. "Yes. Not now. Tomorrow."

They both pretended not to notice that she had begun to shake uncontrollably in the safe haven of his arms. "I'm here, Callie. Whatever it is, it's all right."

"I know," she promised herself, adding a whispered "I'd like to stay here with you tonight."

Thomas kissed the top of Callie's head. "I was hoping you'd say that."

nine

Once upon a time, a mortal man, who lived for a time in Faerie, accidentally ate Faerie food.

It made him very sick, which was not unexpected.

Somewhere, though, in the man's dark mind, he knew he wanted more of the Faerie food that had made him sick—which came as something of a surprise to him.

All the Faerie food he'd eaten by accident, or might have had further access to, had been quickly removed. All, that is, except for three large, deliciously exotic Fey pink apples, which had fallen unnoticed from the dining table to the floor of the mortal man's living room. One apple had settled casually underneath the table. A second apple had rolled across the floor and hid stealthily by the room's wall of windows. The third apple had bounced toward the far side of a cabinet that held the man's beautiful guitar, and was hidden from view.

After he'd been very sick for several days, and then had begun to feel a little better, the man found himself

168

thinking about apples—the Fey apples he'd eaten earlier by misadventure.

Although he had slowly returned to eating mortal food, automatically eating whatever had been prepared to help restore him to health and happiness, his fascination with the pink apples grew. He thought about them when he was awake; he dreamed of them when he slept.

This, too, was not unexpected. For good or ill, all things Fey will have their enchantment.

As he grew stronger, the man left his bed and chose to recline on his sitting roomcouch, to read books and recover. For a whole day, he lay there, absorbed in a book. He slept when he was not reading.

That afternoon he had a particularly vivid dream about pink apples.

And when he woke, it happened that he noticed the large and inviting pink apple sitting on the floor under his table.

The man, of course, rose carefully from the couch, picked up the apple, examined it for a long while. Then he bit into it.

It was as aromatic and delicious as he remembered, and he savored each and every bite. He nibbled at it, wanting to fully experience it almost as much as he wanted to hold off the intoxicating sensation and save some for later.

He settled for eating half of the apple, and placed the remaining half on the table beside his couch. Happy now, he lay back down and continued to read his book.

A short while later, there was a quick knock on his front door. A tall, beautiful Glaistig entered, carrying a basket of mortal food. She glanced at the broadly-smiling man (Faerie food can make mortals a bit giddy), looked around, and saw the half-eaten pink apple on the table.

The Glaistig said a few breathy, well-chosen, multi-syllabic words of profanity, put her basket of food on the table, and hurried away.

169

Not long after that, the Queen of the Faeries, attended by her Lord High Chamberlain—who was also a friend of the mortal man's—arrived in the man's room to assess the situation.

They discovered that the man had eaten the other half of the apple as well. And he wanted another one.

The enchantment had taken hold.

Other Fey food was not all that interesting to him; he only wanted another pink apple, and he did not want to understand why he should not have one. And then another. And yet another, until the end of days.

The Queen and the Chamberlain explained to the man that, while he was not solely to blame for his growing need for pink apples (since he had only accidentally eaten Faerie food in the first place), he was indeed responsible for the effects that he suffered because he had in fact eaten a Fey apple by choice. The man said he understood, but it was clear that he did not care very much about that.

Sadly, the Queen and her Chamberlain left the man alone to deal with the price of his unwise choice.

And so it was that the mortal man, enchanted as he was by the pink apples, stayed alone, and longed for another apple to eat.

He could think of nothing else. His mind and his body twitched irritably with wanting.

Mortal food was delivered to him several times each day, although he had no stomach for it. He asked for pink apples instead, but of course was refused them.

A day later, the man started to feel sick. He did not understand why. He lay on his couch, and wondered how he had come to be ill.

Deciding the room was too dark, he moved to the windows, and opened the curtains to let in the light. As he did so, his foot connected with something on the floor. It was a pink apple.

Happy and rejuvenated by the sight and feel of it, he sat on the floor by his windows, and ate the entire apple with bright sunshine streaming on him.

Several hours went by, and the man began to feel very strange and decidedly unwell.

An hour after that, the man began to sweat, then he began to shake. His mouth dried and soured, his stomach churned, his muscles cramped, and his head felt as though someone had thrust a rusty sword into it once or twice.

When his mortal food was delivered to him that evening, the Selkie who carried it in found him writhing in pain on the floor. She ran for help.

The man's friend, the Lord High Chamberlain, stayed with him for the next three days. The Chamberlain said little, but remained present nevertheless.

In his agony, the man swore. He screamed. He cursed his friends and his gods. He promised never to eat pink apples again, if only he could have one more. He was certain that he was going to die, then he was afraid he wasn't going to die at all. The pain, wrapped in a fear and a hatred that the man could never have anticipated, scorched through his body and his mind like wildfire across an ocean of paper.

He wondered if the hell he suffered would ever end.

On the morning of the fourth day, the man awoke in his bed to find his friend sitting in a chair nearby, watching him intently.

"The worst is over," said the Chamberlain. "You can be free of the torment of pink apples any time you wish, now—provided you choose correctly when the moment of choice comes."

The mortal man groaned, and went back to sleep. He did not want to make a choice about anything. He also did not believe he wanted an apple.

The man got out of bed in the evening of the fourth day. His friend the Chamberlain was in the living room, reading.

The man washed himself, dressed, greeted his friend quietly, and asked for mortal food and water, which was provided for him at once.

After he had eaten, the man felt the need to make music. He moved to the cabinet and took out his cherished guitar.

As he closed the cabinet door, he happened to look down. He saw the third Fey pink apple on the floor.

He bent down, and picked it up. He rolled it around in his hand, and walked back to where his friend was sitting. His friend watched him, with a strange look in his eyes.

The mortal man looked at the apple again. Then he looked at his guitar. Finally he looked at his friend.

A heartbeat later, the man tossed the apple toward his friend. "Here," he said, both sadly and firmly. "Have an apple."

HE READ. HE wrote. He jogged in the woods and through the village, both alone and with silent companions. He played his guitars. He ate. He drank. He slept. Alone with Callie, he danced, talked for hours, took meals, and made love. He went hawking with the Court regularly, and hosted the weekly poker games in his rooms with a growing number of friends. He laughed more now, and far more easily, than he had probably ever laughed in his life.

Since his return from Edinburgh with the Queen, Thomas had come to understand that even though he knew a couple of his Fey friends' True Names (Swiftaine's and Arrendel's among them), he would never use them, out of courtesy for the Folk and respect for Faerie Law.

The Game is the Game, Callie had told him in all seriousness when they'd returned from Upworld, and Thomas took her words to heart. After that, he retrained himself to think of his friends as he'd named them. It wasn't that difficult, either, because as his circle at Elvenhome grew, everyone had grown used the names he'd given them, no matter how strange or random they were. Of course, by this time nearly everyone had experienced Thomas' inexplicable naming conventions. The funny part was that not many of the Folk understood just how bad the names could be. Everyone was having too much of a good time.

Thus, at a cheerful pace, time moved forward. Surprisingly, Thomas Lear, without having to try so hard, learned to be a more balanced, happier, and better version of himself.

THE AFTERNOON SUN was shining into Thomas' sitting room through its long wall of windows. The light sparkled on the guitar Thomas was playing as he sat on a stool that directly faced his couch. He was talking with the pretty Queen's Lady who sat there, watching him.

Thomas enjoyed the Queen's Ladies when he encountered them, usually as a group in Callie's apartments, or in various pairings when they attended Her Grace when she and Thomas went for walks, strolled down into the village, delivered messages or other things from Queen to Court Singer, or met for dinner in the Great Hall. Despite his choice to maintain an exclusive sexual relationship with Callie, Thomas never grew tired of watching Juniper move elegantly (and mostly unclothed), or of wondering what kind of naughty could be achieved with his favorite purple Sylph, Violet (who, much to Callie's amusement, made more than just his heart flutter). He loved listening to Iris manage not only the Queen's Ladies but the Queen herself, and found the rest of the Ladies similarly endearing. He never grew tired of them. He tried hard not to think too much about Lavender; sometimes he succeeded, other times he did not.

Still, Thomas had his favorite Queen's Lady, and it was she who sat with him today. Unlike the wide-eyed, very shy Carnation, who was genuinely if too obviously fascinated by anything and everything Thomas Lear did, said, or sang, and went into virtual paroxysms of breathless delight in his presence, Thomas had found peace and quiet, easy laughter, a passion for Fey as well as mortal history, interesting insights and a strong sounding-board in Orchid.

It had not taken them long to become good friends. She made no demands; she liked him, loved his music, and quietly enjoyed his company. Apart from Terena, whose death he still felt keenly, Thomas had probably spent more time alone with Orchid than with any other female in Elvenhome except for, of course, Callie.

Thomas' fingers were busy on guitar as they talked.

"You're saying," Orchid gaped at him, "that mortal history books lie about mortal history?"

"Sure they do," he admitted. "You've heard the expression 'to the victor go the spoils'?"

Orchid nodded. "So?"

"The *truth* is part of the spoils. It's the people who win who get to decide how to tell the story, and it gets told that way forever after. Don't look so shocked. It's always been that way. Even with oral tradition, long before things were written down, the troubadours would write and sing the tales their patrons wanted to hear, whether they were 'factually accurate' or not."

Taking this in, Orchid nodded slowly. "It makes sense, Thomas. Only I had never considered it before." She frowned. "So how do you know what to believe?"

Laughing, Thomas stopped playing, stretched his fingers, and began playing again. "Now there's a question that has confounded wise men since time began."

Fingers sliding along the frets, he played an obviously wrong note, swore under his breath, and played the phrase again before moving through the rest of the song.

Orchid watched him concentrate, so she remained silent for a few minutes. When he finally noticed that the conversation had halted, he looked over at her.

"Whatever are you doing?" she wondered aloud.

He didn't understand the question, since it was obvious what he was doing. "What do you mean?"

"What are you doing? You've been playing that same song over and over again since I got here," she pointed out.

Thomas understood. "Oh. I'm learning my song."

Orchid didn't understand. "You're learning your song? Your *own* song?"

"Uh-huh." Thomas missed another note, swore again, replayed it correctly, and kept going.

Orchid was attempting to fathom this. "Help me with this one, Thomas, for I'm greatly confused. You wrote a new song..."

Nodding, Thomas played the song faster to see if he could do it. "...and now I have to learn to play it right."

She was quiet for a few more minutes, watching him, and his fingers, more closely. Then she smiled at him broadly. "You wrote your music with one part of yourself, and you play your music with an entirely different part of yourself?"

She laughed when delight when he nodded approvingly. "Exactly right. By playing the new tune over and over, and over again, my fingers are learning what to do so they can play this song the right way every time on their own. It's a little thing called 'muscle memory.' Once muscle memory takes over, I can perform the song with an additional part of myself."

Orchid had it now. "Your voice!"

"That's it," he smiled.

"And your heart, too, I'd imagine," Orchid added with a gentle look at the Court Singer.

Without missing a note, Thomas shrugged. "On my better days, anyway."

As she watched him play the new song again and again, she frowned just a little. "The more I get to know you, Thomas, the more I am convinced that being a mortal must be very complicated indeed."

WHAT THE HELL was tickling the back of his head?

Thomas drank two cups of coffee while he worked on the song about Lavender and her letter. He was emotionally itchy this morning, but it was a harmless itch; it entertained him, and he took it in stride. Something was

175

whispering for his attention. He hadn't figured out what that was, yet, so he worked on another new song instead.

He ignored the tempting distraction as long as he could, then sighed and put the guitar down.

He looked around the living room, and nothing caught his focus, so he got up and walked into his bedroom. He sat on the bed, and looked around.

Nothing unusual looked back at him.

Standing up and stretching, he opened drawers, looked under his bed, and checked out the contents of his armoire, to see if anything interesting leaped into his awareness.

Nothing did.

He glanced at the latest pile of unread books on the floor by his bed. Then he saw his leather overnight bag, sitting sleepily in the corner, on the other side of the nightstand.

He felt a glimmer of curiosity. He hadn't noticed it for a very long time.

Thomas dug around in the bag, grinning at the stuff he'd stashed in there the night he'd first met Callie. It was strange, realizing that some of the things he'd packed had never been used.

At the bottom of the leather bag was a long, brown, thin paper bag. Thomas had no idea what it might be as he reached for it.

He shook the paper bag and turned it upside down. Out fell the penny whistle he'd bought the first time he'd walked alone along the Royal Mile in Edinburgh. He tore off the cellophane, grinned, and sat back down on the bed and began to play with it.

Thomas Lear, Rock Star, was not a very good penny whistle player. But he was in a good mood, and his sudden burst of enthusiasm made up for his utter lack of familiarity with the instrument. The sounds that blew out of the penny whistle were shrill and loud if not remotely melodic. He laughed at himself. *I don't think The Chieftains will be knocking on my door anytime soon.*

176

He laughed some more as he dropped the whistle on the bed.

It was then that he knew what the distracting little itch was all about.

Thomas strolled into the living room, walked to the music cabinet, and opened the lower doors. He came face to face with the harp that Callie had given him when he'd arrived in Elvenhome. He'd touched it once or twice that first day or maybe the next, but otherwise he hadn't paid much attention to it. He felt a twinge of embarrassment; he'd all but forgotten about the pretty thing.

He was looking at it now, though, and the beauty of it, and the urge to learn to play it, filled him with a sense of shimmering delight.

LATER THAT AFTERNOON, Thomas sat on the bench in his garden, beside a small table he'd brought from his rooms. On the table sat the harp, a bottle of beer, a pen and a pad of paper. The beer was his favorite brand, and he looked at the bottle for a moment, then laughed out loud. In his head, he played out the crazy notion of some HobGoblins from the castle Kitchens having to dash Upworld to go shopping, pushing a cart that was nearly as tall as they were, cruising the grocery aisles in search of beer, cheese, steaks, grapefruit juice, peanuts and chips to keep Thomas well fed on mortal food. *Then they'd go through the check-out line...*he laughed again, until his ribs ached. With a happy smile, he turned to the instrument in front of him.

The harp was out of tune. There was nothing Thomas could do about that at the moment, so he studied the harp's structure, construction, and experimented with getting sound out of it. He winced at the sharp and flat notes his fingers plucked from the strings. He needed to figure out how to tune this thing before he started bleeding from the ears.

He'd intended to make some notes on the paper about playing the harp, something he might discover while he was spending time with it. But that wasn't what was happening. Instead, strangely, he was scribbling notes to himself about *meeting* the harp. He knew there was a song lyric lurking in the moment, and he was getting ready to tease it out of his soul and onto the paper. It was just a matter of time. He could sit here all afternoon and quietly revel in whatever creative thing was about to happen.

Thomas toyed with a couple of the strings again, accidentally touching one that was decidedly flat. He groaned aloud and told the harp, "I have got to find something to tune you with."

"Something for which we will all be grateful," a rich baritone voice said, with a distinct hint of amusement.

Thomas turned and looked behind him.

Fifteen feet away, leaning against a tree, stood the High King of Faerie. He was dressed in jeans, black running shoes, and a green shirt. Sunglasses were perched on top his head, and the sun kissed gentle rays of light across his long, dark hair.

Thomas must have been gaping; the King watched him for several seconds, then, realizing what Thomas was reacting to, began to chuckle. "My clothing."

Thomas nodded, speechless. He had only ever seen the King in medieval-looking clothes.

This only made the King laugh more. "This caught you off-guard."

Thomas closed his mouth, and nodded again. It was the King's presence rather than what he was wearing that was the alarming thing, but Thomas, still a little wide-eyed, let it go.

"I was visiting a friend Upworld. The work on restoring her home, her horses, and her belongings has been completed for some time. I wanted to see for myself that all was well."

The Court Singer relaxed a bit, understanding now. "Sheila. From Queensgate."

"Yes." The King tilted his head toward Thomas. "I was walking the path on the far side of your back garden, and I heard the harp. It sounded like you were strangling her, and I couldn't resist coming to see how you are going to torture her next. Is she in dire need of protection from you?"

Frowning, Thomas sounded justly apologetic. "I don't have anything to tune it...*her*...with yet."

"And you don't play."

"Not yet. I'm ready to learn, though."

Thomas stood up and watched as the King, whom he could no longer refer to even in his head as "ScarF," walked over to him.

The deep gray eyes studied him seriously. "I have not had the opportunity to thank you for all that you did to help with the rescue of the man you call 'Guardian.' You put yourself at some risk to get him to safety, and you were of great help to the Queen, and for that I give you my sincere thanks. Is there something you would ask of me, to reward your courage?"

Thomas acknowledged the King's gratitude, but said definitively, "No, of course not. Guardian is my friend. I'm glad I could do something to help."

The King focused on the other man. "I can see that this is so. He is fortunate to have your friendship, Thomas Lear."

"Your Majesty, I didn't do anything much, compared to the things I've heard that you did to end the Mischief—"

"The Folk are terrible gossips. Tales get wilder the more often they are told," the King interjected with a slight shrug.

"—but even if only some of what I heard is true..."

"All that is truly important is that the Mischief has ended, 'Guardian' is safe and well, and done is done." The King did not want to think about any of it, even for a moment. Only his Men knew that memories of his encounter with Mazzin still haunted his sleep. He pushed these thoughts from his mind, and added: "We all do what is required of us, one way or another, whoever we are, yes?"

"Yes," Thomas agreed, perhaps a touch uneasily. "My contribution was minimal, even if it was what was required of me. What you did—"

"—was sufficient." The King looked at the harp sitting on the table. "Nevertheless, perhaps I could do something to honor your kindness. It is our way."

Thomas was uncomfortable at the prospect. "That's really not necessary."

Reading him with such accuracy that Thomas almost blushed, the King laughed. "Oh, I think it is, if only to protect my own ears. *Harp: tune.*"

Instantly, the harp was surrounded by a dance of golden light that vanished almost as quickly as it had appeared.

Intrigued, Thomas turned and reached toward the harp. He ran his fingers carefully along the strings. They were perfectly tuned.

Grinning, he looked back at the King, who was smiling too.

"That sounds about right," Thomas commented with a wry smile. "Nice technique."

"You might," the King suggested, "talk with one of the Queen's Ladies about which of our musicians might be best suited to teach you a few things about playing the harp. For my part, I can offer you this: keep your wrists tucked inward, and keep your thumbs up."

Intrigued, Thomas positioned his wrists and hands and plucked a few of the harp's strings. "Like this?"

The King nodded. "Like that."

"Thank you, Your Majesty," Thomas said with a respectful bow of his head, Rock Star musician to Royal musician.

"Everything is music, Thomas Lear, one way or another. Everything. Despite all else, I cherish the music you have brought to the Folk. Your songs are rare and moving, and we are forever changed by the gifts in them."

Thanking the King seemed a little lame, all things considered, but Thomas did it anyway.

Suddenly, with a mental jolt that nearly dropped him, Thomas noticed that he was standing here talking with the very powerful husband of the woman he loved. He was stunned that he had so easily bypassed all of the other issues between them because they were talking about the harp. As he met the King's eyes, he was jolted again as additional, unbidden insight came flooding into his mind: the King had, for his own reasons, bypassed the other stuff too.

The King turned to leave, then stopped, and looked back at Thomas. "Guardian's lady is quite...*something*, don't you think?"

The question surprised Thomas. "She is. I liked her. A lot."

Eyebrow raised, the King frowned, and Thomas wondered if he'd touched a nerve. He watched the King's face grow serious as he pointed out: "I found her to be stubborn, sarcastic, impractical, strong-willed, impetuous, aggressive, too clever by half, defiant and insufferably shameless."

Thomas didn't know what to make of that. But before he had a heartbeat to consider it, the King laughed and winked at him. He watched as the King took a few steps toward the garden's back gate. "I liked her, too. Very much. She's wonderful. But I suppose he loves her enough to overlook her obvious character flaws." The King chuckled merrily as he walked away.

Thomas couldn't let him go without saying something. "Your Majesty?"

The King turned again.

"Your Majesty, thank you for tuning the harp."

"You're welcome." The King began to say something else, stopped himself, reconsidered it, and finally spoke. "Thomas Lear, I can see much of your heart and mind in your music. So I offer you this in return for the good you have brought to the Fey: if you want to learn to play your harp, there are Folk in Elvenhome who can teach you many fine things. If you want to learn to *know* your harp, the best person for that is *me*."

Across the garden, they stared at each other for a heartbeat or two, each somehow not terribly surprised to see the shadow of a kindred spirit.

Thomas recognized, at once and instinctively, that underneath the cool smoothness of the royal presence, many of the King's passions, frustrations, and private, tortured feelings of failure and self-contempt very closely reflected Thomas' own unspoken self-destructive, raging, pain-filled belief in his own unworthiness.

As if reading Thomas' mind, the King said, "Yes, Thomas Lear, it appears we are more alike than I would have guessed. We seem to care deeply about many of the same things." With a half-smile, he added: "Keep the harp tuned."

The King turned and walked away, all but disappearing in the dazzling sunlight as he finally moved through the garden's back gate.

A delicate shimmer of golden light by the harp caught Thomas' eye just before it vanished. In its place was a thin metal cylinder connected to a straight wooden handle. Thomas lifted the thing, and turned it over in his palm. The end of the cylinder was shaped to fit the pegs that held the harp's strings in place.

The King had given him a tuning key.

It was at that moment, and for no apparent reason, that Thomas Lear, Rock Star and Lover of the High Queen of Faerie, began to realize that it was quite possible that the High King of Faerie was still in love with his wife.

THE GREAT HALL was full tonight; the Folk had gathered to hear him play and sing. He was glad he'd chosen to share the stage with some of his Fey musician friends. He looked around and saw Alice Cooper (a seven-foot-tall Merrow) holding a huge bodhran, Mick Jagger (a short, barrel-shaped Dwarf) on pipes, Van Morrison (a slender Elf) on lute, and Grace Slick (a tiny Pixie with a stunningly-tall green and pink pointy hat) on a miniature flute, all smiling at him. They'd rehearsed for a couple of hours earlier in the day, and they were ready to perform.

Thomas scanned the crowded Hall for Callie, and found her sitting on a long bench, surrounded by her Ladies and other friends. Zodiac sat, still and serene, beside Iris, who kept a watchful eye on the Ladies and their Queen as the audience quieted.

He took a step forward, and addressed the Folk. "Tonight, as promised, you will hear all new songs. We'll sing old songs together next time." His eyes met Callie's across the huge room, and her smile widened as they connected for a second or two before he addressed the audience again. "I finally finished this song last week. We're all friends here," (and the Folk agreed with him vociferously) "so I can tell you the truth. It was a hard song to write, a sad story to tell, because my feelings about it all, and the beautiful lady involved, were sort of tied up in knots.

"You know what I mean, and you know who I'm talking about. At first, I didn't think I knew how to write this song. I do know how to sing it, though. You see, I got this *Letter from a Friend...*"

He nodded to Alice Cooper, who counted a slow, lingering beat, and the music came alive. Thomas took a breath, added his guitar to the wave of sound flowing from the stage, and began to sing about an overpowering, unrequited love, about love rescuing a broken heart, and about love standing quietly by, waiting for another time and place.

Thomas finished with unfeigned tears in his eyes.

There wasn't a dry eye anywhere in the Hall.

When the song was finished, the Folk went wild with applause. And then they wanted to hear the new song again.

He'd told no one, not even Callie, that Lavender's tear-streaked letter of apology—heartbreakingly honest words revealing what Lavender was coming to understand about blinding, desperate love—rested safely in the pocket of his breeches as he played her song a second time.

ONE NIGHT, THOMAS dreamt he was back in Los Angeles, as if he'd never left at all; his life was the same as it had always been. He was fairly certain that he was dreaming, but he was having a good time anyway.

He energetically fucked two pretty B-list actresses who somehow stepped out of his heroically magnified Infamous Tour Suitcase. Afterward, he easily slipped away from the scene as the sweet young things snuggled together in the suitcase and fell asleep.

He had an interesting if somewhat nonsensical conversation with his record producer about projected numbers and new projects and, as usual, only barely acknowledged Jack Grandberg's blonde secretary sitting in the background as he strode cheerfully out of the office.

Seconds later, his lawyer had only good news for him, which confirmed to him that he was, in fact, dreaming. In all the years she'd worked for him, she had rarely told him anything that had made him smile.

He found himself in his business manager's office, too, and signed paperwork that would set a new North American tour in motion, whether he had new songs ready or not, and would pay him a million dollars.

Then he was at home. He roamed his big house in comfortable silence, and ended up in the music room. A quick check in some of the drawers and behind some books told him that there were no drugs stashed in the places where he usually kept them.

Before he could decide if this perplexed him, he felt someone else's presence.

He turned and saw Callie, dressed in Upworld clothes but—incongruously—with her distinctive royal markings dancing slowly on her skin. She was sitting at the piano, looking at him, unveiled amusement beaming from her dark, knowing eyes.

Just as he was about to ask her what she was doing here, and why she was wearing jeans and regal body art at the same time, he heard acoustic and bass guitars playing behind him, and he swung around.

184

His band mates, Chance and Rick, were standing on a glittering stage before a vast, cheering audience. They were starting to play a song, one of *his* songs, and he wanted to join them. He was hungry to perform, hungrier than he'd been in what suddenly felt like an eternity. He took a step toward the stage, then turned back and looked at Callie, who was smiling and wiggling her fingers in an oddly casual goodbye.

Torn between the stage and the High Queen of Faerie, he could only stand there feeling completely miserable as the music swelled and swept over him while Callie stood up from the piano, still wiggling her fingers, and faded away.

He woke slowly, wrapped in a sadness he could not easily explain to himself.

It was just after dawn. He was in Callie's bed, curled up beside her. Feeling empty, he tried to fill the unfathomable void by listening to her soft, steady breathing. He inched closer to her, drinking in her scent and the contours and the colors of her as he sought comfort in the warmth of her sleeping body.

As he watched, the delicate ivy design around her wrist gently, almost possessively, slid up her arm and curled up on her bare shoulder.

For the first time since he'd come to Elvenhome, he found himself aching for familiar things, the familiar things of his other—no, his *real*—life.

He reminded himself that he was not miserable, although in this moment he found himself unexpectedly lonely and feeling a little lost. Thomas Lear slowly realized that he was incredibly, painfully, unimaginably homesick.

ten

SUSANNAH WOKE, HER eyes dreamily focused on the shapeless flicker on her bedroom wall. It took her a moment to realize that the dancing burst of light was caused by the small but determined ray of sunshine that had sneaked past the curtains and found the golden willow on the necklace around Susannah's neck. The necklace was part of her now; she rarely took it off.

The sunbeam reminded her of something else, too. *That morning, the sunbeam sparkled on Rex's gold earring, and I saw...*

Her smile was soft and warm as she remembered Rex, the handsome, wonderful man who had spent a night with her in Edinburgh six months ago. She didn't think about him often (well, not too often, anyway), but when she did, she was filled with a quiet glow. Susannah's world had shifted *because* of her time with him. She couldn't exactly put her finger on what had changed inside her, but she was aware that something significant had reshaped itself in her head, and maybe in her heart, too. Who could know for sure?

What she was certain about was that her life, and the way she thought about it, was different now, and somehow Rex had been part of that. And he had given her the willow tree necklace...

The alarm beeped, Susannah rolled over and turned it off, then snuggled back into the sheets as she considered how very much in her life had changed.

186

Two weeks after she'd returned to LA, with nothing substantive to show from the trip to Edinburgh except Thomas Lear's luggage, Jack Grandberg had gone on a skiing vacation. At some point between hitting on ski bunnies, drinking too much, and smoking plenty of weed before heading for the slopes, Jack had collided rather spectacularly with a very stubborn tree, and broke both of his legs in several places, broke his right arm, and knocked out several of his front teeth.

The tree was annoyed, but mostly unharmed.

When Jack got out of the hospital and returned home to Los Angeles, he took an immediate leave of absence from work. He'd had to heal, learn how to walk again, do his physical therapy, and get his teeth replaced. Then he officially promoted Susannah from Glorified Secretary/Production Assistant to Associate Producer, because she knew his job as well as he did, and there was a lot of extra work to do with Jack out of the office.

Ten weeks after that, in a discussion over the phone, Jack promoted Susannah again. She had earned the title, workload, salary, and headaches of a full Producer.

She'd taken the opportunity and run with it. She put all of her energy into her work, and loved every minute. She had a couple of major successes, which made the record company a lot of money, and Susannah got positive attention. A once-famous-but- almost-forgotten musician took her guidance and let her produce his album her way, and he got a Grammy nomination. She discovered a new singer/songwriter, worked with the shy woman extensively on her very first recording, and the singer became "instantly" an overnight success, and won a Grammy for the album Susannah had produced. The name Susannah Rickert was becoming a familiar and "must-know" one in industry circles.

She had a big office next door to Jack's, with a secretary/assistant of her own. She also had a rigorous work schedule, a lot of responsibility, and loved her new world: the creativity, the music, most of the people, and the overall thrill of the things she was able to accomplish.

It felt good.

No, it felt great. There was nothing else like it.

When she'd been Jack's secretary, she had been regarded as annoyingly shy; she was now seen as quiet and thoughtful. She still didn't take drugs, drink much, or sleep around, but these days her peers viewed her as sane, responsible, mature, and healthy, rather than square. There may have been quiet, whispered conjecture about her sex life, but she only shrugged and kept working. She dated a little, but had not met anyone who had pulled her focus from her passion for the music business. She kept her private life private, and if that led to any particular speculation, Susannah didn't care. It wasn't anyone's business that she didn't really have much of a personal life, was it?

But now she had a cat, and she'd bought the small but pretty house in Laurel Canyon that she used to daydream about. She came home to the cat and the house after every long day, dinner meeting, business trip, awards event, or industry party, and she was good with that.

If the biggest secrets of her life were that she was learning to speak French, and that one of the studio musicians was privately teaching her to play the alto flute just for the fun of it, that was all right too.

Susannah stretched extravagantly. Her life was perfect.

Well, almost perfect.

Most of the time.

For only the first time today, Susannah found herself wondering about Thomas Lear. Was he still alive? Where in the world was he? Was he safe? What was he doing? What about the music? Was he writing? Who was he singing to?

She sighed as she got out of bed and put on a bathrobe. It didn't do her any good to think about him. She knew better than anyone else that there were never any real answers to questions about Thomas Lear, which were still coming from the media and the fans with surprising frequency. Jack and Stan had fabricated a basic industry-credible and public-facing picture of what Thomas was

188

currently up to (off on his own, heads-down in Europe for a couple of years, writing and reading and generally getting his life together). Susannah didn't like lying about it, but damage control dictated that they cover for the absent rock star until he decided to resurface (she had to believe that at some point he would show up). They'd give him all kinds of hell later, for all the good it would do.

If not seeing him had helped to soothe and settle some of her more jagged, confused feelings for him, listening to his albums still had the power to fill her with an aching need that always took her breath away.

She gave a fleeting thought to his beautiful silver cuff links, which lived illicitly in the back of her jewelry box. She didn't often touch them, but knowing that they were there made her feel special. *The stuff of dreams...* she mused, with very little of her former wistfulness.

She sighed again, then chuckled at herself and shook her head. Thomas Lear was AWOL, and even if he weren't, she didn't—and would never—swim at the same end of the pool as he did, no matter how successful she might be.

As time moved forward, she realized that she was more and more okay with that. And if her heart swelled every once in a while when she thought about him...

A cat stood in the doorway, its meow plaintive.

Susannah grinned down at him. "Shouldn't *you* get breakfast for *me* once in a while?"

The cat frowned, unimpressed.

Susannah laughed and swept the big Maine Coon up in her arms as she left the bedroom and started her day.

EVEN IF THOMAS noticed that he was beginning to have fleeting thoughts about returning to his life in Los Angeles, he wasn't actually unhappy or lonely. He still had his growing number of friends in Elvenhome. He missed Guardian, although he grudgingly acknowledged the rightness of the Water Faerie's absence, living Upworld with Maggie.

Thomas' deep, comfortable relationship with Callie was wonderful. She was truly the best friend he'd ever had, and was a constantly exciting, delicious and satisfying lover.

He was writing better, too, both lyrically and musically. He tried to sidestep his increasing bouts of missing his life in Los Angeles by hanging out with his friends.

Over the course of a week, as he spent time with the Queen's Ladies both as a group and individually, Thomas learned that the homesickness thing was a natural part of the process of being Callie's Court Singer. Or, at least from the Fey point of view, of being mortal.

"Deep down, mortals crave the familiar," Violet told him in a breathless rush as she fluttered around his head. "Most of them have an underdeveloped sense of adventure, do you agree? I believe that is why they cannot fly."

"Mortals do not wish to change their hats too much, Thomas, and that is fine, even if it is boring," squeaked Rose the next day, nodding her tiny head and her new, big orange-and-yellow pointy hat judiciously.

Shy Carnation met his eyes, her green-and-gold Goblin ones glittering in sympathy. "I love Elvenhome, yet I've longed for my home many times over the years. It is not a very nice feeling, is it? And it is hard to run away from the unhappiness when you are so far away from places your heart loves..."

For her part, when she brought a basket of dinner to him one evening, the arrestingly beautiful Juniper, dripping with ready-to-share sensuality, offered him some erotic and very explicit temporary distractions from the inherent miseries of homesickness. Thomas had gasped a little, laughed, thanked her graciously, and hurried back to his guitar.

The following day, as he waited in silence in Callie's sitting roomwhile she was being dressed for dinner, Dahlia encouraged him with a knowing, Dwarfish smile.

"Do not worry, Thomas. Your world will still be there when you return to it."

Orchid, who sat beside him on a long, wide couch, nodded. "Perhaps you will find that they have missed you far more than you have missed them. That will give you something to look forward to, before you go home again. Before you begin to miss us."

At that moment, Thomas appreciated the fact that he was currently obligated to silence; he did not know what to say. He wondered if Callie's Ladies were right.

So he divided his time between Callie (who, Iris told him with brisk candor, juggled her Queen Stuff to accommodate his rhythms rather than the other way around, which was a first), his friends, and his own space—where he ran, or fed his voracious reading habit, played his guitars and attempted to learn the harp, and happily all but wrote his heart out.

He also continued to host the Friday Afternoon Poker Game. This happy and, probably perhaps-weekly event turned out to be, apart from his hours with Callie, his favorite way to spend time not focused on music.

BY THE END of June, the males-only poker event with the Court Singer was so popular with the Folk that Thomas had to have the dining table in his apartments replaced by a much larger one so that more men could play. It seated fifteen comfortably. Everyone went wild, as only the Fey can: suddenly there were waiting lists, schedules and bribes, even designates in case of unexpected but necessary absences.

Poker, and all its accepted variations—to say nothing of the strange and sometimes mind-crushingly funny deviations and alarming aberrations—swept through Elvenhome, both the Castle and the Village. In due time, the game traveled through the whole of Faerie, and over the years became something of an official pastime in contemporary Fey culture, although Thomas would never know that he was responsible for it.

The Fair Folk were playing poker. In the Great Hall, small groups of eager souls gathered in the evening, and played the nights away. When the Kitchens were cleaned and closed down after meals, Goblins and their less-bright, hard-working Hob cousins settled down to win small stones and wooden buttons from each other. Spriggans and Pixies of both genders seemed particularly adept at the game. Banshees, Elves, Sylphs, Sprites, and Dwarfs began holding tournaments by race, and yearly championships were eventually celebrated across the Kingdoms as merrily as Solstice holidays, and with as much glee and anticipation.

Even the Queen's Ladies played a private game of poker together several times a week, joined, as often as not, by Her Grace.

SEATED AT THE huge dining table in his rooms, Thomas and his friends waited for the last scheduled player to arrive for the game so they could get down to business. All the regulars were there, of course: Thomas, Zodiac, Menace, Scribe, Boston, Irving Berlin (a long-suffering Goblin musician who was teaching Thomas to play his harp), Professor Plum (a striking, web-fingered Merrow, one of the King's Men), and Johnny Carson, a grizzled Gnome who muttered to himself throughout every game and made Thomas laugh in spite of himself.

Among the other players, who chatted as they drank ale and ate Thomas' crisps, peanuts and pretzels (they couldn't really taste them, but they really liked the sound of the crunch), this week's game included two Dwarfs, three Elves, and a short Brownie with backward feet. Voices buzzed around the table in happy expectation.

"Who are we waiting for?" Zodiac asked the group.

The movie-star-handsome Professor Plum replied after he swallowed his ale, "Colonel Mustard. He should be here soon."

Zodiac, seated at the Court Singer's left, shot Thomas a veiled look of despair.

Thomas groaned and whispered, "I've said I was sorry about that."

Zodiac frowned.

"I am!"

"Indeed," Zodiac whispered back.

"When I first met them and realized they were the King's Men, I kind of lost my grip. All I could think of was that board game I used to play when I was a kid..."

"I have now seen that game, no thanks to you, and you are a disgrace," the Lord High Chamberlain hissed, right before he unsuccessfully stifled a chuckle. "How could you name a ten-foot Giant 'Colonel Mustard'? You should be ashamed."

"I know, I know," Thomas admitted with a sigh. "On the other hand, I catch myself secretly wanting to send him to the Billiard Room, with a candlestick and a wrench..."

After a second, Thomas and Zodiac laughed out loud, their voices joining the general hum of the other conversations around them.

With a silent, almost religious focus, Menace reached his long arm across the table, flexed his twitching fingers, and lifted the deck of cards that sat behind Boston's glass of ale. These he shuffled and, as he did, the Folk at the table settled down, ready to begin as soon as the latecomer arrived.

They only had to wait a minute or two. There was a knock at Thomas' front door, which was answered by everyone still seated at the table. "Come in! Hurry up, Colonel Mustard! Come in!"

The door opened, and the final poker player arrived.

He wasn't tall enough or broad enough to be the Giant everyone was waiting for. He would not need the four oversized ottomans waiting for him at the poker table.

The player who gently closed the door and walked toward them wasn't the impatiently-anticipated Colonel Mustard at all.

He was the King.

Thomas' weren't the only eyes that widened in confused surprise, and perhaps a glimmer of uneasiness, as the King moved to the huge empty space beside Menace at the poker table. "Your friend Colonel Mustard sends his apologies," he said easily as he pushed three of the four ottomans out of his way before anyone could rise to assist him. He sat down and got comfortable. "His King required him to take care of some urgent matters and, sadly, he could find no one else to sit in for him at this most enticing poker table." The King's ready and wry smile made everyone relax as he looked around at the group approvingly. "Now...what are we playing?"

There was some debate among the players, followed by merry talk and drinking and crunching as Menace dealt the first hand and told the Folk, "Five-card Stud."

Zodiac leaned toward Thomas and whispered "I believe it is perhaps His Majesty Mr. Green, in the study, with the rope and perhaps the revolver..."

"Shut up," Thomas whispered back, but they were both laughing as they picked up their cards and turned their attention to the game.

"I'm out," Professor Plum said, laying his cards down.

"I'll see your shiny buttons, and I'll raise you three marbles," Boston declared, tossing four shiny buttons and rolling the large black marbles into the center of the table. He looked at Menace, who sat next to him, studying his cards with a calculating intensity.

After a moment, Menace's eyes flashed, and he pushed a large tulip-bulb, two unsharpened pencils with eraser heads, and a baby turtle across the table. "Call," he announced.

The King moved his cards around in his hand, tilted his head, and said, "Call." He added a beautiful wooden pipe, and a small cloth bag that held some sort of fragrant tobacco, to the interesting pot.

"Too much for me," said Scribe, putting his cards down.

"Fold me up like an old shirt and put me away," grumbled Johnny Carson as he dropped his cards on the table with a snort.

The three Elves, seated consecutively, all called (and between them added a flower pot full of dirt and tiny ferns, a necklace, and two pairs of scissors) but did not raise.

The Brownie, disgusted with his hand, shrieked a spontaneous, profane jumble of words when he folded, one that had a different effect than he anticipated; everyone at the table roared with laughter. The ancient Dwarf sitting beside him patted him on the back sympathetically, but he was laughing too. "I am out," he told them.

"Me too," chuckled the younger Dwarf seated on his left.

"Hmmm..." Thomas said, smiling. "I'll see it, Gentlemen." He tossed four guitar picks into the pot. "And I'll raise you...a penny whistle!"

The Folk were duly impressed, so much so that Zodiac ("I've got nothing") and then Boston folded.

Menace ignored everything but his cards. "Call," he said, and pushed a box of crayons, a bottle of ink, and two remaining baby turtles to the center of the table. "And I'm all in," he added, without blinking an eye.

The King watched the turtles walk around the table before he spoke. "Is that how it is?"

"It is," replied the Spriggan evenly.

"Well then," the King said, tossing a small, jewel-encrusted dagger into the pot.

Scribe and the three Elves folded immediately.

Everyone at the table looked at Thomas, who pretended to be daydreaming. "Oh. Sorry. My turn?"

Johnny Carson could be heard above the others. "Yes, man, yes! Where is your brain?"

Thomas glanced at the cards in his hand, seemed to consider something, then grinned as he tossed a paperback copy of *David Copperfield* into the pot. "See it, and raise you Dickens."

Menace crowed with pleasure as he dropped his cards on the table for everyone to see. "Straight to the ten!" he sang out with his raspy voice, and reached greedily for the pot.

"Not so fast," Thomas said as he laid his own cards down. "What can I tell you, Menace? I'm holding Jacks full of nines."

The table applauded with glee, and Thomas bowed.

Then all eyes moved to the King.

His Grace didn't say a word as he placed his cards on the table: three Queens and two Kings.

The players at the table went wild.

Someone yelled in a panic, "Don't let that turtle fall off the table!" Several of the Folk reached for the small turtle teetering on the edge, and it was moved to safety.

"The King's winnings, don't you know," Professor Plum reminded them all.

The King and Thomas eyed each other over the din around them, and then Thomas, unable to help himself, beamed his admiration at Callie's husband. "Well done, Sir."

Returning the smile, the High King of Faerie laughed and helped himself to his winnings, including the tiny turtles.

The cards were collected and handed to Boston for shuffling and dealing.

Amid the shuffling, laughing, drinking and talking, Boston and Zodiac exchanged a private, speculative glance that indicated more than just their mutual astonishment. With supreme eloquence, Zodiac shrugged his shoulders and his eyebrows at the same time, and they got back to the game.

Several hours later, Thomas stood near his place at the poker table and grinned happily as the Friday Afternoon Game wound down. It had been fun, and Thomas was in a good mood. Scribe and the Dwarfs thanked Thomas, waved to everyone, then remembered to bow to the King before they went out the front door. Johnny Carson and the three Elven Folk did the same, leaving Thomas with Boston, Professor Plum, Menace, Zodiac, and the King, all still talking and gathering up their winnings as they finished their drinks, and ate a few more pretzels.

Thomas couldn't help it; he was watching the King, who was laughing at something Boston had just told him.

"I agree with you," said the King, slipping the three small turtles carefully into a yellow bag, and handing it to Professor Plum. "Working with the Northern Cave Trolls to watch and ward the Far Mountains is an excellent idea. But if you plan to meet with them in close quarters, be certain to first talk with Master...Ocelot...He will have something in his herbarium to protect you from their somewhat distressing breath and body odor."

"That," Zodiac added with something of an adolescent snort, "or he will be able to give you something to ingest so that you will not care much about how they smell!"

Mesmerized, Thomas observed the King's movements, and the way he interacted with the Folk. It was true that the King was no longer a handsome man; the horrible scar on his face at seen to that. Yet the Court Singer could see that there was an easy elegance about the King that had nothing to do with the fact of his royalty, and everything to do with the man himself. *Under other circumstances, we might have been friends...*

"Thomas, many thanks for the game. And for the spoils!" Boston grinned and patted his pocket, where he'd placed the stones, marbles and piece of rock salt he'd won.

"Next week!" Thomas replied with a wave as Boston said goodbye to the others, bowed to the King, and left.

The King was talking in a low tone to Professor Plum, who then nodded, and with a cheerful salute to everyone, turned and walked out the door.

Menace was the only person still seated at the table. He was playing Solitaire, oblivious to everyone else.

The King appeared ready to depart as well. Thomas decided that he was both sorry and a bit relieved about the King leaving. But instead of turning toward the door, he strode smoothly over to stand in front of Thomas.

"An excellent afternoon, Thomas Lear, thank you for your hospitality. My thanks, too, for most of the pot."

"For all that your presence was unexpected, Your Majesty, it was a pleasure too," Thomas answered, hoping he was somehow on form. "We were all honored to have you here."

"Great Gods, man...it was a poker game!" the King laughed, waving his hand as if to disperse the requisite verbal regalia. "Still, I have not had this much fun in a long time. Thank you."

"You're welcome."

The King cleared his throat. Zodiac stopped pouring more ale into a glass, and Menace's game of Solitaire was forgotten. They both looked at Thomas and the King. "I should like to ask a favor."

"A favor?" Thomas repeated.

"Yes."

"Okay. Shoot. Um, Your Majesty."

The King chuckled. "That's just the point. Everyone else has a name. The Game dictates that everyone who comes into contact with the Court Singer must be named by him."

Standing behind Thomas, Zodiac paled.

Without missing a beat, the King asked his favor: "Thomas Lear, I understand that you do not use the name you originally gave me." Menace's eyes got very big but he did not move; even his ever-twitching long fingers froze.

The King continued lightly, "Since this is so, I would like you to *rename* me, so that in the event we spend any time in the same place, you will have something to call me besides 'Your Grace' or 'Your Majesty.' Rename me,

Thomas Lear, and I will be able to play poker with you again next time with a new name that will perhaps relax the Folk around the table a bit."

Thomas hoped he was dreaming. He decided he needed clarification. "You want me to name you?"

The King nodded. "Yes."

"Oh, shit…" Zodiac groaned, unaware that he'd spoken aloud.

The King laughed. "Go on then, Thomas Lear. I know your reputation for naming the Folk, and it is not a good one. But I find I am inclined to play this Game after all, and will live by the rules until your Year is over. I am ready."

"Oh, shit…" Zodiac whispered again.

Menace looked from the King to Thomas to Zodiac and back to Thomas, and immediately vanished into the air.

"Your Majesty," Zodiac began, moving toward Thomas and the King, "it might do to have you suggest a name to Thomas, and he can officially name you that…"

Thomas nodded helpfully, perhaps a little desperately.

Amused now, the King shook his head. "No, that is not the way the Game is played, and you know it well, Zodiac. Now Thomas, give me a new name, and I'll be on my way."

Thomas and Zodiac gaped at each other.

"Can I think about it, Your Majesty, and send it to you by messenger?"

"I think not. Proceed, Court Singer. Name your King."

Zodiac bowed. "I regret that I have matters elsewhere that require my attention, Your Grace…if I might excuse myself…"

"Stay," said the King, who managed to cover his enjoyment of the situation, but only barely. "Thomas Lear?"

Thomas' mind was a blank. Every time he almost had an idea, it slipped out of his mental grasp.

"You would keep a King waiting?" the King pressed, with what he hoped passed as a frown.

"No, Your Majesty," Thomas stammered miserably.

"Go on, then," Zodiac urged, wincing.

Thomas groped for the name of an author, a river, a scent, a movie star, a country, a superhero, a British monarch, and a breed of horses, but nothing came. He had named everyone he knew at Elvenhome, and could not think of a name he hadn't already used. There was nothing at all...until...

Both the King and Zodiac saw that Thomas had come up with something. The King looked on with anticipation, while Zodiac watched Thomas in something close to dread.

"I see you have thought of a name," the King prodded. "Out with it."

Biting his lip, Thomas shot Zodiac a look, and decided that his friend would be of no help here. Taking a deep breath, Thomas cringed a little, and said "I played Clue as a kid...it's where I got the names for Professor Plum and Colonel Mustard."

"I am familiar with the game, Thomas Lear."

"All I can come up with is 'Mr. Green'. I'm sorry about that."

"What is wrong with you?!?" Zodiac exploded at Thomas, nearly forgetting that they were standing in front of the King. "Are you insane?"

Thomas glowered at Zodiac. "What you said before got stuck in my brain!" Thomas assumed a very Zodiac-ish pose, and did a passable if overblown impression of the Lord High Chamberlain: "His Majesty Mr. Green, in the Study, with the rope and perhaps the revolver..."

Before Zodiac could raise himself to his full height to respond, the King interrupted.

"Gentlemen, despite your seeming displeasure over the name, as I think about it, I find I rather like it."

Confusion radiated from both Thomas and Zodiac, followed by small rays of relief.

"I shall be called 'Mr. Green' for a short while. It suits me. Thank you, Thomas. I look forward to the next poker game...if I may be permitted to invite myself."

Thomas could only nod, his eyes wide.

"Good day, then, Thomas Lear. Zodiac."

The King turned, and took a few steps toward the door before he stopped. And waited.

It took Thomas an uneasy five seconds, but he understood. "Good day, Mr. Green."

"Good day, Mr. Green," echoed Zodiac.

Satisfied, the King of Faerie nodded his approval, and strode out the front door.

"Oh my God..." mumbled Thomas.

"Wait until Her Grace hears of this! The Folk are going to call our King...I can't even say it!" Zodiac was disgusted. "You are pathetic. It is a wonder that I am willing to get drunk with you."

Thomas met his friend's eyes. "We're going to get drunk?"

"Count on it." Zodiac walked over to the couch, and dropped himself down on it in shock. "'Mr. Green,' Thomas...*really*?" He shook his head sadly. "We need whisky. A lot of it."

eleven

THE MORNING'S CALM sunlight streamed its radiance into Callie's bedroom windows. It slid most provocatively across the bed, eliciting a chuckle from the man lying next to the Queen.

"What...are...you...doing...?" Callie grumbled sleepily, eyes closed.

"Nothing," Thomas said. "I am finding humor in sunbeams...not something I'd ever have had the opportunity or the perspective to do at home."

Callie opened her eyes. He'd done it again: Thomas had referred to Upworld as "home," the way he had when he'd first arrived. She had noticed it the first time he'd done it, was unsure whether he'd realized it. She'd known he was getting homesick, and that he spent more and more time thinking about his life in Los Angeles. It was one of the early signs of the fading of the enchantment, the subtle, silent heralding of the end of a mortal's Year and a Day with the Folk. Callie had experienced it a hundred times, of course, and often she had been glad about it.

She didn't think she was happy about it today. Not with him.

Snuggling up against him, she whispered softly to herself that it probably was time for The Talk. Drifting back to sleep, she considered that it was also time for a grand picnic.

ON A SUMMERY day, the Queen of Faerie hosted a festival to celebrate the sunshine. And to celebrate Thomas Lear, too.

The Folk from the Village of Elvenhome joined the Folk from the Castle for the event. They feasted and shopped, played music and games, danced and altogether enjoyed themselves in the same field where the Fey Battle of Bannockburn had been played out months before.

There was much merry activity. Pavilion tents were everywhere; food and drink were plentiful. Pixies of both genders went wild buying new hats in the milliner's tent, and the cobbler's tent was filled to overflowing with Goblins eager for new footwear.

Thomas had been granted the Queen's permission not only to speak freely to everyone he chose to from sunrise through moonshine that day, but also to participate in the fun, rather than simply observe it.

Participate he did. Callie and her Ladies laughed gaily as they watched Thomas fail an archery contest, and later win a foot race across the field. He brought flowers to each of the Queen's Ladies, and gallantly took them shopping in turns. While strolling down a row of vendors with Rose, Orchid and Violet, he stopped and bought Callie a small, perfectly-formed sliced geode that held a sea of tiny, beautiful pink crystals.

He danced with everyone who approached him, including a shy male Gnome who wanted to ask him about his poetry. Thomas also was introduced to the remaining King's Men he hadn't met, and renamed them as poorly as he'd renamed almost everyone else. Although they were never in close proximity, Thomas saw the King several times during the festival, moving easily among his people, talking and listening and laughing, inspecting the goods in tents, and winning a horse race.

The day's feast was spread across more than three dozen huge trestle tables; Thomas stayed away from them, and ate happily from a small, overflowing table that held crisps, fresh fruit, cheeses, crackers, beef, chicken, ale, water, wine, whisky, bread and cakes from Upworld.

Zodiac and Thomas, sitting in the sunshine with tankards of ale, were joined by Boston, Colonel Mustard, and Master Ocelot.

"It is good to be festive with friends," the Master said, sitting down on the grass beside Boston, and lifting his own tankard for refilling.

"It is also good to get drunk with friends," laughed Colonel Mustard.

"Is that not what I said?" winked the Master. "Thomas, have you been writing new songs?"

Thomas, watching the Folk around him, didn't hear Master Ocelot speak. The Master looked questioningly at Zodiac and Boston. "Is something wrong?"

"Not at all, Master," Zodiac responded. "Thomas cannot hear you because he is, at this very moment, working on a song."

Boston found this fascinating. "Really?"

The Lord High Chamberlain nodded, the soul of wisdom and serenity. "I have come to know him well, and I am experienced in these things. He is writing, in his mind."

Thomas' dark eyes flickered as he watched the activity across the field. "True."

The others were much impressed, and applauded Zodiac's perceptive understanding of the Court Singer.

"On the other hand," Thomas remarked casually as he took another long drink of his ale, "I could just be getting drunk and ignoring everyone."

Zodiac was thereafter mocked by his friends, including Thomas, for the rest of the day.

A HUNDRED SMALL bonfires met the sunset. All around the field, there was music, singing, laughter, and talk as the Folk relaxed in half a hundred little groups, and rejoiced in the merriment of the festival.

Seated by the fire, next to the Queen, Thomas yawned.

"Talking to everyone, and running around all day, has tired you," she observed, her tone placid.

"Maybe," he said. "But it's been fun."

Boston and Juniper rose together. The Glaistig replied to the Court Singer even as she stared into the rich warmth of Boston's eyes. "That was the point, Thomas, right?"

Chuckling, the rest of the Queen's Ladies began to get up and move away from the Queen's fire, to meet up with other friends and lovers. Amid wishes for a good night all around, Zodiac at last rose from his place beside Thomas, and put out his hand to help Iris to her feet.

"Will you be in need of anything else at present, Your Grace?" Zodiac asked.

The Queen smiled. "Not for a while, my friend. Thank you."

Iris still held Zodiac's hand. "We'll be off, then," she grinned and waved goodnight to Callie.

Minutes later, the Queen and her Court Singer were alone by their bonfire. The star-filled night settled in above and around them.

Callie studied Thomas for a few seconds, and then murmured "I need to speak with you about something important."

He glanced at her, and gave her a wry smile. "I'm a little drunk, Callie. Maybe not the best time for a chat."

"Oh, I don't know...I think that a warm night under the summer stars, in a moment of quiet, and you tinged with just the right touch of drunkenness might be the perfect time for us to have this conversation."

He groaned. "No, Callie."

"Yes, Thomas," she countered.

"Oh God. Am I going to hate this?"

"Of course not."

Thomas sighed, then met her eyes and smiled. "Oh, what the hell." He moved into a position where he could lay by the fire, his head cradled in her lap. "Speak to me, my Queen," he teased, "and I will listen until I've conveniently passed out."

She smacked him playfully on the head, then ran her fingers through his brown curls. Her touch relaxed him, and he smiled up at her.

"Talk to me, Callie."

"It's about timing and your life Upworld." She ignored his wordless shrug. "I know you've begun to feel a bit unhappy and homesick, and I believe it's getting worse, more intense as we get closer to the end of your year and a day."

He frowned, unsure of where she was going with this. "I've been told it's normal."

"It is. You are coming full-circle. I'd gauge that you're probably deeply homesick about half of the time now, when a few weeks ago, it was less than that, simply some stray if somewhat strong pulls. Memories, wishes, and dreams from your other life."

Thomas considered this in an ale-induced daze.

Callie watched the flames in front of them. "As your time grows short here, the enchantment begins to get...sleepy."

He chuckled. "I keep forgetting that I'm enchanted. Officially enchanted. Like I wouldn't have fallen in love with you without it, Callie. As if."

The Queen stroked his hair affectionately. "Even so, Thomas." She took a breath. "Things will begin to change."

"Change?"

"A little, at first, starting now."

He closed his eyes, and nestled closer against her. "What are you going to do, detox me?"

"In a way, yes."

Thomas' eyes flew open, but he was too drowsy, too mildly drunk, and too comfortable to sit up and gape at her.

"It will go like this: you and I will begin to spend a little less time together. And when we do spend time together, apart from the more playful aspects of our relationship, we will use much of our time to get you ready for your return to your former life."

"Yeah? Get me ready how? Bizarre life lessons, Fey style?"

She wrinkled up her nose. "That doesn't sound like fun at all, does it?"

"Callie, please don't tell me you're going to do something creepy like...like having me prove I'm not as really shallow as I seem to be about feminine beauty. By maybe tricking me into dinner, dancing and, um, *breakfast* with a back-footed, great-great-grandmother Gnome or something...?"

"I hadn't thought of that. But I do believe dear old Martha Washington is rather sweet on you, so if you want to go into the village and visit her at the candle shop for a couple nights, you should do that."

Thomas shuddered, then laughed. "Thanks, but I think I've got a healthy enough perspective without having to go quite that far."

Callie lifted an eyebrow at him.

"I have friends now who are from many Faerie races. Different species, even. I think it's fair to say that I'm far less dismissive of anyone than I ever was. Although I admit that I may have had a slightly less-enlightened view of all that before I got here." His eyes twinkled with a sudden thought. "But, you know, if I could figure out how to have sex with a Sylph that was maybe Violet's size..."

"Well, if you wanted me to shrink you a little..." She chuckled.

He gasped before he laughed. "Funny, Callie. Very funny."

"All part of the service," she whispered, hoping that she sounded lighter about it all than she felt.

Thomas watched her for a minute, trying to read her. "What do you think could possibly make me ready to leave you?" he asked in a somber, if not sober, voice. "I know that once I'm back at home, I'm going to miss you. God, I can't even imagine how much."

"The point," Callie said carefully, "is to send you back in such a way that you can hold on to the things you've learned here: the way you see yourself now, the way you function alone and around others. We'll all help where we can. That way, you can ever be the very best version of Thomas Lear, be happy and well in the new life you'll create for yourself. That has always been Faerie's gift to its Court Singers."

He had listened carefully. "But what about us? You and me?"

Callie sighed. *Had this ever been easy?* she wondered. *Only occasionally*...and memories of the Court Singers she couldn't wait to get rid of made her smile and helped her regain her balance.

"Thomas, in a short while, you'll never think of Elvenhome or the Folk here. I'll be a faint memory, a dream, too. And then you'll forget me altogether."

"No."

"That's the way of enchantment."

"Unacceptable."

She laughed out loud at the stubborn tone in his sleepy voice. "But that is the way."

He struggled to sit up. Once he was seated beside her, he searched her face for the truth of it, and to his dismay, saw it in her eyes. "I'll never see you again?"

"No." His face fell. "And yes." He stared at her. "There may come a time, perhaps many years from now, when you will call for me, and I will answer." She took his hand, and held it tightly in both of her own. If there was a faint, shimmering green glow around her, he was not able to see it. "Thomas, my dear love, I will make you a promise. When your world fails you, when your heart truly fails you, when your life fails you, remember that I am a friend who loves you. When your need is True, call for me, and I will do all in my power to come to you."

There were tears in his eyes, but he was unaware of them. "If I have forgotten you, Callie...if I've forgotten you, how will I know to call for you? How will I know what to do?"

With a shining smile that rivaled the light of the night's brightest star, she turned, put her arms around his neck and leaned her head against his so that she could whisper in his ear. "Do not worry about forgetting this. You will forget it. I'm going to tell you now, and you will only hold it for a few seconds. Know that a part of you will hold the knowledge until you need it." She kissed him on the cheek, and spoke very softly. "Here's what you will do..."

AFTERWARD, THEY WALKED, hand in hand, back to the Castle. They'd been silent for the first half of the walk, each cloaked in private thoughts.

Finally, Thomas voiced what he'd been thinking. "Callie, what about Michael MacAllistair? You remember him. Court Singer, still around, definitely didn't forget you."

Callie gave Thomas' hand a little squeeze. "True. He lives his life, and he remembers his time in Elvenhome with us."

"So he's still enchanted?"

"No."

"But he remembers you. He still has feelings for you."

"Yes. Before he left, Thomas, I offered him the choice of remembering or not, and he chose to remember, even though it has cost him much in his other life."

It seemed simple enough to Thomas, then. "Well, I'll make the same choice. Problem solved. Best of both worlds!"

"My offer to Michael was a mistake, Dearest One. It seemed like a good idea at the time, but it wasn't, and it caused harm, which I will not allow to happen again."

"But—"

"No, Thomas. And that's an end to it."

Callie slid her hand from Thomas', and stuck it in the pocket of her gown, and they walked, not speaking as the Queen remembered her folly, and the Court Singer wondered about it all.

Several minutes later, he couldn't stand it any longer. He had to know, and understand, too.

"Why, Callie? Why did you offer to let him remember? Had you done that with any of the others?"

She sighed, a deep, sad sound that echoed long regrets. "Michael gave me one of the best true friendships I'd ever had. Since the time of the King." She slid her arm through Thomas' for comfort. "I knew that Michael was in love with me. I made it clear, though, that we could only continue as friends after his year.

"I should never have done it. And wouldn't have, on any other day. In an unguarded moment, after a series of events that once mattered but no longer do, I offered him the choice so that I might not have to give up the precious friendship when the enchantment was over."

"And?" he prompted, when she'd been quiet for a minute.

"And once you open the door to enchantment, you have no choice but to walk through it. The results were, of course, disastrous all around. He never moved very far from the notion that if he waited long enough, I would come to him, and stay. And that colored the way he lived his life, and all other choices he made. For my part, I lost the dear friend I'd sought to keep, because I knew I was wrong in the first place, and knew that seeing him occasionally Upworld would only make things worse."

Callie sounded so unhappy now that Thomas stopped, put his other arm around her, and gave her a kiss. "You know, it's kind of a relief to know that you're not perfect all the time, Callie." He touched her face, stroking her cheek until she smiled.

They made their way to Thomas' back garden. They opened the gate, and strolled toward the front, past the tree that Lavender had become. Each greeted her in their own silent way as they passed by.

"What if I kept in touch with Maggie and Guardian? I could come back to Scotland and see them every once in a while—"

They reached the bench, and sat down.

Callie shook her head sadly. "No, Thomas. You won't remember Maggie, or my cousin. You will remember that you came to Scotland, that you spent a year away from Los Angeles, and that you returned and got on with your life."

"Oh, no. Don't make me give *them* up, too. They're Upworld, Callie. I think Maggie and I could be good friends. And Guardian...Arrendel..."

She shook her head again, but said nothing.

Thomas' mind whirled in frustrated circles. Out of the mental chaos, he grabbed onto a notion that had often bothered him for the past month. He hadn't known what to do about it, so had said nothing, but the words spilled out of him now in a stream of frustration and vague panic: "How in the hell am I going to explain where I've been and what I've been doing?"

At this, Callie laughed, her tension and sadness swept away by the befuddled look in his eyes. "Thomas!" she giggled helplessly. "I have told you this before. Of all of the mortals I've ever met, you are the only one about whom I have no qualms about the necessity of creating credible fiction. You have spent much of your life creating stories you can find comfort in. You are utterly convincing. You have the enviable capacity to fully believe the stories you tell yourself about anything and everything. It's one of your great strengths."

He did not know whether to be relieved, insulted, or amused.

This made Callie laugh more.

"Thomas, love...be merry. All is well. You, my dear, are going to be fine. Your old life will welcome you with open arms, and you will be ready for it. I promise."

She hugged him, and stroked his face until he smiled at her.

"This is too weird, Callie."

"Just so," she agreed. "Still, I would like to spend the rest of this night in your bed."

"Well...all right, I suppose..." he teased.

They rose from the bench and, with an arm around each other, headed for the door to Thomas' bedroom.

"One more thing..." Callie began.

He almost managed sarcasm, but he began to laugh. "Oh God, now what, woman?"

"Before your Year is over, I will show you my Tower Room. It's something I do. It gives me a special memory of my Court Singer that will last forever."

"Wow...the Queen's Very Own Private 'Do-Not-Disturb' Tower Room?"

She kicked his shin as they reached the bedroom door. "The very one. And I'll show you my treasures. You may choose any one thing you see there, and take it with you out of Faerie and back into your world as a...remembrance."

"Seriously?"

"Yes."

"A souvenir of a place and a time I am not going to remember?"

"Yes."

"That doesn't make any sense, Callie."

"I have news for you Thomas."

"What?"

"Enchantment doesn't have to make sense. It simply *is*."

Before Thomas could respond, Callie leaned against him and kissed him hard. "Now shut up, and let's go to bed."

GOD, BUT HE wanted a long, hot shower and to reacquaint himself with the joys of modern plumbing. He wanted to watch a basketball game on TV. He wanted to get his hands on his own piano so much that he could have howled in frustration. He wanted a real burrito. He missed the ocean, and the beaches. He wanted to eat at all of his favorite restaurants. He wanted to talk to the guys in the band. He spent what seemed like hours having imaginary conversations with Chance and Rick, where he apologized for having been such an obnoxious asshole, and they grudgingly forgave him. He wanted to drive his cars. He wanted his own hairstylist to cut his hair, even though Iris had always done a good job and even massaged his head like a professional. He missed his house, he missed his friends, he missed the layers of his life he had rarely thought about in the years before coming to Faerie. He wanted to read the Sunday Los Angeles Times, fight with a producer, talk himself silly doing an interview with Rolling Stone. He wanted to watch porn. He wanted to see his bank balances. He wanted Myra Butler to make him breakfast and fondly tell him to grow the hell up. He wanted to be Thomas Lear, Rock Star again.

On the other hand, he wanted to spend every moment with Callie, laughing, fucking, talking, dreaming, making all kinds of merry. He also wanted to spend every moment with the guitars and the harp. He wanted to play poker with his friends, and imagine what kinds of things would show up in the center of the table: a bowl of rock salt, a bundle of exotic feathers (Thomas didn't want to consider from whom the feathers were drawn), a chunk of silver... He wanted to talk with Zodiac about the ways of the worlds. He wanted to get to know Orchid even better. He wanted to take a run every day with Violet zooming ahead of him with her purple wings fluttering. He wanted to spend time with Lavender in her new form, and her letter, too, and let the confused honesty of her love teach him something. He wanted to approach the King and talk with him about many things, especially the grace that was Terena, whom Thomas still missed. He wanted to hang out with Guardian and Maggie in the Highlands to see True Love alive and well. He wanted to fill his heart with the unfettered merriment and music that can only be fully experienced around the Fey.

He began to see incrementally less of the Queen, and he struggled to take this in stride. Thus, he spent much of his solitary time in an almost insatiable frenzy of poetry and musical composition. He wrote feverishly to make sense of the worlds around and inside him. He needed to ease the aching, and did it in the only way he ever would again: not with drugs, or self-hatred, or unfocused rage, or misery, but through the act of writing. He would, as he always had in better days in his past, open his heart and mind to the words and the music, let them flow over and through him until he was satisfied with the places they took him. He was finding it easier to tell the truths that had been held captive in his soul. He discovered that he was ready to dream new dreams, ask himself new questions. He was no longer afraid.

The songs he wrote were pure, passionate magic.

Was he feeling things more intensely, seeing everything around him more clearly? Did his emotions slide too often from one side of his life to the other? He struggled through a personal haze that was not exactly illness or depression, but often seemed like it. Sometimes he couldn't sleep, too caught up in putting all the newly-acknowledged, barely unearthed pieces of himself together.

He yearned painfully for the happy, familiar things in both of his lives, and was startled by the realization that he finally understood exactly who he was in each of them.

Thomas Lear was just a man, automatically and effortlessly worthy of any life he chose, like everyone else in the worlds. He marveled at the variety of personal hells it had taken him to reach this understanding. He got it now, and knew he'd never need to question it. He wondered how he'd managed to spend so much of his time agonizing over something so fundamental and immutable.

In the past three weeks he'd completed the lyrics for nine new songs: "Fire and Candle," "My Lady Harp," "The Truth About Apples," "Ladies of the Garden," and "All Your Heart Needs to Know" to express his deepening feelings about one side of his life, and "She Sings Sad Songs," "The Prodigal," "I Will Remember The Love," and

"Welcome Me Home" to handle his increasingly wistful sentiments about the other.

He had never written this much, this well, this consistently in so short a time in his entire career. He was telling his stories, and it was a pleasure beyond description. It still cost him something deeply personal, but it no longer caused him pain. There was only satisfaction that he was working, and that the work itself was good.

With delightful abandon, he laughed at himself.

Thomas laughed for a very long time, until his sides ached and his jaw hurt.

Then he put on his shoes, walked out his front door, and went looking for Callie.

twelve

nce upon a time, on a stormy evening deep in the Highlands of Scotland, a child braved wind and rain as she went out to her family's barn to comfort the horses. She knew they must surely have been frightened by the sounds of thunder and the flashes of bright light that tore through the darkness.

The child, a ten-year-old whose name was Jane, lifted her lamp high above her head as she closed the barn door behind her and approached the horses as they stood quietly in their stalls.

"I thought ye'd be worrit by the dreadful noise," she called out as she walked toward them. "But I've heard not one of ye cry out."

She stopped suddenly when she saw that her three horses were rubbing their heads in turn against a fourth horse, who stood calmly outside the stalls, accepting their attention.

Jane had never seen a horse as large as the stranger. He was a magnificent grey-white stallion standing nearly sixteen hands high. He turned to watch Jane, who had frozen in mid-step; his intelligent brown eyes studied her. He nickered in soft invitation, and after a moment she moved slowly toward him.

"Who are ye? Ye're very handsome; but how did ye get inside, and where do ye belong?" Jane asked, as if the stallion could answer her. He nodded his head, indicating a dark corner by the farthest stall. Jane's eyes followed his gaze.

A shimmering of green light came from the corner, and a soft voice said, "He belongs with me."

Then a beautiful lady, dressed in a dark cape over a long, flowing green velvet gown, stepped gracefully out of the shadows and smiled at Jane.

Jane's startled eyes moved from the horse to the beautiful lady and back again. She could not decide which of them was more of a marvel.

"Ye and yon stallion are the reason my horses are not afraid of this frightful storm," Jane said, matter-of-factly.

"True," said the Lady. "We reminded them that the storm need not trouble them. They kindly permitted us to rest in the barn for a short while."

Jane stared at the Lady. "Ye're magic, aren't ye?" she asked boldly, although her eyes were wide with wonder.

"Some would say so," the Lady laughed.

Jane raised an eyebrow, which was no mean feat since her eyes were already open quite as wide as they would go. "And would they be right?" she countered, her hope rising.

The Lady clapped her hands in delight. "They would," she confirmed with a wink.

The girl now stood between the stallion and the Lady. "Ye're a princess! A fairy princess, are ye not!" As she spoke the words, Jane realized how much she wanted them to be true.

The Lady shook her head, but there was a merry twinkle in her brown eyes. "No, not a Faerie princess, not any longer. I am the Queen now. But then, you knew it all along, did you not?"

The Queen of Faerie, for so she was, held her hand out to Jane, who took it without hesitation. "What is your name?" she asked the girl.

"Jane," said the child. "And this is our farm, my Da's and Ma's and mine. These horses are Mae and Gilly and Thorn."

"So they told us," the Queen said. "Very polite and clever horses they are, too."

Jane placed the lamp on the corner of a tack box; it had grown too heavy in her small hand. The Queen of the Faeries was in her barn! She could barely contain her excitement, but her mind was crowding with questions. Being a practical girl, she asked some of them. "Why are ye here?"

The Queen gathered her soft green skirts and sat down in the hay with a cheerful sigh. "Cassane," and she indicated her stallion with a nod of her chin, "has a stone bruise on his hoof, and needed to rest before we continue on our journey."

"Where are ye going, Yer Majesty?" Jane's question was polite.

"Home," replied the Queen.

"But do ye not live in Elfland? It is in all the tales..." Jane blurted, before she could remember her manners.

"We do, Jane. We were on our way when Cassane stumbled."

Cassane snorted at the Queen in unveiled disgust, and shook his head in defiance.

"All right," snapped the Queen, but she wasn't truly angry. "I will own my part of it, but I am not the one who limped away from the encounter, am I?"

The horse made a sound that reminded Jane of the words her father sometimes used that earned a hard look from her mother. Jane giggled behind her hand, so as not to insult the noble stallion.

The Queen arched an eyebrow at Cassane. "See that? Even Jane recognizes your bad language. You should be ashamed, truly."

Cassane looked away from the Queen, and studied a neat pile of hay on the other side of the barn.

The Queen smiled back at Jane. "We should not be here much longer. Cassane is rested enough that we can leave within the hour."

Thunder crackled overhead. "But what about the rain? Ye could catch yer death!"

"It is not far, and Cassane will be careful, will you not, my dear?" The Queen emphasized the word "careful" when she spoke to the horse, who blew a long, glowering breath through his lips at her. "We will hardly get wet at all."

"Because of magic?" Jane wondered aloud.

"Just so. Because of magic," the Queen conceded, patting Jane's arm. "I think you had better go back to the house, Jane; we would not want anyone wondering what has become of you."

"Very well," Jane said , not wanting to leave. "But do ye have need of anything, Yer Majesty? Food, or water? Or a blanket for Cassane? Ye are welcome to whatever we have..."

"That welcome is the greatest gift you could offer on this cold, wet night. We are most grateful. We have need of nothing else.

"Go now, and be safe and warm in your bed." The Queen lifted the lamp from the top of the tack box and handed it back to the girl.

Obediently, Jane accepted the lamp, curtsied to the Queen, then patted Cassane cautiously, memorizing his beautiful face. She was rewarded with what she always believed later was the horse's smile of approval.

When she reached the barn door, Jane turned and asked the Queen wistfully, "Do ye ever think ye'll be back this way again, Yer Majesty?"

"It seems most likely, Jane," replied the Queen with a chuckle.

"Well, then, I hope to see ye again, Yer Majesty, so we can talk more. Good night, then, and safe journey home." Jane closed the barn door behind her and hurried back to the house in the pouring rain.

When Jane crept to the barn early the next morning to feed the horses, the rain had stopped. She hoped against all hoping that she would find the Queen and Cassane still there, but they were gone.

Jane patted each of her horses, and kissed them before she gave them their breakfast oats. "Did Cassane tell ye where they were going? How to find Elfland? She said it wasn't far. Do ye know where they went?"

Mae, Gilly and Thorn never told Jane where the Queen and Cassane had gone.

And Jane never told her father and mother that the Queen of Faerie had spent part of a rainy night in their barn. Not that they would have believed her if she had told them. Jane knew that her parents would not know how.

That day, her busy father walked past the dark corner the Queen had stepped out of the night before, oblivious to the faint sparkling of green light that hovered in the air.

But Jane could see it still shimmering, the evidence of the Queen's presence that would remain for another day before evaporating altogether.

Jane kept her knowledge of the visit by the Queen of Faerie to herself for most of her long life. She eventually inherited the family farm, married a good man, and raised a family of her own with him. Over the years, she told her daughters many times the story of the night the Queen of Faerie and her stallion stayed in the barn.

For the whole of her life, she kept a watchful eye and a safe, ready room for an unheralded visit from the Queen. Jane never gave up her dream of welcoming the Queen as she moved to and from Elfland.

Jane's youngest daughter, Jeanne, was enthralled by the oft-told tale of the rainy-night encounter; the child grew up waiting for a visit by the Queen. With that in mind, Jeanne, when she grew up and eventually inherited the farm and raised her own family, had a cottage built near the barn as a guest house intended for use only by the Queen of Faerie.

And who is to say that, over the generations, the Queen did not come to stay from time to time?

IT WAS GOING to be a peaceful day, Thomas thought as he closed the book he had been reading. He sat on the couch in his living room, legs stretched out in front of him, feet on the coffee table. His mood was entirely neutral; he felt as strongly about returning to Los Angeles as he did about staying put here in Elvenhome. Nothing was clawing at him. He was calm, rested, cheerful, and relaxed.

He considered heading for the Library and getting a few more books. He also considered changing his tunic and breeches and going for a solitary run. Or he could play his guitars, or mess around with his harp. He knew that a jam session with some of his Fey musician buddies could be arranged without much effort.

The next Friday Afternoon Poker Game was two days away. He grinned when he thought about it. He (and everyone else, including His Grace Mr. Green) had lost spectacularly to Menace three weeks ago. The Spriggan was as natural a player as he was an unnatural one. He treated the game like a secret religion, which invited all kinds of teasing that Menace completely ignored.

Mr. Green, Thomas noted, was developing a distinct preference for Texas Hold 'Em. There was a sideline pool going about when Johnny Carson would end up roaring frustrated profanity specifically directed at Mr. Green. Zodiac had a lot of coin riding on that one, Boston too. Thomas could hardly wait for this week's game. He ignored the stray thought that it would be the last one...

Thomas almost could not believe that his year and a day would be over in only three days' time. On the other hand, he was getting a little excited about returning home. He focused on Los Angeles to keep himself from having too many thoughts about the fact that he was leaving all of his Fey friends, and most of all Callie, so very soon.

He forced his mind to switch tracks, and it did.

Today Callie would be engaged with Queen Stuff until dinner, so he was content to be on his own. He had come to realize how much he enjoyed the quiet around him, and the quiet within himself; this was something he would take with him when he left Faerie. He had learned to be still, and was comfortable not speaking to anyone for surprisingly long periods of time. He marveled at how much, and how essentially, he had changed.

Sitting back on the couch, he made up his mind to head for the Library in a while. Right now, he was going to try to think of something to give Callie as a remembrance gift.

They were going to spend time in the Queen's Tower Room the day after tomorrow. She'd told him that he could take away any object he saw there as a token of her affection. It still seemed strange to him that he would take something of hers to remind him of her, when she seemed certain that he would be *unable* to remember her after he left. He wasn't sure she was right about that, really. How could he forget anything about her, or anything about this year? Even if she was right (and he acknowledged that there was, of course, a chance of that), he had written songs here about people he knew and cared about. Certainly the new songs, inspired by his time with the High Queen of Faerie and all of her Folk, would remind him of his life among them. They'd have to, wouldn't they?

223

He'd taken her seriously, though, when she'd insisted that he write down everything he'd composed this year. He recognized the determined look in her eyes, and decided that he was not going to take chances, despite his strong conviction that he'd remember everything on his own. Hell, he remembered stuff he'd written when he was in his twenties, really terrible stuff he'd never played for anyone. Still, Thomas gave Callie points for taking care of the music, even if her concerns were unnecessary. He mentally thanked her, and thought about the blank book he'd begun to fill with carefully-notated sheet music: all the completed songs, but also the stray melody lines, the lyrics he hadn't composed music for, even ideas he'd had that hadn't turned into anything yet. He had it all, in his head as well as on paper. He could never forget his music, but it pleased him to please her, and there it was.

There was a knock on his front door. He got up off the couch, and answered it.

Professor Plum was at the door. Thomas waved him in with a smile.

"Hi." Thomas said.

"Hello, Thomas," Professor Plum greeted him. "Mr. Green sent me. He invites you to attend him in his rooms."

"What?" Thomas' brain had stalled a little at the unexpected mention of Mr. Green. *Attend* him?

"Mr. Green," Professor Plum repeated with the courtesy of a seasoned courtier. "Mr. Green would like you to join him." The handsome Merrow's eyes twinkled with merriment. "Now, Thomas, if you please."

Thomas did not know what to do with this information.

"Come, my friend. I shall accompany you."

It was true that Thomas and Mr. Green were getting to know each other a bit better over cards, but apart from their first encounter a year ago, and the more recent one five weeks ago, they had never spoken in a private setting. Going to the King's rooms meant that Thomas would be unable to speak. He wasn't sure if this was a good thing or a bad thing. Surely, all things considered, it could go either way, couldn't it? He looked at Professor Plum again, and tried to sound like he wasn't nervous, wondering where Callie was, or Zodiac. "I guess we go see Mr. Green."

"All is well, Thomas. There is nothing to fear," the King's Man told him, with a smile of amused reassurance. "Bring your harp."

Ten minutes later, Thomas, carrying his harp, dashed behind Professor Plum, who moved through the corridors and up a spiral staircase. At the top of the stairs, Professor Plum made a left turn and said to Thomas, "Hurry along, Thomas. This way."

Thomas wasn't sure why they were scurrying through the castle. He knew he'd never been in this area before. The King's apartments had to be located around here, almost opposite from where Callie's were located. He wanted to slow down and look around, but Professor Plum was having none of that.

"Come *on*, Thomas! Speed!"

The King's Man darted through what appeared to be a gathering crowd. Thomas followed him. He did not want to get lost because he did not have permission to speak. He jogged after Professor Plum.

Folk had crowded the corridor, but moved aside as Professor Plum stepped around them, with Thomas coming up behind, up to a closed door. Stopping and catching his breath, Professor Plum turned to face Thomas, and smiled. "Wait, now."

Thomas looked around at all the Folk gathered here in the hallway. There were quiet rumblings of conversation, but he couldn't quite get the gist. Why was everyone standing here? What *was* this place?

And then he heard it.

It began as almost a whisper of sound, and took shape in a heartbeat.

A harp whispered, made a soft promise, and began to sing.

225

The Folk in the hallway were instantly silent, inhaling the music.

The harp's whisper grew bolder, then almost whimsical as it hinted at the magic to come.

Thomas watched the Folk. Some had closed their eyes, others had joyous tears running down their faces, but everyone was caught up in the song of the harp.

He listened as a musician as well as part of the audience, and felt every note. The melody was playful and bright even as it inched toward a different kind of emotion. A quieter, almost wistful tone rose from behind the happier one, then stepped in front of it.

Thomas gasped, along with many of his neighbors.

The song was vibrant, but it was also sweetly sad. Pain and loss, yearning, hoping, and dreaming wove themselves achingly into the sound. Thomas felt it all, and trembled in empathy with the harper. The playing of the gorgeous piece was flawless, and Thomas could only imagine what the instrument must look like. He marveled that what he was hearing could come from an instrument similar to the one he held in his arms.

And then Thomas tasted it; there was passion, love, anger and, somehow, *joy* dancing in the music sung by the harp. Tinged with longing, the harper's heart was wide open. Thomas could have wept.

When it was over, the hallway was enveloped in silence for a long moment, followed by applause and cheers in a language Thomas could not understand. Then, as if by some tacit understanding, the Folk began to disengage and go about their business.

He watched them move away, and then looked at Professor Plum. Thomas very nearly forgot about his obligation to silence. He needed to know what it was he'd just heard, and where it had come from. Part of his mind was trying to memorize the complex melodies that had taken his breath away, while his heart was holding on to what the skill and the soul of the musician had made him feel. Thomas was both excited about what he'd heard, and also humbled by the complex magnificence it. He wondered if he could make his companion understand.

Professor Plum gave him a warm smile. He, too, had been touched by the harp's song. "Come, Thomas," he said, opening the door in front of them. "It is even more profound when you know the harper."

Thomas took a deep breath, reminded himself once again that he could not speak, and followed Professor Plum through the door, into the apartments of the King.

There were seven King's Men in attendance, some seated and talking, two serving, one entering from another door. The King himself was sitting on a long, backless couch.

Thomas scanned the room at once for the musician who had just played for the King, but in the room there were only Mr. Green and his Men. He didn't see a harp anywhere. Where had the harper gone? He wanted to invite the musician to his place and talk about...

Mr. Green nodded a greeting at Thomas, but addressed Professor Plum. "Why are you here now? I asked you to bring him at nightfall."

Professor Plum smiled at his King. "He is early."

"So I see," said Mr. Green.

Professor Plum laughed. "I thought Thomas might enjoy the music, Sire. Nor did I want to miss it."

Thomas was still looking around for the harper.

Mr. Green sighed.

"I apologize, Thomas Lear. I did have a plan. I had hoped that you'd already have permission to speak before you arrived. I can't blame him, though. He knows I only ever play eight songs in a sitting, and it has been a long time since I played where anyone else can hear." He nodded at his Man. "Professor Plum, take the Court Singer with you, go and find one of the Queen's Ladies, and ask her to ask the Queen to granted leave for him to speak while he is here."

Professor Plum bowed, then turned to leave, indicating that Thomas should follow.

The Court Singer's mind was occupied with something else: *Holy shit...the harper whose music had so enthralled him was His Grace, Mr. Green.*

Thomas raced his fingers over the harp to get Mr. Green's and Professor Plum's immediate attention. When they were both looking at him in surprise, Thomas shook his head violently, and pointed to Professor Plum.

"You don't want me to go?" his friend asked. "You don't want us to ask for permission for you to speak?"

Thomas shook his head again, slower this time, so they could read his firm intention. *I don't want to talk, and mess this up. I want to listen, and learn. Right now.*

Mr. Green watched Thomas for a moment, then smiled. "You're certain?"

Thomas nodded, grateful to be understood. He sank into a chair. The consummate musician/poet in Thomas studied the King, his eyes wide and filled with respect and fascination. If he could have spoken, he would have admitted that he was staggered by the eloquent beauty of what he had heard. What he couldn't have said out loud was how deeply moved he was by the visible, inexpressible elegance and utter majesty in the soul of the man who sat across from him.

Mr. Green studied Thomas carefully. "Are you certain that you will not forget that you need to be silent? I would not wish to be the unwitting instrument that caused you to break your obligation."

Thomas nodded once, and met Mr. Green's eyes with a determined look.

One of the unseen benefits of being forcibly schooled to silence is that I have actually learned to shut up and listen, Thomas thought, mentally beaming his words at his host. He did not want to waste the opportunity to hear anything that Mr. Green might have to say.

"Well then," Mr. Green said in almost a whisper, "perhaps it is time for us to talk about harps. Rather, for

228

me to talk about harps, and for you to listen and learn." If Thomas noticed that Mr. Green sighed, or that he may have somehow heard Thomas' thought, the Court Singer chose not to acknowledge it.

Mr. Green gestured to a Dwarf who stood by a stained-glass door. The Dwarf went through the door and, a moment later, returned and handed him the King's harp, and with a deep bow, left again.

It was a beautiful instrument, made of a hardwood Thomas had never seen before. There was a tree engraved on and around the harp's front pillar.

Thomas sat and watched, fascinated by the thing. It struck him that the King's harp had a distinct aura of timelessness; it looked new and untouched, eager to be played for the first time, and all but shimmered in awareness of its own allure. At the same time, the harp gave Thomas the subtle impression that she was wise beyond her years and long-loved, often-played, and cherished for time out of memory.

"A beauty, is she not?" asked Mr. Green.

Thomas nodded, transfixed by the energy he sensed in the instrument.

"I have belonged to this harp for...a very long while," Mr. Green said with a wry smile. "A long time, but somehow never too long a time." He beckoned Thomas to move closer, to a seat nearer his own. "So you can see what I'm going to teach you."

Thomas rose from his chair and carried his harp to where Mr. Green had pointed. He sat down.

Mr. Green appraised Thomas' harp. "Very pretty indeed. Is this the one Her Grace gave you?"

Thomas nodded again.

"It has a sweet soul. Her Grace chose well." Mr. Green looked at Thomas. "Have you begun to truly know this harp? Does she know your touch?"

Thomas shrugged, then frowned.

"That's all right, I meant no offense. The knowing of a harp takes time, and you have been attending to other

229

things. I am not criticizing." Eyeing Thomas, Mr. Green asked again: "Wouldn't you prefer to be able to speak? We can do this later today, or perhaps we could move to your rooms now."

Thomas shook his head in a firm negative, and indicated that Mr. Green should continue. Mr. Green watched Thomas for another moment, and then he made a decision.

"Very well, Thomas Lear. I will show you something about the harp that no one else can teach you."

It was not like any of the hundreds of formal or casual music lessons Thomas had had throughout his life, either as a child, a tense teen, or as a professional musician. He watched, listened, and imitated Mr. Green.

"With your head and your heart, together," Mr. Green said for the fourth time, patiently watching Thomas attempt to grasp the concept. "Together. As when, I'd imagine, you are composing your songs, or getting ready to sing them to the Folk. Together!"

It took more time than expected. But when Thomas finally opened his mind and his heart at the same time, and moved his hands along the strings as instructed, the harp in Thomas's lap sang sweetly, a smooth sound of love, desire, and joy that Thomas could have lost himself in.

The Court Singer grinned, feeling ridiculously proud of himself. This was fun.

"I do not often give instruction, Thomas Lear," Mr. Green chuckled, "But it is a pleasure indeed to show you how to know your harp." He was impressed that Thomas was such a quick study. It made sense to him, since the Court Singer's heart and mind were filled with music. The King noted to himself the presence of a depth of music Thomas hadn't heard within himself yet, music that waited patiently to be felt and composed.

Eventually, after a few lame attempts, Thomas got the sense of what Mr. Green was showing him, and he smiled as he mirrored Mr. Green and added clear, sweet notes to the basic melody that his host teased from his own harp.

"Don't touch the strings as if she were a wanton woman, Thomas Lear," Mr. Green reminded him. "She is not simply solid matter, she is spirit. She is not a guitar, she is a harp. You must discover the *nature* of a harp. She does not want to be stroked; she wishes to be firmly, confidently plucked."

It was all Thomas could do to not laugh out loud. Instead, he bit his lip hard and focused on what he was doing.

Mr. Green was delighted by how well Thomas was able to move from basic instruction to a solid understanding of what the harp needed. He was pleased when Thomas played almost-recognizable renditions of three songs from the *Dangerous Blue Eyes* album.

If the Court Singer could have spoken, and if he and Mr. Green had compared opinions, it might have been debatable which of them had enjoyed the royal harp lesson more.

"I did not plan to talk to you about the nature of harps, and yet here we are," Mr. Green began, as he handed his beautiful harp back to the Dwarf, who carried it away. "You seem to be of a mind to hear me, for reasons of your own. I assume it has something to do with the close of your time here as Court Singer."

Thomas shrugged, his eyes filled with questions he would not have known how to ask even if he could have spoken.

"I have played many harps over the long years. I think you will agree that there are certain instruments, your own guitar you brought from Upworld, for example, that we would chose above all others. Although I think you'll also agree that it often serves us to play our music on any instrument that comes to us.

"I see that you understand. I can admit it freely, Thomas Lear: I have only truly cherished one harp for the whole of my life. I honor that harp as no other, whether I make music with her, or stand aside and know she is being played by another harper.

"Over the years when I abandoned the King's harp for…music of another kind, or lived in a way that denied the music she made, nothing ever altered the truth of the matter. The King's harp is filled with life, with love, and magic, whoever plays her, for however long. And her enchanting music makes her song all the more beautiful."

Mr. Green's smile was gentle, directed more at himself than for Thomas' benefit. Thomas' gaze was glued to Mr. Green's face; Mr. Green was looking out the window. "Losing sight of the music itself, and pulling away from the source of our music, is a choice that we make, often in confusion and misguided frustration. If there is a tragedy, it is that we unwittingly persuade ourselves that the instrument we love, one that best reveals the radiance of our songs, can no longer make the music that we know is in us, and we cleverly, angrily, defiantly shut the beloved instrument away, without realizing that the instrument remains alive and well on its own. We are fools; it is ourselves, and our own music, that we have shut away."

Mr. Green looked back at Thomas, his smile a little sheepish now. He mentally shook himself. "Harps. Interesting souls, no? By the Light, we may as well have been drinking, Thomas Lear, for all I've rambled." He gestured, and Professor Plum brought a tray to the table beside Mr. Green: two goblets, two carafes of wine. Professor Plum poured from one carafe, and served Mr. Green a goblet with a bow. Then he poured wine from the second carafe and handed the second goblet to Thomas. "French, Thomas. *Drink, free from care.*"

The Court Singer nodded his thanks to both his friend the Professor and Mr. Green. The two musicians saluted each other with their goblets, and drank in a companionable silence.

Thomas' mind was not silent, however. It whirled in circles, absorbing everything Mr. Green had said. He also thought about the things Mr. Green *hadn't* said, and the context in which he'd placed his stunningly direct metaphor. Lyrics and melody lines flooded his brain at the same time, too, and he thought he might drown in the overlay of emotion that filled him. He felt guilt and compassion, respect and wry humor, laughter and loss, sadness and joy, irony and victory, love, desire, wisdom, understanding and conviction—all at once.

And, while it startled him, he realized that he didn't mind a bit. He just sat back, and drank it all in.

Someone Thomas did not recognize, a middle-aged Brownie with big, backward feet, scurried to stand before Mr. Green. "Sire..."

Mr. Green sighed. "Yes, yes, I know." He smiled at Thomas. "I regret that our one-sided conversation must come to a close, Thomas Lear. Professor Plum will escort you back to your apartments, if you like." He rose, and so did Thomas. "Extraordinary that you never spoke aloud, although I suppose I didn't give you much opportunity, did I?"

Thomas smiled broadly, and bowed his thanks.

"For the harp lesson?"

Thomas nodded. His gaze darted to the furnishings around them, visually searching for what he wanted. He moved to a table that had a pen, ink, and paper sitting on it. He thought for a few seconds, nodded to himself, then put pen into ink and then to paper, and scribbled a quick note.

When he finished, he picked up his note, walked back to where Mr. Green was standing, and handed it to him. Mr. Green watched Thomas return to collect to his harp, lift it, and walk back toward His Grace. Then Thomas bent down, and placed the beautiful harp that Callie had given him at Mr. Green's feet, a look of open respect shining in his dark eyes.

Mr. Green looked down at the piece of paper in his hand, and read it.

Thank you, Your Majesty. Done is done. I think I almost understand.

Mr. Green's gray eyes met Thomas' brown ones. His voice came in a whisper. "Are you certain of that, Thomas Lear?"

Thomas nodded, and slowly offered Mr. Green his hand in friendship.

The Court Singer and the High King of Faerie shook hands.

"It may be that you are, at that." Mr. Green took a breath. "But finish the song. For her sake. And for yours as well."

Thomas' face wrinkled in genuine consternation. If he'd had a revelation over the past hour or so, Mr. Green had just confused the matter considerably. Questions and denials danced in Thomas' eyes as he willed Mr. Green to see the problem.

Mr. Green understood. "If there is jealousy, or anything else for that matter, on my part, it is of little consequence. That is merely the way of it." He squeezed Thomas' hand for emphasis. "Know that all is well in the way of enchantment. You must finish what you have begun, my friend. For the sake of *all* of the music, Court Singer, finish the song, and finish it well."

thirteen

DOES HE SEEM distracted? Orchid asked herself as she, Violet and Rose watched Thomas address the thing called "pizza" that had been brought to him two minutes before. The Ladies were pleased to be keeping Thomas company while he waited for the Queen to visit for the night.

It occurred to Orchid that perhaps he was thinking, with mixed emotions, about his journey home and his parting from Her Grace. Something in his eyes told her that although Thomas was laughing and talking, there was much on his mind.

"But you said the pizza is all wrong, Thomas," a confused Rose was saying, scratching her head underneath her tall blue hat.

The Court Singer nodded, his voice pretending theatrical sadness, while his face was alive with laughter (and a touch of fascination) as he poked at the pizza with his finger. "It *is* all wrong. These are huge chunks of pepperoni, too big to get into your mouth. The skin's still on the onion. If the crust was any thinner, it would be a cracker. The sauce is close, but not quite right. The cheese didn't melt very much, and I'm afraid to think about why. There are supposed to be sliced olives here. I think they might be grapes, which is just a little creepy..."

Violet fluttered on her purple wings in front of Thomas' face as he inspected the pizza, which had been presented on a large serving platter. "If it is not what you want, tell Zodiac, and he will have it taken away."

"Can't do that," Thomas said. "I mentioned pizza to him about a week ago, and I have no doubt he made a great effort to manage getting the ingredients and a recipe...I doubt the Castle's within anyone's delivery range." This made him laugh. "I know that everything about this pizza came from Upworld, and everyone tried...can you imagine Hobs attempting to order one in person from a pizzeria? God, what I'd give to see that!"

There had even been a short-lived, creative but useless plan to have pizza delivered to Sheila at Queensgate Inn, and dash it through the Portal.

"If it is not what you wanted, you should tell Zodiac," Orchid repeated, eyeing the strange thing with suspicion.

"Well, it's not, exactly," Thomas had to admit. He looked at the pizza some more, gently swept Violet out of the way with his hand and, with a dubious look on his face, lifted a slice.

He took a bite out of it.

He chewed tentatively, swallowed, and took another bite.

Six Fey eyes watched him in wonder, waiting while he finished the slice and then, to their amazement, immediately reached for another.

"Thomas!" Rose exclaimed, her voice shrill in disbelief. "If it is 'all wrong,' why are you eating it?"

He shrugged at them, and then winked. "Because, Ladies, like it or not, pizza is pizza."

Later, they sat around and chatted. Thomas told them a little about his spontaneous harp lesson with Mr. Green.

"And you played your harp with the King?" Orchid gasped in astonishment.

"I did. Well, *he* played, and I sort of tagged along." Thomas' eyes grew bright. "I learned a lot today."

The Ladies drank Faerie wine from the large carafe they'd brought with them, and Thomas drank a lusty cabernet. He was sprawled on the couch, with his feet up, Violet hovering above his sneakers. Orchid and Rose shared one of the big chairs, relaxed and happy.

"You were going to tell Thomas the gossip," Violet reminded Rose.

"The gossip?" Rose asked, her face a blank when she looked at Violet, then at Orchid, and back at Violet. "Which gossip? Oh yes! The gossip!"

Thomas put down his goblet. "There's gossip?"

"Oh my, yes!" Rose assured him with many nods of her head. "We have heard that there is every chance that Swiftaine—oops, you know, Swiftaine..." She looked at Orchid for help. "What is his other name?"

"'Menace'," Orchid reminded her.

"That's right! 'Menace' will be knighted by Their Majesties at the Winter Solstice this year! He'll be Sir...um...Menace!"

"For his service in defending and protecting Lord Guardian's Lady Maggie during the terrible doings Upworld, during the Mischief," Violet added, with an approving nod.

"It has been several hundred years since Their Majesties have rewarded anyone in this way, so there will be a huge celebration," said Orchid. "The hope is that Lord Guardian will return to Elvenhome for the event."

Laughing, Violet did a summersault in the air. "The *gossip* is that we all hope he will bring Lady Maggie with him!"

A small part of Thomas wished that he would be here to see Guardian and Maggie again. He let the thought go, grudgingly, and changed the subject.

"You know that I'm going to the Queen's Tower Room tomorrow," he began, and gave them his best smile. "Can you tell me what I'm going to see?"

"You shall see it tomorrow, no doubt," Rose giggled.

"I have something in mind. I'd like to surprise her. I'm going to need your help. I need information, you know, to make the surprise work." He thought for a moment, considering possibilities. "What does she keep in there? Do those things have stories?"

"Everything in her Room has a story, Thomas," Orchid said with an air of affectionate solemnity. "Perhaps Her Grace would prefer to tell you herself about things she shows you."

Considering this, Thomas nodded. "You may be right about that. I would not like to spoil her fun, even for the sake of a surprise."

Violet, Rose and Orchid looked at each other, excitement growing and radiating around them. Violet moved to a position close to the top of Thomas' head, and studied his face, examining his intention. "Might the surprise be a new song?" she asked, the thought making her breathless.

Caught out, Thomas nodded. "The last song I'll write in Faerie," he told them.

The Queen's Ladies met each other's eyes, and after what seemed like a long moment, all agreed to help Thomas with his surprise for Her Grace.

"Allow me, Ladies," Thomas said, and he sat up and poured Faerie wine into their goblets, and the saucy little cabernet into his own. He flashed them a most charming smile as he settled back into the couch. "Now...tell me magical, romantic tales of the Queen's Tower Room. Come, come, Ladies! Details! I need details!"

THE NEXT DAY, the Queen sat on the luxurious couch in her Tower Room and looked around approvingly. "Very nice," she said to Iris and Dahlia, who had just finished dusting and straightening things a little. "I appreciate your help. It has been some time since I've had anyone in here, and I wanted all to be ready for Thomas' visit."

Iris smiled at Callie. "I know this is hard for you, Your Grace. It heralds the truth that your year with your Singer

238

is coming to a close. This time is always particularly bittersweet, is it not?"

"I think it depends on the Singer," Dahlia murmured, eliciting a chuckle from Iris and the Queen.

"I daresay it does. This time is indeed bittersweet," Callie nodded. "But today is a good day, and Thomas will see where I spend my private time. We will have a lovely afternoon."

"There will be time for sadness later. There always is," Iris reminded Her Grace quietly.

Callie shrugged and said nothing.

"Come along, Dahlia," Iris admonished the Dwarf princess who, dust-towel in hand, stood staring in adoration at a framed pencil sketch of the Queen. "Thomas will be here soon, and Her Grace has no further need of either of us."

Iris nodded at Callie, and was followed out by Dahlia, who bowed to the Queen as she passed.

Callie was alone. She sighed with contentment. She loved it here: her refuge, her retreat, her cheerful escape, her cave, her corner, and her playroom. She rarely shared it. Most of her Court Singers had spent time in it (if ever) only once. Her Ladies, her friends, her councilors, and even her husband had understood her need for a space untouched by anyone else's energy, and few entered the spacious, airy, light-filled space, which was filled with the wealth of Callie's personal life.

She wanted Thomas to come here, and to get a deeper sense of who she was through what he saw collected in the room. She wanted him to know her well, even if it was only for this afternoon. What would he glimpse of her that he hadn't known about her before? They had come to understand each other. They had spent much time together talking and touching. She would have said that Thomas Lear might know her better than any of the other Court Singers she'd brought here. He might even know her more completely than anyone else ever had, except for Arrendel and Garrhyn, and perhaps Ban.

She knew the truth of this, too, that knowing him well, and loving him deeply, would make their parting that much more painful.

He would grieve the loss of her, and miss her—for a few long heartbeats. Then the enchantment would fade away, and he would forget her.

But she would always remember. And remembering, she would ache for him.

The knock on the door snapped her into the present, moved her away from thoughts of the pain that awaited her when he was gone, and into the pleasure of spending time with the man she loved.

"Come," Callie called, rising from the couch with a genuine smile. This was going to be fun. She would hold the memories of this day close to her heart.

The door opened, and Carnation, Juniper, Orchid and Violet entered, surrounding Thomas, who was carrying the guitar Callie had given him. They all looked at the Queen expectantly.

Callie opened her right hand, and green light flickered in the Tower Room. "You are free to speak here, Thomas, from this moment until the time you return to your own rooms."

Thomas bowed to his Queen, exchanged a few easy pleasantries with the Ladies around him, and then stepped into the round Tower Room. The Ladies bowed to Callie, and left, chatting as they went down the Tower's staircase.

"Welcome, my dear," Callie began, as Thomas stood the guitar against the wall, then strode across the floor to kiss her hello.

Her smile was radiant when he released her. "I'm ready for my tour, Your Grace," Thomas declared. He walked over to the North window and looked out. "Wow. Great view."

Callie looked out the window, too. "Yes. You can see the village from here. And the far end of the forest."

The views from all four windows impressed Thomas. "It must be beautiful under the moon," he said as he looked west. "Imagine moonlight, stars, and this view."

"Yes, it can be breathtaking. It's also peaceful, and quiet at times, and noisy and busy at other times. I can sit and watch from any of these windows and love everything I see."

He understood. "You can be unreachable for a time, with the Folk knowing you're watching them, watching over them, and resting up from past Queen Stuff so you can deal with present and future Queen Stuff."

"Something like that," she agreed.

For the next hour, Callie showed Thomas some of her treasures.

He looked at the books in her glass-fronted bookcase, books written and bound by hand, stories told and thoughts revealed that had never been published. He was fascinated. At her request, he sat on the couch beside her and read several poems aloud from one of the oldest books in her collection. He did his best to not be mesmerized, but confessed with a grin that it was probably too late for him not to be, all things considered.

Thomas was impressed by the delicate sketch in black ink of Elvenhome Castle that hung above the fireplace. When Callie revealed to him who had created it, Thomas looked at it again, with awe and delight. There was a drawing of Callie hung above a tall dresser at the west side of the round Room that looked as though it could have been drawn yesterday.

"Not three hundred years ago?" Callie asked.

"No," Thomas said, stunned.

"Yes," she laughed.

Thomas was especially taken with the bronze-and-stone cup Callie had received as a gift from Dwarf friends long ago. He loved watching her show off her vast collection of jewelry and precious stones. He liked looking at the small pieces of sculpture, the paintings, the things he'd consider knick-knacks if they had belonged to anyone else. Here, they were on the scale of museum-quality properties, combined with the sense of deeply personal belonging. Everything was beautiful, and everything was very much a part of Callie.

His eyes widened in appreciation of the in-laid amethyst design on a small, round table that had to be older than he could imagine, and an instrument that looked like a kind of mandolin. The carving on its neck was a detailed design of a large bird in flight. It had to be priceless.

"That belonged to my grandfather's youngest brother. He was a troubadour of some renown in his time." Callie indicated that he could pick up the instrument and play with it, but he shook his head and took a step away; it was too wondrous a thing for Thomas to feel comfortable about touching. Callie ran her fingers over the strings for him, and Thomas smiled at the delicate sound.

"Hey, where's all of your needlework?" Thomas asked, looking around. "I thought you'd have some hanging on your walls."

"I give most of it away," she admitted. They moved to the huge armoire in the south of the Room, and Callie opened doors and drawers, and showed him. She was proud of the needlework, and pleased about his interest in it. There were about a dozen pieces in various stages of completion, and Callie had stories about each one. She opened drawers, showing him fine silk threads, delicate linens, and drawings she wanted to reproduce on them.

They were still sitting on the couch talking about the last of the needle work projects when there was a double-knock on the door. Carnation entered the Room with a broad smile, carrying a tray that held two goblets and a bottle of wine. "Crackers, and cheese, too, from Upworld," she added.

After Carnation had gone, Callie poured wine and reminded Thomas about taking something from her Tower Room as a remembrance. "Have you seen anything specific that you'd like to have?"

"I don't need to take anything, Callie. Seeing it all, and learning about where it came from, is more than enough."

"You must choose and take something. It's tradition. An important one, for me."

"All right. But I would hate to think I'd take something from here, and then have you decide once I'm gone that you didn't want to part with it."

"Don't worry about that. It won't happen."

"Okay. I'll give it some thought." He stood up, walked over to his guitar, and brought it back to the couch.

He sang to her for the next hour, and then they made love as the day slid into a sweet, blue-gray dusk.

"Choose something, Thomas," she said later, indicating the treasures in the Room. "*The Gift honors the Giver*, as my people used to say."

"All right," he said, more to placate her than anything else. He felt that he already had everything he could ever need from her, but couldn't find a way to tell her so that wouldn't sound incredibly lame.

He got up from the couch, kissed her as she lay there, and took a last stroll around the spectacular room, looking for something innocuous that would honor her.

Everything looked too important, too valuable, to potentially precious to her. He didn't want to take anything away.

He decided to go for simple.

He moved toward the armoire that held her needlework supplies and unfinished projects. That seemed like a safe bet, so he slowed as he approached the huge collection of drawers and doors, and stopped, then looked back at his Queen.

Callie beamed with pleasure, and nodded permission for him to look inside.

Thomas studied the armoire. Several of the drawers were still open, as were three smaller doors, and one large one.

One of the small doors was open, but only a crack. He opened it the rest of the way, and reached inside. His hand fell on a small, wooden casket, a little larger than his hand. Callie had not shown him this when she had let look at all of her needlework.

He pulled the casket toward him. It opened easily when he raised the lid.

When Thomas saw what was inside, his heart skipped a beat. He had never seen anything like it before.

In that instant, he knew what he would take with him from Elvenhome that belonged to Callie. He pulled the casket out of the armoire, opened it wider, and felt his heart beat faster and stronger. "Here, Callie. This. I'll take this with me, to remember you."

Thomas turned and showed her what he held in his hands.

Callie's heart stopped. Her face went pale, her eyes filled with confusion and utter disbelief. *No...*

In the casket rested the Moonsong Harp that Garrhyn had given her the night before they were married. They had danced in the garden, under the stars, to music this harp had played for them. She had known it was in the armoire, of course, but she had believed it was well-protected, covered up with linen and other sundries.

She had not specifically mentioned it, nor had she shown him the small casket. It never occurred to her that he would see it, much less choose to take it.

Thomas was thrilled. "Callie, this is wonderful! And it will remind me of the harp you gave me." He looked over at her, and saw that something was wrong. "Callie? What is it?"

She didn't trust herself to speak. She shook her head and tried to look cheerful.

"I don't have to take it, if it's important to you."

She wanted to stand up and cry out *No! No! Not that!* but she could not refuse to let him take the small, sweet harp. The rule of enchantment bound her as firmly to itself as she had bound him for the past year. Although it was tearing her apart, Callie had no choice but to allow Thomas to take the precious harp out of her Room, out of her kingdom, and out of her life.

She nodded her head, and Thomas smiled as he turned toward the door to leave. "I'll see you at dinner...your apartments, or mine?"

The Queen took a breath, and forced herself to speak, a trembling but valiant smile tugging its way to her mouth. She whispered it; it was the only thing she could have said, as she watched Thomas holding the Moonsong harp with a carefree grin on his face.

"Mine."

"WHEN WOULD YOU like your dinner served tonight, Your Grace?" Iris asked as she brushed Callie's hair. "Is Thomas still coming, or are you too upset?"

"Oh, he will be here, and I'm glad of it."

"Will you tell him about the Moonsong Harp, then?"

The Queen sighed. "No. I won't. Done is done."

"Your Grace—"

"Enough. Let's talk about the feast, shall we?"

Callie disliked goodbyes as much as Thomas did, so she decided that there would be a last feast in Thomas' honor with, as usual, much merriment, laughter, music and dancing. Everyone in Elvenhome, both Village and Castle, was invited to celebrate the Court Singer and his music. The event would go on for a day or two, during which time, Thomas would leave.

Iris put the brush down and, with a critical eye, examined her handiwork on Callie's head. "Your plan is to have all the Folk, and Thomas, too, drink so much that none of us remembers that he's leaving?"

Callie said nothing.

Iris frowned. "And that would be that, Lamb?"

The Queen sighed. "Numb is good." After a heartbeat, Callie couldn't help but smile, then she giggled. Iris laughed too. "Oh, it seems like a good way for the Folk to see him, spend a little fun time with him before he goes, and then keep celebrating after he's gone." She looked at Iris seriously. "Doesn't it?"

"Sure and it does, Your Grace."

"Well then," Callie said, "let's find Zodiac and plan tomorrow's festivities."

"Thomas—will he be singing for us, then?"

This made Callie laugh happily. "Of course. He's 'Thomas Lear, Rock Star,' Iris. He wouldn't have it any other way."

THE FINAL CELEBRATION in honor of the Court Singer was a raging success, the kind of event that the Folk would be talking about for several hundred years afterward.

Orchid sat in her seat at the Queen's Table and watched across the Great Hall as Thomas and the Queen danced to the piping and drumming of the Royal Musicians.

Orchid knew she would never forget the things she'd seen at this gathering. Although it was in truth a farewell party, everyone was having a wonderful time. All evening, Folk approached Thomas and shook his hand, or patted his arm, or even hugged him. Tonight was the public goodbye; more private goodbyes with close friends would be said in the morning, and then Thomas would leave Faerie and...

But Orchid did not want to think about that right now. She shook her head, as if to clear it of unhappy thoughts, and watched two pretty Wood Elves kiss Thomas on the cheek.

Yes, it was obvious that the Queen's choice of Court Singer this time was one of her best ever. Everyone liked Thomas, and loved his music.

Orchid's sigh was more wistful than sad. The music had begun again, and across the Hall, Juniper danced with Boston. The beautiful Glaistig moved in provocative, clearly seductive ways that made Orchid gasp in shy delight. The Selkie knew she wasn't the only one who watched the sensual Queen's Lady as she all but floated in Boston's arms. It was so pretty to watch.

Menace was shuffling cards at his place at one of the nearby trestle tables. He shuffled them faster and faster, with his eyes closed. Orchid was amazed by this, also very impressed.

When the dance was over, HobGoblins carried huge trays of food in from the Kitchens, and the Folk moved to tables, and ate as they talked and laughed.

The Queen and Thomas started toward the Queen's Table. Zodiac popped into the space at the Queen's left shoulder, and she stopped to speak with him. Thomas smiled at them both, and walked toward the High Table where Orchid sat.

Just before he was close enough for Orchid to greet him, Professor Plum strode purposefully over to him, whispered in his ear, and the two turned and walked to the other side of the Great Hall.

Orchid followed them with her eyes, twisting in her seat to track them. Where were they going?

Ah, she thought after a long moment. *There.*

The King, surrounded by four of his Men, had entered the Hall from a side door. By the time most of the Folk were aware of his presence, Thomas and Professor Plum had reached him. Both bowed.

The King and Thomas talked for several minutes. Orchid couldn't tell what they were saying. She could only see that both the King and the Court Singer wore serious expressions, and that their conversation was clearly private. Professor Plum had turned his back and was acting as a subtle wall to keep interruptions away.

Just as Orchid was about to get nervous on Thomas' behalf, the King stepped back, slapped Thomas on the back, and the two began to laugh heartily. She could see that both Thomas and and the King had said the word "poker," and remembered that the final Friday Afternoon Poker Game had been held earlier in the day. Intrigued but no longer concerned, Orchid poured more wine into her goblet, and smiled as Thomas made his way back across the Hall. After a minute, he reached the Queen, took Her Grace by the hand, and led her back to the table, chatting and laughing, and sometimes shaking hands with Folk he encountered along the way.

Orchid wondered how well the poker game had gone. Last week Thomas had won a very pregnant cat, which he had (Zodiac said) carefully managed to lose to Menace before the game was over. Gossip had it that Menace was thrilled at the prospect of kittens. Orchid hoped he would know what to do with them when they were born. Perhaps she could help.

She was glad to see that Thomas was having such a grand time. She hoped that the Queen was enjoying herself as much as she seemed to be, but she doubted it. In private, Her Grace was taking the coming separation from Thomas rather hard, although she was determined to appear cheerful.

Only the Queen's Ladies knew otherwise, of course, but they would never betray their beloved Queen's feelings. And for their part, the Ladies were going to miss Thomas very much, too. It was almost too sad to think about.

Orchid sighed again, in contentment this time, as Thomas and Her Grace returned to the table. A HobGoblin brought a heavy tray of mortal food to the Court Singer.

There was much dancing, courtesy of the music provided by several groups of musicians. Over the course of the evening, Thomas danced with all of the Queen's Ladies, and managed to only blush twice while dancing with Juniper.

When he danced with Callie again, he held her close and whispered to her. Enchanted by their affection for each other, the Folk watched as Her Grace and the Court Singer moved elegantly on the open floor. When the dance was done, the happy Folk applauded and cheered their Queen and her lover before returning to the floor to do some wild and wonderful dancing of their own.

Later, Thomas stood in the center of the mostly-cleared Queen's High Table, and played a few songs for the crowded Hall. He sang a couple of his favorite pre-Elvenhome Lear songs, including "Dangerous Blue Eyes," only now he looked down toward where Callie sat, and sang about brown eyes instead.

He also sang the song about Terena, the one he'd written about Lavender, and the first song he'd ever written for Callie.

And then Thomas Lear, Professional Rock Star, Lover of the Queen of Faerie, and also a Friend of a Wise and Gifted Harper, played the song whose lyrics he had finished only this afternoon. He had not yet played it for anyone.

It was about love, letting go and, interestingly, a lonely musician and his magnificent, elusive, much-cherished harp. The song told the story about one day when the harp played for him on its own, when he did not have the strength and courage to play it himself. The song was called "Minstrel's Lady."

When Thomas finished singing "Minstrel's Lady," the Folk applauded and stomped their feet, banged stoneware cups against the trestle tables, and danced around in glee. "More! More! More!" they shouted. "Give us more, Thomas! More music! More!"

From where he stood on the table, he could not see Callie and her Ladies, who were seated at the far end, below his direct line of vision. He loved this new song. He hoped that the Folk – and his Queen – liked it, too.

Standing high above everyone, Thomas' eyes scanned the gathering. At another High Table, at the opposite end of the huge Hall, Mr. Green sat with his Men, and several of their own ladies, enjoying the feast and the Folk and the music. Mr. Green was still visibly moved by what he'd heard Thomas sing and play.

Across the huge Hall, the Court Singer's eyes met and held Mr. Green's eyes. Thomas' studied, professional stage smile slid into a private, personal one, and Mr. Green raised an eyebrow.

"More, Thomas! More!" roared the crowd.

Thomas addressed the Folk, but his gaze kept returning to Mr. Green. "I am something of a minstrel, but I confess that I am no true harper, though perhaps, with five hundred years of practice..." (here the Folk laughed heartily) "...I might be, someday," Thomas began, and the Folk grew quiet, to hear him. "No, I am no harper. I am a simple, mortal Court Singer who lives for his guitar and his music. Like you, the music means everything to me."

There was quiet mass agreement throughout the Hall.

"And yet," continued Thomas, still meeting Mr. Green's gray eyes across the Hall, "I think I have learned that there is much more to music, and to magic, than I ever dreamed.

"You have each and all, in your way, helped me to see magic and music in different lights, for new reasons, and I will be forever changed by that." Thomas couldn't help it; he laughed. "Whether on the morrow I remember it specifically, or not."

He moved to get down from the table upon which he'd been standing for quite some time. "I need whisky, and some merry music! Aren't there a bunch of pipers in the Hall somewhere?"

And with that, Thomas jumped from the table, and a band of pipers, led by Count Basie, began to play from the King's end of the Hall. He handed his guitar to a HobGoblin standing nearby, who would carefully return it to its place in the cabinet in his apartments.

Thomas walked down to where Callie was seated, and sat down beside her. He put his arm around her, and after a few seconds, tried to read her mind. He couldn't.

With uncharacteristic coyness, he asked her what she was thinking about.

"Your new song, of course," she said, giving him a kiss on the cheek. "That was a surprise."

He couldn't help himself. "A good surprise, or...?"

She smiled. "A good surprise. Several surprises. The song is beautiful, and moving, and so...I don't know what. I'd like to hear it again, later."

He was happy to have pleased her.

She met his gaze and chuckled, a delightful, wicked sound. "And although I believe I have an appreciation for the vast and varied company you keep, Court Singer, and I approve of you spending time with the Folk, I must confess that I was not aware of the scope and depth, shall we say, of your growing circle of friends and admirers."

He held his breath. "Have I done something wrong?"

The look on his face made her laugh. "Oh, no! All is well. It is only that I suspect that this is one of the very few times in our history that a Court Singer has ever spent any real time alone with...your 'Mr. Green'...and has come away without a broken bone, or a bruised or sprained something, or a nervous tick, or an attack of the terrors, or the request to have guards posted..."

With a half-smile, Thomas watched Callie as she laughed, and wondered for a fast second if she was really only kidding.

IT WAS TWO hours before dawn. The three Queen's Ladies, who had dutifully attended Her Grace tonight by staying in the wide alcove that sheltered the royal bed chamber beyond, were solemn, and far too quiet.

A sleepy-looking Iris entered the alcove, and looked at Carnation, Juniper and Violet. Their beds had not been slept in; Carnation and Juniper were sitting on a couch. "What's this? Awake yet? And quiet as the grave, not like any one of you. Drink too much at the feast, did you? I know I did."

Violet fluttered in place, beside Juniper's right shoulder. "Not nearly enough," she said, her eyes looking as sad as her voice sounded.

Iris studied the three. "What's amiss, then?"

Not one of the Ladies met her eyes. Carnation stared at her hands, Juniper looked out the window into the

251

grayish darkness, and Violet spiraled upward, evading Iris' gaze.

"Someone tell me at once: Is Her Grace well?"

The Ladies confirmed at once that the Queen was indeed well, and in the next room.

"What, then?" Iris attempted to remain patient.

The Ladies looked at each other. After a long moment, Juniper began, her voice quiet. "Thomas is with Her Grace. After they closed the door, they talked for a while, about nothing specific. She did not require us, and we were content to wait upon her out here, as ever."

"And?" Iris asked.

"After a time, they made love," Violet whispered. "For a long time."

More silence.

Iris hissed in confused frustration. "*And?*"

Carnation looked up at Iris, misery in her eyes. "And after, Her Grace began to cry."

"And was Thomas still with her?"

The three Ladies nodded.

The Elder Lady was exasperated now. "And did he then comfort her?"

Juniper frowned. "He couldn't."

"He couldn't," Violet repeated, with a tremor in her breathy little voice.

Iris did not understand. She knew the Queen was extremely sad about the end of Thomas' year. It was to be expected, since she had fallen in love with him, poor Lamb. Iris was certain that the Queen would get over it in time. She always did.

"Whyever could Thomas not comfort Her Grace's sorrow?"

Carnation closed her eyes, and her voice cracked. "Because he was crying, too."

fourteen

CALLIE STOOD ALONE in Thomas' back garden, and listened to the faint hum of mixed laughter and conversation coming from the group gathered in Thomas' apartments. Friends were saying goodbye, and Callie was content to give them time without her.

She'd needed the break. She had to prepare herself for her last walk with the man she loved. There were so many things she still wanted to say to him. She had to get control of herself, to make sure she came to the end of this tale having done all of it right. She reminded herself of the moment when she had unwisely offered the choice to Michael MacAllistair. That had been a moment too much like this one, when her heart ached, and she faced loneliness again. She had to keep her mind clear, and ignore the crying of her heart so that Thomas could return to his life, and she could return to hers, too.

Her life. Without him.

This was the down side of the enchantment; she knew it well. She would pay the cost of forever carrying the memories of the year they had spent together. He would be free of it before the sun set on this day. She would suffer for a while, and eventually all thoughts of him would be sweet, with occasional twinges of sadness. And need.

She shook her head, and walked further into the garden.

Earlier this morning, looking only a little worse for the emotional strain of the night they'd shared, the Queen and her Court Singer had left the Queen's bed and moved through the castle to Thomas' apartments. Invitations had been sent the day before to specific people Thomas wanted to see before he left. They had begun arriving an hour ago.

Yesterday's farewell feast was still going on in the Great Hall. Callie knew it would carry on all day long. Thomas was being well-celebrated. She couldn't help but smile.

A distinct burst of group laughter danced toward the garden and pulled her focus again. When she had excused herself and left the growing party in the living room, Master Ocelot had just come in the front door. He joined all of the Queen's Ladies, several of the King's Men— including Professor Plum, who had built a strong bond with Thomas over poker, of all things—and Zodiac, Boston and Menace. It seemed that Thomas had made more friends in Elvenhome than any other Court Singer except perhaps Michael MacAllistair, who had (if truth be told) come to her less personally encumbered than Thomas. Michael had the broader, more open heart; Thomas the deeper, more poetic one.

Callie had been blessed with wonderful mortal lovers twice in a row.

She sighed now, and found herself strolling toward the tree that had once been, and still was, her dear friend Lady Sonorielle, named "Lavender" by Thomas Lear. A pretty tree, and in this moment, a comfort to Callie.

"I haven't replaced you, you know," the Queen told the tree off-handishly.

I know. Sweet of you, but unnecessary.

"How tree-like you have become, Sonorielle," Callie almost laughed. "Are you ready to consider rejoining the Court?"

Of course not. I am only beginning my rest.

"All right." It had been worth a shot. "Thomas' year and a day is over today. But you knew that."

I did.

"There is so much..." Callie began, feeling her resolve to remain strong and focused quaver. "I don't want him to go. I miss Arrendel. I do not understand Thomas' relationship with the King. *That* has never happened before. I don't understand *my* relationship with the King, either..." And then Callie began to giggle. "By the Light, I sound remarkably like Arrendel's Maggie!"

What troubles you most?

Callie ran her hand along the tree's trunk. "Thomas is leaving. I didn't expect to love him, not like this. And he has chosen to take the Moonsong Harp with him. I will lose them both this day, Sonorielle, and I cannot understand how this has happened."

You are parting with the Moonsong Harp. It was not a question.

"It would seem so. Strange, is it not?"

He chose it from the Tower Room?

"Yes."

That has always been a foolish but romantic ritual, Your Grace.

"Undeniably, today." The Queen sighed. "Still, I believe I know his heart. I think he may return the Harp to me before he leaves. He has an interesting sense of timing, and carries romance in his soul. It is like him to want to surprise me with the return of it."

I would not put too much hope into that, Your Grace. Love can have much magic in it, or very little in it, but I think that does not matter. Perhaps Love simply IS. Your hope might be disappointed. He might not think to return the Harp. Perhaps he needs it more than you do. Still, I would hate to see you unhappy.

"When did you get so wise, Sonorielle?"

Rhetorical question, Your Grace?

Nodding, Callie smirked at herself, and turned as she heard sound coming toward her.

The other seven of the Queen's Ladies surrounded her a minute later.

"Everyone has gone, except Professor Plum. As soon as we stepped away, they put their heads together and started laughing," Iris reported. "I heard the words 'poker game'."

Rose's tall, orange pointy hat bobbed above her sweet face. "Your Grace?"

"Yes, Rose?"

"Professor Plum just informed Thomas that Mr. Green has come to say goodbye."

Callie knew she shouldn't have been surprised by this, yet somehow she was. It was easy, however, in light of the heaviness of everything else that she carried today, to leave that piece of it alone. She knew she wouldn't ask Thomas about it. She didn't need to.

On the other hand, ever eager for gossip, her Ladies wanted to know what was going on in Thomas' living room, what he and the King were saying to each other, and what it all meant. She waited for the Ladies to realize she wasn't going back inside.

Violet fluttered in the air beside Callie's face. "Are you not returning to Thomas, then, Your Grace, to be present while Thomas and the King speak?"

"What do you think I should do?" she asked her Ladies, to distract them.

As usual, they all started talking at once. The sound of their combined voices soothed her heart. She let them go on for a few minutes, and then put her hand up. They quieted at once.

"Let Thomas and the King have their time to talk. In the meanwhile, you can tell me what you were all laughing about in there, before."

Carnation smiled. "Thomas does not believe that he will forget us. He said he is much smarter than your enchantment, and knows his own mind." The Ladies laughed again. "He is sure of it, and thinks we are daft!"

256

"He said he has an exceptional memory, and that we are, of course, unforgettable," Violet volunteered. "I think he meant me, especially."

Dahlia added, "It is sweet that he does not want to forget us. He thinks he can remember because of Michael, doesn't he?"

"It is my fault he does not believe he will lose his memories of us," said Callie. "But that does not alter the truth of it." She turned to Juniper. "Are all of Thomas' belongings packed and ready?"

Juniper nodded.

"And you are certain that he has written down all of his music, and that it is safely among his things?"

"Yes, Your Grace."

"And Zodiac has told him that everything will be at Queensgate when he arrives there? His guitar, as well?"

"Yes, Your Grace," Orchid said. "I heard Zodiac tell him that the things that he left at the hotel in Edinburgh were retrieved long ago, and would be at his home in America. Someone from Thomas' other life collected them for him last year."

"What did Thomas say to that?"

"He made some remark about 'Faerie spy networks' that I did not understand," Iris admitted.

"But he made himself laugh," Rose pointed out. "It was funny to see him laughing all by himself. Zodiac was a bit unsettled by it, though."

"That was funny, too, Your Grace," Carnation giggled. "His face went red and he sputtered rather a lot."

"Which only made Thomas laugh more," Violet's breathless little voice giggled. "And Zodiac got even redder and called him a 'flaming twit'! Then they hugged each other, and Zodiac popped out of the room in a noisy burst of light."

"Zodiac does not like being laughed at, which is why he should be laughed at as often as possible," chuckled Iris. "Forgive me for saying so, Your Grace, but it will be

257

good to have our True Names back after today. I miss calling your red-faced Lord High Chamberlain 'Carraherne' in private."

Callie frowned only a little, and the other Ladies groaned at Iris' remark. Yes, it was time for this Game to end. But oh...

There was only one thing left to do, and as Callie watched Thomas come out of the bedroom door and move to join them all in the garden, she took a deep breath and prepared herself to do it.

Thomas kissed each of the Queen's Ladies goodbye, taking a little longer to hug Orchid before he smiled one last time, waved, and watched in silence as they walked away as a group. Not one of them looked back.

Without a word, Callie indicated the tree that had been the Elf called Lavender. Thomas strode over to it, and put his hands on the trunk.

"Goodbye, Lavender," he whispered. "Thank you. I'm sorry for causing you pain. I hope you find whatever it is that you're looking for. Thank you."

He walked back to where Callie stood, facing away from him. "Thanks. I would have forgotten."

She smiled at him. "Are you ready?"

"Yes and no," he admitted.

"Then we should probably start," Callie replied. She took his hand, and they walked out of Thomas' garden.

"Callie?"

"Hmmm?"

"I've been thinking."

"Yes?"

"The Rhymer."

"What about him?"

"One of his names was 'Thomas Learmont.' My name is Thomas Lear."

"Yes. Isn't that a strange and wonderful coincidence? We have had this bit of conversation before, have we not?"

"Well..."

"What, Thomas?"

"When The Rhymer came to the end of his time in Faerie, you gave him a gift. You made him 'True Tom,' and he was able to see the future and, according to some of the legends, could only speak the truth...for the rest of his life."

"And?"

"And I've wondered if you were going to do something like that to me."

Silence.

"Callie?"

"I would never do something like that to you, Thomas."

Silence.

Then: "Why not?"

"Because you love your fiction, and will continue to create it in your music. I do not think you will have the same need to create it in your true life, from now on. I would not have you lose your need for creative fiction, though. It is closely tied to who you are."

"Oh." For a second, he could not decide if he was relieved or disappointed.

Callie laughed. "Oh Thomas, you no longer need the fiction to save yourself. You only need it to feed the places in your soul that hold the music you haven't written yet."

"And to explain to the whole world where I've been for a year," he groaned playfully.

They held hands in fragile silence as they walked toward the wood.

Dressed once more in his favorite jeans, the brown cashmere sweater, sneakers, and his black leather bomber's jacket, Thomas tried to remember who he'd been the last time he'd walked around in these clothes, exactly a year and a day ago. He found, to his faint amusement, that the tied-in-knots, frightened, bitterly angry, confused, and—he could admit it now—pathetic man he'd been had not vanished completely.

He had merely grown up, opened himself to love, and had found himself worthy. He was, at long last, almost entirely comfortable with Thomas Lear.

He would have no trouble with who he was, now, no matter what happened to him when he re-entered his "other" life. For reasons he chose not to consider at present, Thomas thought of the post-Faerie world he was returning to as the "other" one. He sadly acknowledged to himself that it would be his *only* one soon enough.

Beside him, Callie walked with her hand in his, her eyes focused on the ground, her mind closed to him, her heart wide open. Thomas stole a glance at her, memorizing again the beautiful designs that decorated the skin of her face, hands and arms. Her living, moving royal markings had startled and almost offended him at first, he remembered. Forever ago, that moment after they'd arrived in Faerie, as she slid from Cassane's tall back and touched the ground, her clothing had changed, and her lovely face was somehow covered with colorful shapes and lines that had not been there seconds before. His disapproval had shown in his eyes, had changed to annoyance when she had all but laughed at him.

If he could have an hour more with her for every time she'd laughed at him since that first evening in the bar at the Caledonian...

His breath caught in his throat, and she looked over at him, eyebrow raised.

Thomas exhaled, regained his balance, and squeezed her hand.

They walked on.

Callie was wearing a simple but elegant long-sleeved, light-green gown that was subtly cinched with a dark green cord. The sunshine around them made the highlights in her hair sparkle. He wanted to reach over and touch her hair, but he resisted the urge. He knew that if he slid his fingers into the long tresses of the woman he loved, the provisional courage that carried him toward his departure would shatter and fail him.

Not for the first time today, Thomas regretted that they would not need Cassane for this trip. The ride on the stallion would have added precious minutes to the time they had left.

Reading his mind, Callie made a sound that could have been a chuckle on any other day. "If Cassane could see me weep over a simple goodbye, Thomas, he would have had a difficult time not plaguing me with irrepressible teasing. I would not give him that satisfaction."

"Good call," Thomas' voice cracked.

She smiled up at him, a soft grin that required no effort but had little joy behind it.

He couldn't help it; he choked. "Callie, Callie...what am I going to do with you?" His artificial smile was replaced with a strangled frown. "What am I going to do with*out* you?"

She had nothing to give him now except truth buoyed by all the love that was in her. "You will do all the things you were meant to do. Only I believe you'll do them better. You will be happier, perhaps. More grounded and far less self-destructive. Your music will be sharper and sweeter, your words truer, with the power to touch, to hold, to heal and to love. You and your music have changed, Thomas, yet only in that you and your music are more your own than they could have been without the time you spent here."

"Time spent with you," Thomas corrected her in a whisper, and kissed her hand.

Callie nodded, and managed a dazzling smile.

They had arrived at the wood, and Thomas recognized the two great oak trees that guarded the Portal between Elvenhome and Upworld, which he had used three times since he'd arrived in Faerie with Callie a year ago. She was inching toward them, and Thomas realized that he was walking even more slowly than she was.

261

In a moment, they were standing in front of the Portal. Thomas could feel a quiet but insistent energy flowing in the space between the trees. He wasn't afraid of it, but he was trembling anyway.

"It is better not to wait." Callie advised.

"What will happen?" He tried, and failed, to sound casual.

"Just walk through the gateway that these noble trees open for you. You will find yourself on the edge of the wood just beyond Queensgate Inn. Sheila is waiting for you there. You will find all of your belongings and your guitar, as well as the things you've chosen take with you from Elvenhome, safely at the Inn, where you will spend this night. Tomorrow you will be driven to Edinburgh, and then you will return to Los Angeles by any method you and your people decide. Everything is arranged, Thomas. All you need to do is rest, and then make contact with your world. Those who matter will surely welcome you back to the life you left."

He shook his head. "You've taken care of everything, haven't you?"

The tart look in her eyes made his chest ache. "I have done this a time or two, you know." She squeezed his hand. "One thing more. Remember, in this moment, the instructions I gave you concerning how to reach me once you are back in your own world."

"Callie, you said I wouldn't remember how to do it."

"You won't, at least not consciously. Your choice to find me will be triggered by something outside of your control. You may never have need of it, and that is well, too. But if you do, reach for me, and I will come to you." She slipped her hand out of his, and touched his face. "Think of the instructions. Think of how to call for me."

Thomas thought of it, etching the knowledge sharply into his mind.

A fast snap of green light clicked around them. Thomas squinted at the flash, and Callie took his hand again.

"I won't forget how to call you, Callie," he said, determination tightening his features.

You already have, she thought. *You just don't know it yet.*

Nodding toward the trees that guarded the Portal, he asked, "How long will it take me to get to Sheila?"

"About ten seconds."

Thomas squinted hard into the sunlit wood to locate Sheila. "What? You mean she's standing right there, and I just can't see her?"

Callie laughed. "Something like that. Call it 'a trick of the light'."

"I would have, a year ago. Not now, though. Now it almost makes sense, God help me."

"I have found that every journey homeward, wherever home may be, seems swifter than the journey away from home. Your swift journey begins here."

He was staring at the ancient trees in front of him. A thought struck him. "Wait...if I walk through here...and out...to Upworld, can't I come back to Elvenhome the same way?"

She patted his arm. "Nice thought, but no. Making your way easily from Faerie never means you can easily find the way back in. That's the way of it for mortals, and since the wrong done by the Mischief, the gateways between the worlds are more vigilantly watched and warded." She sighed, and tried to smile. "You have graced my world with your sweet presence. And now our time is finished. Go in peace, my friend and my love."

"But..." he began. He was not ready to go.

"Our goodbyes have been spoken. There is nothing left to do." She shot him a most suggestive wink, then tried to smile. "Unless..." she prompted.

"Unless what?"

She studied him and realized that, despite everything, he was not going to surprise her with the Moonsong Harp after all. It had never occurred to him, and in truth, there was no real reason that it should have. She took a deep breath, and let her hope fly away.

Bending down, Thomas reached into the grass and picked up a small, sharp stone. Standing, he showed it to Callie. "May I take this?"

She looked at the stone in his hand, then touched it. "I thank you for asking. And if it will please you, yes, it can accompany you on your journey."

"Thanks, Callie." He took a step closer to the trees; he was in front of the Portal. "Callie...?"

"Yes?"

"I love you." He turned, took her in his arms, and kissed her. His growing anticipation for returning home mingled with his agony over leaving her, and it shattered them both. At last they pulled away from each other, and their eyes met.

"I love you too, Thomas. Now go. And do not look back."

Thomas Lear, Mortal Rock Star and suddenly Former Lover of the Legendary High Queen of Faerie, furtively dug the sharp, jagged surface of the stone into the palm of his hand until he felt his skin break and he knew he was bleeding. He stuffed his injured hand into his jacket pocket, and strode through the warding trees.

Green light crackled around him and, in a flash, he was gone.

Callie stood there for a long moment, and let out a deep breath. A dozen conflicting thoughts sped through her mind, and there was yet another one pulsing in her heart. Squaring her shoulders, she decided not to give in to any thought. She could afford a small space of time to herself. If she was going to be able to move past her love for (and, she groaned to herself, her *need* for) Thomas, she would have to begin at once, before the pain of parting fully settled in.

"Damn," said the High Queen of Faerie, as tears flooded her enchanting brown eyes.

Before those tears could fall, a spontaneous blaze of bright green light burned for a mile around and above her as she shifted herself into a large orange-and-black butterfly, and flew resolutely away.

SHE SAT IN her Tower Room and focused hard as she stitched gray and blue silk thread into clouds on the pearl-white linen in her lap. The morning sun shone in through the East windows. On any other day, she would revel in the light, and in the ever-fragrant air that danced around her.

She would not let her mind wander. She would spend her full attention on her stitchery. Her world could wait a day; it had to. At present, she had nothing left to give. There was only sadness, grief, and a sense of loss she would never have imagined possible, the like of which she had only experienced once before.

She would not think about Thomas Lear. She would not think of the Moonsong Harp that he had taken away with him.

She could not allow herself to make room in her mind, or her heart, for anything but needlework.

There was a tentative knock at the door. She knew that her friend wanted to protect her privacy today, but he had a confirmation to deliver.

Ban, the head of the Queen's Council, known a short while ago as "Boston," waited a moment, then walked into the Tower Room. He knew her well, and understood that she had few, if any, words this day. She would not waste them.

"There is confirmation. He took the train from Edinburgh to London, boarded the plane at Heathrow, Your Grace," he told her, with an approving smile. "He wore dark glasses, was recognized in first class, was polite, and then ignored everyone. It would seem that he has not forgotten how to be a famous rock star."

The High Queen of Faerie did not look up from her needlework.

"You chose well, my Queen, and we all thank you. As it turned out, he was everything we needed him to be," he began, his voice kind.

"And everything *I* needed him to be, too," the Queen murmured to her needlework.

"Even so, Your Grace, all was done as it was meant to be done. The giving and the taking, the lessons, timing, and the goodness of it all. No more and no less than what was required."

The Queen closed her eyes. "And no more, and no less than what was yearned for," she admitted unhappily.

Ever patient, he waited, sharing her pain, because there was nothing else he could do for her.

She was too wise, and far too experienced, to be entirely miserable and distraught. Still, there was a chasm of wretched sadness in her that would take more than simple time and distance to heal. When at last she opened her eyes and spoke to him, her voice was dulled with grief. "Ah, Ban, perhaps I was wrong this time. Perhaps I should have asked him to stay. Perhaps he would have chosen to stay."

Ban bowed to his Queen and, turning, moved to the door. Looking back over his shoulder as he opened it, he gave her a small, affectionate smile. "*'Perhaps'* is a cruel game, Lass. No one ever completely wins it, eh?" He nodded at her, and left without a word, closing the door behind him.

Taking a deep breath, the Queen turned around in her chair, and stared with longing at Thomas' guitar, the one she'd had made for him. Silent now, it stood fifteen feet behind her, upright against the oak bench where he'd last sat and played it for her. Somehow that seemed like weeks ago.

She trembled, feeling cold and alone and, not surprisingly, bitter. He would not be here to sing his songs for her and the Folk. There would be no more laughter shared after glorious lovemaking, no more quiet walks under the stars, no more wandering around in stories of his past, no more kisses, no touching.

266

Unguarded, her breath came out in a sob.

But despite the anguish of this day, she knew that she would survive the loss of him. She knew, too, that there would, in time, be other Court Singers. Above all, she knew that she would mourn her loss of Thomas Lear, that she would feel the cold and lonely depths of that loss for a very long time.

She wrapped herself in the glowing awareness that his presence in Elvenhome for the enchanted year and a day had not changed only him for the better; it had, in fact, subtly altered her as well. Having known him well and loved him, she, too, had been transformed by the experience. She would remain so until the end of days.

"I miss you," she whispered, her dark eyes filling again with heavy tears that did nothing to soothe the burning ache in her heart. "I will always miss you, Thomas."

fifteen

Once upon a time, in the land known to some as Faerie, there lived, for a time, a mortal man whose sole purpose was to serve the High Queen, and sing to her and her people.

In his own land, he was a maker and singer of beautiful songs. It had been for this reason that she had chosen him for her particular brand of enchantment. He was not the first mortal to so serve the High Queen of Faerie, and it was unlikely that he would be the last.

The singer fell deeply in love with the dazzling Queen, as is often the case with mortals. It was not a surprise to the Fair Folk that he would do so.

What was, however, a surprise to one and all was that the Queen, despite her obligations to the contrary, returned his love in kind, loved him perhaps more than she had loved any other *mortal who had fallen under her enchantment for seven hundred years.*

Their love was not the stuff of legend. It was simply a matter of fact. The Queen healed and fed the mortal singer's sad and hungry soul by exposing her own lonely need.

In return, he blessed her with the creation of his sweetest and best music. He learned to let his love for her touch and awaken the melodies and the words he needed to speak, writing and singing songs that had been buried deep inside his restless heart.

Through his love for her, he freed himself.

Together they filled each other's dark places, and knew joy and contentment and easy laughter, as well as the searing passions of love...for the space of a year and a day.

When the appointed time for their parting arrived, the mortal was torn equally between his love for the Queen and his increasing need to return to the life he had left behind.

For her part, the Queen resolved to let him go. She was refreshed, and ready to resume her responsibilities to her land and to her people.

Their parting was a time for tears and laughter, which they gave to each other as freely as they had given their love. They stood at the very edge of Faerie and shared a final, binding kiss before they turned away and moved back into their respective worlds.

Having had much experience with mortal singers, the Queen sighed, brushed a single, diamond-bright tear from her cheek, whispered green magic into the air. This she sent after her lover on a breeze, then returned to her castle in silence.

Having had no other experience with Queens, the mortal singer stepped out of Faerie with a sharp ache in his chest, which was soothed by a soft, green light he had not seen, only felt and vaguely recognized.

He re-entered his former life refreshed, and ready to be a more contented man, for he was, to his amazement, finally at peace with himself.

He flowed easily back into the stream of his life, and as he did so, he began to forget the Queen and his year and a day in Faerie. That first week in his home, as he rested from his journey and planned his new life, he could recall her face, her voice and her touch when he wrote his lyrical poetry. In a very short time, however, he did not find himself thinking about her at all. His memories were shrouded in a soft green light he could not see.

At first, she came to him in dreams, or perhaps he went looking for her in them. In any case, their meetings were few, and faded away as time passed.

A month later, he no longer recalled her face, her name, or the gifts she had given him. She became an abstraction. He truly did not remember their time together; he began to believe that he had imagined her. And yet he was consumed by a raw, aching emptiness that he could not explain.

He lived the rest of his days with the need to ease and fill that emptiness with something bright, beautiful, and good. He gave himself fully to the single thing that really mattered to him, gave him peace and a reason to continue. In truth, although he tried to appear otherwise, he lived only for his music, and ached for a magic he could not find.

He wrote songs for and about his bright and illusive fantasy lover, and his feelings about her. His fame never diminished. If anything, he became more famous, but he found that he did not care very much.

If his private yearning for the kind of love he needed (and had experienced, but had forgotten) threatened to break him beyond repair, he soothed himself with the magic of his own music.

For the rest of his life, he did not realize for whom he was writing and singing his songs. Whether he sang them in the recording studio, in live concerts, or to himself when he was alone and sad, he believed that they were for his own private salvation.

She knew better.

The ringing of the phone woke Jack Grandberg from a deep sleep. Without opening his eyes, he grabbed the phone and dragged the receiver under the covers to reach his head.

"Jack Grandberg," he muttered, his voice heavy.

"Wake up, Jack, it's Stan."

Jack came a little more awake, but not much. He hadn't talked to Stan Williams in a couple of months. With Thomas Lear gone and out of the picture, there hadn't been any reason for a conversation with his business manager.

"Are you there, Jack? Wake the fuck up!" Stan was impatient.

Jack had only been in bed for a couple of hours; it had been a great party. He groaned. "What time is it?"

"It's 3:30 or so. Are you awake enough to get this?"

"Get what?"

"Our boy's coming home."

Jack woke up a bit more. "What?"

"The prodigal's returning," Stan announced.

"What?"

"Jack, open your eyes and listen: The Absent Mr. Thomas Lear is no longer absent. He's on his way home. In fact, he should be here sometime tonight."

"*What*? Thomas is *back*?"

"Yep. I finished talking to him half an hour ago."

Receiver in hand, Jack sat straight up in bed, eyes wide open, and reached for the lamp on the nightstand, turning it on. "He's alive, the bastard! Fantastic! And...?"

"While details are sketchy, Thomas said he has been in the UK all this time. Says he has about two albums' worth of new songs, and he's ready to get back to work."

"You're shitting me. What's he been doing for a year?"

"Writing songs, apparently." Stan chuckled. "I thought he'd gone away to do drugs and die, or maybe detox. Or maybe had the Mob after him, or some woman's husband. Or several women's husbands. But he's on his way home, and he sounds great."

"Wow," said Jack, his mind fully functioning now, and thinking like a record producer. "New songs? Did he say how many? And are they good?"

"Didn't say how many. We'll find out soon enough. I got him on a commercial flight from Heathrow to JFK, JFK to LAX. He'd already called his housekeeper, and she's going to pick him up at the airport. I told him I'd send a car for him, but he didn't want it. Also didn't want to make a fuss, no press this time, no nothing. He said he

272

just wanted to come home on the sly, and catch up, and then get back to work."

"So..."

"So I'll resurrect the PR plan I told you about, the one I was kicking around last spring. I can use it now. Add a layer of 'Welcome Back to LA,' get him on the talk shows, get Rolling Stone all hot and bothered with an exclusive."

Jack was thinking. "He's okay? He didn't sound sick or strung out?"

"Nope. Not that I could tell. He sounds...hell, he sounds healthy! Weird, huh? Well, we'll see. He's going to hang out at home for a few days, he said, and get his head together, and then get back into it."

It was a little shocking, naturally, but Jack didn't waste time pondering it. Thomas Lear, one of the biggest names on a record label of big names, was coming back, with new songs for the catalog. Jack found himself smiling at the thought of Thomas' solid five-year contract.

"Jack?"

"Yeah, Stan?"

"He's back! Let the good times roll, eh?"

"Yep," Jack agreed. "The next phase of Thomas Lear is about to begin, and it'll be a hell of a ride! Everybody wins!"

Stan's voice chuckled in his ear. "Good luck getting back to sleep now, man. But I had to let you know, so you can get all of your wheels rolling today. Later."

"Bye," Jack replied, his mind racing.

By the time he hung up the phone, Jack had already decided that the smartest thing he could do to add to the excitement and success of Thomas Lear's surprise return was to make sure Thomas' next album made history.

He laughed out loud. It was total a no-brainer. Only one person was creative enough, good enough, and had enough of the industry's attention these days to produce it. It wasn't going to be easy, but it would be a killer combination if he could make it work.

Jack lifted the phone's receiver and dialed. He waited until someone on the other end of the line picked up.

"Hello?" a sleepy voice answered.

"Wakey, wakey, Susannah my love! You'll never guess who's on his way back to town..."

IT WAS MIDNIGHT. In one of the smaller chambers off the Kitchens, a Banshee and her Elfish lover, who was also the Lord High Chamberlain of Elvenhome Castle, shared a casual, quiet supper. They sat at a table, and together reveled in the serenity of near-silence.

"This was an excellent idea," Carraherne said at last. "I sometimes forget that the Kitchens are not wild with activity all the time. The absence of hyperactive HobGoblins dashing around with dishes is quite appealing."

"And no one can easily find us here, should they be looking. I needed peace and some distance from hysteria," the Banshee sighed. "It has been rather a day."

"Oh?" Carraherne said, pouring more wine into her goblet.

The Banshee, whose True Name was Dinaea but had recently been known as "Iris," sighed again. "As is always the case when a Court Singer leaves us, Her Grace has been in a sad and somewhat prickly mood." Carraherne was going to point out that this was nothing out of the ordinary, but Dinaea raised a hand to stop him. "I know. But she is more unhappy, and less consolable, than I have seen her in a very long time. And after today's hysteria..."

"What happened?"

Dinaea took a sip from her goblet, and groaned. "When I walked into Her Grace's rooms this afternoon, three of our Ladies were standing before her, carrying on and crying, apologizing."

Carraherne's eyebrows lifted. Dinaea nodded and continued, her voice taking on a conspiratorial tone. "The Queen has also been suffering over the loss of the Moonsong Harp."

The Lord High Chamberlain gasped. "The Moonsong Harp is missing?"

"Not exactly. Remember to keep this to yourself, Carraherne, or I shall have to thump you. I did not wish to say anything, but here it is: Thomas Lear took the Harp with him when he returned Upworld, a remembrance gift from the Queen."

"She gave him the Moonsong Harp?" Carraherne's voice rose in shock.

"Not precisely. Well, yes. In a way." Dinaea articulated the words slowly. "He chose it when he was in the Queen's Tower Room."

Carraherne looked stunned. "She would never willingly—however did he find it?" He interrupted himself, staring at Dinaea.

"That is the crux of the matter, I daresay. I did not understand it myself until today. Our dear Ladies Sylph, Selkie and pink-hatted Pixie were the ones who told Thomas the romantic tale of the Moonsong Harp, along with several other stories I might have preferred them not to." She saw that Carraherne was about to explode. "Now, now...it was harmless. Thomas asked them about things he might rightfully choose from the Queen's Tower Room, and they told him about many of the Queen's treasures. They meant no mischief, of course. Thomas told them, or so I heard Saff say as she fluttered tearfully around Her Grace's head, that he was looking for inspiration for a new song before he left. Which, in fact, he did write and perform for us. It didn't occur to them to not tell him what he wanted to know. He positioned it as 'research', and they wanted to be helpful."

"Oh dear..."

"Her Grace was not unkind, of course. She waited until Wrense stopped crying. The poor Pixie all but tore her hat into miserable confetti, she was so distressed. It was Raniashin who put the pieces together and discovered that what she and the others had told Thomas that night was how he knew where to look for the Moonsong Harp."

"Her Grace let him take it, though? How is that possible?"

"The rules of enchantment appear to have outwitted us all, Carraherne." Dinaea took a long breath, and pushed her plate away. "The unhappy Ladies begged Her Grace's forgiveness, and naturally she forgave them. Poor Lamb, so much has made her unhappy in so short a time." Dinaea took Carraherne's hand and gave him a faint smile. "The Ladies are still troubled, but they will calm down," she said. "The Queen is suffering the pain of lost love, but will smile again in time. And I, my dear, am ready for our lives to get back to normal again."

She rose, and Carraherne rose with her, his hand still holding hers.

A thought struck him, and his eyes widened. "The King! Does the *King* know that the Moonsong Harp left with Thomas Lear?"

Dinaea shook her head, her eyes wary.

"Great Gods!" Carraherne swore. "If he were to find out...oh, no..."

"Better that he never learns of it. Only the Queen and her Ladies know that the Harp is gone."

"And now I know." Shuddering, Carraherne frowned. "No one else should be told. Nothing good can come of this."

"As usual, my dear, we find ourselves in perfect agreement," Dinaea declared with a tired sigh as they walked through the Kitchens, and in the direction of Carraherne's apartments, since it was long past bedtime.

THE WEEK AFTER Thomas Lear left Elvenhome, Her Grace received a letter.

My Lady—

It seems our world is at last settling back into its familiar rhythms. With mixed emotions, I am grateful for this. Much has happened to our people, and to us, these past months, and yet I find that the happy things have wearied me perhaps as much as the unhappy ones.

We have both lost friends and loved ones. There has been no time to consider the changes. The loss of Terena is hard for me to bear, along with the passing of Emmel and Borril, and too many others. I miss Arrendel sorely, too, as I know you do. Elvenhome seems a smaller, sadder place tonight.

I know you miss Sonorielle's companionship. And you grieve deeply the loss of Thomas Lear. I find that I do, as well, although of course in a different way. It has occurred to me that, under other circumstances, and given a bit more time, he and I might have been friends.

In the morning, I leave Elvenhome for the castle at Elvenmere for several weeks, to grieve, to think, and to regain my dubious footing. When I return, I would like to talk with you about the restoration of some of the kingly responsibilities I long ago abandoned and that you so graciously embraced in my stead.

And perhaps we could spend a quiet evening talking fondly of absent friends.

Time heals, but slowly. Be gentle with yourself, My Lady. Rest your heart, and be well.

—Garrhyn

P.S. The King's Men, Ban and Swiftaine accompany me to Elvenmere. If you have need of any of us, send word at once.

IT WAS PERHAPS a month later that the King and Queen of Faerie regularly began having dinner together once, and sometimes twice, a week. On occasion they were joined by friends, but most often they were served dinner for two by Hobs from the Kitchens, or Queen's Ladies or King's Men, and spent long evenings talking, laughing, remembering, and planning the future for the Kingdoms and the Fair Folk.

Sometimes there was a difference of opinion, and on only one occasion was anger sparked, anger that faded away in the face of easy laughter and a long history of understanding.

Neither the King nor the Queen had envisioned a time when they might again revel in each other's company, but it seemed to the Folk that the time had at last arrived. No one forgot the centuries of conflict, which made the present courteous and amiable royal relationship all the more precious to the inhabitants of Elvenhome, and the other Kingdoms as well.

After sharing dinner alone on a night in the early spring, the King and Queen stood in the King's garden and observed the stars.

"I believe they grow more beautiful every season," the Queen murmured, gazing up into the sky.

He was looking at her. "I cannot but agree."

The moon stepped out from behind deep cloud cover, and shone on them. A glimmer of light caught the Queen's notice, and she looked over at the King.

"You're sparkling," she told him.

"Why thank you, Your Grace. So are you."

She chuckled. "No, no...that's not what I...Garrhyn you're *sparkling*. The moonlight has touched something and..."

He did not understand for a moment, and then realized. "Oh. Yes. I suppose you saw the moonlight touch this." He slid his hand into the slit at the neck of his tunic, and pulled out a gold chain, from which hung a small, golden harp. Face carefully neutral, he showed her, and slid it back under his tunic.

"I have not seen that in a long while," she said, reaching for something to say. The sight of the necklace had surprised her, and she found herself wondering why he would wear it, if there had been a specific reason. To impress her? To inspire guilt, or uneasiness that would initiate a conversation she was not ready to have? She did not want to walk too near old, familiar wounds with him yet. She was not sure he was ready, either.

She did not want to talk about it, not any of it, tonight. Or anytime soon. There were too many things to talk about, things that had remained unspoken forever. No, she did not want to go there, she wanted to remember how to enjoy his company, his friendship, his sense of fun.

She looked back up at the sky, finding the Pleiades very interesting just now.

The King stole a glance at her. He'd been looking away while she wrapped herself in silence. He considered his choices: in this moment, he could say and do nothing, or he could tell her a quiet truth.

The question was this: which quiet truth could he tell her?

He opted for the first one, the deepest one, but he gave it to her with a lightness that he hoped all but disguised the importance of it. "I have never removed the harp from around my neck, from the first night you gave it to me," he said softly. "I have always, and ever, worn it."

Her gaze dropped from the stars to his face. "You've never taken it off?"

The King shook his head, his eyes meeting hers.

"Surely, you must have...when..."

The King continued to shake his head.

"It has never left me. It has always been a part of me."

279

She hazarded a step toward conversation. "We did not speak for centuries, Your Grace. There was no need for you to continue to wear it."

He sighed. "There was need. I confess it; I used it at first to make me feel bound to you, to torture myself for choices made, punish myself for deeds done, and those left undone. I would see it and feel it every day, a reminder that I had failed you, and the Folk, and the land itself.

"As time moved on, it allowed me to stay angry, bitter at what I'd lost by fate and happenstance. It remained with me as a talisman of solitude and self-loathing." He shrugged, and very nearly smiled at her in the darkness. "Eventually, over this past year, I began to understand that I continued to wear it through time because a part of me never stopped loving you, never stopped being proud of you, being amazed by you. I have always loved you. It is likely that I always will."

He was faintly surprised that the admission hadn't hurt him at all. He wondered what that meant, if anything.

The Queen bristled beside him. He could feel her clench, and waited for her to speak.

In a moment she did, in a soft, solemn voice that seemed calm and disinterested. He instinctively knew that she was neither. "And when you spent a century with...with Terena? Did you really wear the harp in those years, Garrhyn, when you belonged to her?"

"I have never *not* worn this necklace, my Lady. Not even when I shared my life with Terena. There has not been a single day in seven hundred years when I have not been touched by this harp you gave me once upon a time."

"Oh," she said, studying him in the moonlight before she turned away. "It is getting late. I should go."

He followed her back inside in unhappy silence, wondering why truth did not truly set anything free. If he did not know where the Queen was standing, how would he be able to navigate the delicate path toward her?

ALONE IN HIS Tower Room, the King of Faerie sprawled in his favorite chair, staring into space, lost in thought.

I should not be thinking about her. But how can I not think about her? It should be enough that we are friends, and can talk almost the way we used to. Almost. I do not know what I want from her, do I?

He knew what he wanted from her. But wanting was one thing; having was another matter. He did not know how to return to the way things had been, at their beginning, although he acknowledged to himself that he would have done anything to find a way to have now what he had lost then.

He was confident that the Queen was enjoying their growing friendship. They were sharing more of their royal duties these days. The time they spent together pleased her, too, or it wouldn't be happening. Even the Folk were happy. Life in Elvenhome was better than it had been in centuries, and all was well.

The King sighed, wishing that his own story had been told differently.

All Faerie tales do not necessarily come true, Maggie, he answered the unasked question, although the idea of Maggie posing such an inquiry nearly made him smile in spite of himself. *Hers had, hadn't it? That was something.*

Suddenly he missed Arrendel deeply. And Emmel. And strangely, it struck him that he missed Thomas Lear, too. Or maybe only the idea of Thomas Lear. No, it wasn't that. He had lost the opportunity to build a friendship with the Court Singer, but the potential had always been there, despite the convoluted circumstances of the musician's presence in Elvenhome.

Every fiber of this tapestry had the Queen's touch on it. He marveled at the intensity of his understanding of this. His own touch was there, but nowhere was it as strong as hers.

He loved her for it. He loved her for all of it.

Hopeless, he grumbled to himself. *You are hopeless. You should be grateful that she lights your days, and has become a friend again.* He shifted in the chair, and tried not to lose the fragile thread of hope he couldn't help but carry inside him. *To have her close beside me only in the Throne Room is better than never having her beside me at all. Our friendship is a welcome change that I shall not demean by wishing my heart had more.*

The trick was going to be resigning himself to his fate, and honoring their friendship, without pushing the woman he loved away with feelings he could not expect her to reciprocate. He would find a way to survive it. He'd already lived without her. He knew how, and could do it again.

But seeing her in the pleasant light of friendship, and laughter, and mutual respect, how could he face not spending private time with her? Done was done; they could not go back, any more than they could resurrect their dead child. He would teach himself to settle for whatever she gave him, and be content.

His eyes roamed the Tower Room, itching for something to comfort his mind. He saw books, treasured paintings, a favorite sculpture. He saw swords on the wall, ancient maps everywhere. He glanced at casks and cabinets, and smiled at a portrait of Cav.

He thought about a book he hadn't read in eighty years, and looked back at the bookcase to see if he could spot the title on the shelf.

And then he saw it.

Garrhyn closed his eyes, squeezed them tightly, shook his head. He opened his eyes, and looked again.

There it was, all but staring back at him.

He forgot to breathe as his mind filled with whirling questions. *How? When? Who had done this? Why had she never said...?*

"Ah," he murmured. Either she didn't know, or had not wanted to tell him. This was getting to be more interesting by the moment.

The King smiled, but it was hard to say whether his smile was tied to distant memories or to his next few hours.

"Fiall!" Garrhyn called to his Man, who attended from the other side of the Tower Room's heavy oak door.

"Sire?" the Gnome called back. No one entered the King's Tower Room without an explicit invitation to do so.

"We have work to do," said Garrhyn, grinning as he opened the door and hurried down the stairs, Fiall close behind him.

Less than an hour later, Garrhyn sat on the dais steps in the King's Presence Chamber, and passively observed the three Folk who stood before him. "Well, Gentlemen?"

The Gentlemen said nothing.

"I take it," the King said with a lightness they didn't trust, "that you believed I wouldn't notice it right away, but that I would indeed notice it at some point. I do not know how long it has been there, but you three have something to do with it."

The Gentlemen were silent, and gave no evidence of understanding what their King was talking about.

The King rose, and moved to stand in front of them. "Allow me to tell you why I know this involves the three of you, although I must admit I might have missed an important connection if it had not been for the Friday Afternoon Poker Games. Which immediately ties our friend Thomas Lear into the picture somehow, too…"

Two of the Gentlemen stiffened, but they all looked straight ahead as the King walked around them.

"This has the scent of something Lord Arrendel would be involved in. But as he is not here, and has not been for a time, I cannot help but think that Swiftaine's active involvement is a likely substitute. In addition, Swiftaine's capacity for stealth—always laudable to some degree, I daresay—could have been a useful tool."

The King looked down at the Spriggan, who made no move, except that his fingers twitched nervously.

283

"And you, Wyand!" The King took his gaze from the Spriggan and moved to stand before the Elf who Thomas had named "Professor Plum." The King groaned in feigned distress. "My own Man a more-than-likely participant in such a scandalous event!"

Wyand found a spot on the wall behind the King's head, and stared at it without blinking.

"Nothing to say, then?"

Wyand tightened his lips.

"I see," said the King.

He moved past Wyand, and in front of the last man he'd called to his Presence Chamber. "Now you...you are the one who knows everything."

Carraherne barely breathed as he met his King's eyes.

"Nothing happens in Elvenhome Castle that you don't know about, Carraherne. It's likely that little happens in the Village that you don't know about."

Carraherne didn't blink.

The King circled the three Folk, shrugged, and went back to the dais steps. As he sat down, he peered at them. "Not a word, Gentlemen?"

Not a word.

The King sighed. "Very well. I shall tell you what I believe may have happened. When I have finished sorting this...*situation*...out, perhaps you will be kind enough to correct my deductions, and clarify for me whatever I have not figured out for myself.

"Here is what I see: someone entered the King's Tower Room without the King's leave, to place an object in there for the King to see. Only I am unclear as to how long the object has been in residence there.

"You are each connected to Thomas Lear in several distinct ways, the convergence of which was the poker game. You were each on good terms with him. Perhaps I can even say that you considered him a friend.

"How am I doing so far?"

No one spoke.

The King sighed, and kept going. "My presumption is that Carraherne managed the timing of getting the object to the Tower Room, that Wyand's work was to make certain that I was occupied and duly distracted so would not notice the change in energy when someone entered there. That leaves Swiftaine, to snap in, then vanish after he placed the object where I'd be likely to see it at some random moment. The only things I have not been able to understand yet are why that *particular* object, and what does Thomas Lear have to do with it?"

The King rose from the dais steps and frowned. A flash of bright golden light zapped around him, and slammed like thunder into the air above Carraherne, Wyand and Swiftaine.

The Lord High Chamberlain and the King's Man shot each other a look.

"I am waiting, Gentlemen..."

HE HAD JUST enough time to pour wine into the jeweled goblets before Fiall knocked once on the door before opening it.

She walked into his Tower Room. Her face wore a quizzical look that he thought was quite becoming. Fiall closed the door and walked down the steps.

It had been many long centuries since she had been in in this Room; she couldn't help but look around. After a minute, she looked back at him, with an amused smile.

"It still looks like you in here, Garrhyn," she told him.

"Ah well. That happens. Does yours still look like you?" he countered politely.

The Queen nodded. "I would say it does."

He picked up the goblets, handed her one, and motioned her to a comfortable chair. She looked around some more as she sat down and settled. The Greencrystal Pendant caught her eye; it was hanging from its long necklace, held by a thin rod, above the East Window, glistening in the sunlight. Brown eyes twinkling, the Queen nodded at the Stone. The Stone shimmered an

285

affectionate flash of golden-green light in response. Queen and Stone smiled, and then the Queen returned her attention to the King.

"Why did you invite me up here? It's been a very long time, Garrhyn," she began.

He cleared his throat, and walked toward a tall bookcase.

"We've had," he said, "a small situation. One that involves you."

"Oh?"

The King bent down and lifted the object from the bottom shelf of the bookcase. "Your Grace, I believe this belongs to you." He held out his hand, and showed her the Moonsong Harp.

sixteen

AT FIRST HE didn't know if the look in her eyes was one of pain, guilt, or relief, but it didn't matter. After a sharp, sudden intake of breath, the Queen grinned, her face reflecting pure happiness.

"Where—?" she began, as the King walked over to her and placed the Moonsong Harp on her open, outstretched palm. "Oh, Garrhyn!"

At its first touch on the Queen's hand, the Harp flickered impatiently. The Queen laughed. "Go on, then. Speak."

The Moonsong Harp all but exploded into frenzied music, telling a tale of stealth, frustration, confusion, and then joy and reunion. The Queen listened intently, waited for the Harp's song to finish before she kissed it, and looked up at the King, who had seated himself on the arm of her chair.

"And that seems to be only part of the tale," Garrhyn chuckled. "I have nearly all the rest of it. A strange story indeed, Your Grace."

The Queen looked away, took a deep breath, and tried to piece the tale together in her own mind. She closed her eyes when Garrhyn touched her on the shoulder and offered, "Shall I tell it to you?"

When she nodded, he told her everything he knew, right up to the point where he'd questioned Carraherne, Swiftaine and Wyand. "But what I do not understand is how Thomas Lear is involved, although certainly he is. He is no thief. I do not believe he stole it, nor do I think he meant to do harm. Yet he had the Harp. Has the Harp not lived in your Tower Room for…time upon time?"

The Queen nodded, and kissed the Harp once more before placing it on the table beside her chair.

"Thomas Lear did not steal the Harp, did he?"

The Queen frowned. "No, he did not. He chose it as a remembrance."

Garrhyn frowned now. He knew that Court Singers did not long recall their time in Faerie. "I do not understand."

So the Queen explained her habit of gifting her Court Singers from the personal contents of her Tower Room. She winced as she admitted that she'd believed Thomas would return it to her before he left, since she knew he had heard its story, and he had to have been aware of how much the Harp meant to her. She admitted to Garrhyn that she had wanted to make Thomas give it back, but that she hadn't because, of course, she had to live under the same rules of enchantment that she had set up for him. "Done was done," she conceded.

For his part, the King was silent as she spoke. Her generosity of spirit, coupled with her innocent wistfulness, all but choked him.

Her eyes asked his for a kind of forgiveness, one for which there were no words.

After several long moments, Garrhyn cleared his throat, steadied himself, and gave the Queen a tiny smile. "It appears that our friend Thomas Lear has attempted to make some playful mischief in his absence."

"How so?" she asked.

"He left the Harp with his clever friends: Carraherne managed the timing, Wyand caused several wily distractions, and Swiftaine planted the Harp up here."

"But why? Why did Thomas not take the Harp with him, as it appeared he did?" The Queen shook her head in vague disbelief. "As I believed he did?"

"Ah," Garrhyn nodded. "Now we come to it." He rose, and took their empty wine goblets to the table for refilling from the carafe. "It seems that Thomas had a purpose, which took me a bit longer to learn from the culprits.'" He walked back to the Queen, returning her filled goblet. "They were not going to tell me, even though I began to roar at them."

"Swiftaine worries when you roar, Garrhyn. You are quite a theatrical force when you wish to be."

The King shrugged. "I gave them every opportunity to come clean, but they were steadfast in their silence. I got ready to bellow at them, knowing that it was likely that Wyand would panic but not speak, Carraherne would ultimately risk popping out of the room, but that Swiftaine would stand still, then cave."

Intrigued now, the Queen leaned toward the King, eyes wide. "And?"

"And just as I was about to shout the walls down, I began to laugh."

"What?"

"Actually, it was more like giggling. The insanity of the moment got the better of me, my dear, and I laughed until I nearly had to sit down," Garrhyn admitted.

"Then what happened?" the Queen wanted to know.

"And then they all started to laugh, too, even Swiftaine, poor old Spriggan. And that," the King declared, "was that. They told me the *why* of it all. Why Thomas chose the Moonsong Harp in particular, how he knew where it was, who he had pressed to get his information. He asked his friends to do what he could not in his absence. He seems to have very much wanted to put you, and me, in the situation in which find ourselves at this very moment: together, talking and laughing, in the presence of the bridegift I gave you forever and forever ago."

She took a deep breath, and beamed at him. "You are a rather clever man, Your Grace."

He nodded at the compliment. "We also have clever friends, Your Grace. And I would say that Thomas Lear is one of them. Quite the romantic, that Court Singer of yours."

"That poker-playing friend of yours is not the only romantic in the vicinity, Garrhyn." The light in her eyes tugged at his heart. She placed her goblet on the table beside the Moonsong Harp, and rose from the chair, her gaze questioning his as she took a step toward him.

"Harp," said the Queen over her shoulder, her eyes still on Garrhyn, "Play for me."

The Harp shivered in silver light, and began to play a sweet tune.

"Your Majesty," the Queen asked as she stood directly in front of the him, "may I have the honor of dancing with the King of the Faeries?"

He froze, and trembled, suddenly chilled by a cold pain that tore deep inside him. Standing, he whispered, "We have not danced together since the night before—" and she quietly said the name with him "—Garrhydan died."

The Queen held out her hands, her invitation unmistakable. "I know. But all that means, really, is that we have not danced for a terribly long time. Perhaps we should rectify that, don't you think, husband?"

The Moonsong Harp sang all the more sweetly when Garrhyn reached for his wife and danced with her in the afternoon sunlight.

THE MESSENGER ARRIVED. He was ushered into the Queen's Presence Chamber without a word. Her Grace entered as soon as the doors were closed behind the messenger, and guards were posted to assure privacy.

Shortly thereafter, the messenger was sent on his way, coins jingling in his pocket. The only sign that he had been in the castle at all was the large, covered basket he'd left behind.

That evening, when the King arrived at the Queen's apartments for dinner, she took him to her study and showed him the basket, her eyes shining with delight.

She handed him a note:

> *In loving gratitude for the return of the Moonsong Harp, and the happy memories (both past and present) it conjures every time it sings.*

Touched, the King smiled.

The Queen pointed to the covered basket.

The three Wolfhound puppies waiting inside were adorable, and bonded to him almost immediately. For the rest of their long lives, Luna, Harper and Dancer made it their business to follow His Grace almost everywhere he went.

In time, it was once again said in the kingdoms of Faerie, *If you seek the King, look for the Queen.*

They ruled together, they worked, talked and danced together. They hawked and went riding and read together, they made love and slept together, they played with the dogs and hosted feasts together, happier than they had ever been. Life in the kingdoms was at its zenith, with no sign of change, or reason to do so. The lives of the Folk were consistently filled with music and merriment.

ONE DAY, THE Queen started into the huge sitting room area of the Royal Apartments she shared with her husband and stopped, smiling as she watched the King, who was seated comfortably on one of the couches, tapping his foot to the rhythm of the guitar riff he was listening to. A year-old wolfhound slept on the floor nearby, undisturbed by the movement. When the guitar riff was over, the King hummed along with the melody rising from the song on the record album he was listening to.

The Queen was not at all surprised to hear the voice of Thomas Lear, singing the last verse of "I Don't Think That I Can Love You."

Garrhyn smiled when he saw her. "Isn't it time," he suggested, "for you to entertain the notion of another Court Singer?"

The Queen smiled back at him, all sweetness and serenity. "Shut up, Garrhyn."

"As my Queen commands," laughed the King.

She sat down beside him. "Dinaea tells me that Sir Swiftaine requests permission to go Upworld to visit Arrendel and Maggie."

"And?"

"And I think Maggie will send him back to us in a box if he shows up on her doorstep without having asked first."

Garrhyn laughed. "Quite right."

"Shall we give him permission to ask Maggie's permission, then?"

"As soon as possible. Once that Spriggan gets something in his mind, he will not rest until he resolves it. He will drive us mad in the interim."

"My thought exactly."

Thomas Lear began to sing "All I Need Tonight."

The Queen stroked her husband's cheek affectionately. "You have been thinking about Thomas again," she said.

"Aye," he answered. "Every so often it strikes me that if I had had more time with him, I could have become a much better poker player."

The Queen's eyebrows lifted. "Truly?"

"Yes." Garrhyn settled back on the couch, and pulled the Queen against him in a cozy snuggle. "If there had been more time, I could have taught him to play the harp. I could have shown him much. And learned from him, too. He has a gift with words and music—"

"Not unlike your own, in your way, my love," the Queen pointed out.

"But there wasn't time, was there? It was a full year, and I had some changing to do before I could understand the man's value. It didn't take you so long, though, and I'm glad of it. "

The Queen kissed her husband. "You are so wonderful."

"I know it. Practical, too," he teased. "The Folk benefitted from his presence, you benefitted from his presence..."

"Indeed I did," she teased back.

"—and I benefitted as well. You made an excellent choice, my Lady, and we are all the better for it."

They listened to Thomas sing the rest of his song. It was the last song on the album. When it was over, Fiall came into the sitting room, and took the needle off of the record, lifted the vinyl carefully, and slid it into its cover before he replaced it on a shelf. Bowing at his Lord and Lady, he left them alone.

"I liked him," remarked the King. "And if there had been more time—"

The Queen pulled a little away from him, and looked into his face. "Why are you obsessed about this? Thomas has been gone for a year."

"Have you sent anyone to check on him? To see how his life is moving?"

"No, of course not," she told him, her eyes serious. "That is not the way."

The King nodded. "I know. But I wonder about him. Often."

"Why? His time with us is done. I grieved the loss for a while, too. And after that, my heart found its true home again."

He put his arms around her. "And mine has come home as well. For which I am most grateful. And yet..."

"And yet what?"

293

"And yet, my Lady, I cannot help but think that if things had been different, then he and I might have been fast friends." He rubbed his cheek against hers. "I think I blame you for the timing issue."

She sat up and gaped at him. "Me? You blame *me*?"

"Certainly," Garrhyn confirmed with a wicked grin. "If you were still keeping your Court Singers for seven years, rather than just the puny *one* year, Thomas and I might have been tight as brothers. Whatever possessed you to change from seven years in Faerie to one? The literature does not speak to this..."

She gasped in mock insult, and then laughed. "You are an evil man, Garrhyn and, at the moment, a terrible husband. I find I like the combination, though."

The Terrible Husband sighed, mild frustration making his face seem intense. "There were many things I would like to have shown him, things that might have made his music that much more True. I could have taught him...by the gods, my dear, sometimes thinking about what I cannot tell him makes me sad, as if he were the adult son I never had..."

A huge flash of wild, fire-golden light burst spontaneously into the room, hurled itself around the King and Queen in a roar of thunder, then surrounded the King, flying into his fingertips and his chest.

Neither of them spoke. They simply looked into each other's eyes, as the realization shone around them. The King touched his chest where the light had blazed into him. The Queen touched his hand, then squeezed it. Then they began to smile.

Later it was said that everyone in Elvenhome understood at once. The day got brighter. The sunlight was warmer, or so it seemed. The forest was greener, the sky bluer, the air more fragrant.

Everyone knew immediately what had changed; there was no need for an explanation. The curse that Garrhyn had screamed in a rage from his Tower Room seven centuries earlier had finally been laid to rest:

By flower and tree
By night and morn
Until I have a son
No child in my kingdom shall be born.

"The adult son you never had, eh?" the Queen murmured.

"Well, you know what I mean."

"We *all* know what you mean," she said, her dark eyes brimming with love.

Garrhyn's smiled beamed. And then he noticed for the first time that the tension on the scarred right side of his face was somehow less strained and uncomfortable than he was accustomed to. He laughed, and silently embraced a layer of redemption he had not believed possible.

Done, he thought, *is done.*

He wondered if he was going to smile forever now. Looking at his wife, it seemed likely.

THERE WAS A feast, of course, to celebrate the healing of Elvenhome. A place was set for Thomas (in absentia) at the High Table, in honor of his masterful work in inspiring the King to save his people yet again. The dancing, eating, singing, and drinking went on for more than a week. And throughout the course of the celebration, everyone reverted back to the use of the strange and sometimes mystifyingly alarming names that Thomas had given them.

Naturally, there were dozens of games of poker played in the Great Hall in Thomas' honor.

Even more naturally, there were hundreds of Fair Folk in Elvenhome making babies.

In their bed, the Queen lay in the King's arms and told him that she had never been happier. "I find that it is worth everything to me to have you speak my True Name in the dark, my dearest friend, King, and husband."

By candlelight, he traced the regal markings as they moved on her face, neck, chest and arms. Then he kissed her, and whispered her True Name one more time as he reached for her.

The Folk say that Faerie tales come true. They should know.

seventeen

THOMAS LEAR RODE the elevator down from the twenty-fifth floor. He had just finished a third meeting with the record label's marketing and advertising managers. It had gone well. There would be a photo shoot next week for the new album. He'd approved all the press junkets and interviews they'd suggested, and everyone was satisfied. That in itself was weird.

He remembered how he'd always felt about the business side of the music industry, how he'd automatically bristled at what the label wanted, and how he'd done his best to be a pain in the ass in the vain hope that they'd all leave him alone. They never did, no matter how obnoxious and demanding he'd been. This struck him as funny now. He didn't seem to mind much about how large of a fuss the label was going to make about him and the new album.

The recording work was nearly finished. He'd spent weeks in the studio with his new producer, and they were both pleased with the way it was coming together.

The elevator stopped on the nineteenth floor, and half a dozen people got on. One of the passengers, an older guy Thomas recognized as a studio musician, caught his eye, and they smiled at each other.

The elevator stopped on the eighteenth floor. Most of the passengers got off here, and one came on.

Susannah Rickert stepped into the elevator, carrying two folders and a pen. She nodded at a woman she knew, then smiled at Thomas. "Hi," she said, her tone light and friendly.

"Hi," Thomas replied, and watched as Susannah opened one of the files and glanced at something, then closed the file again.

She was looking very pretty today, Thomas decided as he covertly studied her. Her blonde hair barely hit the collar of her blue silk blouse. He'd always preferred long hair on women, but Susannah's seemed perfect. He had found himself staring at her hair a few times too many while they'd talked about the album, been in the studio, met with musicians and arrangers...

Thomas found it hard to believe that his amazing producer was the same woman who'd been Jack Grandberg's secretary for as long as he'd been signed with the label. He'd vaguely known her for four years. She had been a familiar if not-too-interesting face in Jack's office, one that he'd largely ignored. Who knew she was going to turn out to be one of the industry's best, most creative producers? Her reputation was certainly growing, and her interest in world music was getting more attention. She was a shining mover and shaker. He'd learned from spending the last month working closely with her that music was much more than simply business with her. She understood the music.

She understood *his* music.

The thought floored him. She'd proven it more than once, talking through layers of the melodies, gently sifting through the lyrics, and making recommendations about musical arrangement, timing, and tone. One night they'd sat in her office until midnight talking about the subtext of one of his newer songs, "Letter from A Friend." He groaned to himself; he'd had to make up a lot of the substance he'd contributed to that conversation. He was glad that he'd read all of his mysterious, but carefully-compiled, notes. He used what he'd read to feed the fiction he told about the personal side of the writing and composition. It had never been his habit to write anything down, he had never needed to. But he had the notebook with thirty-two completed songs, and more poetry and snatches of notation in his own sloppy handwriting, to prove it. It bothered him more than a little that he didn't remember a goddamned thing about having written the new songs, or the experiences, feelings, and processes that had inspired them. Still, they were obviously his own, and he knew them well: heart, mind, voice and fingers.

Somehow, talking with Susannah Rickert about them had made them more real for him, only he would never tell her that, any more than he would tell her that he believed his songs were made even better for her enchanting touches on them.

And here he was, standing less than six feet from her in the elevator. Susannah took a deep breath, held it for a heartbeat or two, and steadied herself. Why had she thought that working with Thomas Lear directly, instead of supporting Jack's work with him, would finally scour the unanswerable feelings she had about him and his music? If anything, she'd come to appreciate him—*like* him—more than she'd imagined was possible. His music made her feel...oh hell, it just made her *feel*.

He'd calmed down since he'd been back, seemed more focused. Obviously he was easier with himself. Not so angry, or so wildly unhappy...

He'd given up recreational drugs. She had been around him enough to know that he didn't do coke or even smoke pot. She liked him better this way.

She also liked that he respected her work on his beautiful, touching, painfully honest and very-Thomas-Lear songs. The process was going well, and the resulting album would be one of his best. She was certain of it.

Susannah had learned to sit across a table from Thomas Lear, talk business and music, and not fall all over herself about him the way she had when she first went to work for Jack. It had taken her several personally nerve-wracking encounters with Thomas before she could eat a casual meal with him when they got hungry in the middle of a work session. She was cursed with a nervous stomach.

He knew Jack had sent her to Edinburgh to look for him when he'd disappeared. That was not a secret, although they hadn't discussed it. But there were secrets, of course. She wondered if *he* ever wondered what had happened to his expensive silver cuff links. A blush heated her face for a moment. She took another breath, and wished she could actually follow through on her long-standing daydream of talking with him outside of the work paradigm. She'd come far, she was a successful record producer. She was proud of how hard she'd worked, and she loved her job.

The rewards were astonishing, and she was in an elevator with Thomas Lear! But she would never be in his league, could never rise (or fall?) to meet his impossible expectations for personal friendship.

Or partnership. She had to get over that. She bit her lip as the elevator stopped on the tenth floor.

Everyone got out. Everyone, that is, except Thomas and Susannah.

The elevator doors closed, and they descended.

Thomas took a deep breath.

Susannah took a deep breath.

"You know, if you were as smart as everyone thinks you are, you'd want to go out with me. We could have a lot in common. It might be fun."

"Really?"

"Really."

"Are you asking me out?"

"I might be."

"Does it matter which of us asks?"

"No."

"Oh."

"Oh?"

"If you ask me out, I'd be inclined to say yes."

"In that case, then – would you like to have dinner with me tonight?"

A pause.

"Yes."

By tacit agreement, neither Thomas nor Susannah ever admitted publicly who asked whom out on their first date.

He's not what you'd expect. An almost essentially different Thomas Lear: A year away changed the music and the man.

Thomas Lear: The Rolling Stone Article (March, 1977)

by Casey Tourlin

It's a too-often-proved fact of life that, in the clutches of the ravenous beast that is the music industry, artists have to be visible and readily audible on a constant basis, and not just on the radio. If you're not recording and touring and selling, you're as close to dead as it matters. Everyone gets that.

Everyone, apparently, except singer-songwriter Thomas Lear, who appears to have once again broken the established rules and flipped off The Way Things Are. As usual, he's done it in his own time and in his own way, effortlessly resurrecting and recreating himself without too much fuss and aggravation. He has made what can only be called a triumphant return into an overcrowded arena where you just don't get

301

back in once you've left the spotlight for a quick trip to the men's room.

He's back—and he's here to stay.

Eighteen months ago, after a grueling but highly successful North American tour, he dropped completely out of sight. No one, not even his band mates, knew where he'd gone, or why. When he resurfaced six months ago, he reunited with his band. Then he walked into the studio, worked hard with high-powered producer Susannah Rickert, and walked out again with what is possibly his best and most provocative album to date, the instant double platinum "The Rhymer Returns."

What made this spontaneous prodigal son vanish from the music scene, where he's been an undeniable force of nature for the last decade and a half? Where the hell did he go? What was he doing? How did he pull off such a smooth comeback in an unforgiving business that punishes private—if not downright mysterious—sabbaticals? What's behind the undeniable magic of the new album? And what's next for this beloved folk icon and rock troubadour?

CT: Your "Dangerous Blue Eyes" Tour, in the spring and summer of 1975, was a blowout success. People were still talking about it, still wanting more, when you disappeared. Not only were you not on TV, in the studio, or on stage, you were nowhere to be found. What was that all about?

TL: The Blue Eyes Tour was great, a lot of fun to do, every night. The band was something else. They played like love on fire. But at the end, since we were burning up the stage every night, we got tired. It happens to everyone. Then we were so tired, we couldn't even look at each other anymore. We got ourselves messed up every night after the show, and that only made everything worse. I got lost someplace between the booze and the drugs, and then things started to crash. I don't think I even remember playing the last two weeks of the tour.

CT: The stories that were circulating about the Blue Eyes Tour have become the stuff of legend. Great reviews, though. It was sold out every night, in every city, right?

TL: That's what I heard. And about the reviews, that was cool, they made the label happy. (He laughs.) And of course, if the label is happy, *everyone's* happy. Except I wasn't happy.

CT: What happened?

TL: After a while, stuff just felt wrong, I felt wrong, so I decided to get the hell out of Los Angeles.

CT: Where did you go?

TL: Europe.

CT: Europe? Where?

TL: Scotland. Beautiful country. I was happy and busy there. Got a lot of work done.

CT: You have been more than high-profile for the better part of ten years, fifteen even. You lived a year in Scotland and no one knew you were there?

TL: Oh, some people knew where I was. (His eyes shine.) I just stayed pretty much out of sight, and spent the time really getting into my own head, getting into the music.

CT: And the result of that year was "The Rhymer Returns" album? Not a bad way to spend the time, writing songs like that.

TL: Yeah.

CT: The music is raw and intense, and seems almost, I don't know, kind of "other-worldly," in a way. Would you say that's a Scottish influence on an American songwriter?

TL: How could there not be? The Scots have a passionate and sometimes sad history. I think that passion and sadness, and pride, too, lives in the air around them. They have a strong literary history, too. I don't think you can be there for any length of time and not feel a combination of these things. And there's more to it...there's energy there, and light, and for want of a better term, maybe a magic that I found intriguing.

CT: There's Scotch there, as well.

TL (He laughs): Yeah, well, there's that.

CT: Have you become a connoisseur of single-malt?

TL: Oh no. But I know what I like. (He laughs again)

CT: What about drugs? You say you and the band were "messed up" after the shows.

TL: Yeah, we were.

CT: Rumor has it that you no longer do coke, or even smoke weed. True?

TL: True.

CT: Really?

TL: Yeah. I stopped using when I was in Scotland. It took me a while, but I finally figured out I couldn't write if I was fucked up, so eventually I stopped getting fucked up. The difference was a huge surprise. Seems simple logic now, but it was a bigger deal then.

CT: Did you spend time in a rehab facility?

TL (A cryptic smile): More or less. It's enough that I'm done with that shit.

CT: Alcohol, too?

TL (He laughs outright): Hell no. I developed a fondness for excellent single-malt. Just enough of a fondness, anyway. Too much of it, it gets in the way of the music, and I am not willing to go there anymore.

CT: Your change in lifestyle seems to have paid off, personally as well as professionally. Did you have any idea that "The Rhymer Returns" would be such a huge success?

TL: Yeah. (He laughs) I've been doing this a long time, and I know what's good. A couple of years ago, I knew when the writing wasn't what it needed to be, and that was the beginning of the end of my rope. When I came home, and looked at the work I'd done when I was away, I knew I had done it right. I'm actually really proud of the result.

CT: Where did the title come from?

TL: It's kind of a personal in-joke. Comes from a 13th-century Scottish myth, about a folk hero, Thomas the Rhymer. I never paid much attention to him, although I've always known the story. Not a lot of people know this, but I have a Master's degree in Medieval Lit from UC Berkeley, so I knew the literature pretty well. Anyway, I think it's fair to say that I took a little history from Thomas the Rhymer, spent some time with him, and the result was "The Rhymer Returns." Kind of takes care of him, and of me, too.

CT: The images that you paint in these songs, the intensity of emotion, feels like vintage Lear. But it's mixed with a sense something else, too, of fairytales that come true. One or two kind of mystic stories with uneasy endings. The blend seems both familiar and compellingly new, all at the same time. It's like we recognize you, only there's an added layer of something we can almost see, only not quite. But we can feel it. Tell us about that.

TL: The writing was private, it was my own story of coming back to myself, and finding that I was stronger and better for the road I had walked. On the other hand, these songs

307

leave me with an overwhelming sense of ethereal reality. Like being firmly grounded, but knowing in your heart that you know how to fly, want to fly, even – but also recognize that it's not necessary, and feeling good about that. The magic of not needing magic, maybe?

CT: I'd say that audiences feel much the same way. The record sales speak for themselves. Did you know "Rhymer" would go double platinum?

TL: We were pretty sure it would, yeah.

CT: No surprise there, then?

TL: Yeah. But only one surprise. It took a whole day longer than we anticipated. (He grins.)

CT: What's next for you?

TL: Easy. I'm going to sit around and count my money. No, not really. We're planning the American Rhymer Tour right now, and will hit the road sometime in early summer. I'm still writing songs, and hope to go back into the studio this time next year. And I'll do that for as long as it stays fun.

CT: Your producer is a bright light in the business, with an impressive portfolio of success in a relatively short time.

What's it like to work with Susannah Rickert?

TL: It's great...almost as much fun as playing with Susannah Rickert. (He laughs.) She listened to the new songs, and she—and this shocked me—she understood them, deep down. And more than that, she knew when to crank up the intensity, when to turn it in on itself, and when to leave it behind. Better than anyone else, even me, sometimes.

CT: Word is that you'll be working with her on future albums.

TL: Most likely. She's good to have around, both professionally and personally. Especially personally.

CT: Congratulations. So is it fair to say you have finally found the deep, essential, passionate, storybook love you've been writing about all these years? Your lyrics would be a hard thing to live up to.

TL: In my view, art should reflect life, not the other way around. And love is many things all at the same time – it's happy, it's sad, it's energizing, it lays waste to you, it's passive and active, it sings, it screams, it's celibate, it orgasms, it dances, and it weeps. Love is what it is, and it's all those things, and more. Finding yourself in a position to share all the things that love is—with a special person – is what it's all about. It's something that we can all live up to, if we want it. And I want it, doesn't everyone?

THEY SAT ON the porch of the private rented house on Kawai, and looked out at the ocean, sipping margaritas and talking as the sun set.

"So how long did Jack make you stay in Scotland looking for me?"

Susannah settled into her chaise lounge and smiled at him. "A week. It's a beautiful city, but I didn't really have time to appreciate it. It was kind of intense, and mostly a blur now." She touched her necklace, smiling to herself. "A nice blur, but a blur nevertheless."

"I can't believe the stuff he had you doing back then," Thomas chuckled.

"You don't even want to know some of the things I had to get into," she groaned.

"You're probably right about that."

"Trust me."

"I do," he told her, serious for a moment.

She looked at him closely for a minute, accepting his admission and loving him for it. "I heard you up early this morning. Did you finish the new song?"

"Almost. The lyric's not quite right. Getting there."

"The guitar sounded good. I'm just glad you didn't hang out with the piano, or I'd have had to get up."

"That might have been fun, Susannah..."

She laughed. "Shut up." She reached for his hand, and squeezed it playfully. "So really: where were you for a whole year, Thomas?"

He was quiet. "Would you believe me if I told you I can't recall a thing? That I have absolutely no idea, other than Edinburgh?"

"At first? No, I wouldn't have believed you. Now I do, though." *Goddamn drugs*, she thought, more sad than bitter about the year they'd taken away from him.

I lost a whole year of my life, Thomas was thinking, *but whatever the hell happened during that year has made me better and happier, rather than letting me destroy myself. I know that much. Who was I with? What did I do? How did I learn what I've learned? Why don't I know where I was?*

"If it helps," Susannah said, kissing his hand as she pulled his focus from his darkening thoughts, "Whatever you were doing for that year away, and whoever you were with, I like you much better now."

"Me too," he confessed, and leaned over to kiss her, letting his recurring, unspoken ache to remember what had happened in Scotland slide away as he lost himself in the safety of her smile.

Lear a 2001 Inductee into the Songwriters Hall of Fame

(The Seattle Times, 2001)

Last week, the Songwriters Hall of Fame released the list of its inductees for 2001, and superstar Thomas Lear is on it, along with his longtime friends Eric Clapton and Paul Williams, and pals Willie Nelson, Dolly Parton, and Dianne Warren. "I'm delighted and honored to be included in this year's Hall of Fame roster with so many gifted songwriters," he said during a telephone interview today. "I hadn't expected it. It was a cool surprise."

It's been a year of cool surprises for the singer-songwriter. The recently-released tribute double album "Lear & Many Friends" has already gone gold. "It's a fun DVD, I like it a lot, and I didn't have to do anything this time around, other than listen to everyone else work. And they're all pretty good songs, too," he laughs. "Don't know about some of the singing though. I told Eric [Clapton] his gentle and bittersweet version of 'What I Need Tonight' made me nervous as hell. I think he does it better than I do. And the extra guitar stuff he did in the middle is killer."

The Academy of Motion Picture Arts and Sciences had some news that surprised Lear, too. He's been nominated for two Oscars, one for Best Score and one for Best Song, for his work on last year's hugely successful film "Her Autumn Afternoons."

The ever-youthful Lear, who will turn 66 this fall, was in Seattle yesterday for an AIDS Research benefit, sponsored by Bailey-Boushay House. He donated two of his signature guitars, which raised $180K.

The beloved folk and rock icon is busy preparing for his eight-week/24-city US tour, which kicks off next week in Seattle. "There are a couple of new songs, but mostly it's the old songs, the ones I can still remember the words to," he joked. "But it'll be a lot of fun."

Lear and his wife of twenty years, famed Los Angeles record producer Susannah Rickert, split their time between homes in LA, New Orleans, and on the Washington State coast. "I love living in Washington," he said. "I don't know which is better – the people or the coffee.

But after the tour I'll spend a lot of time figuring that out."

Does he have any plans to put the music away and rest on his impressive pile of laurels? It doesn't appear so. "I can't put the music aside. It's how I explain the world to myself. My take on the whole thing is probably skewed all to hell, but it works for me. And it keeps me out of trouble, which is always a good thing. My plan is to sing and play in public until they make me stop. And then I'll just sing in the shower, until Susannah makes me stop."

Apart from his music, he admits that he would rather be reading a book than doing just about anything else; he reads several books simultaneously, "like flipping channels on the TV." He took up jogging after returning to Los Angeles after his now-legendary mysterious year-long disappearance in 1975. "These days I run and listen to books on tape. That way I've got everybody's words bouncing around in my head, and that's usually been able to take the edge off—and keep me going."

ELTON JOHN THREW Eric Clapton a birthday party in March 2003, at his home in Los Angeles. As usual, everyone was there.

Thomas Lear and Susannah Rickert chatted with old friends and associates, drank champagne, and had a good time.

"I'm glad you changed your mind and decided to come," Susannah told her husband when they had a brief moment to themselves while the party buzzed around them. "You've been a little off all week. I was hoping hanging out with everybody would be good for you." She wrinkled up her face at him playfully. "You need a little fun."

Fun came immediately in the form of Al Stewart, who had been good friends with both Thomas and Susannah for a decade or two. After kissing Susannah and grinning at Thomas, Al said, "Guys, I brought a friend, and Thomas, he's asked me more than once to introduce you."

Al stepped aside, and a strikingly handsome man with long gray hair and sparkling blue eyes stood beside him. The man looked at Thomas with a gaze that could only be described as expectant, but a second after seeing no recognition in Thomas' dark eyes, toned it down to polite curiosity and greeting.

Al patted the man on the shoulder. "Thomas, this is my friend Michael MacAllistair. He keeps up the troubadour tradition all over Scotland, has for about a hundred years. I've known him forever."

"But don't hold that against me," Michael laughed, his Glaswegian accent merry as he and Thomas shook hands.

"Musician, songwriter, and singer," said Al helpfully. "Stays put in Scotland, plays guitar like he knows what he's doing, and keeps the pubs singing."

"And the whisky flowing," Al and Michael said together, and laughed.

"My wife, Susannah," Thomas said, and Susannah and Michael exchanged pleasant smiles.

Thomas was trying to place Michael in the industry. He couldn't, exactly. "I know your name, but I don't think I know your work," he apologized.

"Yes you do, you just don't remember," Susannah offered. She smiled at Al and Michael as she spoke to her husband. "He writes wonderful and sometimes funny historical pieces." She turned to talk to Michael. "I especially like 'You Could Be a Plantagenet.' You also played on three of Al's albums, or was it four? And you played lead guitar on his concert tour last year, right?"

Michael nodded, surprised. "I'm stunned that you even know about that."

Al poked Michael in the ribs. "We should have introduced Susannah as Susannah Rickert. She's only *secondarily* Thomas' better half."

Thomas groaned, and then joined in the laughter. "It's true. So what are you doing these days, Michael?"

Susannah and Al went to get more champagne, and left the two men alone.

"To tell you the truth, most of the time I sit at home and read detective novels. I've a nice home in the Highlands, and life is pretty quiet, but I've come to like it that way. You know what I mean."

Thomas nodded in agreement. "I still play the guitars, most every day, but it's for me now. I get out and raise the level of intelligence from the stage every so often, but I've gotten to the age where I'd just as soon sing a song or two and go home. God, if I'd have thought such a thing were possible thirty years ago—"

"—you'd have drunk yourself to death like the rest of us would have," finished Al as Susannah handed Michael a glass of champagne, and passed another one to Thomas. "I can't imagine doing anything but writing songs and playing them. I'll probably do it for the rest of my life."

Thomas agreed. "I think most of us feel that way." He turned to Susannah. "Just promise me you won't let me turn into the Geriatric Guitarist on stage, eh?"

"Pretty safe bet there, Lear," Susannah chuckled. "But I think you've got a little while to go yet."

"Still," Thomas returned, only half-kidding, "Rock musicians don't retire...they just play quieter, in smaller venues until they can't remember more than three chords. Then you've got to put them out of your misery."

"Oh God!" Al laughed, and the three musicians raised their glasses and drank a toast to Rock Star Rot.

When the chuckling and groaning died down, Susannah remembered a question she'd wanted to ask Al about wine. They put their heads together and talked about Al's second-favorite subject.

Michael was looking at Thomas as though he very much wanted to say something.

Thomas raised an eyebrow. "Michael?"

Michael's studied gaze moved over Thomas, and he seemed to struggle with a decision for a fraction of an instant. Then he took a breath, smiled brightly, and said, "It's a pleasure to meet you, Thomas. I'm a great admirer of your work, especially the vintage stuff."

"Thanks," replied Thomas.

Michael took a small step forward. "I am most especially fond of your work on 'The Rhymer Returns.' I think it's the most...enchanting...music I've ever heard. It sounds strange to say it out loud, especially to the man who wrote it, but what the hell: it has haunted me for years."

Thomas nodded at the compliment. "Truth be told, it haunts me, too."

"Where," Michael asked carefully, "did it come from?"

Thomas had been answering this question for more than twenty-five years. "Place and time, I guess. It's where my head was when I spent that year away. The magic of Scotland crept in when I wasn't looking, and carried me away."

Slowly, Michael nodded his head, his eyes intense and serious. "I understand."

Thomas wasn't convinced that Michael did, since he didn't himself, but he let it go.

"Beautiful, enchanting songs," Michael said.

"Thanks."

"...so I'll send you a bottle, Suze, and if you like it, I'll send you a case. Fair enough?" Al was saying.

"Works for me," Susannah said, giving him a kiss on the cheek. "Thank you!"

"Hey Al!" a voice called from the other side of the room.

Al looked over his shoulder, and saw someone waving at him. "Oh shit – I've got to talk to him. See you later, guys. Come on, Michael, let me introduce you to a real pain in the ass." With smooth, hasty goodbyes, Al and Michael turned and made their way through the sea of party guests.

"Nice guy, Michael," Susannah remarked as she sipped her champagne.

"Yeah," Thomas said, watching him.

"What?" she asked. "You've got the strangest look on your face."

Thomas pulled his eyes away from Michael and looked at her. "No I don't."

"Yes, you do. You can't see the look in your face, Hon. What's wrong?"

"Oh, nothing. Let's go find EJ and the birthday boy." He smiled at Susannah as he tried to toss the weird thought away, but it wouldn't go. He'd only just met Michael MacAllistair, but the man seemed to have looked at him as though Thomas should have recognized him from somewhere.

As he and Susannah walked through the room to find Clapton, Thomas pushed down the sudden urge to go back and ask Michael if they had met at some point during that lost year in Scotland. It occurred to him that, as much as he might want to know, he might *not* want to know. It might be best left alone.

But if that was true, why did his heart ache all of a sudden?

Eric Clapton, Rock Star Birthday Boy, was laughing at a joke, and nodded at Thomas as he and Susannah approached the buffet table that held the enormous, guitar-shaped birthday cake that looked remarkably like Clapton's "Blackie".

Thomas cleared his throat, put on his best public smile, and slid into his well-practiced, charming professional persona, leaving the troubling heartache behind as he joined the laughter and conversation with his friends.

EIGHT WEEKS LATER, while at home in Los Angeles and changing a string on one of his guitars, Thomas collapsed and lay unconscious in the living room for perhaps ten minutes before being discovered by Susannah. He was rushed to UCLA Medical Center. The prognosis was not good.

The doctor explained it to Susannah as gently as possible. Thomas had suffered a ruptured aortic aneurysm; he had bled into his abdomen and lost a substantial amount of blood. He only barely survived the emergency surgery the situation required. He was in a coma. The doctor did not like the rock star's immediate chances.

Susannah called friends, the guys in the band, and the family spokesperson, and told them only as much as she thought they should know. Friends could come by as they chose, if they could do so without press inquiries. The spokesperson let the media know generally what had happened, played it down, and announced that Thomas was "resting comfortably." There would be no mention of coma, or of the nearness of death. For added privacy, a plainclothes security guard was posted surreptitiously in the neighborhood of Thomas' hospital room, with a list of permissible visitors.

The first three days and nights, Susannah never left him. She had her knitting, a daunting stack of paperwork from the office, and half a dozen books. She'd read one of his least favorites aloud to Thomas, wistfully hoping to inspire him to come out of the coma and articulate his annoyance at her choice.

He didn't wake.

Doctors came in and went out, nurses stayed ahead of every need, and friends stopped by, tried to comfort her, and left sadly.

THOMAS HAD BEEN in the coma for nine days when he opened his eyes and very carefully looked around to determine where the hell he was and why he felt so bad.

It didn't take Susannah long to look up from her knitting and see that he was awake.

"Hello, Sweetheart," she said, rising from her chair and reaching for the call button to summon a nurse. "Are you all the way awake?"

Thomas opened his mouth to speak, and then realized there was a tube in his mouth. Confused and more than a little unnerved, he frowned, but nodded. His eyes asked her a handful of questions he couldn't actually frame.

Not being able to talk with her triggered a distant thought that he couldn't quite reach. He gave it up, and focused on his wife.

"Do me a favor," Susannah said, her heart beating fast and her eyes filling. "Just lie there, and wait until we have you looked at. I'll tell you everything in a little while, Thomas. Just lie there and breathe, okay?" She took his hand and squeezed it hard.

He was glad they'd taken the tubes out of his nose and mouth, and he was mostly able to ignore the sounds of the machinery that monitored his body. The drugs kept him fuzzy and fairly quiet, but despite the sedated calm they supplied, his mind whirled in too many directions.

Was his life over? Was this *it*? He wasn't sure, especially after the rough day he'd had yesterday, that he wasn't about to die. If he was, well, shit...but okay. Had he done everything he'd wanted to do? Had he been everything he'd wanted to be?

Most importantly, in terms of the work of his lifetime, had he said everything he'd wanted to say? Had everything been sung?

It isn't sitting right, he thought between drug-induced naps. *Something is missing. Something huge. Goddammit!*

He didn't know what it was, but it was essential. The emotional ache he could not touch would not go away, no matter how he positioned it to himself.

The more he thought about it, the more his soul twisted in on itself. For probably the first time in decades, he felt lost, alone, troubled, confused beyond endurance, and unable to bear it. He knew no one, not even Susannah, would understand what he was trying to navigate inside his head.

He needed help, but he didn't know where to turn.

And then he did.

Just like that.

The realization rose over him like a warm blanket being drawn up to cover and protect him from cold thoughts.

He remembered. And remembering, said her name in his mind only once, took a deep breath, and went to sleep feeling safer than he had since he'd awakened in the hospital.

"I'M GOING TO have an ugly scar," Thomas complained two days later.

"Yes, I know," Susannah said patiently. "I don't know if the ocean of nineteen-year-old females who worship you are going to be able to cope with that," she added with a playful snicker.

"Still," he groaned. "The cut's nasty too. It's ugly, what I can see of it. And it hurts."

"It helped keep you alive. At least so far," his wife said in a tartly menacing way that made him smile in spite of himself. "It won't be the worst scar in the world, Hon. No one will see it but you and me."

Thomas looked at her with a smirk. "I guess I should have told you about the nude spread I agreed to do for Playgirl Magazine next month."

"Playgirl? I was under the impression the nude spread was for AARP."

"Ouch. I hate you, Mrs. Lear," Thomas said. "You're only funnier than me because I'm on drugs right now."

Susannah kissed him. "I am only funnier than you are, Mr. Lear, because...well, because I'm funnier than you are." She ran her fingers over his face. "I do love you, you know."

"Smart girl." He kissed her fingers and smiled at her. "And about my scar?"

"Yes?"

"It wouldn't be the ugliest scar anyone ever had to face." He slid her sleeve up, and ran his own fingers along the long-faded scar on the inside of her left forearm. "Some sweetheart of a lady told me once that scars aren't who we are, they're just where we've been."

He reached for her, and kissed her arm. Then he slid her sleeve back into place, and then gathered her into his arms, pulling her against him in the hospital bed. Careful of tubes and things, he held her close and reminded her about how very much he loved her.

Susannah was sitting beside Thomas' bed, engrossed in a book, when she was disturbed by a light but persistent tapping on the door. She rose, dropped the book on the chair, and walked out into the corridor.

The plainclothes security guard whispered something to her and tilted his head to indicate what he was talking about.

The woman looked to be about thirty-five years old. Long, dark hair, loose curls at the waist, golden highlights visible even in the dimness of the hospital corridor. The woman's compelling brown eyes watched her with a sense of something Susannah didn't have words for; she could only recognize that there was kindness, patience, and compassion there.

"Mrs. Lear, she says she's an *old friend* of his." The security guard looked uncomfortable, as though he were about to witness a family drama heading for a cat fight.

Susannah had never seen this woman before. Nor had Thomas ever mentioned anyone like her, and his wife was all but certain she knew, or at least knew about, every one of Thomas' friends, male and female, including his old girlfriends.

This very attractive woman was not old enough to be one of Thomas' old friends.

Susannah was too tired, and too sad, to give this situation much more thought. She sighed, and shook her head at the security guard, and turned to go back into Thomas' room.

"I'm Callie," the woman said, her voice soft and faintly musical. "I really am an old friend of his."

Susannah turned back, and studied the woman. "He doesn't know you," she murmured.

To Susannah's chagrin and confusion, the woman laughed lightly, and gave Susannah the tiniest of smiles. "Truly spoken! He didn't remember me, until a short while ago."

This was the wrong day to play games with one of Thomas' fans, or whoever this woman was. Susannah didn't have the strength to deal with it, and was just about to tell the other woman so, she tilted her head ever so slightly, to gently scratch a place toward the top of her head, which moved her long tresses a bit.

That was when Susannah saw top of the woman's ear.

Or rather, she corrected herself, the *tip* of the woman's ear.

It was delicately pointed, and it was an awfully long way from where it should have been.

Susannah had seen an ear or two like this one before.

In 1975.

In Edinburgh.

In bed, with a handsome man called Rex, a man whose kindness and wisdom had helped her to make room for good changes in her life. The man who had given her a necklace that she had worn almost every day since he'd put it around her neck. She touched the small tree in wonder, almost forgetting to breathe as she saw the pieces of something unimaginable come together in front of her.

Her encounter with Rex, the man with the beautiful, pointed ears she'd never had the courage to ask about, had happened in 1975.

1975 was the year Thomas was in missing in Scotland, living the year he didn't remember. Jack had sent her to look for Thomas in Edinburgh...

Susannah looked nervously at the other woman. "What did you say your name was?"

"It won't mean anything to you," she replied. "But my name is Callie."

The Scottish accent was unmistakable.

Oh my God...

Trembling, Susannah beckoned to Callie, and together they went into Thomas' room, and closed the door behind them.

They moved the two guest chairs away from Thomas' bed so that he would sleep without interruption.

"You are part of what he can't remember," Susannah whispered, not certain if she was excited to have a finger on the truth, or worried about what she might learn. "Thomas spent time with you during that year he was away. He doesn't remember anything about it, but you were there, weren't you?" Susannah's eyes grew wide, as the realization hit her. "You're too young, though. It was such a long time ago."

Callie nodded but said nothing.

Susannah kept talking; she couldn't make herself stop. "It was you. You're the elusive one he's been writing about all these years, the secret love he couldn't quite reach for. You're the ghost in so many of his love songs! Oh my God...you actually exist!"

Callie shrugged. "It's a long story, but it's a nice one."

"And he really doesn't remember," Susannah told her, the comment almost but not quite a question.

"I know. He wasn't supposed to. He didn't need the memories as much as he needed what he learned from the experience."

This was true. Susannah was well aware of the difference in Thomas after he'd returned from his year away. She had fallen in love with the updated, much easier to deal with version of Thomas Lear, Rock Star. And Callie had contributed to that in some way.

"How is he?" Callie asked, her voice gentle.

"Good days and bad days. I thought the immediate danger was past, but the ruptured aneurysm seems to have triggered some other issues. They say he might be all right for a while, but I am not so sure. I don't know why, but I didn't see this coming. Silly, I know..."

Callie's dark eyes flashed with sympathy. "Things are what they are, and done is done. But only when it *is* done, I'd say."

Susannah shivered helplessly. "Why are you here? I don't know you, and didn't call you. We've kept the news pretty quiet. How did you know to come, and know to come *here*? Why now?"

"Thomas asked me to."

Susannah thought about this for a long moment, strangling her immediate reaction. She looked at Callie, then looked over at the sleeping Thomas, and finally back at Callie again. "I don't understand."

"Would you like to?"

"I honestly don't know." Susannah made a sound that tried to sound like a laugh.

"In that case," Callie told her with a sweet smile, "I think you and I are going to be fine together." She nodded at Susannah. "I'm going to tell you a wee story."

Susannah's sigh was wistful. She was trying not to seem as sad and tired as she felt. "Does it have a happy ending?"

"I don't think it has an ending at all," Callie said.

eighteen

Hours later, Susannah had gone home to get some much-needed sleep, and Callie sat alone in the chair by Thomas' bed, watching him. He had aged, but he was still handsome. She felt a small tug on her heart, and knew that she would always have feelings for him. She wondered how much he would remember when he woke and saw her sitting there. Most of it, she reasoned. Not all, but most.

It was enough.

He opened his eyes just before dawn, and lay there looking at her as though he knew he was only dreaming.

"Hello, Thomas..."

They talked, pausing only when a doctor or nurse entered to do something for him. He did not want to eat, and he was unwilling to sleep, even after he had exhausted himself with conversation.

He fell asleep several times anyway.

Susannah returned in the late afternoon and listened as Callie and Thomas talked, entering the conversation when invited to, or when she had something to ask or to say. Every once in a while, Thomas reached for Susannah's hand and held it while the talking continued.

"Can I do that?" Thomas was asking Callie, his voice noticeably weaker. "Look everything over, and actually make the decision about what happens next?" This had not occurred to him before.

Callie laughed at him then, a merry sound not unlike bells chiming in a sunny spring wind. "Thomas, it's *your* life, filled with your dreams, your music, your passions, your memories. You can do with it anything you wish, whenever you wish."

He smiled at her, almost faint with the aching, and whispered, "Oh, then, Callie, I wish...I wish..."

And he fell asleep again.

CALLIE AND SUSANNAH talked long into the night.

"Do you think you can help him?" Susannah asked, handing Callie a cup of steaming hot tea she'd gotten from the nurse's station kitchen.

"He doesn't need my help. He needs to give himself what he needs."

Susannah couldn't understand. "Then why—"

"Why did he call for me?"

Susannah nodded.

"Because it's part of the story, Susannah. His story, your story, and mine as well."

Susannah thought this over. "There's got to be more to it than that, Callie."

"Perhaps there doesn't."

"He seems to think you can do something to help him," Susannah pointed out, not unkindly.

"Think of me as a small bridge, nothing more. Helping his journey along over some rough water...oh, that's a terrible metaphor!" Callie laughed.

Susannah laughed too, and made a face. "No offense, but it is kind of scary that I get that."

Both women watched Thomas sleep. He twitched a bit, his eyes moving in the depths of his dream.

"Did you love him very much?" Susannah asked, without taking her eyes off her husband.

"In my way, I did," Callie answered her honestly. "For a time."

"I love him, Callie," Susannah said. "I fell in love with the music first, believing that he had to be the man in his songs. Boy was I disappointed when I first met him. He was kind of a jackass. No, more of a total prick." Susannah grinned with amused fondness at the memories. "The music moved me, like it moves everyone. But I needed him to be the man in the songs. He wasn't. I couldn't understand it. I also couldn't give up on him, or my feelings for him. And then, when he came back from Scotland..." Susannah trailed off, remembering.

"And then...?" Callie prompted.

"And then, he still wasn't exactly the romantic man in the songs. But he was sweet, and smart, and wonderful, and funny, and so many other things. And I had the privilege and pleasure of working with him on that first album after he came back. While we worked together, I fell in love with the man he really is." She chuckled. "Sometimes he's the man in the songs, sensitive and connected and all that. But mostly he's Thomas."

"It took some time and some work, but he figured out that that was all he ever needed to be." Callie patted Susannah's arm. "I'm very glad you have had each other. His music was already wonderful, brilliant, and beautiful. But once you touched it, it sparkled! Has anyone ever genuinely thanked you for that?"

Susannah's eyes welled up. "Not in so many words. He's the artist. I'm the craftsman, I think. But thank you for saying that. It means something special to me."

IN SILENCE, THE sun rose. Susannah stretched, exhausted. "I should go home and go to bed," she told Callie. "I can come back around noon. Did you want to come back to the house with me and get some rest? You haven't really been out of here since you arrived."

Callie was studying Thomas, who was still sleeping. "No, Susannah, not yet. I think we should stay for a little while longer, okay?"

327

"Okay," Susannah replied, stifling a yawn. "But I need some serious coffee. I'm going to go find a barista. Can I get you something?"

"Sure. Anything," Callie said, still watching Thomas.

Susannah noticed the look on her face, and glanced at Thomas. "Callie, what's wrong?"

"Not a thing," Callie reassured her. "Go get the coffee. It's your turn, isn't it?"

"It is." Susannah stretched a little more, and went in search of caffeine.

Callie sat on the bed beside Thomas, took his hand, and squeezed it. "Good morning, Court Singer," she said.

Thomas opened his eyes, and grinned when he was able to focus on her. He looked alarmingly fragile. "Where's Susannah?"

"Getting real coffee. She'll be right back. How did you sleep?"

Thomas thought about this. "I dreamt a lot." He looked into Callie's dark brown eyes. "I remembered a lot about my year in Elvenhome. I remembered people I'd completely forgotten about. Arrendel, Maggie, the King...my God, Callie, how's...how's 'Mr. Green'?"

"Mr. Green is quite well, and sends his best wishes."

"Are you happy? Are you both happy? Together?" Thomas wanted to know.

Callie nodded. "We are."

"I'm glad," Thomas said, and he meant it.

Then he looked at her, hesitantly at first, then directly, seriously. "I'm going to die soon, aren't I?"

She let out a long breath, and put a matter-of-fact tone into her voice. "You are going to read a new book; the chapters in this one are done. Well-read, appreciated, but done. You are in the space between songs on the album; the previous song is nearly over, but the next one's a heartbeat away."

He got quiet. "Maybe I should never have left Faerie."

"We both know that's not true, Thomas. But for you, I might still be without my Mr. Green. Without your time spent with us, you would never have survived beyond 1975, and you certainly wouldn't have had a life with Susannah. And all the rest of it, the music...because you chose well, the world has the music of Thomas Lear." She took his hand. "I am so glad we met, we loved, and we parted friends."

"I'm going to die," he said, trying out the words.

"No, you're not. You're simply going to change. New words, new music."

He considered this. "Nothing else makes sense, does it? Wow."

She shook her head, and smiled as she held his trembling hand.

When Susannah came back with the lattes, Callie gratefully accepted hers, excused herself, and took a walk outside the hospital. She needed the fresh air to clear her head and steady her heart, and she wanted to give Susannah and Thomas time to say goodbye in their own way.

She re-entered Thomas' room almost half an hour later, and found them holding hands and talking. They were both a little teary, but they were all right. Susannah looked strong, and Thomas seemed peaceful. They watched as Callie walked over to Thomas' bed.

"I'm going to walk a little of the way with you, Thomas, and then you're on your own."

"Looking for more music," he said.

"That's right," Susannah said. "And you'll find it, Hon. You always do."

Thomas Lear, Rock Star, smiled at the two women he'd loved most, closed his eyes, and went in search of a new story.

The machinery monitoring Thomas began to make alarming noises.

Susannah buried her face in her hands, and began to weep.

Callie's eyes filled with tears, and she let them fall as she flicked her right hand toward Thomas' body, showering him with glittering green light.

While Susannah cried, her hands over her eyes, a glittering green shadow of Thomas Lear rose gracefully from the bed, smiled happily at Callie as he touched her shoulder, and then bent down and kissed the top of Susannah's head. Then the shadow turned and walked toward the window as it faded away.

Susannah wiped her face, took a tissue out of her pocket, and blew her nose.

A nurse rushed in, examined Thomas, then turned the noisy machinery off. "I'm so very sorry, Mrs. Lear," the nurse said. "He's gone. Can I get someone for you?"

Susannah took a deep breath. "No, thank you. But we'd like to sit here with him for a little while, if that is all right."

The nurse nodded sympathetically, and left.

Callie and Susannah sat in silence, staring at Thomas.

"It's over," Susannah said at last. "He's gone. I knew it might come to this, but I don't think I really believed it. I didn't expect to have to..." Her eyes filled with tears. "He's gone."

"He's gone," Callie repeated. "But in a way, of course, he'll always be around."

Susannah sighed and sniffled a little. "The end of a story," she said dully.

Callie smiled. "The story never ends."

"Do you believe that? Seriously?"

Callie nodded.

"Even right now? We're here, and he's dead, Callie. This story's over."

"If you wish to think so, then it is. But I don't think so."

"I wish you could prove it," Susannah said, feeling an empty sadness moving toward her. She leaned down and put her shoes on. As she did, the willow necklace, the one piece of jewelry she'd worn nearly every day since she had received it as a gift once upon a time, fell forward from inside her blouse. The tiny golden tree flickered as a ray of early-morning sunshine touched it.

Noticing it, Callie's eyebrow lifted in surprise, and then she began to chuckle. The chuckle turned into easy, happy laughter.

The sound startled Susannah, who looked over at her new friend with shock and uncertainty all over her face. "What's funny, Callie? How can you be laughing at a time like this?"

Callie beamed at Susannah. "You wanted proof that the story never ends?"

Susannah shot a fast look at Thomas' dear face, and nodded her head fiercely.

Callie met Susannah's eye, then pointed at Susannah's necklace. "I do not quite know how it can be so, but I see that you have met my husband."

epilogue

Maggie turned off the television with a sad sigh. She sat quietly, remembering that once upon a time, she'd met a rock star.

"...and I would know, LORD Arrendel, since I am a Knight and, technically, you are not." Arrendel and Swiftaine came in through the front door of the cottage, hungry after spending most of the day in Arrendel's workshop, and arguing philosophically about Faerie heraldry. As usual, Arrendel was right but, also as usual, Swiftaine was louder.

One look at Maggie, and Arrendel knew something was wrong.

"Maggie?" he asked as he slid onto the couch beside her. The brave Sir Swiftaine stood in the middle of the room, fingers twitching, eyes scouting for unexpected danger that he could conquer in a knightly way.

"It was just on the news. The BBC is reporting that Thomas Lear died today in Los Angeles, Arrendel."

Arrendel put his arms around Maggie, and they held each other for a long while, each letting strong memories wash over them. For a moment it seemed as though mere weeks had elapsed since they'd seen him, rather than decades.

"I hope the Queen was there with him," Maggie murmured at last. "Rhymer routine or not, I mean. It makes the thought of it easier to bear."

"He was a terrible chess player," Arrendel said, the beginnings of a smile playing on his lips. "And I had heard that he cheated at backgammon, but didn't cheat very well."

"He was a good poker player, though," Sir Swiftaine added. "And once I won an entire litter of kittens from him with a royal flush."

"Gentlemen," Maggie said, sitting up and clearing the emotion from her throat, "you are talking about one of the greatest songwriters of a generation. Chess, backgammon and poker do not signify in this particular conversation."

"Yes they do, Maggie," the Spriggan insisted. "He did more than write and sing songs. A lot more. He gave us music *and* poker."

Maggie closed her eyes and shook her head, then lay back against Arrendel.

"He was a good friend to us," he said, his voice low. "I avoided the temptation a dozen times to go to him and renew the friendship, but I thought about it often."

"I wonder if he ever knew that he was the last of the Court Singers in Faerie," Maggie said. "I think he might have liked knowing that. He really was very much in love with her, you know. And obviously he wanted her to be happy when he was gone...from Elvenhome, I mean."

"Thomas was a surprising man, likely as surprising to himself as he was to everyone else," Arrendel chuckled. "As I recall, the last time she and Garrhyn spoke of him in my presence, they said he was well and happy."

"When was that?"

"Four years ago, when you and I went back for that visit."

"Oh. I never heard that."

"No, you were still sleeping off the journey."

It made sense to her now. "Got it."

Sir Swiftaine had walked over to stand in front of them, by the coffee table. "Are you thinking of going to the funeral?" he asked Arrendel.

Arrendel looked at Maggie before he answered Swiftaine. "No. There is no need for that. We do not know his wife, she does not know about us, and so there is no one there we need to comfort and support. We will remember Thomas here at home, even as we wish him well on his next journey."

The Spriggan considered this, then nodded his agreement as he was struck with an idea. "We could have a poker game in his honor. A big one! A tournament! It could go on for days!"

Maggie and Arrendel both stifled a laugh. She buried her face in his neck, and whispered loudly enough for Swiftaine's benefit, "If you can catch him, I'll drop the vacuum cleaner on him."

"I heard that..." Swiftaine grumbled, and evaporated in a huff.

The Water Faerie smirked. "You've gotten good at clearing the room, Maggie."

"I have, haven't I?" she laughed. "About Thomas, though. I hope he found everything he was looking for. I hope he was happy, and joyful, and satisfied with the way his story played out."

"Me, too."

"And I wanted to tell you something, before I saw the news and got distracted about Thomas. I've got the beginnings of a brand-new faerie tale bubbling in my brain."

He knew she was happiest when she was caught up in thinking about her stories. "What's it about?"

"Oh, I don't know all the details yet. You know how I am about the writing. I'll give it a little too much thought and make myself crazy. But I think it's about time I started writing about us, you and me."

Trying not to smile, Arrendel pretended to study her, eyebrows raised.

Maggie grinned. "It'll be fun! And when I get to things I probably shouldn't talk about, I'll do what I always do to get the story told. I'll just make it up as I go along."

THE END

Find more by Lisa Courtney
Web: http://www.courtneyink.com
twitter: @courtney_ink
Amazon: http://www.amazon.com/-/e/B009I4465E

Acknowledgements

It's my habit to write personal thank-you notes by hand (my grandmother insisted upon it, and I'm still a little neurotic about that).

That said, here is another thank-you note, sort of. Less personal than usual, and not by hand, but honest and heart-felt nevertheless.

Thank you, **Ellen Kushner**, for writing *Thomas the Rhymer*, and for the cover artwork by **Tom Canty**. The cover caught my eye at first glance, and The Rhymer took up residence in my head and never went on vacation. He simply waited for me to catch up with the magic.

Thank you, **Gordon Lightfoot**, for the lyrics and music that have been and continue to be part of the soundtrack that is my life. My love for your work fed my need to make Thomas Lear's songs worthy of you, and of me as well.

Quieter but sincere thanks to **Frey** and **Henley**, too, who taught me a little bit about composition and performance that I would never have grasped on my own.

Special thanks to **Paul Camelia**, my own Arrendel, for giving me plenty of room to do what I do.

Most of all, thank you, **Ladies of the Book**, who listened and read and watched me pace and fret, waited while I put the project down for a couple of years, and were the best emotional and creative support imaginable when I picked the thing back up and got serious about it again. And you **Ladies** who handled the production to get Thomas Lear and his friends (and, uh-oh, *me*) out there—there aren't words, not really. I love you all, and thank you so very much: especially

Stacey Eck

Jane Mackinnon

Kristie Lundberg

Sally Sloley

337

Brenda Potts

Nancy Monson

Shari Wetherby

Rebecca Stevenson

and my beloved godmother **Betty** (even though she never took to Thomas, and suggested about two dozen times over the years that I kill him off because she did *not* like his attitude; I got even with her by giving her surname to Susannah, with the desired effect of annoying Betty ever so slightly, and potentially forever).

www.ingramcontent.com/pod-product-compliance
Lightning Source LLC
Chambersburg PA
CBHW060356260626
47160CB00006B/2333